Surviving Red

Book One

Jana` Chantel

About Right Media Group | Detroit, MI | 2019

About Right Media Group, LLC.
http://www.aboutrightmedia.com

Surviving Red
Copyright © 2019 Jana` Chantel

Library of Congress Cataloging-in-Publication Data
Names: Chantel, Jana`, 1988—author.
Title: Surviving Red/ Jana` Chantel
Description: Detroit: About Right Media Group, LLc. 2019. | Series: Surviving Red; 1
Identifiers: LCCN 2019905417 (print) |
ISBN 978-1-7330788-2-5 (ebook) | ISBN 978-1-7330788-0-1 (hardcover) | ISBN 978-1-7330788-1-8 (paperback)
Subjects: | BISAC: FICTION/ Science Fiction/Apocalyptic & Post-Apocalyptic. | FICTION/ Science Fiction/ Action & Adventure. | FICTION/African American/General.
Classification: LCC 2019905417 (print)
LC record available at https://lccn.loc.gov/2019905417

Cover design by Moe Balinger and Fred Evans
Book Design by Jana` Evans

Printed in the United States of America
10 9 8 7 6 5 4

For Fred

~1~

Jade leaned against the bathroom door, holding onto her chest. Fear struck her body. It was happening again. It had been sixty days since her last attack, and she had been very cautious ever since. Because of her medical debt, she had to avoid hospitals at all cost, or she'd be discovered. She shut her eyes and focused on breathing. The sensation of an elephant sitting on her chest wouldn't let up.

"Shit," she said to herself.

She realized she had to stop this asthma attack naturally. Jade went through the abandoned house, her current residence, looking for something to help. Ginger root or honey, but she knew she wouldn't find it in the house. The house lacked electricity for at least ten years, the time everything went wrong. Jade didn't know what exactly happened and why everything started to go wrong, but it did. So, for ten years, the world had been living in chaos.

Jade had to go out and hunt for something that would help her asthma. She grabbed her scarf, wrapped it around her mouth and nose, and headed out to look. Jade called her current living situation, the apocalypse. Some people thought it was pre-apocalyptic. Others thought it was post. Jade was convinced they were living in the thick of it. Unexplainable things were happening in the world: uncommon natural disasters, blackouts, robberies, killings. There were significant earthquakes that could sometimes be felt around the country. There were rolling blackouts that lasted for years. Eventually, only government buildings had resources to keep the power on. Everywhere else was darkness. The most vital and essential things, such as food and medicine, were hard to obtain. Everything turned chaotic—hectic. Medical costs skyrocketed. The use of medical care became practically illegal. Those who could afford it were the ones who could get it.

That was hardly anyone.

Jade decided to check the houses a few blocks away from her home. She scavenged through the houses nearby for any goods and knew they didn't contain any treasures.

No matter how many times she walked outside, the streets seemed eerie to her. What used to be well-manicured lawns, now looked like roads from third world countries. All the houses and buildings were currently abandoned. Most of them had parts of the roof, or the side of the building missing. What wasn't standing was now a pile of rubble. The once beautiful blue skies were a hint of omnipresent orange. The Midwestern weather turned into a consistently warm atmosphere, which was something to get used to since she lived in Michigan. On rare occasions, it would be so hot that ash would fall from the sky.

Jade was in hell.

The two-story, brick house on the corner looked promising. Jade scanned the area to make sure nothing seemed suspicious or out of the ordinary. Everything appeared in order, but she still went inside cautiously. The front door creaked as she opened it. A coat of dust welcomed her. She pulled the scarf tighter around her nose and mouth.

"Great," she muttered.

This was just what she needed—something to agitate her asthma even more. She paused for a moment—debating if she should retreat or not. She was already this far; she figured she should see it through. The door closed shut behind her. The bare light from outside gave her enough light to see. Her search began in the kitchen. Jade looked through the refrigerator, the cabinets, and the pantries. Nothing was found.

The bathroom upstairs was the next target. Jade looked through the medicine cabinets. She was looking for anything—anything that would help with her attack. If Jade found an inhaler, that would be a jackpot. She hadn't seen one of those in over a year.

Jade searched for the next room, which was a nursery. Her chances were slim, but she checked the room anyways. A quick glance around the crib showed nothing but a green and yellow cover set that laid inside. A mobile of smiling jungle animals sat on top. Jade continued to look around the nursery. She noticed that, apart from the dust, everything seemed brand new. That meant that the baby wasn't born when everything went wrong. Jade sympathized for the mother. Bringing a baby into this kind of chaos was unimaginable. She wondered if the baby was a boy or a girl. The room was painted light green, along with everything else there. Judging from the gender-neutral colors, Jade figured that the parents didn't know the sex of the baby either.

The master bedroom was Jade's last stop. It was small, but the furniture was arranged where she could move around comfortably. She checked the top of the dresser and all its drawers. She found articles of clothing that she desperately needed, but nothing that would resolve the issue at hand. Jade shoved the clothes and a pair of boots into her bag and prepared to leave, but something caught her eye.

On the nightstand, draped across a picture frame of a happily married couple, was a rosary. It had black beads, and a gold cross hung from it. Jade picked it up and ran her fingers over each bead. She wasn't Catholic, but she did believe in a higher being. Right now, she could use a renewed strength in her faith.

Voices interrupted Jade's silent reflection. Judging by the sound, they were just outside the front porch. There was a group of them. Jade put the rosary around her neck and quickly, yet quietly, hid in the closet. The closet was deep and very dark. Jade maneuvered past clothes and shoes as she made her way to the back. She hid behind some jackets and dresses as the intruders entered the house. Jade's hand grasped the handle of her knife, which was strapped around her thigh.

Her breathing was quiet and slow.

Since the chaos had broken out, violence had tripled—if not more. Killings, robberies, and rapes were happening more and more—especially with the lack of essentials. Apart from the misuse of medical care, there was no one around to enforce the other laws. It was every man for their self. So, if you had anything of value, like food, water, etc., you had to be prepared to fight or even kill for it. Jade had her share of run-ins with these threats, so she knew her way around a knife.

"Look for anything of value," a male voice said. "Spread out!" A variety of footsteps moved about the house.

Jade was still.

"Ain't shit in the kitchen!"

"Nothing in the bathroom!"

"You think someone might be hiding out here?" someone else said.

"Sucks for them if they are."

More footsteps were heard as another person entered. "'member the last group we ran into?"

"Yeah, those ladies weren't so lucky."

"But I was!" another male's voice boomed with laughter.

"Check upstairs!" Footsteps ran up the stairs—it sounded like two people.

"Aww, they were gonna have a baby," a female voice said.

"Who cares? Just find some valuables." There was silence for a moment—just the sound of rumbling. "Nothing, check the other room."

"Hurry the hell up, people!" the leader yelled.

"Ok, ok!" the woman said. "Geesh, what's his hurry?"

"No idea."

Jade could hear the slamming of drawers and doors throughout the house. She positioned herself closer to the corner wall in the closet. Her breathing became very still. Just like she predicted the closet door opened. She made sure that she wasn't in a position where light could hit her.

"Damn," the woman said. "These people had no taste in clothing."

Jade's hand grasped tighter around her knife's handle as the woman made her way further inside.

"That's not what we came for," her partner said.

"Move out!" the leader yelled. "There's other houses to hit!"

The woman smacked her lips and slammed the door. Jade heard their footsteps go downstairs and out of the house. She waited for a moment. The front door closed. She started to breathe normally—hard and ragged. Finally, she came out of the closet. Someone hit her from behind as soon as she stepped out. Jade fell to the floor.

"Surprise, bitch!"

Jade looked up at the woman and kicked her as she launched at her. The woman stumbled back. She was about to yell out to the others when Jade kicked her in between her legs. The woman doubled over. Jade jumped up and was able to block a punch from the woman in time. She returned a blow, and the woman stumbled back. The woman quickly recovered and tackled Jade. They both went tumbling back into the dresser. Jade kneed her in the face. The woman grabbed a bat and started swinging it at Jade.

Jade pulled out her knife.

The woman smiled. "She's come to play."

"Jesus, will you shut the hell up."

The woman came charging with the bat. Jade moved her body to the side—her arm protecting her head. Jade caught the blow on the shoulder. She grabbed the bat and pulled the woman closer to her. She gave the woman a quick cut on her stomach. The woman jumped back, a little surprised that Jade cut her. Taking advantage of her being caught off guard, Jade pulled the woman's hair and bashed her head against the dresser. The woman dropped to the floor—unconscious.

Jade looked around, took some of the clothes the woman was criticizing earlier, and tied her up to the bedpost with them. She tied a scarf around her mouth so she wouldn't scream when she woke up.

"Lyanna!"

Jade rushed to the bedroom window and saw that one of the guys were heading back that way. She looked back at the woman, who was called Lyanna, and saw that she was still knocked out. Jade rushed out of the room and downstairs. She went out the back door and hopped over the fence.

Jade ran for her life.

"Lyanna!" she heard again in the distance.

Jade kept running until she had to stop. She held her chest, "Shit." She had to go to the hospital. At this point, it was inevitable.

~2~

Jade stood a few blocks away from the hospital—the emergency entrance in sight. She was scoping the place out to see what their security was like. How often did security make a patrol? Did they run your name before or after they took care of you? These were just some of the things she needed to know before she did what she had to do. Unfortunately, she didn't see how the staff operated inside. It was a huge risk to take, but she had to take it or die.

Making her way to the emergency entrance, each step was getting harder and harder to take. Her breaths were getting shorter. The stress of entering the hospital was making it harder. It was now or never. She would figure something out once inside. She always did.

The hospitals had drastically changed. Back when everything was normal, there were people in and out of the hospital. Busy for those who worked there. Now hospitals were a dead zone for the living. Hardly anyone went in for medical emergencies anymore.

As things deteriorated, medical care and equipment became rare and expensive. The government still had little control over people and implemented a law regarding treatment compensation: no payment, no treatment. People thought it was a joke until the government released the DCs, an aggressive task force that captures and imprisons those in medical debt, known as debtors.

Horror stories began to float around—DC officers abusing their power, torturing people, doing unspeakable things. The government didn't seem to care. At this point, the only major crime to commit was to abuse the medical system.

A cruel world.

Jade pressed on. She walked up to the registration desk. Two women sat behind the counter flipping through old magazines, which they've probably read a thousand times. Their bored expressions made them look like twins. It was a struggle for Jade to catch her next breath.

"May I help you?" one of the women asked. By her tone, she seemed very uninterested.

"I'm-having-a-asth-"

"Name?"

"Sarah-Blane," Jade saw that it was the name of the woman who owned the abandoned house. She had several aliases and was glad to add this to her roster.

One of the women typed her name on the computer while the other put a wrist band around Jade's wrist.

"Come around back," one of them said.

The door next to the desk opened, and a male nurse greeted Jade. "What brings you in today?" he took her blood pressure.

"Asthma-attack," Jade relaxed a little. She was still in an abandoned area, so the security wasn't that tight.

"Ok, let's get you that breathing treatment," he put Jade into an exam room. "Be right back."

Jade sat on the exam table with her head hanging low, and her eyes closed. She focused on breathing. Jade just needed to get through this treatment and sneak out before they figured out who she really was. Hopefully, she could score something along the way. There was a small knock at the door.

"Ms. Blane?" a younger man came into the room. "How are you feeling today?"

"Been-better."

"I hear you're having an asthma attack."

Jade nodded.

"Ok well, the doctor should be with you shortly. I just need to get some information from you first. Where are you currently staying?"

"In-between-houses. My-aunt-stays-on-the-west-side."

"Address?"

"It's-it's-it's," Jade swayed a little as if she was about to pass out.

"Ok, ok, I'll get that from you later. I just need a drop of your blood," the guy pricked Jade's finger and added her blood droplets on a slide. "The doctor will be with you shortly."

Jade figured she had about 45 minutes. Hospitals used people's blood samples to determine who they were and if they owed any medical expenses. When people realized that the new medical law was real, they started to use fake names. The government required that hospitals take blood samples and run them through a database to see if they owed any money. Hard to trick the system when they have your DNA.

"Ms. Blane," the doctor entered. "I have your breathing treatment."

Jade gave a fake smile.

He set up the machine and handed her the mouthpiece. "I'll be back to check on you."

Jade closed her eyes and inhaled. She was relieved to be receiving treatment. Her lungs welcomed them. For a moment she didn't think about anything. Not the state of the world. Not the consequences she would face if she got caught. She let her mind roam free. She thought about the place she used to visit when things were good. It was a field by her house. It had this beautiful Gilead tree. She would lay under it when she wanted to escape from everyone. It was her safe haven—her home. Oh, how she wished she could go back there.

The tightness in her chest began to lighten up. She was able to breathe more easily. The medicine in the breathing machine was getting low. Jade sat up. She had to plan for her escape. She listened out for voices outside her door. Any moment now they were going to see that she was a debtor and the DCs would be there to get her.

The machine started to whistle—letting her know that it was all out of medicine. Jade jumped off the examination table and wrapped her scarf around her face so that she was unrecognizable. She quickly searched the cabinets and drawers in the room. Rubber gloves, face masks, Band-Aids, and alcohol pads were stuffed in her bag. Jade took a deep breath and headed for the door.

She cracked open the door a little to see if she saw or heard anybody nearby. Everyone sounded far away. She walked out of the room, quietly and quickly. The nurses at the nurses' station could be heard talking.

"Did the identity confirmation come back for exam room 3?"

"Need a couple more minutes."

Jade kneeled and leaned against the wall. She made sure that they couldn't see her and then moved quickly.

"You think she's a debtor?"

"Call the DCs."

"Just leave her be, will ya."

"It's the law, Stacey. I'm not getting imprisoned to protect some debtor."

"Look where we are?! Everyone's a debtor!"

"Not my problem, *Stacey*."

Jade managed to turn right down a corridor without being seen. She started looking for exit signs.

"We're supposed to help people. Heal them. Not imprison them for their sickness," Stacey said.

"You're just emotional because we had to report that mother and her child."

"And it wasn't right!"

Stacey's co-worker ignored her last comment and began scrolling through the computer. An alert popped up. "Jade Willer!"

"What?"

"It's Jade Willer, get security!"

Jade was at the end of the corridor. She made a left down another hall and began to jog.

"Just let her go!"

"No chance in hell Stacey!"

A couple more turns down two more corridors and then she hit the jackpot. Jade saw a cart with five boxes of inhalers on them and another with half eaten food. They both were left unattended. They were abandoned once it was alerted that a debtor was in the building. With one quick, swift movement, Jade loaded the goods in her bag. She spotted an exit door up ahead and went into an outright sprint. She burst through the door and into the night.

She kept running until she was miles away from the hospital.

She kept running until she couldn't run anymore.

~3~

For the first time in a long time, Jade actually felt relaxed. She found a house to stay in that was close to the city, but far enough to avoid the DCs. Most of her days were spent sleeping and reflecting on life before the madness. For the most part, she was an average teen. She had friends. A boyfriend, Vincent. A lovely family, whom she missed dearly and now realized that she'd completely taken them for granted. She sat up from the floor in one of the rooms she was sleeping in. She rested her hand on her forehead. She tried not to think about her overbearing mother. It killed her to think about her loving, caring father. And oh, the affectionate laugh of her little sister! How she wished she could hear her laugh again. Jade hadn't seen her family in a while. Long before things started going bad.

Jade got up and started looking around for some hygienic items.

"You're so damn selfish!" Jade recalled her mother saying. She had just come back four hours after curfew. She was nonchalant about the situation and about causing her family such worry.

"We thought you were dead or something!"

"What's the big deal?" Jade laughed. "I'm here now so relax."

Her father shook his head, and her sister shifted in her seat. Jade was in her rebellious phase, and she was wreaking havoc on her family.

"Were you out with Vincent again?"

Jade didn't answer her mother.

"I'm tired of this shit, Jade! I told you I don't trust that boy!

"Ma chill out!"

"What the hell were y'all doing at 2'oclock in the morning!"

"None of your business!"

"Enough, Jade!" Jade stood stunned. Her father never raised his voice before. He approached her with his hand out. "Give me your phone."

"What?"

"Give me your phone now. You will get it back by the end of summer."

"Are you kidding me?! You guys are overreacting!" Jade clutched her phone in her hand.

"You've been gone for hours without a word, and we're overreacting?!" her mother intervened.

Jade's father didn't wait for another word. He forcefully snatched the phone out of Jade's hand. She stood there, fuming. She and her parents continued to have their shouting match about unfairness, worry, and selfishness.

"Why don't you just leave Jade?!" her 12-year-old sister yelled at the top of her lungs.

Jade felt like she was just punched in the gut. "What?"

"Just leave! You act like you don't wanna be here!"

Jade stared at her sister. *Has she been that hard to deal with? So hard that her sister wanted her gone for good?* Her parents were silent—neither confirming nor denying the situation.

"Just go!" her sister yelled. She got in Jade's face. "Leave!"

Jade slowly backed away. "Sorry I'm such a burden!" Jade ran away from home. No one went after her that night.

Jade slammed the medicine cabinet so hard that the mirror cracked. "Great, that's another 7 years of bad luck."

She stared at her reflection through the cracked piece of glass. She changed so much since then. Her once straightened hair was now in a curly, kinky state. Her dark brown skin that was once graced with makeup now showed all her flaws that she used to hate—particularly her freckles. Her brown eyes mostly stayed the same, but what was once happiness that lied behind them was replaced with sadness and anger.

She began searching through the cabinet under the sink. "Where the hell is the tissue and soap?"

Thinking about her family always put her in a bad mood. How could she have been so stupid? She had a loving, caring, supportive family, and she took them for granted. Even though her parents begged many times for her to return home, Jade lived on her own for about a year before everything went wrong.

It felt like it was yesterday. Jade was sleeping at a friend's house, who was out of town when the house started to shake. She jumped up and manage to avoid the things that were falling. It was hard to believe that she was experiencing an earthquake—she was living in Michigan after all. Running outside, she saw all the neighbors fleeing about. The guy down the street got smashed by a tree that was in his front yard. The old lady next door fell inside a large crack that appeared in the middle of the street. A house collapsed with a family trapped inside. Their screams were agonizing.

Jade was terrified.

She was all alone.

Jade tried to look for her family after the first natural disaster, but her house no longer stood. She searched for them for about a month, when finally, an old neighbor told her that they died trying to save the elderly woman down the street. Jade couldn't believe it. When she asked about her sister, the neighbor couldn't give her an answer. Jade steadily looked for her after that. She checked every FEMA shelter that was within a 50-mile radius, but no one ever seen nor heard from her.

After countless more of natural disasters, robberies, and looting, the FEMA shelters were left abandoned. Workers were starting to get more concerned about themselves and their families than those who were eventually robbing them. Jade began to lose hope once the shelters began to shut down. She tried to keep looking for her sister, but after a while, her attention focused on staying off the DCs radar.

Jade figured that her sister was dead.

"I need soap and fucking tissue!"

Tears ran down her face. She was young then and didn't know any better. When everything started to go wrong, she was alone. Her family wasn't there to love her, to comfort her, to support her. She shook her feelings off. She needed to focus on the task at hand. And that was finding soap and tissue. It had been weeks since she used those items and she couldn't bear her smell any longer. She kicked the cabinet's door—realizing that she would have to go out and search for them. She put on her boots, wrapped her scarf around her nose and mouth, and headed out.

It was quiet out.

Jade never really saw a lot of people anyway, but today was a little too quiet. It was an eerie quiet. Walking three blocks over, she quickly dismissed the strange feeling that she had in the pit of her stomach. She looked through a few houses and came up empty. There was no soap or tissue to be found anywhere. Jade knew what she had to do, and she dreaded it.

The only places that had all the essential needs for survival were hospitals and government buildings—all the places that run your name. Jade sat on a porch to think for a minute. Although she was rationing, she was running low on food. Her little trip to the hospital was over a month ago. She thought about where to go.

There was an Urgent Care facility that was two miles away. She could go there. There was always less security at an Urgent Care facility because they had less essential equipment than a hospital. And what was even better was that she was still on the poor part of town. She figured security would be even less if any at all.

It was final: she would go to the Urgent Care facility. She would find tissue, soap, food, and anything else that was of good use. If she could get more inhalers, a breathing machine, or albuterol, that would be even better. Jade started off the porch.

"No!" a piercing scream came from behind her. She quickly turned around to see no one there.

More screams and gunshots followed. Jade ran to the backyard and stopped in front of the garage. There were DC officers. Debtors were trying to flee from them. They were doing a sweep—rounding everyone up and running their names to see who was in debt. But in this part of the city, they knew that everyone was a debtor.

A woman was out running a couple of DC officers, but she tripped on something, and they pinned her down. She let out an agonizing scream. The woman struggled against them as much as she could, until a DC officer hit her in the head with a baton.

Jade stood there, frozen.

This was the first time she'd been close to the DCs since she watched her boyfriend and his family get taken away. She knew that she should run—put as much distance between her and the DCs as she could, but she couldn't move.

"What are you doing?!" a guy yelled to her, breaking her out of her trance. He was in the yard next door. "GO!"

Jade took off running. The guy was right behind her. She ran in the direction towards the Urgent Care facility. The plan was for her to stock up on supplies and get as far away from the city as she could. Jade glanced down each street and saw that the DCs were doing a sweep. They were hitting the entire neighborhood simultaneously, collecting as many debtors as they could.

The scene reminded her of the last time she saw her boyfriend, Vincent. She had been surviving with him and his family after the new medical law was implemented. They've been moving from house to house trying to avoid the DCs. Unfortunately, with Vincent's father battle with cancer and her issues with asthma, it was hard for them to stay off the DCs radar.

It was a year after the new medical law had been enforced, and Jade and Vincent's father were at $100,000 apiece. Jade and Vincent were leaving out of an abandoned house when they saw his family being rounded up by DC officers. They both froze. Vincent pushed her into some bushes.

"Stay here and don't come out until the coast is clear."

Tears filled her eyes. "Don't."

"Jade, please, just stay here," he turned to leave but stopped. "I love you."

"I love you too," she took a moment to really look at him. It felt like the

first time in years. His flawless, olive skin; his bright smile; his beautiful chiseled face; and she never noticed how much facial hair he had for a 17-year-old. He was her first love, and she had a sinking feeling when he walked away.

That was the last time she saw him. He was beaten unconscious and dragged away by the DCs. Two weeks later Jade heard that Vincent's family died. A couple of months after that, she got word that Vincent became a bounty hunter for the DCs. She couldn't believe it. Bounty hunters hunted debtors in return for food and shelter from the DCs. You didn't need any specialized training to be a bounty hunter—only debt free. Jade couldn't understand why Vincent would do that. She feared running into him again.

Unbelievably, Jade was able to avoid the attention of the DCs. There were so many people squatting in the abandoned houses that it was a little too much for them to handle. Her breaths were getting shorter and shorter. Her asthma was becoming agitated from running and stress. She was about two blocks away from Urgent Care. It was noticeably peaceful. Jade figured she was ok here. She stopped abruptly—her hands on her knees.

"You ok?"

"Sh-it," it was the guy who told her to run. She didn't notice that he was behind her the whole time. Jade reached in the side of her boot and pulled out an inhaler. She took two quick puffs.

"You ok?" he asked again.

Jade nodded. She took slow breaths. The tightness in her chest loosened up. She was able to breathe more easily. She readjusted her scarf—to keep dust and peering eyes out. She started walking toward the Urgent Care.

"Where you going?" the guy followed her.

"To Urgent Care," she looked over at the guy. He looked rough. He had long shaggy, disheveled brown hair, and a thick beard with eyebrows to match. His ivory skin looked well-tanned, but Jade could tell that he was tired and suffering.

"Why?"

"I'm gonna steal some supplies and get the hell out of the city."

"Are you crazy?"

She turned around to face him. "These inhalers aren't gonna last forever."

They stood in silence for a minute. Jade eventually resumed walking. The guy fidgeted with his hands for a moment. "I have diabetes," he said as he caught up to her. "Insulin would be nice."

"And some food."

"Ok," he said. "But we gotta be careful."

"I wouldn't be doing it if I wasn't."

"I'm David by the way."

"Jade."

They both walked towards the Urgent Care. Jade scanned the area for signs of any DCs.

"Well this suck," David said.

"You think the DCs will be here?" Jade asked, ignoring his last comment.

"Probably," he looked around. He caught Jade's eye. He smiled. She frowned at him—not knowing why he was smiling. David cleared his throat. "You know I hear that America is the only country that *still* charges for medical treatment."

"Riveting," Jade never really concerned herself with what was going on around the world. She only involved herself with how she was going to get by day to day.

"Yeah, Canada, Switzerland, New Zealand. They're like safe havens for medical needs."

"How can you be so sure?"

"I can't, but it seems like any place is better than here. I mean the world is ending and all America can think about is how to capitalize on the last essential resources."

"Well, what choice do we have?"

"We can fight. Or leave. Hell, anything would be better than staying here."

Jade didn't say anything. She just gave David a strange look. He was sharing a lot for someone she just met.

"Sorry," he said. "I haven't had the opportunity to share my thoughts with anyone else."

"Don't wor...shit," they both stopped walking. The entrance of the Urgent Care facility was guarded by a group of DC officers. There was a line of debtors who were getting their names checked.

"Don't run," David whispered. "Just turn around and walk away slowly."

Jade readjusted her scarf and kept her breath still. They turned around and began walking away. Jade prayed that they would get away unnoticed. She ran her hands over the beads of her rosary.

"Don't you wanna get out of this fucked-up country?" David whispered. "Or at least fight against this shit?"

Jade never thought about leaving or fighting against the government. She just learned how to adapt and survive. "Can we just foc—"

"Hey! Stop right there!" They both turned around and saw a DC officer running towards them.

"Run!"

They took off running. David went left, Jade went right. She ran a couple blocks and then turned into an alley. Jade hopped over a fence and ran a few more blocks. She ran down four more blocks and made a left. Halfway down the block, a force hit her right side, causing her to fall in a front yard. She believed that it was a DC officer who tackled her to the ground.

"Get off of ME!!" she managed to kick the guy in the face. He flew back, blood pouring from his nose. Jade got weak once she realized who it was.

Vincent stared at her with anger in his eyes. "You lil' bitch!" he yelled as he stood, each sound flinging blood in the small space of air, separating Jade from her attacker. As he stumbled forward, he managed an efficient kick to Jade's stomach.

"Vincent," she managed to get out. She tried to gasp for air. She got up—only to stumble a few paces and fall again. Her asthma was triggered. It was hard to breathe. Jade was convinced that this was the end for her. She was going to die right there. Vincent laughed.

"Having trouble there, Jade?" he dragged her into the street by her hair.

"Vincent, please," tears streamed down her face. This was not the same guy that she used to love. Jade always wondered what it would've been like running into him again after all these years. She prayed that it wasn't like this.

"Yeah, my family begged too," he said, letting her hair go. A couple of DC officers began to approach them. Vincent kneeled on top of her. "Imagine how I felt when my mother died because of you and my father."

"Hold her down!" a DC officer ordered.

Vincent held her arms down with his knees. Jade kicked, screamed, and struggled against him. He still managed to prick her finger. They ran her name.

"No need to run her," Vincent said, staring down at her with dead eyes.

"Jade Willer, $600,000. I see you've had no problem racking up your debt Jade. Even after my mother got your treatments under her name. You just had to keep going. No matter if she was in debt. Selfish bitch!" He punched her.

Jade could feel the blood running from her lip.

She remembered that argument. It was the day his family was taken away. He wanted his mother to stop using her name to get Jade her breathing treatments. Vincent and his mother were in good health. His father and Jade not so much. His mother was using her name for both Jade and Vincent's father. She collected a lot of debt because of that, which was why she was taken by the DCs along with Vincent's father.

Her results came back to the officers. "Cuff her."

"No!" Jade kicked and struggled as one of the officers tried to cuff her.

Suddenly Vincent fell to the ground. Someone had tackled him. Jade watched as the two guys wrestled on the ground. Without any hesitation, she elbowed the DC officer that tried to handcuff her. He fell to the ground, and she kicked him until he was unconscious.

The other officer made his way to her—baton in hand. Jade pulled out her knife and charged at him. She gave a slice to his baton hand, and he immediately dropped it. Slamming him to the ground, Jade began punching him until he was unconscious.

Jade looked over at Vincent and the other guy wrestling. She realized that it was David. Vincent had gotten the upper hand and was now on top of David, punching him furiously. Jade jumped on his back and wrapped her arm around his neck. He fell backward, landing on top of her. It felt like the wind had been knocked out of her. David took one of the DCs batons and hit Vincent on the head—knocking him out.

David helped Jade off the ground. "We gotta go."

Jade reached down in her boot and took out her inhaler. "Thanks-for-that," she said in between puffs.

"Don't mention it," he wiped the blood from his nose.

They saw another group of DC officers running toward them; they ran in the opposite direction. They cut through side streets, backyards, and alleys. The city was chaotic. Debtors were running for their lives—young and old.

They turned down another alley and hid behind a dumpster as more officers passed by. They watched as they dragged a lady down the street by her hair. She screamed in agony as they forced her into a debtor transport van. There were several people chained in the back. They shoved the woman onto a bench and handcuffed her hands and feet to it. Once the officers closed the doors, Jade and David could hear courageous voices screaming and shouting.

"Corruption!"

"Please let me out!"

"Greed!"

"Get me out of here!"

"Capitalism!"

"Please! Someone help me!"

David shook his head. "Don't you wanna fight against this?"

"I'm just here to survive," How could she fight? Jade was only one person. She just looked out for herself. She had become so desensitized. For that, she felt ashamed.

No wonder Vincent hated her.

A piercing scream broke up their discussion.

Jade froze.

A DC officer was dragging a young girl away. The young girl put up an intense fight and was subjected to blows from the officer. Jade was horrified. All she could see was her sister receiving the severe violence from the officer. Jade knew that the young girl wasn't her sister—her sister would've been a woman by now, but the young girl reminded Jade so much of her. Her short, pixie hair disheveled as she shook her head back and forth in resistance. Her big brown eyes looked around frantically for someone to save her. Her small, narrow nose scrunched up every time the officer punched her petite frame.

Jade was in shock. She couldn't believe what she was seeing. Why did they have to deal with this? With everything else they had to go through once the world fell apart, why were the very same people integral in rebuilding the world being beaten, tortured, ripped apart from their families, and murdered for trying to survive?

Jade's haggard breathing calmed. Her shock turned into anger. Her anger turned into hatred. She just wanted to escape—escape from everything. She wished for her family. She wished for Vincent to love her again. She wished for the world not to end. She wished for Canada, for Switzerland, for New Zealand. She wished for rebellion towards the DCs and the government. Before she knew it, she stepped from behind the dumpster.

The world around her slowed.

The debtors' yelling and screams seemed incoherent. The DCs attacked their victims in a robotic motion. It seemed like the young girl's beating was even more brutal than before. It was as if it was all a dream, but Jade's heart and mind told her differently. Her eyes met the young girls— they pleaded for help. The knife left Jade's hand so effortlessly—the blade giving the tips of her fingers a kiss goodbye. She didn't think. She just reacted. All she saw was an innocent young girl who looked so much like her sister. She was in danger—being apprehended by a DC officer.

So, the knife left Jade's hand—the blade kissing her fingertips.

The knife went into the officer's chest, and his body froze. His eyes bulged, and he stared at Jade—right into her eyes. He stared at her knowing he was dead. Jade wondered if he would be able to pay for the hospital fees to save his life. His look told her he wouldn't.

Crimson blood oozed down his chest. He dropped the young girl and stumbled back. Without warning, he went down like a fallen tree. Jade stood in disbelief for a moment—her first kill. She had run-ins with people before, but she was always able to fight them off and escape. Something changed. She could no longer just stand by and watch as injustice and corruption unfold. She had to make a stance.

Jade stared at the young girl. "No more surviving," she said more to herself.

~4~

*N*o *more surviving.*

"No more surviving," Jade felt like she was dreaming.

No, correction, she felt like she had an out-of-body experience. She stared at the dead DC officer—blood oozing down his chest, her knife sticking out. She had just killed someone. Jade never did that before, but the risk was worth it. She stared at the little girl who reminded her so much of her sister. Jade had to save her. She couldn't watch the little girl fall victim to the cruel DC.

Jade forgot for a moment exactly where she was. She forgot that the DCs were doing a sweep and gathering all debtors who were in their mist. She forgot about David, her 45-minute-partner, who had helped her out of some close calls. She forgot about her fear of being caught. Everything was forgotten—only for a moment.

The DCs were still doing their sweep, and someone was bound to stumble across them and the dead officer soon. Jade would never be off their radar. She would always be a wanted woman.

"Christ," David mumbled.

Jade glanced down at the dead officer and then back at the little girl. She looked around at the chaos that surrounded her. A woman peeked from behind a nearby dumpster. They had to move. Someone was bound to alert the DCs about the dead officer soon. With one swift movement, Jade took the knife out of the officer's chest and grabbed the little girl's hand.

"We gotta move!" she yelled back to David as she led the little girl away.

David stopped staring at the officer's dead body. "Right." He followed. They ran down streets and alleys trying to avoid the DC.

Jade was worried that the DC officers would figure out what she had done. She couldn't imagine the consequences behind the discovery. They had to get out of sight. Jade stopped for a moment behind a house. Her chest was tightening again, and she needed to take two puffs of her inhaler. She looked around. They needed somewhere to hide. A warehouse was just up ahead.

"We-can-hide-in-there."

"You ok?" David asked. Jade nodded. "Ok, let's go."

The three of them ran towards the warehouse—hiding behind dumpsters, garages, and abandoned cars along the way. The scenery was getting more intense by the minute. Debtors and DC officers swarmed the streets. Jade felt very uneasy. She needed to get out of sight. She felt like someone would know what she did if they saw her. They hid behind an abandoned car just a block away from the warehouse.

Jade and David scoped the area out. It didn't look like there were any

DC officers around, but they still waited for a moment. Jade glanced over at the little girl; she seemed very weak and badly bruised. It was surprising to see how severely injured the little girl was. Jade remembered the beating being severe, but not *that* severe.

"You good?" Jade asked her.

"Yeah," the little girl mumbled.

"Time to move. Stay close," David led the way, the girl followed, and Jade took the back.

The warehouse had five floors; Jade thought the fifth floor would be the best hiding spot. Darkness was falling, and she hoped that it would help hide them.

"Stay here," David instructed. "I'll go further inside to see if it's clear."

The girl sat down in the doorway.

"You sure you good?" Jade asked again.

"Yeah just tired," she rested her head against the door frame. "Thank you for saving me."

"You're welcome," that felt like a meaningless thing to say for saving someone's life. "What's your name?"

"Raina."

"That's a beautiful name. I'm Jade." Raina nodded and sighed. "How old are you?"

"Eleven."

"Where's your family?"

"It's just been my mom and me, but she was taken away by the DCs a while ago."

"I'm so sorry."

David came back to them. "It's all clear."

Jade and Raina followed him. They went up to the fifth floor and barricaded themselves in a corner office. The sound of the chaos was finally dying down. Jade crept to the only window in the office. She kneeled so she wouldn't be visible. She didn't see anyone out on the streets anymore. Screams could still be heard as the sound of the DC trucks rolled away.

It really looked like a war zone out there. Jade noticed some blood on the street, along with articles of clothing and shoes. Just then a guy, a teenager maybe, sprinted pass. A DC officer was right on his tail. The officer stopped and withdrew his gun.

"Stop!"

The guy kept running. The DC officer fired his gun. Jade ducked down. The guy screamed out in pain. A DC truck pulled up. More officers arrived and loaded the guy in the DC truck. The guy's protest could be heard as the truck drove away. Jade's heart sank. She couldn't save them all.

Jade looked back out the window and saw that the truck was gone. "I think we might be good."

"I can't believe you killed that guy," David said.

"Yeah well, you said I should make a stand."

"Yeah but..."

"But what?"

David said nothing.

"Are you suggesting that I should've let him take the girl?"

"No, I'm not..."

"I don't feel good about what I've done, but I would've felt a whole lot worse if I haven't done anything at all."

"I'm not saying what you did was wrong," David explained. "It was just so sudden, that's all."

"Yeah well, it's clear that the DC isn't showing any mercy," Jade glanced over at Raina, who was now sleeping soundlessly in the corner across the room. "I wonder what she has."

"Huh?"

"She's a debtor...I wonder what she has."

David shook his head. "I can't believe they're taking children."

"The only thing that matters to them is if you're in the red."

David slid down to the floor.

"How you holding up?" Jade asked.

"A little weak."

Jade dug in her backpack and took out some peanut butter crackers she stole from the hospital a month ago. She figured that David's blood sugar was getting low. She handed them to him.

"Thank you."

"We should probably get some rest."

David nodded as he munched down on the crackers.

~5~

Jade, David, and Raina spent the next couple of days hiding out in the warehouse. DC officers were still flooding the streets—doing sweeps and something else. David and Jade tried to figure out what they were doing, but they both guessed what it could've been.

"We gotta move," Jade was trying not to panic.

"We don't know if that's why they're out," David tried to calm her.

"I've never seen them out like this," Raina was peeking out the window. "It has to be because of the dead officer."

Jade began to pace back and forth. This was bad. The DCs was searching for her. She was going to get caught, and she knew it. She couldn't imagine what they were going to do to her. There was sure to be an endless amount of torture before they eventually killed her.

Jade heard the rumors about DC officers torturing people in prison. A guy who broke an officer's nose was waterboarded for three days straight. Then there were the rumors about prisoners being tortured by electrocution, solitary, starvation, and sleep deprivation. However, the stories about the abuse of women prisoners are what frightened Jade the most. There was an endless amount of sexual assault that women endured there.

She wouldn't last a day in there.

To make matters worse, Jade was now on Bossman's radar, and that terrified her. Bossman was the one in charge of the DC task force. He called all the shots and made all the rules. No one knew his real name, but they knew how vicious he could be. No debtor has survived when they've dealt with Bossman. They said he'd torture debtors for days, sometimes weeks or even months. He'll have you begging and wishing for death before he eventually put you out of your misery.

What terrified Jade, even more, was Bossman's right-hand man, Razor. Jade didn't know who was crazier. Razor was said to have more violent outburst than Bossman, and his explosions were usually more lethal. Sometimes Razor would spend days torturing debtors before Bossman came to finish them off. Now they were looking for her. Jade couldn't have been the only person that killed a DC officer.

It's just no one has ever survived.

"Once darkness hits, I'll go out and see what's going on," David said.

"But what if you get seen?"

"Trust me, I won't," he paused for a moment. "Plus, we need food and supplies."

Jade agreed. Her supplies were running low now that she was sharing it with two other people. "Be careful."

"In the meantime, I think you two should hide out in another room."

Jade and Raina agreed to hide out in a supply closet in the basement, in case someone came in looking around.

"I'll be back soon," David said as he left.

Jade and Raina sat on the closet floor in silence. It would've been pitch black, but David gave them a glow stick that he found in one of the rooms. Jade took out her knives and arranged them in front of her. She wiped them down with her scarf. She did this whenever she got bored, which was often. Her motto: a clean knife was a good knife. She noticed Raina looking at them.

"Were they a gift?"

"No, I found them one day when I was scavenging through a house."

Jade remembered it like it was yesterday. It was weeks since Vincent and his family were taken by the DCs and she had her first encounter with some shady people. She barely escaped—with the help of an aluminum bat. Jade hid out in a house, miles away from where she was attacked, for about a month.

One day she finally made it up to the attic—after spending days going through their closets, drawers, and medicine cabinets. The room upstairs appeared to be a study. The dad was obviously a hunter considering all the stuffed animals and animal heads that decorated the room. The knives were in a glass display case, which was coated with dust. Jade took them out and stared at them in awe. They were so beautiful to her. Lions were roaring out at her. She loved lions. It wasn't clear if she loved them because they were her zodiac sign, or because she saw them as a symbol of strength. Nevertheless, seeing those knives gave her hope, it gave her power, it gave her a sense of security.

"Can I see one?"

Jade handed Raina one.

Raina stared at the handle. "Cool! It has a picture of a lion roaring." She looked up at Jade, smiling.

"Yeah, I thought that was cool too."

"What's the handle made out of?"

"Pearl, I think."

Raina handed back the knife. "They're beautiful."

"Thank you," she strapped them back across her thighs—two knives on each leg.

Jade remembered when she first started practicing with them. The dad's study had a dartboard hanging on the back of the door, and Jade would spend hours, sometimes days, practicing her throw. She used the stuffed bear and lion as combat practice too. Although they couldn't fight back, she found herself becoming pretty good.

The other days were spent on running. Running around the block endlessly. Running up and down the basement stairs. Although these weren't wise choices, it helped Jade go the distance before her asthma really started bothering her. She finally found out how well her practicing was going when a group came scavenging at the house she was in. They didn't expect her to be so skillful.

"I'm sorry by the way."

"For what?" Jade said, coming back to her current situation.

Raina shrugged. "For causing you all this trouble. Now they're looking for you."

"They were already looking for me. Besides, I couldn't let the officer take you."

"Why did you save me?"

"You're a child," Jade paused. "And you remind me of my lil' sister."

"Were you two close?"

Jade was silent. She was too ashamed to answer.

"Is she still alive?"

"The last time I saw her was 11 years ago. She was 12."

"What was her name?"

"Helena."

"That's a pretty name."

"Yes, it was."

They were silent for a moment. Both lost in their own thoughts. Jade thought about her sister, Helena. She missed her so much. She could've been a better sister to her. But she was all about herself.

"You're a debtor, right?" Jade asked, trying to pull her thoughts somewhere else.

"Yeah, I have leukemia."

Jade was taken aback. She knew that whatever Raina had had to be serious, but she never thought it was *that* serious. "I'm so sorry," she managed to say.

Raina laughed. "It's ok."

"How old were you when you found out?"

"One, the same time everything went to shit. Just my luck, right?"

"You don't have any brothers or sisters?"

"Nah, like I said, it was always my mom and me...until a while ago."

Jade nodded.

"But hey...I'm surviving."

"Yeah, that's the problem."

They sat the rest of the time in silence. Raina eventually fell asleep. After a while, Jade began to doze off too—until she heard some footsteps at the top of the stairs. She quickly covered up the glow stick and awoke Raina with her hand over her mouth. She took out her knife as the footsteps got closer.

"Jade, it's me, David." Jade still had her knife out—in case someone was making him say that. "I'm gonna open the door now."

Once the door was open Jade saw David with his hands in the air—as if he already knew she would be on edge.

"There's no one with me," he continued. "Just me."

Raina walked out of the closet and looked around. "He's alone."

Jade walked out of the closet. "Sorry."

"Don't apologize."

"So, did you find anything?" Raina asked once they were back in their usual hiding room.

"Lots," David emptied a bag of canned goods. They each took a can for themselves. Jade had green beans. "I came across a storm shelter. It was untouched."

"That's weird," Jade said.

He got uneasy for a moment. "I found something else too." David took out a piece of paper from his pocket and unfolded it. He handed it to Jade. "I think you might wanna see this."

Jade took the paper and saw her face staring back at her. There she was in sketch form. Her brown eyes, her cocoa skin, her small and pointy nose—her red scarf! The word "wanted" was capitalized right above her picture, and her full name "Jade Willer" was at the bottom. Jade figured that someone told the DC she was the one who killed the officer—maybe that woman behind the dumpster. They probably tortured it out of her.

"These are all around town," David said.

Jade nodded.

"We should probably move out tomorrow night."

"Ok," she said weakly.

~6~

Surprisingly Jade slept peacefully that night—even after she knew that the DCs were really after her. She had no nightmares about being caught. Instead, she dreamt about her sister Helena. It was more of a recollection than a dream. It was the day Jade and Helena went to the park. Jade was 14, and Helena was 10. They ran around for hours playing with each other. Jade pushed Helena on the swings—her pixie hair blowing in the wind. They hung off the monkey bars and climbed on the jungle gym. They ended their day eating ice cream on their front porch.

"Jade," Helena said, licking on her bomb pop popsicle. "Promise we'll do this all the time."

"Promise," Jade said, eating her fudgsicle.

They never did.

Jade hung out with her friends and got a boyfriend. After a while, the only thing that Jade and Helena did was fight. Helena was nothing but an annoying little sister at that point.

"Jade! Jade!" a faint voice yelled. Someone was shaking her. Jade saw the silhouette of Raina running around grabbing things.

"Jade! Get up!" David yelled.

Jade jumped up. "What's going on?"

"They're raiding the building next door," David packed up the last bit of the canned food. "We gotta move."

Jade quickly put on her boots and wrapped her scarf around her nose and mouth. She crept to the window and peeked out. There was a DC raid truck across the street. Two officers were standing in front of the building, keeping watch.

"Can we go out the back?" Raina said.

"Maybe out of the loading dock area," Jade suggested.

"Ok good," David looked at Jade for a moment. "Maybe you should take that scarf off?"

"Yeah if you want me to have an asthma attack every second."

"Well at least throw this on," he handed her a black hoodie.

Jade put it on and pulled its hood up.

"Alright, let's get out of here," he led the way. They quietly made their way to the first floor. They stood in the dark shadows for a moment to see if anyone was inside or coming near.

Jade came out of their hiding place and signaled that the coast was clear.

"Where we gonna go?" Raina asked. Jade put her finger to her lips—suggesting that they should be quieter.

"The storm shelter I found," David whispered. "It's like half a mile away."

"Let's go," they reached the loading dock, and Jade cracked open the door.

"I'll go first," David suggested.

"Be careful," Raina said.

"I will. Three taps on the door mean it's safe. Be ready."

Jade took out two knives.

Raina looked around and found a pipe. She looked at Jade. "Just in case." They heard three quick taps on the door.

"Move," Jade opened the door slowly—her knife at the ready. David was standing on the other side.

"We'll have to take a long way," he said. "We gotta move quietly and quickly."

"Lead the way."

They dashed between houses, cars, and dumpsters. A swarm of DC officers was hitting the surrounding buildings across the street. Jade's heart was racing. She couldn't believe it. They were looking for her. Really looking! She was going to get caught eventually. David couldn't keep her hidden forever. A part of her felt sorry for putting him in this situation. He didn't need any more attention from the DC—neither did Raina. She just needed to get somewhere—somewhere the DC couldn't see her, then she could decide if she should take off or not.

"Orders are to take Willer alive. She is dangerous and killed one of our own. Move out," a DC officer said.

"We gotta go," David said. They ran behind a nearby dumpster until the coast was clear. David signaled to move forward, and they ran around the block away from DCs eyes.

They ran through more blocks that were DC-free. Occasionally, they stopped so Jade could catch her breath. Her inhalers were running low, and she was trying to ration them.

"Good to go?" David would ask after a few minutes.

Jade would nod.

"Good, we're almost there," they ran a few more blocks and then came to a sudden halt.

"Shit!" they all whispered. DC officers were swarming the streets.

"Let me guess, the storm shelter is on this street?" Jade asked.

"You know it."

"What are we gonna do?" fear was in Raina's eyes.

"We sneak past," David was scoping the scene. "Jade, you stay behind me, and Raina, you follow behind her. Jade is who they really want."

They took in the scene and waited for a precise moment. They were now in sync with one another. They automatically stopped at any object that shielded them from the DCs sight. They all knew just when to start moving without anyone saying anything.

"Just a couple more houses," they were now behind a shed.

Everything was going smoothly until a pipe hit the ground and rolled. Jade turned to see Raina on the ground. She had tripped on a protruding crack. Tears were forming in Raina's eyes.

"I got movement at 9 o' clock!"

Jade ran over and helped Raina up.

"I'm sorry," Raina whispered. Her voice was shaky.

"It's ok," Jade hurried and grabbed the pipe. Just then, a DC officer rounded the corner and locked eyes on her. Jade froze for a minute.

"I have visual on the target!" he yelled over the radio.

Jade swung the pipe and hit the DC officer on his knee cap. He went down, screaming in pain. "Run!" Jade yelled, pulling Raina with her.

"Follow me!"

They jumped over a fence and started running. David was in front while Raina and Jade followed. DC trucks sped towards them. They ran even faster.

"We're close!" David yelled. "It's right there!"

Jade could see the storm shelter—their temporary safe haven. Its steel door could provide them with protection. They were closer now.

Ten feet.

Nine feet.

Eight feet.

Then something fell on Jade. She stopped to look down at it. It covered her whole body. Light brown stuff coated her hands, her face, her nose, and mouth. Her chest tightened.

It was dust.

They dumped dust on her. The DC found out that she was asthmatic and used that against her. David and Raina turned around.

"No!" David ran towards Jade as she fell to the ground.

Jade couldn't breathe. She had a full-blown asthma attack. David picked her up and ran towards the shelter. Jade gasped for air, but nothing was coming through. She made a scary gasping sound. It was tough not to panic, but the lack of air was making that difficult.

A door opened and closed. David put Jade on the floor. They were in the storm shelter. He reached down in her boot and took out an inhaler. He handed it to her. Jade shook her head.

"Jade please."

It was useless, but she took two puffs to ease his mind. It didn't help. Banging started on the door. The DC officers were trying to break in. Jade's gasping increased. Her eyes got bigger as if they were about to pop out of their sockets.

"Hang in there, Jade," David encouraged. "Don't give up on me now!"

"Jade," Raina had tears falling from her eyes. The banging was getting louder and louder. "We gotta do something!"

Just then they heard an explosion. The DC officers were shouting. Then gunshots began to go off. It sounded like a war was going on outside. They all stood still—nothing but Jade's gasping to fill the air. She was focusing on not passing out, better yet dying. Just then it went silent for a moment, followed by another explosion. The storm shelter door flew open.

A group of people dressed in all black rushed in.

"What did they do to her?" the leader demanded. Raina choked on her words and couldn't respond. "I need an answer now!"

"She's having an asthma attack," David said.

"We need Keeper!" the leader said.

"Are you the Black Deficit?" Raina asked.

"Yes. You're in luck, kid."

A guy ran in from outside. "Don't worry, boss, I brought it." The guy dropped down next to Jade and pulled out a nebulizer, hooked it up, and put a breathing mask on her. "Don't worry Jade, I gotcha covered."

He started the machine, and Jade felt the medicine slowly drift into her airways. She finally drifted into unconsciousness.

~7~

Jade felt like she was dreaming, but she was just drifting in and out of consciousness.

"What did they do to her?"

"Threw dust on her," David said.

"Shit, they're starting to prey on our weaknesses."

Jade drifted back out, where she was welcomed to Helena's laughter. They were at the park, and Jade was pushing her on the swings.

Helena tilted her head back. "Let's do this forever."

"Forever."

"Put her in the medic wing."

"How long do you think she'll be out?"

"Push higher Jade. Higher!" Jade pushed Helena higher on the swings. Helena laughed with glee. "You're the best sister ever!"

"She needs another breathing treatment."

"Right away boss."

Jade could feel the medicated mist enter her lungs as she and Helena chased each other around.

"Catch me, Jade!"

"Is she gonna be ok?" Raina asked.

"Only time will tell, but I think she'll be fine."

"Catch me, Jade!" Jade ran after her little sister, but she just couldn't catch her. No matter how fast she ran, she just couldn't catch up with her.

"Catch me, Jade!" Jade ran faster. "Catch me!" Jade ran faster and faster and faster. She ran until she couldn't run anymore.

"Helena!" she yelled.

Beep.

"Helena!"

Beep.

"HELENA!"

Jade jumped up out of her sleep.

"It's ok, Jade," Raina was sitting next to her. A look of concern was in her eyes. "You just had a bad dream."

Jade looked around her surroundings. She was hooked up to an I.V., and a machine was monitoring her heart rate. It looked like she was in a medical ward in part of a building.

"Where are we?"

"At our headquarters," a muscular guy entered the room. He reminded Jade of someone who was in the army. He had a crew cut, and tattoos ran up down both of his arms. She could tell that he was the leader. His facial structure was strong and dominant. His eyes were bold and hopeful. He didn't live in the same world that she did.

"Headquarters?"

"Yes, the Black Deficit's headquarters."

"The rebel group?"

"You seemed surprised."

Jade shrugged. "Thought you guys were a myth that's all. And what kind of a name is the Black Deficit anyway? Seems like an oxymoron."

"That's the thanks we get for saving you?"

"Just telling the truth," she disconnected herself from the heart monitor. "Nonetheless, thank you for saving me."

"I'm Jackson, one of the leaders of the Black Deficit."

"Jade."

"We know who you are," a woman who strongly resembled Jackson entered the room. She looked like his twin. Jade saw all of Jackson's features in her—even down to the crew cut. But you could still see her femininity. "You caused quite a stir around here."

"Sorry?"

"The dead DC officer, you've really raised morale around here."

"Glad I can help."

"Love the sarcasm."

"Come now, Beverly, let's give Jade here some rest," Jackson said. "We'll be back to check on you later."

Jade watched them leave out of the room. She had a funny feeling about them. What were they up to? Why did they save her? Jade tried to remember what all happened before but couldn't. She looked over at Raina. "How long have I been out?"

"About a few days."

"Glad to see you're up," David walked in.

"Glad to see you're ok...what happened?"

"They threw a bag of dust on you," he said in disgust. "Those bastards are using our health conditions against us."

"As if imprisonment and torture weren't enough." They were silent for a moment. "How they treating y'all here?"

"Good."

"It's nice not having to look over your shoulder all the time," Raina said.

"Oh yeah?" Jade had her doubts about them.

For years she heard the myths and rumors about the Black Deficit. They supposedly formed a year after the DC started imprisoning debtors. They were to help debtors, but Jade never saw them in action. With all the sweeps and innocent people being taken away by the DC, not once did she see nor hear about the Black Deficit coming out to help. As far as she was concerned, the Black Deficit was only good at one thing—hiding.

"Why you think they saved me?"

David lowered his voice. "My guess is that they want something from you."

Jade rested her head back on her pillow. "You may be right."

"Hey Jade, how ya doing?" a guy asked as he walked into the room.

"Fine," it came out like a question.

"Are ya now?"

Jade had a little recollection of him. "You're the one that gave me a breathing treatment?"

The guy laughed. "Try loads. The DC really fucked you up. I'm Keeper by the way."

"Jade."

"Oh, I know," Keeper started taking her vitals. Jade studied him for a moment. His hair was jet black and spiky. He had tattoos all over his arms and neck. He wore a lip ring. Jade noticed that he wore four watches—one of which had a chart of numbers attached to it.

"What's up with the...wait a minute do those actually work?!" Jade couldn't contain her excitement. She hasn't seen any kind of watch, clock, or anything electrical work for a decade—apart from government buildings.

Keeper laughed. "Yes, they work."

"How?"

"Well once everything started going to shit, I started stacking up on watches, calendars, and batteries. With the end of the world coming, the most important thing you wanna do is keep up with time," he jotted something's down in a notebook.

"So what time is it now?" It's been so long since Jade actually knew the answer to that question.

"It's 2:45 p.m. on Wednesday, July 4th. Happy Independence Day!" he said sarcastically.

Jade looked over at Raina, who was in wide-eyed shock like she was.

"Is that how you got your name?"

"Kind of," he laughed. "I was a bit OCD before the world started going to hell. I was always obsessed with times, dates, and facts. Keeper is a nickname from my old life. It's a nice reminder, ya know?"

Jade nodded.

"Sit up for me please," Jade obeyed. Keeper placed a stethoscope on Jade's back—right near her lungs, "Take a deep breath...and out...hmm."

"What's wrong?"

"Ya sound ok, but could be better," he looked over his notebook. "I'm gonna give ya another breathing treatment. Ya should be tip-top after that."

"Thanks."

"No problem Jade," Keeper walked out, leaving Jade to her breathing treatment.

The medicated mist entered Jade's lungs with a warm welcome.

"Did he just say tip-top?" Raina asked. Jade smiled at her.

After a while, Jade eventually fell into a dreamless sleep. She felt relaxed, even in her sleep. It's been a long time since she felt like that.

**

Jade suddenly woke up to the smell of food. Beverly was standing at the end of her bed when she opened her eyes.

"You look like you could eat."

"I could."

"Come on, follow me."

Jade got up and slowly put on her boots. She followed Beverly out of the hospital ward. They were in a warehouse. "What city are we in?"

"Niles, just on the borderline of Michigan, the DCs don't really travel this far out."

They arrived in the cafeteria area. David and Raina were already at a table with Jackson, Keeper, and other people.

"Nice to see you out of bed," Jackson greeted her.

"Nice to be out," Jade took a seat in between Raina and David. Keeper sat a tray of chicken nuggets and chocolate pudding in front of her. "Thank you," Jade dug in.

"I told you, you looked hungry," Beverly chuckled.

Jade gave her a weak smile and quickly finished her food. "So, what you want from me?"

"Well you get straight to the point," Jackson said.

"There had to be a reason. You aren't known for rescue missions."

"That's because we're just now gathering people to conduct them," Beverly said.

"Look," Jackson jumped in. "Not a lot of people are comfortable fighting against the DCs. Some just want to survive."

"It took a lot of prep time to get this started—recruiting, gathering supplies, and working on experimental drugs."

Jade looked over at Raina and saw that she wore a confused expression. David sat with his arms folded—taking in as much information as he could.

"Our father was a pharmaceutical scientist. He discovered and experimented with medicine all the time. He started developing and distributing drugs once the DCs started carting people away. He was helping a lot of people. Sadly, he was killed by them a few years ago."

"I'm so sorry." Jade looked back and forth between the brother and sister duo.

"Jackson and I have been coming up with more drugs that will help people. We're still trying to keep his mission alive."

"But the DC needs to be overthrown and so does the government who put them there. To do that we need people."

"Where does Jade fit in all of this?" David asked.

"Well, Jackson and I aren't exactly on the DCs radar. We're not in any medical debt."

"Must be nice," Raina mumbled.

"The only people who will be more than happy to fight against the DCs are the ones who are being tortured and beaten by them."

"And the only way for us to free them is to find one of their prisons."

"So...you need me to get caught," Jade finally caught on.

"They want you to be the bait," David shook his head in disbelief.

"That's too dangerous," Raina objected.

"Well actually they'll torture her before they kill her," Keeper said.

"Oh, that's a relief!" David snapped.

"We'll get there before they lay a finger on her," Jackson said.

"But you can't guarantee that!"

"You don't think we'll supply her with weapons?" Beverly said.

"And the DC will find it in a second."

"Ya don't think we've thought of that?" Keeper asked insulted. "Jade tap yo left foot twice for me please."

Jade tapped her left foot twice, and a small compartment opened, which held her knives. "What the hell?!"

"Holy crap!" Raina was surprised.

"They will go undetected when you're searched. Ya inhalers are in ya right boot."

"Jade will be able to defend herself."

"So, Jade," Jackson said. "Will you help us?"

"You think some hidden knives and medicine is going to raise the odds? You should let her think about it for a moment," David interjected.

Jackson and Beverly look out each other for a moment. "Fair enough. We'll leave you to your thoughts," Jackson said, getting up. The rest of the people followed and left David, Raina, and Jade at the table.

"Jade, you can't do this," David said once they were gone.

"You're the one who said that we need to fight against this."

"Yeah, but not at your expense."

"It's too dangerous Jade," Raina said.

"It's always gonna be too dangerous," Jade sat and reflected for a moment. She thought about the previous sweep. All those people chained in the back on that DC truck. What was their fate? Days of torture? Beatings? Rapes? It would've been easier for them to just die before they reached the prison.

That was almost her fate. Jade didn't want to experience that feeling ever again. She didn't want anyone to feel that. To do that, Jade had to sacrifice herself. Surprisingly she was ok with that.

"This is war, and sacrifices gotta be made. We need people who are willing to fight." Jade figured seeing how the DC treated prisoners would motivate her, even more, to fight against them.

David sighed. Jade could see his frustration and disappointment with this whole situation. A tense silence hung in the air before he spoke.

"I'll be right behind you, making sure nothing goes wrong."

"Thank you, David."

Jade, David, and Raina found Jackson, Beverly, Keeper, and the rest of the crew in the artillery section of the warehouse. Guns lined the walls, along with knives, grenades, and other kinds of weaponry. Seeing how heavily equipped they were, made Jade a bit angry. Here they were with heavy firearms while other people were out there suffering and falling victim to the DC. She struggled to push her feelings to the side. She was working towards evening the playing field.

Jackson was sitting, talking to a group of people, he stood when he saw them.

"I'll do it."

~8~

It was going to take at least a week before they got everything together for the mission. Jade took that time to familiarize herself with the Black Deficits' headquarters. She spent a bit of time with Keeper in his invention room, as he called it, looking over the things he's created. He'd come up with some unique gadgets, from things that could carry and conceal weaponry, to things that could administer medicine quickly and proficiently.

"How did you learn how to make all of this stuff?" Jade asked while browsing around.

Keeper smiled. "It's something that I've been doing since I was a kid. I was always inventing shit. It drove my parents' nuts!"

"They alive?"

"My dad took off when I was six. My mom was taken by the DCs a few years ago. She died a year later from breast cancer."

"I'm so sorry." At least she didn't die by the DCs hand, Jade thought to herself. "My parents are no longer alive, either. They died trying to help an elderly neighbor during a disaster. That was just how they were...the helpful kind." Jade realized that she was veering off course. "Sorry."

"No, it's fine...it makes us stronger," Keeper tinkered with a gadget. "Anyways, I was eventually discovered by Jackson's and Beverly's dad, Dr. Blackwell. He found me hiding out in a school. I had some of my gadgets with me, and he was very interested...he saved my life."

Keeper put the gadget down and walked over to another workstation. Jade picked up the device and toyed with it in her hand. She didn't know what the purpose of the foreign object was.

"He didn't make it though," Keeper continued on. "Rumor has it, he was tortured and killed by Razor."

"Another debtor," Jade assumed.

"No, he was doing something worse than being in the red. He was making medicine that was helping people with their sickness and diseases. The government didn't want that, so they took him out."

Jade gazed off for a moment. She couldn't believe the world she was living in. So cruel. So unfair. So unjust. They would rather have people living in the red than getting better. Although she didn't know him, Jade knew that losing Dr. Blackwell was a considerable loss to them all. She just hoped that Jackson and Beverly were equipped for the job.

"Don't worry," Keeper said, reading her thoughts. "Jackson and Beverly have been taught well. Since birth actually."

"That's reassuring, given that I'm risking my life," Jade wasn't sure if she meant it or not. It just seemed like the appropriate thing to say at that moment.

When she wasn't in Keeper's invention room, Jade spent some quiet time on the roof—looking out at the view. The Black Deficit's headquarters was miles away from the closest town, so it was surrounded by trees and open fields. It looked peaceful. It allowed Jade to escape for a moment. She was grateful to turn her brain off and not think about what she had to do. Sometimes Raina would come up to the roof and talk with her—when she felt strong enough.

"My mom called me her miracle child because she had me so late," Raina said one day. "She used to say that I was a special "seed gift," which I later found out it meant a donor baby...every minute with her was fun."

Jade watched her as she stared across the field. It was eerie how much she reminded her of Helena. Raina was scrunching her nose up, and Jade remembered how Helena use to do that.

"We used to play this game," Raina continued. "She called it Nourish Detectives, we would go into different houses and buildings, and try to find as much food as we could. The one who found the most got promoted...I was a Captain."

Raina stopped talking for a moment. Jade watched her. She realized that Raina was crying. Jade pulled her into her arms.

"I never realized how bad off we were. I mean, I knew that things were bad, but she made it seem like everything was ok. That this was just life."

Jade wished she had someone shielding her from the evils that were going on today.

"Do you know what it was like before everything went to hell?" there was longing in Raina's eyes. "They used to go shopping, to the movies, out to eat at restaurants, bowling...they had fun."

"I know," Jade admitted. She was guilty of doing all those things. "I know it's hard for you to grow up in a situation like this."

"You have no idea," Raina rolled her eyes and shook her head.

Jade smiled a bit. That was such preadolescent behavior.

"You and David are the only people I've been around since my mom," she stared into Jade's eyes. "Please don't go Jade."

"Trust me, I don't wanna go Raina, but I gotta. There's a bigger picture in this world, but we're living in fear, and that's exactly where they want us to be. But their beliefs are more malignant than our own bodies, and it's time we break away from that."

Jade spent the remaining of her time hunting or at least learning how to hunt, with David. She was convinced that she was just terrible at it. She walked too loud, and her wheezing would scare all the prey away. But no matter how much she protested, David insisted that she should learn. They would spend hours out in the woods. Although they spent most of their time talking instead of hunting.

Jade enjoyed getting to know David more. He was a nice guy. She learned that he was from Canada. He had come to Michigan to meet some relatives for a hunting trip in Denver, but they never made it to him. Crazy storms like hurricanes and tornadoes kept all their flights grounded. And he couldn't get out of Michigan. He's been here ever since.

"Do you know what happened to your parents?"

"No clue, but I'm sure they're better off than me."

A few years after the DCs were enforcing and imprisoning people, debtors began to flee out of Michigan by crossing the Detroit River. It was getting so bad that they set up a DC border task force. Now anyone who tried to pass was automatically imprisoned, whether you were in the red or black.

"You ever tried to flee? Before they set up the border patrol."

"Loads," David admitted. "But I would run into the DCs every time. The number of people that were fleeing then...it just attracted too much attention."

Jade felt sorry for him. The world was ending, and David just wanted to be home with his family. Who wouldn't want that? Jade had wished that she was with her family when things went to shit. It was the presence of a family that brought you comfort during trying times.

"I eventually gave up after a very close call with an officer. It's all about trying to stay alive now," David paused for a moment when he heard a twig snap. It was a while before he resumed walking. "So, who was that guy that was trying to take you in?"

"When we first met?" Jade knew he was talking about Vincent, but she wanted to avoid that topic.

"Yeah, the bounty hunter. He seemed familiar with you."

"My ex-boyfriend, his name is Vincent."

David stopped, eyes wide. "Your ex is a bounty hunter...talk about an ex from hell."

"Tell me about it."

"The break-up was pretty bad, huh?"

"I wouldn't even call it a break-up," Jade didn't know what to call it. "The last time I saw him, he and his family were being taken away by the DCs." Jade stopped walking and sat down by a fallen tree trunk. David sat beside her.

"So why does he hate you so much?"

"I was surviving with him and his parents. His father had pancreatic cancer, and my asthma was spiraling out of control. We were getting into some serious medical debt. So, Vincent's mother started getting his father's treatments under her name. Meanwhile, I was just going deeper and deeper in debt," Jade paused for a moment and stared off. She was so young and petty then.

"I started complaining, saying that no one was helping me. Vincent and I got into so many arguments about him getting me treatments in his name, but he always said that someone had to stay clean in the group. So,

I started complaining more, telling them that they all were willing to let me die. Eventually, his mother started getting me treatments in her name."

Jade hung her head in shame. David's eyes were on her.

"What happened to them?"

"His dad died from cancer. I heard it was excruciating. His mother was so stricken with grief and depression that she ended up committing suicide shortly after."

"That wasn't your fault, Jade."

A few tears escaped her eyes. "Don't try to comfort me, David. I know it's my fault." The way she saw it, Vincent had every right to hate her.

"This a fucked-up time. You gotta do what you gotta do to survive. That asshole should've been helping you, not his mom. That's on him."

Jade smiled a little. She didn't really feel any better, it was more of a show for David.

He laughed and shook his head. "And then he sells out and becomes a bounty hunter."

Jade got up. "Like you said, you gotta do what you gotta do." David followed her, and they continued their hunting.

**

Jackson and Beverly went over the mission the night before. They would drop Jade off in a heavily DC area, and she would get captured by them. The DCs would take her to the prison while the Black Deficit followed by a tracking device that would be hidden inside of Jade's boot. Jade would go inside the prison, and the Black Deficit would break her and the rest of the prisoners out. Then the uprising would begin. It seemed simple enough. But Jade was still nervous.

"How you feeling?" Raina asked. They were in their room.

"Nervous," Jade admitted. She was trying not to cause an asthma attack from her stress.

"Same here," Raina doodled aimlessly on a piece of paper. Jade could see the lousy shading of the woman Raina was sketching. Raina's hand was shaking as she gripped the pencil.

Keeper walked in their room. "Ya must be stressing." He sat down the nebulizer. "I figured ya could use another breathing treatment."

"You-know-me-too-well."

Keeper smiled while he set up the machine. "There ya are."

"Thank-you," Jade just took one treatment.

"Don't worry too much," David said. "I'm gonna be there behind you with the rest of them."

"I-know-I'm-just-wondering..."

"We'll get to you before anything happens."

Jade just nodded. Everyone kept telling her that, but honestly, no one knew precisely what the DCs were going to do to her once they got a hold of her. They might just kill her on sight. Or they might start torturing her right then and there. Jade didn't know which one she was most afraid of.

"I'm gonna take a shower," she said after her breathing treatment was done.

"Jade," David stopped her. "If you don't wanna do this, just say the word. We'll be gone before the morning."

"No, it's something I gotta do David."

He nodded.

Jade headed to the bathroom. The steam from the shower melted her stress away. She had to do this. Too many people have been abused, tortured, and died by the DCs hands. And for what? Health treatment? It wasn't right, and someone needed to make a stand against them. To do that they needed people—a lot of people. Jade could do this. She just had to be brave and hold on to her courage to get through this mission.

When Jade got back to her room, she found Raina lying down in her bed. Her back was turned to Jade. She was crying.

"You ok?" Jade asked.

Raina turned towards her—her eyes red and puffy. "According to Keeper's time, I haven't seen my mother in three months. That's 90 days. There's no telling what they've done to her. I'm scared, Jade. I'm scared that you're gonna go in there and never come out."

"Hey," Jade wrapped her arms around Raina. "I promise I'll come back to you. I'll do everything in my power to do so," Jade looked over and saw multiple sketches of a woman who looked just like Raina lying all over Raina's bed. "Is this your mother?"

Raina nodded.

"If she's in there, I'll do my best to bring her back to you," Jade gave Raina a light kiss on her forehead. "Now let's get to bed," she tucked Raina in. "Goodnight little munchkin."

"What the hell is a munchkin?"

~9~

Jade sat in the back of the Black Deficit's van silently praying. Her fingertips moved across each bead of her rosary as she prayed. She prayed that everything would go ok. She prayed that she would make it back out. She prayed that the DCs wouldn't torture her too bad before the Black Deficit rescued her. Jade just wanted to get this thing over with.

"We're about three klicks out from the drop site," Jackson told her. Jade nodded. "How you feeling?"

"Like I'm going to prison."

"Don't worry, everything will be fine."

"Is that what you tell all the prisoners?"

Jackson nodded. "I know you're a bit nervous."

Jade laughed. "A bit?"

"But I promise we will get to you before anything bad happens."

Jade nodded again.

"We need to get ready," Beverly called out.

"Ok," Jackson sat down next to Jade. "Remember that your knives are in your left boot and your inhalers are in your right. We'll be able to communicate with you through your earpiece at all times."

"We're arriving at the drop site," Keeper said.

"Are you ready?"

Jade took a deep breath. "Yeah."

"You'll be two klicks away from the heavily patrolled area. You'll go into that area and get caught. We'll be at your six once you're taken."

"Right," Jade honestly wasn't paying attention to what Jackson was saying. She was wrapping her head around what she was getting ready to get into. She was about to face the DC head-on by herself. Bravery was needed.

The van had stopped. "We're here," Beverly said.

"Good luck, Jade," Jackson said.

Jade wrapped her scarf around her nose and mouth, and then exited the van.

It seemed too bright outside. Jade had been cooped up in the Black Deficit's headquarters for a few weeks, and she had gotten used to the fluorescent lights. She was blinded for a moment—her hand was the only thing to provide her a small amount of shade.

"You better get going. See you on the other side," they drove off in the opposite direction.

Jade stood there for a moment recollecting her thoughts. She had no idea where she was. Her best bet was to keep going straight. Eventually, she would run across something or someone.

"Ok, this is happening," she kept saying to herself from time to time. "This is *really* happening."

Jade walked by endless amounts of vacant fields. It was looking like the Black Deficit was given a bad tip, but 15 minutes later she came across a row of abandon houses. The neighborhood looked like the typical suburban neighborhood, but only destroyed by time and unnatural disasters.

Jade didn't know what to do next. So, going by her instincts, she began to scavenge through some of the houses. She found a few good clothing items that would be useful, some hygienic items, and some prescription drugs. Then a noise came from outside. It sounded like trucks. Jade walked out of the house. She stood on the porch and tried to pinpoint where exactly they were coming from. She walked in the middle of the street to get a better listen. A truck turned down the road just a couple of blocks away. As it got closer to her, it stopped. Two DC officers got out. Jade backed away slowly.

"We have visual on the target!"

Jade began to run. She couldn't help it. Instincts took over. She cut across a yard and hopped the fence to the backyard.

"Jade, what are you doing?" Jackson said in her ear. "You have to let them catch you."

She understood that, but she couldn't help it. Her brain was telling her to run. Hopping two more fences, Jade ended up hiding out in a garage. She tried to block out Jackson's voice in her ear. He was telling her that she had to stop running and surrender. Jade disagreed. She needed to be scared. She needed to run. She needed to make it look real.

As she sat there thinking about it, it would look suspicious if she didn't run. Jade had to resist. She had to fight. It was hard to tell if the DCs were nearby. A truck roared, but she couldn't pinpoint where it was coming from because Jackson was shouting commands in her ear.

"Would you please shut up!" Jade finally yelled. "I know what I'm doing."

Jade looked around the garage to find some type of weapon. Her knives were a last resort. A wooden bat sat in the corner. She grabbed it and walked outside. It sounded like the trucks were a block over. She would get caught, but she would put up a big fight first. Jade crouched down on the side of a house as she saw another truck turn down the street. She crept her way to the back. The truck stopped, and the doors closed.

"She's here somewhere," one of them said.

"It's now or never," she said to herself. Jade took a deep breath and ran. She ran from the backyard to the front, and across the street—right in front of the officers.

"Visual 12 o'clock!"

Jade ran without looking behind her, but she knew that they were right behind. That didn't worry her, she just kept running. When she felt one of the officers touch her, she turned and hit him in the knee with the bat. He went down with a groan. Jade quickly went for the other one by striking him in the stomach. Once they were both down, she ran and hid in a nearby shed. Jade quickly tapped her right foot and took out one of her inhalers. She took a couple of puffs.

"Ok, Jade, it's time to surrender," Jackson said.

Jade listened out for a minute. More trucks were coming. They were getting back up. The time was coming for her to get caught.

"You can do this," she kept saying, "You can do this."

A group of footsteps was nearby. "I think she went this way."

"Spread out!"

Jade stood silently still as she heard them walkabout. She took a deep breath and counted to ten. Someone walked past the shed. Jade charged out and tackled an officer to the ground. They wrestled for a moment, but he managed to get on top of her. She was able to kick him in the groin and then in the face. She got up and started running.

"I see her!"

"She's heading north, north!"

"Ok, Jade!" Jackson yelled in her ear. "I think you've made your point!"

But Jade kept running—until the ground started shaking.

At first, it was a little tremor that turned into a massive shake. Jade fell on the ground. A crack was splitting open behind her. She tried to get up and run, but she only got a couple of feet before falling again. It was an earthquake, and it felt like it was going to be a lethal one. That didn't stop the DC officers, though. A few of them used that moment to try to get to her. The crack was getting closer to her, so she began to crawl as fast as she could.

Jackson told her to hold on tight and be careful. The advice did her little good, though. She was outside and unable to take cover anywhere. A couple of houses were collapsing around her. She tried to fight her fear, but she was sure that this was her end. It was either the earthquake or the DCs.

The crack was getting close to her, and it started opening further— revealing a gaping hole. Jade jumped up and began to run as fast, and as long as she could. She leaped over the hole. She successfully made it over with a tumble landing. Then someone pulled on her leg, causing her to slide to the edge of the hole. Jade avoided falling in by quickly grabbing the post of an old mailbox.

A DC officer tried to jump over the hole to get to Jade, but the hole split opened wider than he anticipated, and he was close to falling in. He was hanging off the edge—Jade's leg keeping him from falling in. Jade tried to shake him off, but that just made him tighten his grip. The officer was clinging for dear life.

The earthquake finally subsided. Jade tried to pull herself up, but the weight of the officer was making it hard. The other officers were composing themselves and heading her way. She started shaking the DC officer off her leg, but he pulled on her leg harder—pulling her further down. Tightening her grip of the post, Jade gave the officer a sharp kick to the head. He loosened his grasp, and she gave him another kick. He lost his grip and fell down the hole—screaming on the way down.

Jade pulled herself up as quickly as she could and sprinted away from the remaining DC officers. She kept on running until something hard hit her on the right and another on the left. Two officers tackled her at the same time. Jade struggled and resisted.

"Get off of m—,"

Everything went black.

Jade could faintly hear Jackson calling her name.

~10~

J**ade** drifted in and out of consciousness. The DC officers sprayed her with something that knocked her out. She was weak and making that scary gasping sound again, like when the DCs threw dust on her.

"I think it's triggering an asthma attack."

"Give her a treatment. We need her alive."

"Jade," she heard Jackson say. "Jade, if you can hear me, we are right behind you."

"We need to get her out of there!" David yelled in the background.

Jade moved her arms a little and realized that they were handcuffed, and so were her legs. She pretended to still be out of it.

"I can't wait until we get her to Bossman," an officer said.

Another officer laughed. "I'm pretty sure he has some interesting things in store for her."

Jade could feel the medicated mist flow into her lungs. She breathed in as much as she could. She was going to need all the strength she could get.

The truck slowed down.

"Ok Jade, it looks like you're approaching the prison," Jackson said.

"Get her up."

Someone kicked her. "Move it, Willer!"

Jade pretended to open her eyes for the first time. A DC officer pointed a gun at her, while another officer uncuffed her.

"Don't you dare try anything."

"We're almost there, Jade," Jackson reported.

"Are you sure you searched her?"

"She's clean," the officer said as he handcuffed Jade's hands in the front of her.

"Move," the gunman pushed her.

Jade walked to the truck's door as it stopped. The passenger and driver door opened and closed. One of them opened the door while the other pointed their gun at her.

"Out of the van Willer!"

"Don't do anything, Jade," Jackson warned.

Jade didn't plan on it, especially not with guns on her. There was nothing she could do. She just had to wait for David and the Black Deficit to get there—that is if they made it there in time. A lot of yelling was coming from the DC prison. One of the officers pushed Jade to indicate that she should start walking. She tried to push aside her fear and convince herself that everything will be alright.

"Packaging is being delivered," one of the officers said. "All officers be advised."

The prison gate opened, and they were greeted with more armed officers. "Is she all clear?"

"Would we bring her in if she wasn't?" They gave him a doubtful look. He sighed and rolled his eyes. "Well, check her if you don't believe me."

A female officer patted Jade down and frowned when she didn't find anything.

"I told you."

"Move it," the female officer told Jade—ignoring the last comment.

They entered two more gates when Jade was hit with an aggressive stench. It smelled like sweat, must, blood, urine, and feces. Jade tried not to gag.

"Enjoying the aroma Willer?" a guard asked. "Betta get used to it.

There were about 15 people in each cell throughout the prison. They all looked beaten, lost, and hopeless. There was absolute fear in their eyes. A lot of them stared at Jade through their cell. Some seemed shocked to see her. Jade struggled to see if Raina's mother was there.

Wanted posters of Jade hung everywhere in the prison. At the end of the main hall was a flight of stairs. It went up five levels.

"High-level," a guard yelled out.

"High-level!"

They were going to the area that housed the high, threatening prisoners. Although Jade wondered who was more dangerous to the DCs than her right now. She was curious about what they did to the prisoners in the high-level unit. She'd find out soon enough. They led her to a cell down at the end of the hall.

"Last stop Willer," one of the guards opened the cell door and pushed her inside. The room was bare and had no windows. It was pitch black when they slammed the door behind her.

"Don't worry Jade," Jackson said over the earpiece. "We're still making our way to you."

Jade ignored him and sat down on the floor. How could she be here? Ever since she went into the red, she's made it a point to avoid being captured at all cost. Yet, here she was volunteering to be in this position. And to make matters worse, she was currently the most wanted debtor there. That terrified her the greatest. What did they do to the most wanted debtors? Jade suddenly pulled away from her thoughts. Someone was crying. It sounded like it was coming from the next room. Jade crawled her way around the small room until she found a vent on the back wall.

She listened to the person crying—too afraid to say anything. It seemed like a private moment. "Are you ok?" Jade eventually asked.

She couldn't help it. The woman sounded like she was in so much pain. More pain than the DCs could ever inflict.

"No, I lost my daughter a while ago. We got separated during one of the sweeps. I got caught, but I don't know what happened to my daughter. She's not in here, which is good, but I don't know how well she'll do out there alone."

"Are you sick?"

"No, but my daughter has leukemia. I've been using my name to get her treatments once she started getting deeper in the red."

Jade's heart began to race. Was it her? "Raina?"

"Ye-yes," Raina's mother's voice got louder. "Have you seen her? Is she ok?"

"She's fine," Jade reassured. "I...I killed an officer to save her."

Raina's mother sighed in relief. "Thank God."

Jade found herself a little annoyed that the woman didn't seem to care about her killing someone. Sure, it was an officer, but he was still a human being, and Jade was feeling shitty about it.

"Where is she now?" Raina's mother asked. "You're in here, what happened to her?"

Jade whispered. "Look, she's fine. She's back at the Black Deficit's headquarters. I'm here on a rescue mission. Don't worry, I'll get you back to her."

Raina's mother started sobbing uncontrollably. "Thank you."

Jade sat back down on the floor while listening as the woman tried to pull herself together. The anticipation was killing her. How much longer did she have to wait until the DCs came back?

The woman cleared her throat. "I'm Sarah."

"Jade."

"We all know who you are in here, Jade. You're something like a hero to us."

Jade scoffed. "I'm no hero."

"I thought you said you are on a rescue mission?"

"Yeah, I'm the bait."

"You're sacrificing yourself to save us. Sounds like a hero to me."

"The Black Deficit will be here soon," Jade was done with the hero talk. "Be alert and ready to move out when everything goes down."

"I will."

Jade couldn't wait to see Raina's face when she saw her mother. She could tell that she missed her so much. Jade knew how Raina felt. She longed for her family too.

"Eight klicks away, Jade," Jackson updated.

Just then, Jade's cell door opened. The light made her squint. It felt like she had been sitting in the pitch black for hours.

"Let's go, Willer," a woman officer said.

Jade frowned. That voice had some familiarity with it. She stood up and walked to the door. Jade stopped in her tracks once she reached the doorway. It felt like she was punched in the gut. Her eyes were deceiving her. Jade couldn't *really* be looking at her sister. Although she hasn't seen her in over 10 years, Helena looked just as Jade remembered. The nose, the eyes, even the pixie haircut —Helena looked the same.

"Hele—"

"Move it, debtor," Helena said maliciously. Vincent was behind her with a gun. Helena pushed Jade out of the room. "Walk!"

Jade stumbled at first but then began to stroll. It felt like she was dreaming—like she was in a nightmare. How could this be? How could Helena be a DC? There had to be a mistake. Jade needed to abort the mission. There was no way she could fight her little sister.

"You sure you can handle this?" Vincent asked Helena.

"I got this."

Jade looked back to see Helena smirking at her. She turned back around to see a big guy coming out of the room they were walking to. It was Razor. Jade's heart dropped. She took a deep breath and prepared herself mentally. A sharp mind was the only way she was going to get out of this alive. Razor gave Jade a menacing look. The torture was about to begin.

"Ready to party?" he asked Jade.

"I was born ready."

"Shut it, debtor!" Helena pushed her inside the room.

"Glad to see you can handle this," Razor said to Helena.

Jade watched them as they kissed. Vincent handcuffed her to a chair. She looked at Helena with disgust. How could she be one of them? They finally noticed Jade staring at them. She looked around the room. There were hacksaws, drills, hammers, bats, screwdrivers, a towel, buckets of water, and other forms of weapons that were used for torturing.

Where in the hell was the Black Deficit?

Razor followed Jade's gaze and smiled. He cracked his knuckles and neck. "Let the party begin."

Jade never saw his backhand coming. It felt like a brick was thrown in her face. She bit down on her lip to keep from crying out. That only made her mouth bleed more. Vincent laughed behind her. She expected Razor to smack her again, so she braced herself for it. It all hurt the same, but she was able to hide her pain better. He swung once more, but this time, Jade was able to duck. Her foot managed to find its way to his groin in the process. Razor hunched over in pain. Helena and Vincent moved in to contain her, but he stopped them.

Razor laughed as he composed himself. "Well looky here, looks like sis is a fighter," he punched Jade square in the face. It took everything in her not to pass out. He tried to hit her again, but again she ducked—afraid that it would knock her out for sure.

Vincent wrapped his arm around her neck. "Stay still you lil' bitch!"

Jade spat blood in his face. Vincent jumped back in disgust. Razor laughed. Vincent raised his fist.

"Don't you touch her!" Razor warned.

"Did you see what she did?!"

"Enough!" frustration spread across Helena's face. "Handle her."

Razor walked over to the weapons table. Helena joined him. Vincent was busy trying to get all of Jade's blood off him. Jade took that time to retrieve the bobby pin that was hidden in the sleeve of her jacket. She grabbed it last night at the Black Deficit headquarters. She knew she'd need it. All the gadgets Keeper invented, and no one thought to supply her with something that'll get her out of handcuffs. She managed to un-cuff her right hand. She made it look like she was still cuffed. Helena and Razor were still going over weapons they wanted to use.

Vincent was done cleaning himself and was now very irritated. "Any day now."

Razor gave him a menacing look over his shoulder. "Shut it, bounty hunter."

Jade took the distraction to work on freeing her left hand. She was almost there when Helena had picked up a bat from the table. Jade worked faster, but Helena was too quick. She swung the bat and hit Jade in the stomach. Jade hunched over in pain. The wind was knocked out of her. She kept working on freeing her left hand. Helena swung the bat again, and this time, it hit Jade on her shoulders.

"Come on, Helena, show her how it's done!"

Helena swung just as Jade felt the click on her left hand. Jade broke free and caught the bat in mid-swing. Helena kept her grip on the bat. Jade head-butted Helena. Helena stumbled a little.

Vincent moved in to intervene.

"Let them fight," Razor ordered.

Helena managed to slam Jade on the floor near the weapons table. She tried to press the bat down on Jade's throat. Jade kicked Helena off her. Helena flew back, knocking over the weapons table in the process. Jade quickly grabbed a steel link chain that landed near her.

Then the building shook.

The alarms went off.

"Code Red! Code Red!" they heard over the DCs radio.

Vincent and Razor stumbled back further from them. Jade and Helena looked at each other. They both charged. Helena gave a quick jab to Jade's side, but Jade was still able to wrap the chain around Helena's neck. She used Helena as a shield.

"Release her debtor!" both men yelled.

"Shoot her!" Helena cried out. "Shoot her!"

Jade tightened her grip around Helena's neck. "Shut it."

"Jade we're sending another explosion ya way. Try to take cover," Keeper warned in her ear.

Jade backed away, taking Helena with her. She couldn't believe she had a chain wrapped around her sister's throat. It was chaos. Gunshots, yelling and screaming reigned throughout. But then there was a moment, a split second when it all went quiet.

There was a whistle.

Jade slammed Helena down on the floor along with herself. She quickly shielded Helena.

The building shook again—this time more intensely. There was heat. Rubble flew everywhere. Even more screaming, yelling, and moaning rang out. A piece of debris landed on Jade's side—knocking the wind out of her for the second time.

"You ok?" Jade managed to ask through breaths. She un-shielded Helena.

"I'm fine," she grunted as she sat up.

They both assessed their wounds for a moment. Jade didn't see any significant injuries, just minor cuts, and bruises. Helena's face was all scrunched up as she looked over her body. Jade loved that look—her wrinkled nose. Helena always looked that way when she saw something gross or didn't like something.

Jade smiled.

Helena looked over at her with a blank stare. Then she jumped on Jade—trying to choke her.

"Helena...stop," Jade managed to get out.

Helena wouldn't let up. Jade head-butted her, and again once she felt Helena's grip loosen. Jade elbowed her, and Helena fell off her.

"Helena!"

It was Vincent and Razor. There were behind a big piece of rubble. It was only one way out of the room. There was a small hole that Jade could climb out of. But she could hear an officer on the other side. Jade had to move quickly. She gave Helena a final kick to the stomach and ran to the opening. Tapping her left foot twice, Jade took out two knives. As she jumped out of the small hole, she threw a knife at the armed DC officer. He wasn't prepared. The blade went into his throat. Jade pulled it out as she ran past him.

"She's here! She's here somewhere!" Helena yelled.

Jade tapped her right foot and took out her inhaler. She took four puffs.

"I don't care what Bossman says!" Vincent said. "I'm killing that lil' bitch on sight! That's three of us that she's taken out now!"

Jade went further down the hall. "I'm not sure who's listening, but I'm on the 5th floor, and I need back up quick."

"I'm on my way, Jade!" David responded.

"Jade, try to meet us at the top of the stairs," Keeper said.

"On it," Jade crouched down and hid behind a big piece of the ceiling that had fallen. She was listening out for Helena and the others.

"She's 'round here somewhere," one of them whispered.

Jade started going down another hall, trying to be quiet, stepping over rubble along the way. She hoped she'd find the stairs soon. Jade wasn't sure where she was going, but she needed to get out of there. There was no way she could face her sister again. Hurting her sister was hard. There were mixed emotions. She was thrilled to see Helena again—alive. But she was furious. How could Helena be a DC officer? How could she torture and terrorize innocent people? How could she be the enemy?

There was a blow to the side of Jade's face. She stumbled back.

Helena was smirking at her. "I got her." She punched her again, so hard that Jade's mouth was bleeding.

Jade spat and smirked at her. "We drawing blood now?"

"You got no idea."

Helena swung again at Jade, but she ducked and punched Helena in the side and again in the face. Helena stumbled back. She charged and punched Jade in the stomach. Helena pulled her by the hair and was getting ready to hit Jade again when Jade cut her arm. She stumbled back and looked at Jade in shock.

"I thought we were drawing blood?" Jade teased.

Helena charged at Jade again. This time she did a spin kick but missed. Jade punched her in the stomach. Helena punched her in the face. Jade kneed her. Helena tackled her, and they both wrestled around on the floor.

"I fucking hate you," Helena kept muttering.

Jade kicked her off, and Helena slammed against the wall. Jade's chest was tightening. She quickly tapped her right foot and pulled out her inhaler. Helena gave her an evil smile. Jade brought the inhaler up to her mouth as Helena jumped on her and started punching Jade repeatedly. Jade took two quick puffs but couldn't tell if it helped. She gave Helena a swift, little cut across her cheek. Helena stumbled back and looked at Jade in shock again. Jade took another two quick puffs. She dropped the inhaler back in her boot and jumped up. They both stared at each other for a moment. They were ready to charge at each other again when they heard gunshots coming from down the hall.

"Jade!"

"Helena!"

They both ran toward the fight. The Black Deficit members were having a battle with a group of DC officers and Vincent. Jade saw Keeper on the ground; a DC officer was kicking him. She rushed over and jumped on his back. She wrapped her arm around his neck as Keeper got off the ground. The officer tried to shake Jade off. Keeper swung a bat and hit the officer in the stomach. The DC officer stumbled back and hit the wall, causing Jade to slam her head. She fell. Keeper rushed over and helped her up.

"Ya ok?"

Jade rubbed the back of her head and nodded. She looked around and saw that they were by the stairs. She was relieved. It was time to get out of there.

"Jade!" Sarah was getting beaten by a DC officer. Jade didn't think. She just reacted. Her knife left her hand and went into the DCs chest. It felt like déjà vu. Jade smiled a little. That was four down now. She started to walk over to Sarah, but she went tumbling down the stairs.

"JADE!" Keeper yelled.

Helena snuck in some punches when the stairs weren't beating Jade up. It was clear how much Helena hated her. They stopped at a landing. Helena was about to jump on top of Jade, but Jade kicked her in the face, she flew back against the gate and fell unconscious. Jade's right arm was dangling, and searing pain ran through it. Her shoulder popped out of its socket when she went tumbling down the stairs.

"JADE!!" Keeper and Sarah were running down the stairs toward her. David was at the bottom.

DCs were swarming, and Helena was moaning and getting up. Keeper and Sarah reached her, and they started running down the stairs towards David.

Jackson came right behind him. "Time to go!".

They started running out toward the van where the others were. Jade looked behind her and saw the DCs chasing them. She spotted Helena among them.

"We're almost there!" Jackson called out over his shoulder.

Ten school buses were outside. They were jammed pack with the prisoners. As they reached outside, their van pulled up in front of them, and Beverly opened the back door.

"Get in!" They all filed in, Jade the last one.

"Jade!" Helena was sprinting towards the van.

"Go!" Beverly yelled out to the driver.

"Jade!"

The driver sped off, but Helena kept running and screaming her name. Jade was stunned. She couldn't believe that her sister held so much hatred toward her, but a part of her couldn't be angry. Jade deserved it.

"We're two and a half klicks out," Beverly said. "It's time to put her down." Beverly was about to point a gun at Helena.

"No!" Jade pushed Beverly. She looked back at Helena. "That's my sister." She watched as Helena chased after her with so much hatred in her heart.

"That's my sister."

~11~

Jade didn't expect to see Helena at her best friend's house. Her friend had called her and said she wanted to talk to Jade. When she got there, she was greeted at the door by Helena. It was close to a year since the last time she saw her—since she ran away from home.

"Please come back, Jade," Helena pleaded. "It's not the same without you. And with all of this weird stuff going on...we just wanna be a family again."

Jade heard all this before. After the first unnatural, but not as devastating earthquake, Jade's parents found her at Vincent's house and begged her to come home. But she enjoyed her freedom. She enjoyed doing what she wanted and not following anyone's rules. So, she declined their invitation back to the "normal" middle-class family. Despite the strange events. Jade wanted to remain on her own.

"We miss you, Jade. We're all worried about you."

Jade smiled at her sister and hugged her. "I'm fine, Helena." Helena didn't look pleased. "I'm tired of living under mom and dad's rules. I like my freedom."

"Something weird is going on here, Jade. A lot of people are dying. We just wanna be together."

Jade heard about that. She didn't take it seriously. "Helena nothing is going on. Just go back home. I can take care of myself."

Helena's eyes watered. "Please Jade."

"No, Helena, I'll come to see you later." But later never came.

Now, a little more than a decade later, Jade gazed off in the distance, looking at her sister chase after her. They were three miles out from the DCs prison, but Helena was still chasing after them on foot. She was slowing down, but she was nowhere near close to stopping.

"You ok?" David asked.

"No," tears rolled down Jade's face. She was in a lot of pain. Her arm was throbbing, but her heart hurt more. She let her sister down. Jade couldn't blame Helena for her anger.

"Jade," Beverly said. "Let me pop your shoulder back in place."

Jade nodded. She watched her sister fall back even further from them. Helena was getting tired but determined not to give up. Jade bit down on her lip as Beverly popped her shoulder back in her socket. She cried out in pain.

"Better?"

Jade nodded. She sat down and watched the silhouette of her sister. Beverly sat down next to her.

"Your sister's a DC."

Jade didn't respond.

"How the hell that happen?"

Helena's silhouette was slowing fading into the background.

"Looks like she's finally giving up," Beverly said. She looked over at Jade, waiting for her to respond. "We've been driving for 20 minutes now...that's a long time to be sprinting." Beverly sighed and rolled her eyes. "*Something* was fueling her to keep going."

"It's anger," Jade rubbed her shoulder. "She hates me."

"Is that the reason she became a DC officer?"

"I dunno. She and I lost touch long before the world ended."

"Why would anyone lose touch with their own sister?"

"Let's give her some rest," David interjected. "She was captured, beaten, and tortured.

Beverly nodded, got up, and went to the front of the van.

"Thanks."

"No problem. I'll leave you to your thoughts."

Jade didn't want to think. Her mind was racing, and she wished that it would stop. She wanted to stop thinking about Helena being a DC officer. She wanted to stop thinking about the hate and disgust that Helena displayed towards her. She wanted to stop thinking about how she let Helena and her parents down. Jade just wanted to sleep—sleep forever. Eventually, she drifted off.

David woke her when they arrived at headquarters. Jade looked around for a moment. The prisoners were getting off the buses and being greeted by more of the Black Deficit members. They warily got off the bus and went inside. Jade couldn't blame the prisoners for their suspiciousness. The Black Deficit was always a myth to them—to her anyway.

"You coming?" David asked.

"I'm gonna wait a little bit," Jade didn't want to face the prisoners at the moment. She wanted to go straight to her room and hide.

She sat in the back of the van and continued to watch as the prisoners steadily filed in. Jackson and Beverly were standing off to the side, talking. They had to be talking about her and Helena. A debtor whose sister is a DC officer. How could they not be talking about them? They probably wanted her to leave. Jade would cause them too much trouble. She had to figure out her next move.

Helena would be looking for her relentlessly. She had to figure out what area would be suitable for her to hide. David would probably try to come with her. She hoped she could convince him to stay. If something happened to him because of her, she would feel so guilty. There were already enough people hating her.

Jade took a deep breath and got out of the van. The plan was to make a quick beeline to her room. People would probably want to stop and talk to her, but she was hoping she could make an excuse to get away. She walked into the Black Deficit's headquarters. Surprisingly Beverly and Jackson didn't say anything to her when she passed by.

The hallways were swarmed with Black Deficit members and prisoners. Jade was hopeful that she could get away undetected through all the chaos. She noticed that some of the prisoners stopped talking and stared at her when she passed by. There was no doubt that they were talking about her and her DC officer sister. They probably heard the news. As a matter of fact, they probably knew that her sister was a DC officer before she did. They must've listened to some of Helena's conversations with her coworkers. Once Jade killed that officer, her name must have come up.

Jade made it back to her room without incident. No one bothered to speak to her. She didn't know if it was because everyone was too occupied with all the new changes or if they were just too scared to say anything to her. Either way, she really didn't care. She rubbed her shoulder. Her whole body was sore. That tumble down the stairs really did some more damaged than she thought.

Plus, her encounter with Razor, Vincent, and Helena really didn't help either. She caught a glimpse of herself in the mirror. It scared her for a moment. Her right eye was black and puffy from when Razor punched her. Cuts were on her face and lips, and she had bruises that no doubt came from Razor's hand.

Razor.

How did her sister end up with him? That mystery seemed to bother Jade more than wondering how Helena became a DC officer. Jade needed to get out of her head for a moment. Stripping out of her clothes, crawling into her bed, Jade quickly fell into a deep sleep.

~12~

Jade kept having nightmares about being tortured by Vincent, Helena, and Razor. Her dreams about Vincent and Helena weren't as scary as her nightmare with Razor. It was just something about him and his presence that terrified her.

In her nightmare, Razor came for her at the Black Deficit's headquarters. The lookouts spotted him, and chaos reigned on the inside of the halls. Jade grabbed her knives and rushed to the window to see where he was. He stood not too far from the main gate. His whole body was tensed—hands clenched.

Jade was angry and terrified at the same time. She took a deep breath, wrapped her scarf around her nose and mouth, took two knives out of her thigh strap, and headed out the door.

Razor was alone. However, he was still known as the most psychotic and ruthless DC officer around, so a part of her was afraid to face him. The two members keeping watch slowly opened the gate. They opened it just enough for her to slip through.

When she stepped all the way through the gate, the members hurried up and closed it shut—locking it. They were determined not to let anyone through. Jade was surprised that Razor didn't attack her as soon as she stepped out. Instead, he stood there, glaring at her with an evil smirk on his face.

"What you want?"

"To make Helena happy," Razor's smirk got bigger as he charged at her.

Jade quickly threw one of her knives, but it barely missed him. He turned out to be quicker than she imagined. Before she knew it, his arm was around her neck, and he was slamming her to the ground. Her other knife dropped out of her hand upon impact. She elbowed him in the stomach, and he loosened his grip. She was able to get away from him, and she rushed to her fallen knife. Sadly, she wasn't fast enough. He was back on her before she could reach her knife.

Razor jabbed her in her side. Jade hunched over in pain. She saw his fist coming toward her again, and she tried to brace herself for the impact, but her jaw still seared with pain. Jade reacted fast by tackling him to the ground. She tried to pin down his arms, but again, he was too quick for her. He managed to get the upper hand and once more had her by the throat. This time his grip was much tighter.

Jade began to panic. Her heart started racing. Her chest began to tighten. She tried hard to loosen his grip, but her hands were pinned down, and she couldn't move her legs much. The look of satisfaction in Razor's eyes terrified Jade. She was about to die, but from what? Strangulation or asthma attack?

Either way, she couldn't breathe, and there was no way out of it. She was getting weak. Her eyes were getting heavy. What was the point of fighting? Helena wanted this, and Jade owed it to her. She accepted her fate and closed her eyes.

Then darkness.

**

The medicated mist entered Jade's body. There was something on her face. She quickly sat up and touched the mask. It wasn't a mask for a nebulizer. In fact, she didn't hear the nebulizer running at all, but she was getting a breathing treatment. That she knew for sure.

The mask was made of some sort of plastic. It was more durable and stronger than the flimsy plastic that usually makes the nebulizer mask. And this mask went all the way around her head, which the others didn't. Jade reached to take it off.

"No Jade don't," Keeper sat in the corner

"Why not?"

"Ya had asthma attacks back to back."

"I have?"

"Yeah, something was upsetting ya and triggering ya attacks."

"Well, nightmares about being tortured and killed will do that to you," Jade touched the mask again. "What is this thing?"

"It's something new I'm working on. I call it the combat nebulizer. It'll help when ya fighting or just going outside."

"Seems more durable than the regular face mask."

"It's made from polycarbonate material. Ya know, like the plastic that they use for police shields. This mask should last in battle."

"Sounds good to me," Jade laid back down. "How long have I been out?"

"A day and a half."

"Wow, didn't mean to sleep that long."

"Well, you've been through a lot."

"Probably not as much as the prisoners."

"Actually, the prisoners are adjusting fine. Some better than others, but we're getting there. Raina is happy to be reunited with her mother again."

"I'm glad that one happy reunion happened out of all of this."

"Well, I think everyone is happy about being free."

"What about fighting? Are they happy about that too?"

"Beverly and Jackson haven't exactly approached that subject yet. I think they're allowing them time to recuperate first."

"Sounds like a good idea, but what happens to those who don't wanna fight?"

"Sadly, I don't have an answer for that."

Jade nodded. She closed her eyes for a moment and allowed the medication to flow to her lungs. For some reason, she couldn't shake her dream about Razor. There was a strong feeling that she was going to cross paths with him again. She was dreading it. A part of her felt like she should leave the headquarters, especially with the prisoners there now. She didn't want to subject them to one of their tormentors again. As long as she was there, no one would be safe, and she couldn't bear the thought of having their blood on her hands.

Keeper walked over to her. "Let me check ya vitals."

Jade sat up and let Keeper do his thing. She took a good look at him and noticed some bruises on his face and arms. There was a huge knot on his forehead. "How you feeling?"

He noticed that she was looking at his bruises. "Been better. Still sore."

"Same here," Jade reached up and touched her right eye. It was still puffy, but it felt like it went down some.

"I put some ice on it while ya were sleeping."

"Thanks for that."

"I never got a chance to thank ya...for helping me with that DC officer."

"No problem."

"I think ya good. Ya can take off the mask. Here let me help."

Jade lifted and allowed him to take the mask off. Cold air rushed to her face. She realized that she had been sweating. She wondered how long she had that thing on. Keeper took the mask and put it in a box that was on her dresser. Jade got up out of bed and stretched. She instantly regretted it. Her body was still sore.

Keeper turned toward her then quickly turned away. "Umm, Jade?"

Jade noticed that she didn't have any clothes on. She forgot that she had taken them off before laying down. Jade saw her pants and shirt nearby. She quickly put them on.

"Don't tell me you never seen a naked woman before?" she teased.

Keeper blushed a little. "No, but I'm not sure ya wanted me to see ya naked."

Jade shrugged. "So what's the verdict on my situation?"

"Whatcha mean?"

"Am I getting kicked out of here...because of my sister?"

"Christ Jade, no. Why would we?"

"I figured I would bring too much heat."

"Jade, we've been at war with the DCs long before ya killed that officer. Plus, breaking those prisoners out probably brought more heat on us than ya ever could."

"If you say so."

"Besides, I'm sure ya not the only person to have a family member on the other side. It's all about survival now. Some people feel like they gotta do what they gotta do."

"I guess so."

"Ya should come out and get something to eat. Some fresh air might be nice too."

"Later, I don't really feel like talking to anyone right now."

"I understand," Keeper headed for the door. "But don't stay hiding in here too long." He left out and closed the door behind him.

Jade knew she couldn't stay in her room forever, but she wanted to prolong her encounter with the others just a little while longer. It all seemed pointless though because she smelled like she could use a nice hot shower. She sighed and grabbed a towel. It was off to the communal bathrooms.

She walked out of her room just when a group of prisoners was walking by. They froze for a moment when they saw her. Fear and terror were in their eyes. She gave them a smile, but their expression didn't change. She realized that she was in their way, so she stepped aside.

"Sorry."

"She looks just like her," one of them whimpered.

Jade waited until they were out of sight before she walked toward the bathrooms. She prayed that she wouldn't run into anyone else. That prayer was in vain. It was way too many people living there now for her not to run into anyone. She mostly passed some Black Deficit members, and all of them just said hi to her.

Unfortunately, the bathroom was filled with prisoners. It made sense. It's been years since most of them bathed. Everyone who was in line stopped talking when she came in. Those who were in the shower hurried to clean themselves and got out.

Great, she was being avoided like the plague.

"Jade!" Raina ran towards her. "I'm so glad you're awake," she wrapped her arms around Jade's waist.

Jade looked to see everyone staring at her and Raina. She smiled a little. "I'm glad to be awake. You ok?"

Tears ran down Raina's face. She didn't say anything. She just nodded.

Jade laughed a little. "You sure? Because it doesn't look like it right now."

"Thank you for bringing my mother back to me," Raina hugged Jade tighter.

"I told you I would, didn't I?" Jade could feel Raina nodding her head. Just then, Raina's mother, Sarah, walked in.

"I take it that Raina has said thank you."

Jade laughed.

"Well, prepare yourself, Jade, because you're about to get another hug," Sarah walked over and hugged her. It all felt weird. Jade hasn't felt affection for a long time. "Thank you for taking care of my daughter."

"It was no problem at all."

Sarah let go and looked at everyone who was staring. "This woman saved my daughter's life. She killed that officer because they were trying to take my daughter away."

No one said anything. They just looked at Jade one last time and then looked away.

"Don't worry about them. They just need to warm up to you."

"They seem terrified of me."

"Well, your sister was a real piece of work. It doesn't help that you look like her."

"She was that bad?"

A woman who was in front of them quickly turned around. "Bad? Bad isn't the word for her. She participated in beatings and the tortures.

Especially with that husband of hers."

"Husband?"

"Yeah husband, hell you met him. Razor."

"He's her husband?" They were married. How could Helena be married to him?

"Yo sista ain't a real woman," another prisoner chimed in. "She turned a blind eye while women were in there being raped."

"And she seemed to do stuff for no reason," Sarah added. "She beat this one woman because she 'looked at her wrong' and she put me in the high level just because she could."

Jade didn't know what to say. "I'm so sorry. I know that's not enough, but truly, I am. I'm sorry for everything that you've been through." A few of them just mumbled and turned away. They continued to wait their turn for the shower.

"Don't worry Jade," Sarah whispered. "They'll see soon enough that you're nothing like your sister."

But they didn't understand. Helena was the sweet one. Jade was the uncaring, selfish one. They had it all wrong. They didn't know the *real* Helena. That was all Jade's fault. If she would've just gone home with Helena that day, none of this would've been happening. Helena would've been with her. She would still be sweet. She would still be innocent. She wouldn't be beating and torturing people. She wouldn't be idly standing by while women were being violated. People wouldn't be terrified of her. People would love and adore her.

Before she knew it, it was her turn for the shower. Jade turned it on and made sure it was steaming hot. She needed pain. She wanted to turn her thoughts somewhere else entirely. It was impossible for her to zone out all the way because she felt eyes on her. The prisoners were no doubt, taking this opportunity to get a real good look at her.

So, she quickly washed up and headed out. Going over to the dressing area, she dried off and put on her clothes. The glances felt like daggers hitting Jade's back. She tried not to get frustrated, but she stormed out of the bathroom, nonetheless. It surprised her to see David waiting by the door.

He smiled. "Wanna go hunting?"

"God, yes." At that moment, she thanked God for him.

~13~

Jade welcomed the fresh air. She didn't realize how much she missed it until she stepped out and let the wind hit her face. Jade never really paid any attention to the wind— not lately anyway. Her mind was always preoccupied with something else, that she never paid attention to the simple things.

David didn't say anything to her as they walked to their spot in the woods. Jade could tell that his mind was elsewhere. She left him to his thoughts. She focused more on the smaller things. Throughout all the chaos and mayhem, the trees were still able to keep its beauty. There were signs of unnatural disasters, but the forest was still beautiful and mystic.

Squirrels, rabbits, and birds passed by them. Jade wished she could be them. To not have a care in the world. All they did was eat, sleep, reproduce, and survive. They didn't have to worry about medical debt.

They didn't have to worry about being hunted down by the DCs. They lived care-free. Jade was so focused on the animals that she didn't even notice that David stopped walking.

"You ok?"

"Yeah."

He raised his eyebrows. "Are you sure? Because if I just found out that my sister was a DC officer, I would be freaking out right now."

"Oh, that."

"Yeah that," David smiled.

"I'm shocked. Disappointed. Hurt. Guilty. Ashamed...it's all my fault."

"I think you're too hard on yourself."

"If I were with her none of this would've happened. She wouldn't have been all alone, and she wouldn't have ended up a DC officer."

"Yeah, but she would've been on the brutal end of them. I dunno which scenario is worst, but being on the brutal end isn't all that sweet."

"Exactly, and she's doing that to innocent people. Some of the prisoners told me how cruel she was to them. She tortured them. Beat them. She even turned a blind eye to women who were being raped. Her being a DC officer is not a good scenario in my book. She would've been better off being on the run with me."

"But you're not accountable for your sister's actions, Jade."

"Yeah, but all of this could've been avoided."

"You can't say that for sure. Who knows, you both could've ended up DC officers."

"Doubt it."

"But you can't say that for sure."

"All I know is that I need to make things right."

"And how you gonna do that?"

"By breaking her out of there and kicking her ass."

David burst out laughing. Jade smiled. She couldn't blame him for laughing. The idea was ridiculous, but honestly, she didn't know what else to do. A good ass kicking might knock some sense back into Helena's head. Jade just wanted her sister to go back being that sweet little girl.

"Well if you gonna go through with that crazy plan, count me in."

"Will do."

"Christ Jade, your ex is a bounty hunter and your sister is a DC officer."

"Wish you were me?"

"Hell no."

"How you feeling anyway?"

"I'm good. Better than I've been in a long time. Keeper gives me all these little gadgets to make sure that my blood sugar doesn't get low. And it administers insulin when I need it."

"Yeah, he just made me something called a combat nebulizer. It's a portable mask that's made from the same plastic that's used for police shields. He says it's ideal for when I'm fighting or just outside."

"Sounds like a great invention. He gave me this watch," David held up his wrist. It looked like an old sports watch. One that was waterproof. "I can prick my finger on the winding stem, and it reads my blood sugar level. If it's low, it automatically gives me a shot of insulin."

"Gotta love Keeper and his inventions."

"Gotta love him," David smiled at her. Jade gave him a nervous smile back. An awkward silence hung in the air. She was unclear about her future. She was unclear about *their* future there.

"So, do you think Jackson and Beverly are gonna kick me out?"

"It's hard to tell. I know they've been on edge lately. I think they're just worried about the kickback from the prison break. It'll be messed up if they did kick you out though."

"Well, I'm prepared for it. I already have a plan in case they do," Jade planned on hiding out in Niles and eventually making her way across the state line.

"Well, I'll be right there with you."

"No, David, I can't ask you to do that."

"You don't need to ask me."

"There are great benefits to living with the Black Deficit. Life will be easier for you here."

"I've made it this far without them. Besides, I don't wanna be a part of a group who will kick someone else out because they have a family member on the other side. You can't be the only one dealing with this kind of scenario."

"Yeah, Keeper said the same thing."

"You're not getting rid of me that easily," he smiled as he got out their hunting bows. "Like it or not, you're stuck with me." He handed Jade her bow, along with some arrows.

David pinned a target sign on a tree and walked back over to Jade. He stood behind her as she drew back her bow. She held her breath as he placed his hands on her waist.

"Now, let's work on your shooting."

**

Jade and David stayed out hunting for hours. Every minute of it was enjoyed. Jade felt so carefree when she was with David. He had a way of making her forget about all her problems—and she had a lot. The vibe he brought just did something to her. There was peace. There was relief. There was security. She wondered how she ever got along without him.

The sun was setting when they were finally heading back.

"Thanks, David, I really needed that."

"Don't mention it. Same time tomorrow?"

"Definitely."

Jade and David walked passed the prisoners' sleeping quarters. She sped up a little—trying to avoid the prisoners. She just had a great day and didn't want it ruined with another horror story about her sister.

"Jade!" a prisoner called out.

Jade didn't recall seeing her in the showers this morning. "Yeah."

"Can I talk to you?"

"I'm sorry, I'm really tired right now."

"It'll only take a minute," the lady said. "It's important."

Jade sighed. "Ok."

"Follow me."

Jade expected to follow her back to the sleeping quarters, but they walked past it. They were heading toward the Black Deficit's briefing room. What was going on? If they were going to the briefing room, then it must've been important. Jackson and the rest of the Black Deficit had to know about it. She was right. When they entered the room, Jackson, Beverly, Keeper, and other members were there. She and David took a seat.

The lady walked to the front of the room and joined the rest of some unrecognizable prisoners.

"Jade, I'm Vicky," she pointed to the people next to her. "This is Paul, Johnathan, Will, and Kim. We were surviving with your sister before she became a DC officer."

Jade's heart raced. "What?"

"We found her shortly after your parents died, and we took her in. We were takers...robbers rather. Helena never participated in the robberies, she was too afraid. So, she was our lookout."

Jade tensed up. She wasn't going to like what she was about to hear.

She needed to keep her composure. Vicky and her crew couldn't be trusted.

"Once the DCs began to heavily flood the area, we began robbing them. We knew that they had some essential items for surviving on them, and as they were doing sweeps, they became easy targets. They usually left their vehicles unattended when they were rounding up debtors. We would clean them out. And if there was a guard by the trucks, then we usually took them by force."

"You ever killed any of them?" Jade asked.

"No, just wounded," the guy named Johnathan replied.

"We eventually started stalking a few of them," Vicky continued. "The really nasty ones. We figured we were doing some type of justice by robbing the officers who abused the debtors the most."

"Razor," Jade whispered.

Vicky slowly nodded her head. "He was Helena's mark."

"Were you fucking crazy!"

"It was time for her to carry her weight," the girl Kim said.

"I don't give a damn about her weight!" Jade jumped out of her chair, but David held her back. The girl Kim hid behind Johnathan.

"Calm down, Jade," David said. Jade shrugged him off.

"I'm sorry, Jade," tears threatened to leave Vicky's eyes.

The guy Paul cleared his throat. "We have video footage of that day. We thought you might wanna see it."

"Video footage?"

"Yeah, whenever someone was doing a robbery, we put a hidden camera on them in case they needed help." Guilty glances were exchanged around the group. They didn't help Helena that day.

"Put it on."

"Jade, are you sure about this?" David asked.

"I need to know," she couldn't figure out Helena's and Razor's relationship. He was a monster. No, the devil. How could her sister end up with someone like that?

"We noticed that Razor would go down to this lake every day to swim. He was always alone. He never told the other officers where he was," Vicky explained as Paul set up the footage. "We figured he'd be less threatening alone."

"Testing, testing. Can you all hear me?" Helena's voice came across the speakers. Jade's heart stopped. That was the Helena she remembered. The sweet, caring, loving girl.

"Yes, we can hear you," Vicky said. "Do you have the target in sight?"

"Yeah, I see him."

Jade could see a figure in the back, standing on the pier. Jade remembered that lake. It was Crooked Lake. It was just north of the city—about a four-hour drive. Jade's parents used to take them there every summer. She remembered pushing Helena on the tire swing just in front of the lake house that they rented.

"I don't think I can do this," Helena's scared voice said.

"You have to," Vicky said coldly. "If you're gonna remain in this group you gotta do your part."

Helena sighed. "Approaching target."

As Helena walked closer, Jade could see Razor more clearly. He appeared to be scarier than she remembered. Something was missing. When she was in the torture room with him, he didn't seem as vicious as he appeared now.

"Hello there," Helena said nervously. "Mind if I take a swim here?"

Razor looked at her sternly. His beard was thick and untamed. Tattoos lined his arms and neck, but there was one tattoo that was missing. Jade remembered it when he was punching her. It was a vine of roses on his forearm. She thought it was beautiful—sweet. It was so different from his other tattoos.

"Depends," he said.

"On?"

He snatched Helena's arm. She gasped. He pricked her finger and walked over to the truck. He was running her name.

Helena took off her jacket and laid it down. Jade could see her. There she was. Her sweet, sweet baby sister. It was her. The *real* Helena. The pixie haircut. The innocent face. The kind and caring young woman. Helena rubbed her hands together and shifted back and forth.

"You're all clear, Ms. Willer."

"I know," Helena walked to the end of the pier and sat down. She took off her shoes and let her feet dangle.

Razor took a seat next to her. "Never seen you here before."

"Never had the chance to come by."

"And why is that?"

"Been too busy trying to survive. Trying to find food. Trying to find shelter. Trying not to get killed in the next natural disaster."

Razor nodded. "I see how that could hold you up."

"It sure can." They stared off at the water for the moment. Jade could see that Helena didn't know how to go on.

"Must be nice being a DC officer," she finally said.

Razor smirked. "Yeah, nice."

Helena laughed a little. That quirky, loving laugh. Just then, Jade knew that Razor was hooked. "I mean, you all get food, shelter, clothing, and protection. In times like these, that's nice to have."

Razor looked over at her, and the camera zoomed in. Someone from the crew was controlling the camera on Helena's jacket. He took his hand and began rubbing her cheek. Helena froze. Shocked at what was happening.

"Is there no one protecting you?" he asked in a tone that shocked Jade.

Jade gasped. It felt like she was just punched in the stomach by Razor. She looked over at David with wide eyes.

"What's wrong?"

"He loves her," that's what was missing. When she was in that torture room, it was love that she saw from Razor. He loved her sister. Genuinely and sincerely in love that her presence alone was enough for him.

"No," Helena said. "Which leaves me to do what I gotta do to survive."And just like Razor, Jade never saw it coming. Helena was so smooth and swift as she sliced the knife across Razor's forearm. The choice in weaponry ran in the family.

Razor quickly moved his hand from Helena's cheek to his forearm. His face became confused, angry, and then disappointed. Helena sliced at him again. He jumped up. Blood was oozing down is arm profusely. Jade wondered if Helena hit a major vein or artery. Razor was getting woozy and was looking like he was about to faint.

"Ok Helena," Vicky said. "Grab the goods and get out of there."

"There's so much blood," Helena whispered. Jade was wondering how Helena was still standing. The sight of blood usually made her faint.

Just then Razor fell over in the lake unconscious.

"Oh my God, no!" Helena jumped in after him. Vicky protested, but Helena ignored her.

"Don't pass out, don't pass out, don't pass out," Helena kept telling herself as she dragged Razor to shore. She thanked God that she kept needles and thread in her pockets. Helena began trying to stitch up the cuts on Razor's arm.

Once she was done, she got some water to clean off the blood. Helena waited about 10 minutes for Razor to come to. His eyes fluttered open.

"I'm sorry. I'm so sorry. Please don't hurt me."

Razor looked around for a moment and then down at his arm. He stood up—towering over Helena.

"It's ok, I won't," he began to caress her cheek as he had done before. Then he brought his head down to hers. Jade could see Helena relax a little. And then he placed his lips softly on hers. Razor stared at her for a moment. "It's such a shame."

"What is?"

"That you never got a chance to swim." Just then a scary looking guy got out of the truck. He was bald and very muscular.

Helena froze.

Razor rubbed his forearm. "You won't like the water now."

"Help! Help! HELP!!!" Helena screamed as the bald guy dragged her by her hair into the water.

Vicky and the other crew members were arguing on whether they should save her or not. The bald guy held Helena under water. Helena struggled to get out of his grasp. Razor looked away as if he couldn't bear the sight.

Jade gripped tightly on the edge of the desk. It was taking all her strength not to jump over the table and attack every one of the crew members. They left Helena behind. Too afraid that they would get attack by Razor and his people.

The bald guy was now punching Helena and throwing her around.

"Please stop," she pleaded. "Please, I can't take anymore."

The guy held her back underwater as Razor casually sat on the shore. When Helena stopped splashing the guy pulled her up by her neck and began choking her. Once she started going limp, he threw her on the shore. She fell near Razor. Helena slowly began crawling away while gasping for air. The bald guy frowned as he followed behind her.

"What's wrong?" Razor asked.

"She's not fighting back anymore."

"God," she croaked. "Please forgive me."

Tears ran down Jade's face. Her sister was accepting her fate. She was accepting death.

"Cut it off," David said.

"No," Jade objected.

"You're wheezing, Jade. You need a breathing treatment."

"Keep-it-rolling," she gritted.

The bald guy smirked. "So it's death you want." He kicked Helena in the stomach. She stopped crawling. "I'm happy to oblige."

He began kicking and punching Helena some more. Once she stopped trying to get away, he grabbed her neck and started strangling her.

"Enough," Razor said. The guy didn't stop. Helena just laid there still— life slowly leaving her body. Razor jumped up. "I said enough!"

"I'm finishing the job," his grip got tighter around Helena's neck.

Razor charged at the guy, knocking him off Helena. They began tussling on the ground. Razor managed to get on top and started bashing the guy's head in on a rock. Blood squirted from the guy's head. Razor didn't stop until the guy's body went lifeless. Razor went still. He slowly took in the scene. He looked at Helena's unconscious body. Without any hesitation, he went over and picked her up.

"I'm so sorry," he whispered to her. He put Helena in his truck and drove off.

The footage ended. Silence filled the room.

"Keeper," Jackson finally said. "Bring Jade's nebulizer."

"Sure-thing boss," Keeper brought in the regular nebulizer machine. Jade took her treatment while Vicky's group frantically tried to explain themselves.

"I'm so sorry, Jade. We just kind of freaked out. None of us have ever been in that much trouble before."

"Razor really freaked us out," Paul explained. "We didn't know how to handle him. And the bald guy...well, you saw him. He was ruthless!"

"And you thought my sister could handle him?"

"Your sister was sweet and innocent," Will said. "We thought he would let his guard down with her. And he did, until..."

"Until she went along with that idiotic plan of yours."

"That wasn't even the freaky part though," Vicky added. "The next morning, we found Helena back in her room, asleep in her bed. He put her there."

"He knew where we were hiding out," Johnathan said.

"How do you know that?" David asked.

"She told us," Kim interjected. "She said that he knew what we were up to. He knew that we were going around robbing DC officers. He was watching us for weeks. He knew that Helena was supposed to attack him. He just wanted to see if she had it in her."

"Of course, we started packing up our shit and heading to another hideout," Vicky said. "But he was right there at our front door. He ignored all of us and looked right at Helena. He asked her if she wanted to come with him. He promised that he would keep her safe and she would never have to worry about surviving again. And surprisingly, she went with him. She didn't hesitate or anything."

Jade just sat there, stunned.

Razor promised to protect Helena, and that was all it took for her to go with him. Jade couldn't be all that upset. Razor kept his promise. He protected Helena and kept her safe. That was more than what she did for her.

"So, how did you end up in prison?" Beverly asked. "You all aren't debtors."

"After a couple of years of just scavenging to survive we went back to robbing DCs," Johnathan explained.

"And who should we run into on our first day of robbing?"

"Razor and Helena," Vicky's group said in unison.

"Talk about bad timing," Keeper said.

Vicky looked at Jade. "She was a completely different person then. She was hostile and cold."

"She was like the female version of Razor," Kim said. "Which made sense. Because by then, they were married."

"I know you have a ton of questions, Jade," Vicky explained. "I just wanna give you the answer on how Helena and Razor met. And how she became a DC officer. I feel like it's all my fault."

Jade stood up. "It's not your fault, Vicky. If there's anyone to blame, it is me. But thank you. This does answer a few of my questions." Jade looked around the room. "Now if you all please excuse me, I need some time alone in my room."

Jade didn't wait for anyone to respond. She quickly walked back to her room. There were planning and preparation that needed to be done. She needed to work on her shooting with David, as well as combat training with her knife. Jade knew what she had to do. If she wanted Helena back, *really back*, she had to kill Razor.

That was what she was going to do.

~14~

Jade spent weeks preparing for her encounter with Razor. She didn't know how, but she knew that she was going to face him again. When that time came, she wanted to be sure that she could kill him. So, countless hours were spent on practicing archery with David. She wore her combat nebulizer to get used to it. It didn't take long. Jade found it very helpful.

Most of Jade's time was spent doing combat fighting and working with her knives. She practiced a lot with the Black Deficit members, particularly with the male members. A lot of her fights targeted the guys that were around Razor's build. She had to be able to overpower them if she was going to have any shot at killing him.

For the most part, she was able to handle them easily. Sometimes it got a little intense. Jade would have the upper hand in the combat, and usually, the male egos started to kick in. She had one member in a nice choke hold that he couldn't get out of for a while. When some prisoners stopped and stared, he mumbled some curse words and elbowed Jade right in the face. It was so hard that it knocked her out. She walked around with a swollen cheek and a knot on the back of her head for days.

"You gotta slow down, Jade," David held an ice pack to her face. "You're gonna kill yourself."

"I can't. I gotta be ready for Razor."

"Jade, you probably won't even run into Razor again," David had been saying that for days now, and it was starting to annoy her. She knew she would be facing Razor soon. Her gut was telling her so. And her gut was never wrong. Jade had to keep working on her fighting.

"Trust me, David, I will see him again."

Jackson and Beverly walked into her room. Jade wasn't that thrilled to see them. They thought she was insane when she told them about Razor. They couldn't see how. For her to run into Razor again, meant that Razor knew where they were. No one wanted to believe that. Jade didn't put it past him. Razor was an intelligent man. If the DCs and the Black Deficit have been fighting like Jackson said they were, then Jade was pretty sure that Razor did some recon on them.

Jade didn't care if no one believed her.

"Jade, you have to stop fighting with the members," Jackson ordered.

"I'm just brushing up on my combat skills."

"Well, it's leaving our members injured," Beverly interjected. She was pissed at Jade.

"The fact that I can injure them so easily shows that they need more combat training as well."

"It's also scaring the prisoners," Jackson interjected before Beverly could say anything else.

"Scaring them?"

"Some of the prisoners got spooked when they saw you get knocked out."

"If that upset them, then how do you expect them to fight?"

Jackson and Beverly still didn't bring up the idea of fighting the DCs to the prisoners. Jade didn't know what was taking them so long. It was now or never. The DCs were sure to retaliate, and they would do it sooner rather than later. The prisoners needed to be trained in combat and the sooner, the better.

"We're giving them time to recover."

"Time that we don't have. While we're sitting here waiting, they're probably loading up and ready to take us out."

"We've weakened them," Beverly's tone was defensive.

"How? All we did was bust out some prisoners from one prison. There are still thousands of prisons out there. Just as overcrowded as that one. What is one break out compared to that?" No one responded.

"And it's not like we weakened their armory. All we did was take away the oppressed from some very aggressive and armed oppressors. And now we're just sitting here twiddling our thumbs while the DCs can avenge themselves."

"We're prepared for them!" Beverly stepped toward Jade. Jade got up from her bed. David held Jade back while Jackson held Beverly.

"Look, Jade, just stop with the fighting," Jackson said calmly.

"Fine."

"Let's go, Beverly," they left out the room, closing the door behind them.

Jade sat back on her bed. David sat next to her, placing the ice pack back on her cheek. He was silent. That was rare for him. Usually, Jade couldn't get him to shut up.

"What? You disagree with what I said too?"

"On the contrary, I agree with you. They really should be training the prisoners. Or at least figuring out who's willing to fight and who isn't. It's been weeks now, and we're here like sitting ducks."

"So, what we do?"

"Don't know. I mean they've let us in, but not really. And they don't seem to take criticism about leadership very well. The fact that you've been able to take down their members that easily is a concern as well."

"He says as he places an ice pack on my face," Jade smiled.

"Yeah, but that was a cheap shot," David returned the smile. "Anyway, we need to decide what we're gonna do."

"We?"

"Yeah, I told you, you can't get rid of me that easily."

"I need to keep practicing."

"Fine. If you're that insistent, we can practice combat fighting out in the woods."

"Thank you."

Over the next couple of days, David and Jade spent their time hunting, fighting, and shooting out in the woods. They spent all day out there. Eventually, a few people started to join them. First, it was Raina and her mother, Sarah. Then some of the women prisoners followed. They began to warm up to Jade during practices. They admired how adamant she was about them learning to protect themselves.

After the women, the male prisoners started coming out. The guys didn't want the women showing them up with their fighting skills. Jackson started to get suspicious when Keeper began joining them out in the woods but didn't bother to say anything. Jade thought that this would finally make them train all the prisoners. Or at least see who is willing and able to fight.

"What's their next move?" Jade asked Keeper one day at practice.

"I don't know."

"Do they plan on breaking out more debtors from other prisons?" a girl, who was getting good at shooting, asked.

"I don't know."

She frowned. "What do you know?" She rolled her eyes and stalked off.

Jade smiled. "She has a point. I thought they kept you in the loop about that stuff."

"If it has nothing to do with me making some kind of gadget, they usually don't consult me."

"You ok with that?"

"It's just how it is."

Jade could tell that Keeper wasn't ok with it. "Who do they consult with then?"

"Usually it's just Jackson and Beverly."

"It's just two members who make all the decisions?" David didn't seem too thrilled about that notion.

"Basically."

"And everyone is ok with that?"

"What can I say? They are *the* members."

"Because who their father was? That doesn't give them the right to make all the decisions. Different skills can be utilized here."

"I know," Keeper was getting agitated. "But what can we do?"

"You can speak up. Say something. This is a group effort, and everyone in the group should be heard."

"Well try telling them that."

Jade knew how well the brother and sister duo took criticism. She started wishing that she could leave from there, but she couldn't. If she left, many people were sure to follow. And she didn't want that. The idea of just her and David going out on their own was more appealing. Light and simple. But as more and more people started showing up for their practices, Jade knew that that option was off the table. Connections were being made. And it's hard to break away when there are connections.

Someone was coming toward them from a distance. By the way that they were dressed, it was a Black Deficit member.

"Shit, it's Beverly," Keeper mumbled.

Jade clutched the knife that was in her hand.

"Play nice, Jade," David warned.

"Only if she does." It was still tensed between her and Beverly. Beverly felt like Jade stepped over some kind of boundary. And she made it known that she didn't approve of Jade and David going out to the woods and fighting.

"This is war," Jade said in their latest argument. "And you expect us to just be sitting on our asses!"

"You do not call the shots here!"

"Newsflash, I didn't ask to be here! You needed me!" Of course, they almost came to blows. David, Jackson, and some other members had to intervene.

Beverly reached them and looked around. She gave everyone a disapproving look. "Mandatory meeting in the mess hall. 5 minutes."

"Aye, aye captain," Jade knew that her comment was petty, but she couldn't help it. Beverly was bringing out the worst in her.

Beverly rolled her eyes and walked away.

Everyone gathered up their things and headed towards the building. Jade, David, and Keeper stayed behind to make sure that they had everything.

"I wonder what's that about," David said.

"No clue."

"It's probably to ban our personal training and force us to rely solely on them," Jade guessed.

They all walked into HQ and to the mess hall. Jade decided to sit in the back, and David joined her. Keeper sat up front with all the other members. Jade looked around at everyone who was in the mess hall. She saw the same look—confusion and fear. She hoped that this was the moment of truth, the Black Deficit would ask the prisoners to stand up and fight with them against the DCs and the government.

Jade couldn't fight with them any longer—at least not on this issue. It felt like she was on thin ice with the members. If they keep arguing on it, she would surely get kicked out. Jackson, Beverly, and some other members were sitting on the stage. Jackson stepped to the microphone and cleared his throat. Everyone in the mess hall fell silent.

"Hello, everyone," he started. "I'm sure you all are wondering why we've called this mandatory meeting here today. We have a few things that we wanted to discuss with you all. First, is your well-being. We hope you all are adjusting very well here. We hope that we are providing you with everything that you need. If you have any requests, please let the members at the back table know," a few people turned around to the members at the back. "They'll be ready for your concerns once the meeting is done. Now, on to the main objective of this assembly."

Jade sat up in her seat. This was the moment of truth. The moment she's been waiting on for weeks.

"We, as the Black Deficit group, believe that it's time to go on the offensive against the DCs and the government that placed them there."

"But to do that we need numbers," Beverly interjected as she stood up. "To fight back, we need people."

Some people started looking around nervously at each other. Jade couldn't gauge how well the conversation was going. Some people looked like they were going to faint at the notion of fighting against the DCs.

"I know this may frighten some of you," Jackson reassured. "And I know some of you may be hesitant to fight against the DCs, but I assure you together we can overcome them."

"But we can only do it together."

"We will properly train you on how to fight and protect yourselves. We have just as much weaponry and equipment as the DCs."

"If not more and more unique."

Jackson glanced over at Beverly. She hesitantly took a step back.

"I know this may be a lot to take in, so we will give you a couple of days to think it over. However, if you know right now that you want to fight, you can line up in front of these members here," Jackson gestured to the members standing in front of the stage.

It went completely silent. At first, everyone looked around at each other—seeing who would get up. Jade was nervous. It was looking like no one was willing to fight. Then a girl stood up and walked to the front. Jade recognized her as one of the girls who came out to the woods—she believed her name was Rachel.

Once Rachel stood, others started to follow. The first was mostly the people who practiced in the woods with Jade and David. Then the others began to file in—Vicky and her crew were among them. Altogether it was about 50 people that stood up ready to fight. It wasn't nearly half of the prisoners, but Jade thought it was a solid start. Jackson thought so too.

"As I said before, take a couple of days to think it over, and we will reconvene here," Jackson smiled. "That's it for now everyone. Again, please address any concerns to the members in the back."

"Excuse me," a woman, who didn't volunteer to fight, stood. "What will happen to those who don't wanna fight? Will we have to leave?"

"Negative. For those who do not wish to fight, you can contribute in other ways. Certain chores and tasks will be vitally important to defeat the DCs. We just want to know where everyone stands so we can proceed."

"But know this," Beverly interjected. "For you to stay here, you will have to contribute in some way." The room fell silent.

Jade shook her head. Some people just really didn't need to be in charge. Jackson stared at his sister in disbelief.

"What my sister means is that we can't secure the objective without each other. We hope that each and every one of you will contribute your strengths to us. With that being said, let us go back to our daily routines, and we will get back to this issue in a couple of days."

Everyone started to get up and head out. Some people lined up in the back to address their concerns to the members. Some people began filing out of the mess hall—most heading back to their rooms.

"Well, if there were more who were willing to fight, Beverly might have just deterred them," Jade said, getting up.

"Yeah, tactfulness doesn't seem to be her strong suit."

"But at least there's some that are willing to fight."

"It's a good start."

Jade and David were getting ready to head to the common room when the alarms started to go off. Everyone looked around frantically. Something was wrong. Something was very wrong. Jade had a strange feeling in her gut.

Then she heard it.

Her name.

~15~

"JADE!"

Jade's heart raced. One of the prisoners came running toward her.

"It's him!" he yelled. "It's Razor!"

Everyone panicked. People started running from the mess hall and to their rooms. Some began to gather up their things, preparing to flee from there. Jade knew what they were thinking about. If Razor was there, then the rest of the DCs weren't too far behind.

Jade looked over at David. "I told you he'd be coming."

"Jade, no!"

"JADE!!" Razor yelled again.

Jade strapped on her knives and gathered up her bow and arrows. This is what she was preparing for. She was more than ready. He was here for her, and she was going to make sure that no one would get hurt because of it.

"This is a trap, Jade."

"There's a strong possibility that it is. But did you think that they'll give up after what I did?"

"No, but—"

"If I don't go out there then he'll force his way in here. No one else is getting hurt because of me." Jade grabbed her combat nebulizer and headed out of the mess hall. Jackson, Beverly, Keeper, and several other members were directing people and trying to keep everyone calm.

"Everyone, head to your bunkers and lock yourselves in!" Jackson kept instructing.

Jade was hoping that she could walk past them without being caught.

"Don't even think about it, Jade," Beverly said. She hoped wrong.

"JADE...JADE....JADE!!!!"

"I'm going out there to distract him. That should give you guys time to secure everyone and prepare for any attack that may be coming."

"She's right," Jackson said. "We need time to prepare. Keeping him focused on her will help us do that."

"So, you're just prepared to sacrifice her then," David said.

"It's not ideal, but it's the best plan we got."

"I'll be fine, David," Jade started towards the door, but stopped. She looked at Jackson and Beverly. "You know I hate to say I told you so, but..."

Beverly rolled her eyes. "Yeah, we know. Just try not to get killed out there."

"Aye, aye, captain."

Jade walked out of the front doors. There, she was greeted by members who were keeping watch. They all looked at her grimly—like they would hate to be her at this moment.

"Is it just him?"

"Looks like it. We don't see anyone else, but they could be miles out. Or hiding somewhere nearby."

Jade nodded. "If you see any more, yell so I can get myself out of there."

"You got it. Good luck."

"JADE!!!"

"Thanks."

Jade put on her nebulizer mask as they opened the gate. The plan was to come out shooting. She didn't want to give him any time or any chance to get the upper hand. Helena was probably close by waiting for her. She couldn't handle them both out there alone.

Taking a deep breath, Jade walked in between the gates before it opened all the way. She saw him. Razor was pacing back and forth. Something was off, but Jade didn't want to pause to think about it. He stopped pacing once he saw her.

"Jade, I ne—" he quickly ducked as Jade's arrow barely missed his head. "Jade, stop!"

Jade didn't listen. She shot off another arrow towards him. This one grazed his left arm.

Razor stepped back and glared at her. "JADE!"

Jade kept running. She drew back another arrow—prepared to shoot. She wasn't going to let up. Razor couldn't get any kind of advantage over her. He wasn't acting how she expected. Although something was off about the whole situation, she wasn't going to use this time to try to figure it out. She shot again and barely missed him.

This time Razor came charging at her. One thing that Jade had over him was speed. She was more agile than him. She was able to pass him and jump on his back. Jade choked him with the handle of her bow. He dropped to the ground and elbowed her repeatedly in the stomach. Jade endured the blows and held her grip on the bow. Finally, Razor head-butted her, and her grip loosened. He managed to get out of her hold, and he rolled over. Jade jumped up to her feet.

"Jade, stop," Razor's hands were up.

Jade didn't listen. She came charging at him full speed. He managed to get up just in time to tackle her by the waist. He punched her, but not as hard as he could. Jade couldn't understand why he was gentle with her, but she dismissed it. She kneed him, and when he stumbled back, she kicked him in the face. Jade jumped up and tackled him to the ground. She punched him a couple of times before he threw her off him. She didn't have enough time to get up before he was on top of her.

"Jade, please stop."

Ignoring him, Jade head-butted Razor as hard as she could. She wasn't expecting the impact to be *that* hard, so she was thrown off by it. Razor quickly fell over. Jade laid still for a moment—trying to collect her bearings. She must've knocked herself out good because she thought she heard Razor crying. She quickly crawled to her bow and pulled out an arrow. There was a pause before Jade got to her feet.

Although her mask was protecting her, Jade could still feel the pain to her lower jaw. Razor was still lying on his side. She quickly got to her feet. Jade drew her bow back and aimed it at him as she walked towards him. Razor was crying and mumbling something. She kicked him, and he rolled on his back.

"He has her," he kept repeating.

"He has who? Who is he?"

"Bossman. He has Helena."

Fear crept through Jade's body. "What you mean? Why does he have her?"

"Because of the breakout and because you escaped," he cried. "I need your help to get her back."

Jade saw the gates opening. The Black Deficit was coming out once they saw she had him down. She pointed the arrow at his head. "Is this a trap?" Her gut told her it wasn't.

"I wouldn't lie about something like this," Razor cried harder. "I gotta get her back." Watching Razor cry convinced her to go. Jade's mind was made up. She had to save her sister.

"They're never gonna let me go with you," she watched as the members filed out heavily armed. "And they're never gonna let you go now that you know where they are."

Razor quickly collected himself. "I can take them all."

"No, we have to do this peacefully."

"We don't have time for peacefully," he grunted. "We gotta move now."

Jade watched as the members got closer. They started to circle around them. She had to figure out a way to do this smoothly. She was already on thin ice with Jackson and Beverly. Mentioning Helena now would surely make a strained relationship even worse. But this was her sister. She already failed her once. Jade refused to fail her again. The members closed in on them—Jackson and Beverly in front.

"On the ground, Razor!" Jackson aimed his gun at Razor's head.

"Jackson wait it's not what you think."

He ignored Jade. "Down on the ground or I'll put you down!"

Razor smirked. "I'll love to see you try." Before Jade could register what was going on, Razor had her knives, and one of them was to her throat. A shiver went down Jade's spine. This was the real Razor. He was going easy on her earlier. "Come any closer, and I will shower you with her blood."

"Jade!" David rushed forward, but Keeper held him back.

"Let her go Razor and get down on the ground!" Beverly barked.

"Sorry sweetheart, you and your members here will have to make me," he pulled Jade's head back even further and pressed the knife harder against her throat. Jade could feel blood trickling down her neck. "Trust me," he whispered. "I just came here for Jade. No one else needs to get hurt."

"I can't let you take her," Jackson stepped forward slowly. "And I can't let you leave."

"Tell me, Jackson, how good will the prisoners' morale be after they see me slice her open right here in front of you?" A lot of the members started looking nervously at each other. "How can they feel safe? Not even the Black Deficit can keep them safe from me."

"I can't let you take her," Jackson repeated. His voice cracked a little.

Razor smiled. "Have it your way then."

Jade could feel the knife slowly glide across her neck. She cried out in pain. Even though the cut was shallow, Jade made it seem like it was more severe.

"Everyone, lower your weapons."

"Jackson!"

"Now, Beverly!"

They all reluctantly put down their weapons.

"That's good," Razor looked at David. "Now Loverboy, gather up her bow and arrows and bring them to me."

David maneuvered around the members collecting Jade's arrows. Once he had them all, he walked over to Razor. "Jade," David's eyes were searching hers—trying to find answers.

"No need to talk Loverboy. The bow and the arrows please."

David handed them to Razor.

Razor slung it across his back. "I assume you brought something to bind me with. Hand it over," Keeper stepped forward. "Give them to

Loverboy here," David took some handcuffs from Keeper. "Now put them on her."

David put the handcuffs around Jade's wrist. He glared at Razor while he did it. "I will be coming after you," he said in a tone that frightened Jade a little.

"Noted," Razor directed his attention to the members. "I kill anyone who follows." Razor began to slowly back away—dragging Jade with him.

Jade had to give it to him, Razor played his role very well. But she was worried about David. David would not stay behind and watch her leave. She had to try to convince Razor to not hurt him. And she had to try to convince David to let her go. It was all stressful. But what stressed her, even more, was the fact that Helena was in danger.

It was all her fault. Because she helped the Black Deficit break out those prisoners, her sister was now paying the price for it. Once again, she failed Helena. But Jade was going to redeem herself. Razor was going to see to that.

Razor held her at knifepoint well into the woods. Once they were out of eyesight, he released her. He pushed her ahead of him. "Run."

They both took off. Razor got ahead of her, and she followed. Jade wasn't sure where they were going, or how long it would even take for them to get there. All she thought about was Helena.

They ran three miles before Jade started noticing that she was getting winded. She panicked a little. Her combat nebulizer, was it running out of medicine? That would be all she needed. Having an asthma attack with only a psycho DC officer as a companion was not ideal. Jade slowed down a little and focused on her breathing. She wasn't paying attention to where she was going and tripped and fell over something. She laid there for a moment—trying to catch her breath. Her wrists were killing her. The handcuffs were still on her, and she'd been running this whole time awkwardly. Razor looked back and saw her on the ground. He ran back to her.

"Sorry," he helped her up. "I forgot I had those on you." He picked the lock and took off the handcuffs.

Jade rubbed her wrist. Razor looked at her neck. It was still a few drops of blood trailing down. He reached in his back pocket and pulled out a handkerchief.

He placed it on her neck. "Sorry about that too. I had to make it look real. You said peacefully. That was as peaceful as I could make it."

Jade held the handkerchief. "Don't worry about it. I'm just glad you didn't hurt anyone."

"How's your breathing? Do you need to slow down?"

"I'm low on medicine for my nebulizer."

"Right," he reached into another pocket. He pulled out an inhaler and threw it to her. "You probably will be needing these too," he gave Jade her knives and bow and arrows back. "We can walk the rest of the way."

"Where's this kindness coming from?"

"You're Helena's sister," he walked off.

Jade watched him for a moment. She took her mask off and put it in her bag with her arrows. It wasn't doing her any good right now anyway. She had it on just about all day, and the medicine needed to be refilled. There wasn't any of it on her. It was back in her room. She didn't plan on going on a trip. She made a mental note to always have extras with her. Putting the inhaler in her pocket, Jade followed Razor.

"You plan to trade me for Helena," she stated once she caught up with him. Jade took her scarf out of her back pocket. She wrapped it around her nose and mouth.

"No."

"No? That seems to be your only option."

"I plan to use you to get Helena."

"Isn't that the same thing?"

"No, I'm not leaving you there to die."

"Why not? You don't owe me anything."

"Believe it or not, Jade, your sister wouldn't be too happy with me if I let you die."

"You're right, I don't believe it."

"And why is that?"

"Because she hates me. And how I hear it, you turned her into a monster."

"Is that what you really think of me? Of her?"

"I heard some of the prisoners' stories. I saw the footage when you and my sister first met."

"Footage, huh?" he paused. He didn't seem too surprised by that statement. "Before I met Helena, yes, I was a monster. I was vicious. I cared only about myself. But after I met your sister, I found love. She taught me how to love and how to care about someone else."

"Yeah, and you taught her how to beat and torture other people."

He stopped abruptly and frowned. "I wasn't always there to protect her, Jade. The other officers could tell what kind of person she was by the smell of her. They anticipated for a moment to pounce. She had to keep up a persona. She had to look like she was one of them.

"It killed her to hurt those people. She tried to protect them as much as she could, especially the women. She used to send some of them to solitary when she heard that some of the male officers were interested in them. She did what she could, but she couldn't save them all."

"Well try telling that to your victims."

"I don't care what they think or how they feel. My only goal is to protect Helena. That's more than I can say about you. I wasn't the one living it up with my boyfriend when she needed help."

Jade felt weak. That was the worst way Razor could hurt her. Her guilt was already eating her up inside. Hearing those words just made it worse. She didn't say anything—she couldn't. She just nodded in agreement.

Razor read her face and sighed. "Look I'm sor—"

It took Jade a moment to realize what happened. Razor was on the ground tussling with someone. The person came out of nowhere. Jade didn't even hear anyone approaching, and apparently, Razor didn't either. Although the person was on top of him, Razor managed to jump up.

"Loverboy," he growled.

Jade realized that David had tackled him to the ground. David jumped up. Razor pulled out a knife. Jade quickly jumped in between them. "David, stop! It's not what you think."

"Out of the way, Jade," David kept his eyes locked on Razor.

"Bossman has my sister. I need to go with him to save her."

"You don't know that for sure! It could be a trap."

"It's my sister. Do you really expect me not to go?"

"So, all of that back there about him slicing you open?"

"It was fake. It was the only way he could get me out of there without anyone getting hurt."

David wouldn't budge. "You completely trust him just like that?"

"It's my sister, David. What would you do if you were in my shoes?"

Jade stood in between them, her eyes pleading with him. David glared at Razor—not trusting him for a second. "Then I'm coming with you."

Razor growled.

"That's the only way!" David shouted.

Just then someone came charging at Razor. He was prepared for it this time. He backhanded them quickly, and the person dropped to the ground. Jade saw that it was Keeper. Razor picked him up by his throat.

Keeper kicked wildly as he struggled to breathe. Jade ran over to them.

"Drop him!" Jade demanded. Razor ignored her. She pushed him as hard as she could. Razor only stumbled back a little, but his grip loosened, and Keeper dropped to the ground. Jade rushed over to him. "You ok?"

Keeper nodded frantically.

"How many more are coming?!" he asked David.

"It's just him and me. The others are probably just now realizing that we're gone."

Razor walked over to Jade and snatched her up by her arm. "Let's go."

"I'm not leaving her."

Razor marched back over to David. "You will be once I'm done with you."

Jade rushed in between them. "There's no use of fighting with them Razor. They're gonna follow either way."

"Fine," he snapped. He pulled Keeper off the ground and stalked off. "Keep up!" he shouted over his shoulder.

~16~

They arrived at an old farmhouse well into the night. They were at least 10 miles away from the Black Deficit's headquarters. Jade was exhausted. The day was long, and it felt never-ending. Most of the day was spent fighting. Her body was sore, and all she wanted to do was lie down. Her asthma was doing ok, surprisingly. She only had to use her inhaler twice during their long journey.

Razor kept a steady pace but made sure that Jade could keep up without upsetting her asthma. She was completely thrown off by him. He wasn't what she expected. The guy she saw in that video wasn't the same guy that walked before her today. Helena really had a powerful effect on him.

Razor walked up the front steps and went inside the farmhouse. Jade, David, and Keeper lingered back for a moment. They were all silent throughout the whole trip. None of them expected to be traveling with a DC officer when they woke up that morning. Jade knew that David probably thought she was crazy for trusting Razor. She probably lost some of Keeper's trust by tricking the Black Deficit. But ever since the world ended, Jade's only goal and mission was to be reunited with her sister again. This was the first step to doing that.

Jade remained at the bottom step—contemplating whether she should go inside or not. She looked back at David and Keeper, who was looking at her.

"Ok," she finally said. "Let me have it."

"Are you fucking crazy?" David snapped. "Just this morning, you were ready to kill him. Now come nightfall you're traveling with him!"

"You're absolutely right," she tried to remain calm. "I can't explain any of this. But I know he's telling the truth. I just have a gut feeling about it."

"Because your gut is always right?"

"I didn't ask you to come, David."

"No, I just thought that he was about to murder you! Excuse me for caring!"

"You have every right to be upset with me. But as you can see, I am ok. You can turn around and go back if you want."

"And leave you alone with him? I don't think so. You may trust him wholeheartedly, but I don't."

Jade didn't say anything. She deserved everything that David was giving her. If the roles were reversed, she would've been pissed with him too. He was the only friend that she had. She hoped that she wouldn't end up losing him.

Keeper stood there expressionless.

"I'm so sorry, Keeper. I wasn't trying to trick any of you. I just wanna help my sister."

"Don't worry about it."

"You're not mad at me?"

"I get it," he smiled a little. "If I were able to save my mother, I would do it, no questions."

"I don't think there's anything wrong with her wanting to save her sister," David interjected. "It's the messenger that worries me."

"Ya can't choose the messenger," Keeper shot back.

"So, you trust him?"

"I trust Jade. And if she trusts him, then I trust him."

Jade was a little relieved. She had grown close to Keeper and enjoyed his company. She was happy that her decision didn't alter their relationship.

David looked back at Jade and Keeper. He shook his head. "Fine."

"Are y'all coming inside?" Razor was on the porch. None of them heard him come outside. "Or do you plan to sleep out here?"

"Sorry," Jade walked up the steps. "There was some stuff we had to clear up first."

Razor looked at David. "Well, I hope it's all clear then."

"We're getting there," Jade walked pass Razor and went inside. The rest followed behind.

Razor had the living room lit up with kerosene lamps. Some bags were lying around, and clothes were strewn about.

Jade turned to Razor. "How long you been here?"

"For a few days," he started to pick up some of the clothes.

"How long have you known about our headquarters?" it was the first time Keeper spoken to Razor.

"Ever since y'all set up shop. It wasn't exactly hard to find. Jackson and Beverly are terrible at figuring out if they're being followed." Jade, David, and Keeper exchanged nervous looks. "Don't worry, I haven't told anyone."

"How come?"

"Because honestly, I didn't think it was important. The Black Deficit really wasn't a big threat to us...not even with the prison break," he looked over at their disappointed faces. Jade was hoping that it all wasn't for nothing.

"Why does Bossman have Helena?" David asked.

"To punish me," Razor dropped the things he was holding and plopped down on the couch. He put his head in his hands. "I was his right-hand man, and I allowed a serious breach to happen over the prison I was in charge of."

"*Was* his right-hand man?" Jade sat down in the armchair across from him.

"You don't expect me to remain the right-hand to a man who kidnapped my wife, do you?"

"Why the pressure on Jade then?"

Razor looked at David like it was obvious. "She killed a DC officer and instrumented a prison break. Do you know what that does to the oppressed?" David was silent. Razor rolled his eyes. "It gives them hope, strength, and courage. The three most dangerous things during the time of war."

"He plans to make an example out of me," Jade tried to accept her fate.

"He'll try. You're proving to be a hard person to catch."

"Other people killed DC officers before."

"But they've never lived another minute to tell it."

"So, what, now you're loyal to the Black Deficit?" David seemed annoyed.

"My loyalty has always been and will always be to Helena."

"What about being a DC officer?"

Jade could tell that David wasn't going to let up until he got all the answers he wanted. Razor stayed surprisingly cool.

"Being a DC officer was just a means of survival. I survived before being an officer, and I will survive after. I'm not worried about that. Right now, my big issue is with Bossman."

"What's the plan?" Jade was eager to get things in motion.

"I just wanna get Helena and get her as far away from him as possible."

"And how you plan on doing that?" there was skepticism in David's voice.

"Well, I didn't plan on having two extra people involved, but the additional pair of hands will be nice. I will bring you all in as my prisoners. Bossman is at the DC headquarters. The place is more of an office than a prison. You and Keeper will more than likely be locked in separate rooms. I doubt there will be any guards there. We're a little scarce since the breakout," he looked over at Jade. "Some were fatally punished for incompetence. I will be taking Jade straight to Bossman. He won't even let me see Helena without her. Once I have Helena, we'll break out of there."

"That doesn't sound like a solid plan."

Razor was a little annoyed with David. "I never said that it was."

"Jade could get hurt."

"She probably will. She might have to take a beating before Bossman even reveals Helena."

"So, the plan is all fine-and-dandy just as long as Jade is taking all the blows."

"I never said it was fine. I'm just explaining the reality of the situation."

"I don't expect to go into this without getting a few bruises and probably some broken bones," Jade stared at the pile of clothes that Razor dropped. "I just wanna be with my sister."

"Like I said before, Jade, I don't plan to leave you there to die."

"Yeah, but with your plan, we could all die."

"I'm ok with that."

"So am I," Jade stated.

David looked between Jade and Razor. "Alright, then."

Razor got up and grabbed one of the bags that were on the floor. He threw it at David's feet. "Eat and get some rest. We head out tomorrow."

"How far is the DC headquarters?" Keeper looked through the bag of food.

"About 40 miles from here," they all looked over at Razor. He smiled. "Don't worry. I have a pick-up truck out back. It's all gassed up and ready to go. You two will have to ride in the bed."

"Jade, where's ya mask?" Keeper asked.

"Oh, right," Jade took the mask out of her arrow bag and handed it to him. "The medicine is out, and I left the rest back at headquarters."

Keeper looked it over. "Where's ya inhaler?"

Jade handed it to him. "It's just this one."

"Hold on," Razor grabbed one the kerosene lamps and went into another room. He came back with another bag. He pulled some more inhalers. "Here you go."

"I think I can use a few of these for the mask."

"She should keep at least one of them on her," Razor pointed out. "She can't come in with it on."

"Good point," Keeper smiled at Jade. "Don't worry, Jade, I gotcha covered."

Jade smiled back. "You always do."

"You wouldn't happen to have any insulin in there, would you?" David asked, warily.

Razor looked surprised. "As a matter a fact I believe I do." He pulled out a few bottles and handed them to him. "I guess you were meant to come after all."

"Thanks."

"Hand those to me, David. I can refill ya watch with them."

"Alright, you all can take this room. I'll take the room off the back door. We leave at first light," Razor gathered up his clothes and left out.

**

The sun was just coming up when they all left in Razor's pick-up. Jade sat in front with Razor while David and Keeper sat in the bed. Her stomach was in knots. She wasn't sure how Helena was going to react to her. Most importantly, she wasn't sure how Bossman was going to respond to her. Severe pain was about to come her way, and Jade was dreading every second of it.

Jade wished to go back. Back to the days when the world was ordinary. Back to the days when she was a good sister. Back to the days when she was a good daughter. Man, she missed her family. If her parents could see her now, what would they think? How would they feel? Probably disappointed. Especially on how her relationship with Helena was now.

She needed to clear her mind. She closed her eyes and let the wind hit her face. It was unseasonably warm. Jade wasn't seasonally prepared for the end of the world. She was used to experiencing all four seasons. Now, you typically experienced one—an ungodly, scorching, hot summer all year round. She has never been a fan of the cold or snow, which was impossible to avoid living in Michigan, but she did miss the holidays and celebrations that usually went along with it.

Jade hated the feeling of being in hell all the time. Her conditions were reminders enough, she didn't want the weather to remind her too. She gazed at the empty neighborhoods that were once flooded with happy people. Now, all that lie behind those doors were people gripped with fear. She was one of them for a very long time. Now all she felt was anger. This new world had taken everything from her.

"Nervous?"

Jade looked over at Razor—who was staring at the road in front of him. It was the first time he spoke since they left that morning.

"A little."

"Of who?"

"Both."

Razor shrugged. "Helena will come around."

"I'm not so sure."

"Trust me. She misses you."

"Sure," she gave him a weak smile.

"So, uh," Razor glanced quickly out of the back window. "What's up with you and Loverboy?"

"David?" Jade asked. Razor nodded. "Nothing. We're just friends."

He smiled sarcastically. "Sure, that's why he hunted me down. Because you're just, 'friends.'"

Jade shrugged. "I dunno what to tell you. That's all we are. We met during one of the sweeps, and we've been together ever since."

"What a wonderful love story."

"I'm not good at love stories."

"Why?"

"One word: Vincent."

"I can't argue with you there. Vincent's a dick."

"I made him that way. His mother was taken away by the DCs because of me. Her death is on my hands."

Razor rolled his eyes. "Damn Jade, I didn't know you were such a buzzkill."

"Sorry for telling the truth."

"You gotta learn how to let the past go. A lot of shit is happening in the present. I think you need to put all of your focus there."

Jade didn't say anything for a while. The words sunk in. Razor had a point—although she hated to admit it. She was stuck in the past. She blamed herself for everything that went wrong, especially relationships.

"You have a point."

"I know I do."

Jade smiled and rolled her eyes.

"Things will get better between you and Helena."

"I really hope so."

Jade looked back out of the window—taking in the depressing scenery. She glanced back at Keeper and David. They were talking and based on David's facial expression, it appeared to be an intense conversation. She caught his eye. He looked at her and smiled. She smiled back. Although they were just friends, Jade was glad that she met him. She hasn't felt cared for in so long. David's been looking out for her like no one else has before. She honestly didn't know what she would do without him.

"We're almost there," Razor said.

"How close?"

"10 minutes."

Jade opened the back window. "We'll be there in 10 minutes guys."

Keeper nodded.

"You ok?" David asked.

"Uh, I've felt better."

"I'll be there with you, Jade. I won't let anything too bad happen to you."

"I know you won't."

"And I won't let anything bad happen to your sister."

Jade smiled. "Thanks."

"You got it."

She closed the window and turned around. Butterflies were in her stomach. Jade didn't want anyone to get hurt. Razor's plan had to go smoothly.

"Exactly how are we getting in again?" It just dawned on her that Razor never went into too much detail on how there were getting in the DC headquarters.

"It's better that you don't know the exact details."

Jade slowly nodded.

"Trust me," he picked up on her hesitation. "The less you know, the more real everything will appear. We have to make it look authentic."

"Right." Jade tried not to feel too leery about not knowing all of the details. She had to trust Razor. Or they'll never get out of this alive. She noticed that the truck was slowing down.

"We're about a half mile out," Razor pulled over to an abandon car garage. "We should walk the rest of the way."

Keeper knocked on the window. Jade opened it. "What's the plan?"

"Hiding the truck here. We're gonna walk there. Can y'all open the garage door?" Razor asked.

"Sure thing," Keeper jumped out the back, and David followed.

They slowly pushed the garage door open. There was no car inside. Razor slowly backed the truck into the garage. The garage was completely empty. Someone had picked the place clean. A lot of businesses were like that. Everyone began to scavenge for any and everything that could hold any value or be useful for survival.

Razor got out of the truck. Jade followed. Keeper and David waited for them out front.

"Alright," Razor closed the garage door. "This is where we'll come once we get out of there. Hopefully, no one will find it and take it while we're gone."

"Ok, how do we go in there?" David asked.

Razor turned and looked at Jade. "Trust me." He stared at Jade intently for a moment. She never saw it coming. A brick hit her face—twice. Jade drop to the ground. She realized that it was Razor's fist that she felt—not a brick.

David and Keeper were fighting with him as she passed out.

~17~

Jade slowly began to come to. Her face hurt. Her body was sore. She must've hit the ground hard after Razor knocked her out. She realized she was moaning out of pain. She reached to touch her face but couldn't. Her hand was handcuffed to something—a chair. Both of her hands were cuffed. She frantically looked around. It was hard to see out of her left eye. It was swollen shut. Jade tried to breathe. She had to remain calm.

Razor didn't betray her. This was all a part of his plan. But his performance was compelling. Jade didn't know what to think, but she had to keep on a brave face. Someone put their hand on her shoulder. She jumped.

"She's up," Razor said.

Someone approached them. They walked past her. "So, it seems."

Bossman was a big man. He was very tall and built like a bodybuilder. He reminded Jade of a professional wrestler she used to watch on TV as a little girl, but scarier. Debtors who usually met Bossman didn't fair so easily. She tried not to think of what was to come.

"I was beginning to think you weren't going to wake."

"Where's Helena?" Razor demanded.

"Straight to business, I see."

"You said Jade for Helena. Well, here she is."

Bossman rolled his eyes. "Yes, yes. Vincent!"

Razor's grip got tighter around Jade's shoulder. Vincent walked through a side door. He dragged Helena along with him. She wasn't visibly hurt—at least Jade could see with her limited vision. However, Helena did seem very spooked and shaken up. There was no telling what Bossman and Vincent were doing to her.

"Take your hands off her," Razor said in a tone that sent chills down Jade's spine. Vincent gave him a smug look. Razor walked towards him. Bossman chuckled.

"I would do as he says," he advised.

Vincent let her go and backed away. Razor took Helena in his arms. He looked her over. Nothing appeared to be out of the ordinary. He stared at her and then kissed her passionately.

"Good to see you both happily reunited," Bossman interrupted. "But I wouldn't have gone through such lengths if you'd brought her to me in the first place."

They all turned their attention to Jade. Her heart raced. What was going to happen next?

"You, my sweet, sweet Jade, have been a thorn in my side," he walked closer to her. "There are 15 cameras above you right now. Say hello to one of them."

Jade looked up and saw the many lenses pointed at her. Fear ran through her veins. She made sure that her emotions weren't visible on her face.

"You know, I've tried to build a perfect solution for the health system without the need for all the bureaucracy and red tape. I thought that was the sole reason why the system stagnated. But you debtors were an anomaly. You, debtors, continue to live on the wrong side of history. For decades I've tried to preserve the limited resources that our country has left. It wasn't easy to get rid of things like pre-existing healthcare and cancer research programs, but we have to focus on the people who are instrumental in rebuilding society." Bossman reached in his pocket and pulled out Jade's inhaler. "You Jade, aren't one of those people."

"That's me," she tried to play it cool. "The anomaly." Jade looked over at Razor and Helena. She couldn't really read Razor, but Helena looked scared for her. Maybe she did care after all.

"This country needs a balance, and you alone are tipping the scale."

Jade looked over at Vincent. "Are you really following this sociopath?"

Bossman chuckled. "Oh, lovely Jade, name calling won't change this situation."

Jade shrugged. "Well, I gave it my best sho—"

Jade shrieked out in pain. It took her a minute to register the knife in her left hand. It went clean through—binding her hand to the arm of the chair. She could hear banging and yelling in the background. It sounded like David. He must've heard her. All she could focus on was the agonizing pain. She blew air out of her mouth as if she was giving birth. She tried not to cry. Bossman began to mock her breathing.

"That's my best shot," Bossman said to Vincent. Vincent smirked. "She kills some of my officers, breaks out debtors from my prison, makes me look like a fool, and she has the nerve to be nonchalant in front of me."

Helena was crying. Razor was holding her back. Vincent remained smirking. David and Keeper were yelling in the background. Jade had to stay strong. She had to keep a brave face.

Bossman walked to her and leaned in her face. "You're going to die today, my sweet Jade."

Jade cocked her head back as far as she could and head-butted him with all her might. Bossman stumbled back. Blood gushed down his nose—it looked broken. He looked at the blood on his hand and then again at Jade. He laughed.

"Whoa!" he laughed even harder—blood spewing about. "That's what I'm talking about! Ballsy! Very ballsy!"

Jade laughed breathlessly. "Might as well draw a little blood before I die."

"Good. My turn," he backhanded her hard. So hard that she fell over sideways in her chair. Her head hit the floor, causing her left eye to hurt even more.

"Stop!" Helena screamed.

Bossman paid her no attention. "Don't tell me you're done already? Come on, your turn, Jade!"

Jade didn't move. She rested her eye on the cold floor and tried to catch her breath. Her right cheek was stinging from his slap. She wasn't sure what he was playing at. Why hasn't he killed her already?

"I said your turn, Jade!"

Vincent cleared his throat. "I believe you said I could have a shot at her, Boss."

Bossman turned towards Vincent. "I know what I said." He returned his attention back to Jade. He looked at her lying on the floor. He walked over and kneeled in front of her. "I believe it's your turn."

"Why?" she closed her eyes.

"Why what?"

"Why are you prolonging this?"

"You're not like the other sick people, Jade. You're a fighter...a survivor. You've proven to be a challenge. I love a challenge," he stood up and towered over her. "Now get up."

Jade laid there a little longer. She was trying to gather all her strength. It became eerily silent in the room. She had to get up. Bossman was growing impatient with her hesitation.

"Jade, please get up," Helena pleaded.

Jade needed to figure out how to get out of the handcuffs. She doubted that Bossman was going to let her out. He viewed her as a fighter. A *real* fighter didn't need help getting out of some type of bondage. Jade turned herself over—placing herself on her knees. She managed to get to her feet. Bossman stared at her as she stood hunched over. Jade was in a wooden chair. She had to break it to free herself.

Keeping her good eye on Bossman, Jade ran backward into the wall. The chair cracked, but the arms were still intact. She threw herself against the wall with full force—never taking her eye off Bossman. The whole chair fell into shambles. The arm of the chair was still attached to her left-hand thanks to the knife. She quickly pulled the knife out her hand—making sure not to flinch.

Bossman smiled proudly at her. Jade wiped the blood off the knife with her shirt. She smiled back at him.

"My turn," she ran toward him. He dodged out of the way, but not before Jade slashed him across his face.

"Vincent!" he looked a little shock that she got him. He didn't expect her to be *that* fast.

Vincent came charging with glee in his eyes. Jade was ready for him. She threw the knife, and it hit him in the shoulder. He yelled out in pain.

Taking advantage of his distraction, she charged at him. Jade punched Vincent twice in the face and then kicked him in the groin. Vincent dropped to the ground, hunched over. Pulling the knife out of his shoulder, Jade kneed him in the face. He cried out again.

The adrenaline was high. Jade was ready to take down every and anyone who was in her path. Bossman stood in the corner—broken nose and a long slash across his face.

Jade stepped over Vincent. "I believe I'm up next, Mr. Bossman."

"I guess so," he ran toward her, but then stumbled. Razor decided to get in on the action. He punched Bossman, but Bossman quickly returned the blow. It turned out to be a full-on tussle. The strikes were intense. The wrestling was lethal. Jade stood, watching them fight for a moment.

"Jade!" Helena yelled, bringing her back to their situation. "We gotta move!"

"Get the guys, Helena! They're David and Keeper." Helena nodded and started to walk out of the room. Vincent went to try to grab her. Jade quickly picked up a piece of wood from the broken chair and flung it at his head. It hit him, and he fell.

"Bitch!"

"Go, Helena!"

Helena ran out of the room. Razor and Bossman continued their fight. Jade slipped the knife in her pocket. She was planning on using that for Bossman. Vincent got up off the floor. He glared at Jade. Hate filled his eyes.

"Let's get on with it," Jade was ready to rid herself of Vincent. He was always going to hate her—no matter what she said or did. She figured it would be better if they just fought it out. The Vincent that she once knew was long gone. The guy who stood before her was far from the guy she used to know.

"I'm gonna enjoy this," he sprinted toward her and knocked her to the ground. Vincent started punching her, but Jade was able to block most of it with her arms. She concentrated on her breathing. Her asthma was getting irritated, and she had no clue where her inhaler or her combat mask was.

Jade took Vincent's blows—waiting patiently for her opportunity to strike. Her moment came when he drew back for another punch. She uppercut him, and he fell over. She kicked him twice in the face and got up. Vincent got up too, holding his mouth. It was bleeding. He spat some of it out. He pulled out a baton that he hung on his belt loop. Jade picked up a broken chair leg. Vincent came swinging with the baton. She dodged a few of them, but he managed to get her on her arm and on her side. He was coming at her with full force. Fighting could be heard outside of the room.

Razor was losing his advantage over Bossman. Jade wasn't sure how Helena, David, and Keeper were doing. They had to get out of there quick, or they were going to be done for.

Jade blocked Vincent's next blow. She swung the chair leg and hit him in his knee cap. He dropped to the ground. She swung again and hit him twice in the face. He fell to the floor—unconscious.

Jade looked over and saw Razor on the ground. Bossman was kicking him profusely. She threw the chair leg, and it hit him in his back. He didn't flinch nor looked her way. She ran toward him and jumped on his back. Putting her arm around his neck, Jade squeezed as tightly as she could. Bossman backed away from Razor. He swung his body wildly, trying to get her off him. She wrapped her legs around his waist. He ran backward slamming her against the wall—knocking the wind out of her. He kept ramming his self against the wall. Jade couldn't catch her breath. She was trying hard not to pass out.

Bossman finally stopped ramming and began to elbow Jade in her side. She kept her grip around his neck. He was getting weaker with each blow. She fetched the knife out of her pocket. Bossman elbowed her again. She drove the knife right below his collar bone. Yelling, Bossman flung her off his back. Jade hit the floor hard—the back of her head slamming against the concrete floor. He lifted his foot to stomp her, but she rolled away quickly. Razor tackled him from the side—slamming him back against the wall. They restarted their punching match, but Razor made sure that he kept hitting the knife deeper into Bossman. This only seemed to piss off Bossman even more. The anger seemed to have fueled his strength. Before she knew it, he had Razor up in the air choking him and slamming him repeatedly to the ground.

Jade ran over and started punching him wherever she could, but he didn't seem fazed by it. Razor was turning bright red, and it looked like his body was going limp. Jade panicked. Helena would be devastated if she lost Razor. Jade couldn't let her sister lose the love of her life. She had to do something quickly. She latched onto the arm that Bossman was choking Razor with. Jade bit down as hard as she could.

Bossman let out a piercing scream and dropped Razor. He tried to shake Jade loose, but she locked her jaws like a pit bull. The taste of blood filled her mouth. Bossman began to elbow her in the back, but she kept her grip. He started punching her in the stomach. She was able to take about four punches before she lost her grip. Bossman kneed her in the face, and she fell to the floor. He kicked her in the stomach, and Jade went flying across the room. Razor was gasping for air. Jade's chest was tightening.

They were in serious trouble.

Jade laid right in front of the open door. There was a fight going on in the hallway. She hoped Helena and the guys were on their way. Bossman was attending to his new wound. His arm was bleeding profusely. She got him good. Jade wondered if she nicked an artery or something. He caught her eye, and anger rose within him. He began to stomp over to her, but Razor grabbed his leg.

"Jade!" David, Keeper, and Helena were running towards her. She saw her weapons in David's hand.

Jade looked over at Bossman and Razor. Bossman was punching Razor in the face.

"Bow!" she managed to get out. Her asthma was in attack mode. David slid her bow and arrows to her. Jade caught them and rolled on her back. She drew her bow and focused.

Bossman's back was to her. Razor was weak and didn't seem to have any more fight left in him. Jade let the arrow go. It hit Bossman on the side of his leg. He dropped to his knees and looked at Jade. She quickly had another arrow ready. It landed in his side, and he fell over.

"Ra-zor," she whispered.

Razor got up and gave Bossman one final kick to the face—knocking him unconscious. He ran over to Jade, picked her up, and threw her over his shoulder. He ran out of the room.

"Jade!" Helena cried out.

"Where's her mask?" Razor asked.

Keeper ran around and put Jade's mask on. "I gotcha Jade."

The medicine hit her lungs as she passed out.

~18~

Jade woke up with the sun hitting her face. She tried to shield her eyes with her hand. Her left eye wasn't that swollen anymore. Where was she? How long has she been out? Someone was lying next to her. Jade lifted herself up. She was in bed. Helena was lying next to her sleep. Jade's heart stopped. *Helena was sleeping next to her.* She really did care about her.

"How are you?"

Jade jumped. She didn't notice Razor sitting in the corner. She winced a little. "Where are we?"

"A safe house. We're ok here."

"How long have I been out?"

"Few days."

"Oh God," she noticed her left hand was wrapped in a bandage.

"Don't worry about it. You really needed the rest."

"He's not dead, is he?"

Razor shook his head. He didn't need to ask who she was talking about. "He's not gonna go down that easy."

"Great," Jade knew Razor was right. There was no way that Bossman was going to go away that quickly.

"Thank you by the way."

Jade looked confused. "For what?"

"Saving my ass back there."

"I didn't save you."

"Jade please, he had me. I wouldn't be here if it weren't for you."

"Well, I'm the reason you were in that position in the first place."

"Jade, just take the damn thank you."

"Right, sorry. You're welcome," Jade looked over at Helena as she turned over. She was still sleeping. Jade smiled a little. Helena still had that sweet, innocent face like when she was a little girl.

"She's been by your side since we got here. I told you she'll come around."

Jade stared at her sister in awe. All these years she thought Helena was dead, but here she was, lying right next to her. This was what Jade wanted for so long—to be with her sister again.

Razor's face tensed up. "She has bruises under her shirt. She won't tell me what happened."

Jade nodded slowly. "We gotta kill him."

He looked over at Helena sleeping. "Yes, we do."

"What's our next move?"

"Well," he paused for a moment. His jaw clenched. "We're gonna need the Black Deficit."

"Um, I wasn't on the best of terms with them before you got there. I dunno if it'll get better once they figure out what I did."

"Don't worry about that. I'll handle it. I just need a sit down with them."

"Dunno how we'll do that. They'll try to kill you on sight."

He gave her a smug smile. "I'm sure they'll *try*."

Jade shook her head. "I can't let anything happen to you."

"And it won't."

"I can't let anything happen to them either."

"Nothing will happen, Jade. I'll try to be as peaceful as I can."

"Thank you."

Helena stirred. "Jade?"

"I'm right here, Helena."

She sat up and rubbed her eyes. "How are you?"

"Sore," Jade reached over and fixed Helena's bed head. "You?"

"Tired."

"That's all?"

Helena looked over at Razor. "He told you about the bruises."

"Course he did."

"It's nothing."

"Helena, let me see," Jade gasped as Helena lifted her shirt. She didn't mean to, the sight just surprised her. Helena was covered with bruises. It looked like she was taking punches daily. "I'm so sorry, Helena," tears escaped Jade's eyes. It was her fault. She didn't realize what the consequences of her actions would be.

"It's ok, Jade."

"No, it's not. It's my fault."

"You came back for me, that's all that matter."

"Are you gonna tell me what happened now?" Razor chimed in.

"It was Vincent."

"He's fucking dead!" Jade wished she would've driven that knife into his heart when she had the chance. "He did that to get to me."

"And Razor," Helena gave him a sad look. "He's always been jealous of you. He wanna prove to Bossman that he could be his right-hand."

Razor nodded slowly. At first, anger rose in his face, but then it was quickly replaced with sadness and disappointment. Jade recognized that look—it was the look of failure. He got up and sat down on the bed next to Helena.

He kissed her forehead. "I'm sorry."

"Not your fault."

He grabbed her face and kissed her on the lips.

Jade turned away—feeling a little awkward. She cleared her throat. "Ok...that's a thing. I'm just gonna leave you two alone."

They didn't say anything. They remained kissing. Jade rushed out of the room—afraid of what she was going to see next.

The house was silent. Jade walked downstairs to find Keeper and David. Keeper was sitting on the couch in the living room. He was packing a bag.

"Hey," Jade sat down on the couch next to him.

"Hey, how ya feeling?"

"Ok."

"Good. I was pretty worried there."

"Yeah me too."

"Not too many people survive an encounter with Bossman."

"Thank God for Razor."

"The way I hear it, he thanks God for ya."

"He's exaggerating."

Keeper smiled and shook his head.

Jade noticed the bag he was packing. "Going somewhere?"

"Back to headquarters."

"Alone?"

"Yeah. Razor thinks that's the best way to approach it and I agree. It'll be easier trying to convince Jackson and Beverly to meet with him if it's just me."

Jade didn't say anything. She just nodded. It wasn't clear how much weight Keeper's words would hold, but she knew it would be a lot heavier if she weren't there when he delivered them.

"Well, good luck."

"Thanks," they heard noises coming from upstairs. Jade looked disgusted. Keeper laughed. "David is in the family room if ya wanna talk to him."

Jade got up. "Yeah, thanks."

Keeper got up too. He threw the backpack over his shoulder. "See ya in a few days."

"Be safe out there."

"I will. And I refilled ya mask. Try to make it last 'til I get back."

Jade watched him leave. She hated the thought of him leaving alone. Somebody should be going with him, but she knew that David would refuse to leave her. Besides, she would be no help to Keeper in terms of convincing Jackson and Beverly. Keeper just had to go alone. That was the only way.

Jade walked to the family room to find David. She opened one of the double doors off the living room. David was sleeping on a fold out couch. Jade closed the door quietly. She didn't want to disturb him. Instead, she took a tour of the house. It looked like a house that was in the suburbs right off the city—the other side of the train tracks kind of thing.

The house looked like it had been renovated—before things started to go bad. Dark stained hardwood floors ran throughout. The kitchen had marble counter tops, stainless steel stove and refrigerator, and a fancy backsplash. Expensive light fixtures hung throughout the house. Jade figured that the home used to be owned by some hipsters—it just had that kind of feel to it.

A library was just off the kitchen. Jade's heart raced. She loved reading. Before she started dating Vincent, she used to read all the time. She walked over to one of the many bookcases and browsed through the books. She found a copy of *The Long Ranger and Tonto Fistfight in Heaven* by Sherman Alexie. Jade loved Sherman Alexie. All his stories had a way of portraying pain and struggle in a beautiful, poignant picture. Opening to the first page, Jade saw that it was signed by him. Oh, how she would have loved to meet him. She wondered how he was faring in this new world. Probably a lot better than she was.

Jade sat down in a big brown leather armchair. She read a couple of short stories and got lost in the world. A part of her felt relieved. The simple act of reading felt so normal to her. It reminded her of the good times. She recalled doing a final essay on this book in her English class. She got an A+ on it. Jade smiled a little. She wasn't such an obnoxious teen after all.

After a while, her eyes got heavy. Jade got up and went into the family room with David. She found herself climbing into bed with him. She wrapped her arms around him and snuggled up to his chest.

"How are you?" he asked in a groggy tone.

"Better."

"Good," he kissed her forehead. Jade smiled and closed her eyes. She felt so safe in his arms—something she hasn't felt in a long time. She quickly drifted off into a dreamless sleep.

**

"Something's wrong. He should be back already," Jade said to Razor. She was sitting at the kitchen island as he leaned against the refrigerator. Razor rolled his eyes.

"Nothing happened Jade," he repeated in what seemed like the hundredth time.

"It's been a week."

"It's a long trek to headquarters."

Jade shook her head. "He shouldn't have gone alone."

"You wouldn't be helping him at all if you went," he sat a cup of chocolate pudding in front of her.

"Why do we even need the Black Deficit's help?" Helena asked as she ate her pudding cup. "Why not just leave here?"

Jade opened her pudding. "And go where?"

"Canada."

"Canada's a myth," Razor said.

"How you know that?" David entered the kitchen.

"I used to work for the government, remember?"

David sat next to Jade at the kitchen island. "But who says that Canada's a myth?"

"The President."

David laughed. "Don't tell me you believe a former plastic surgeon."

"Things may be shitty right now, but I still hold respect for the President of our country."

"You only say that because he implemented that insane medical law and created the psycho DC task force."

"Which I'm no longer a part of."

"Yeah, but not because you think it's wrong."

"Enough," Jade was tired of David's and Razor's debates. That's all she'd heard for the past few days. "I'm worried about Keeper."

"I'm sure he's fine, Jade," David said. "If he doesn't show up in the next couple of days I'll go out and look for him."

"Great, just another person I'll have to worry about," she mumbled.

"What's your plan with the Black Deficit anyway?" Helena asked.

"Help break up the DC task force. We can't live our lives with them still around."

"The world is ending, Razor," Jade said. "Will our lives really be much better?"

"I'll be able to sleep better. And for me, that's enough."

Helena got a little antsy. "I don't know about this Razor."

"I'll make them understand Helena. They have a much better shot with us on their team. They'll see that."

She shook her head. "The prisoners."

"Don't worry about them."

Helena jumped up from her seat and ran upstairs to her room. Jade stared at the empty doorway.

"Don't worry," Razor said. "I'll make her come around. Just give her some space for right now."

Jade nodded. She couldn't imagine what Helena was going through. She had to do some harsh things to survive with the DCs. Things that she would never do in a million years. But that was where they were at in the world. You had to do some despicable things to survive—and survival was a must.

Jade got up. "Be in the library if you need me," she left the guys to continue their debate about the last legs of politics.

She sank into the brown leather armchair. It was becoming her favorite piece of furniture in the house. She cracked open her current read, *The Hunger Games* by Suzanne Collins. Her life was feeling oddly similar to the characters in the book—pain, struggle, the need to just survive. Jade didn't mind getting lost in another person's pain, though. It was her pain that she was trying to get away from. There was only a couple more chapters to read before she picked the next world to get lost in from the bookshelves.

Jade didn't know how much downtime was in her future, so she wanted to take advantage and get as much reading done as she possibly could. She didn't even notice Helena entering the room. Helena squeezed next to Jade in the chair and rested her head on Jade's shoulder.

Jade put her book down. She got uncomfortable for a moment. She and Helena never really talked about what happened between them. They made small talk with each other, but it wasn't anything profound. They just got along to get along.

"I went looking for you." Helena gave Jade a puzzling look. "When everything started going to shit. I went looking for you. When I got back home, the Jacksons from down the street told me what happened to mom and dad. They didn't know what happened to you. So, I kept looking. I went to churches, YMCAs, FEMA shelters. I was searching for months and coming up empty. Eventually, my asthma started getting worse."

"And you eventually stop looking," Helena said.

"...I thought you were dead."

"I get it. I just wish you would've kept looking."

Jade nodded and closed her eyes. "I failed you."

"You did," Helena's bluntness surprised Jade for a moment. "At least that's how I felt for a long time. But as time moved on, I thought I was finally getting over it...until I saw you again."

Jade chuckled. "Yeah."

"But Razor made me see that I couldn't blame you. You were just a kid yourself."

"That's still no excuse."

"Yeah, but it gave me some perspective. The world isn't the same anymore. We do what we gotta do to survive."

Jade got up and paced back and forth. "Yeah, but does that really excuse us from our actions? Can we just do whatever the hell we want because the world is ending?"

Helena laughed. "Jade, let's not get all philosophical. All I'm saying is that I get it. And I forgive you."

Jade paused for a moment. She let Helena's words sink in. Those were the words that Jade was dying to hear. She just wasn't sure if she was worthy of hearing them. But Helena was ready to get past the whole ordeal. So, Jade was glad to accept them.

"Thank you."

Helena got up and hugged Jade. That totally left Jade stunned. This was the first time, in a very long time, that she was able to hug her sister. Jade couldn't control what happened next—she started crying. It first came out as silent tears, but as Helena's hug became tighter, Jade's silent cry became sobs. Helena slowly rocked Jade back and forth to comfort her. This only made Jade cry even more.

"I love you so much, Helena."

Helena chuckled a little. "I love you too."

A quick knock was at the door, and then Razor peeked his head in. Jade quickly wiped away her tears. He took in the scene. A look of confusion swiftly appeared and left his face.

"They're here," he said more so to Jade.

"Ok," Jade's voice cracked a little.

~19~

Tension hung heavy in the air as they sat in the living room. Jade was nervous. It wasn't because of the armed Black Deficit members that surrounded Jackson and Beverly. And it wasn't the guns that were pointed at her, David, Helena, and Razor. Jade was nervous at the eerie calmness of Razor. What was he up to? He never really elaborated on his plan. What exactly did he want with the Black Deficit? Everything was in his hands.

That terrified Jade.

"Glad to see you alive and well, Jade," the sarcasm was heavy in Beverly's voice.

"Yeah, sorry about that. I had to save my sister."

"Who's a DC officer."

"Former DC officer," Helena responded.

Beverly looked at her. "How convenient."

"Enough," Razor interjected. "That's not the reason why I asked you all here today."

"Then, do tell us why we are here."

"Beverly," Jackson grunted. He was not in the mood for her antics.

Razor completely ignored Beverly and her attitude. "I want to offer support." Beverly and Jackson looked at each other confused. Razor sighed and rolled his eyes. "I want to take down Bossman."

"Such a change of heart. A razor getting dull," Beverly said.

Jade looked over at Razor after Beverly's jab. Her heart raced. Razor was literally biting his tongue. Jade could see the veins protruding out of his forehead from where she sat. This had to go peacefully.

"...they tried to kill my wife and me."

"Why should we trust you?" Jackson asked.

"Because I'm the best shot you got. I hold a lot of valuable information."

"So do the prisoners," Beverly shot back.

Razor shrugged her off. "Please, the prisoners don't know shit."

"But the prisoners didn't have a motive," Jackson said.

Razor sighed and looked at the coffee table that sat in between them. He pulled out a knife from his fatigues. He toyed with it in his hands for a moment—all the while staring at his jacket that was laying on the coffee table. He absentmindedly began to stab at the patch the read *Commander*. "I won't be able to live in peace with Bossman roaming around."

Jackson watched Razor stab at his patch for a moment. "We'll need to think about this."

"Think about it?" Beverly asked in disbelief. "We can't trust him, Jackson! He helped kill dad!"

"Enough, Beverly!" Jackson jumped up. "Outside, now!" Beverly jumped up angrily and followed Jackson out the front door. They slammed it shut behind them.

They all sat awkwardly as they listened to Beverly and Jackson's shouting match. Jade watched the Black Deficit members guarding the door. She recognized a few of them as her former sparring partners. It felt like they were throwing daggers at her. Jade cleared her throat. She looked over at Helena and Razor. She couldn't really read their faces. David looked bored, and Keeper looked a little nervous for some reason.

The brother and sister shouting match got louder. Razor blew out air in frustration. He stood up and walked toward the members guarding the door.

"Let them know that this offer won't be on the table for long." One of the members reluctantly went outside to deliver the message. Razor turned around and walked out of the living room.

"Where you going?" Jade called after him.

"To rest."

Helena followed him. "Get us when they're ready."

Jade slowly got up as well. She headed for the library. David and Keeper followed her. She sank down into her favorite brown leather armchair. David sat on the arm. Keeper sat in the chair across from them.

"How was your trip?" Jade asked. She was so relieved to see him. She thought something had gone wrong.

"Long."

"You ok?" David asked. "You seem a little off."

"They're not too happy with me," he looked at Jade. "For going with ya instead of reporting ya. They no longer trust me."

"I didn't mean to get you into any trouble."

"It's cool. I honestly think I lasted this long because of my inventions."

"Well they're stupid," Jade said. "You're more valuable than your inventions."

Keeper smiled a little. "Thanks, Jade. It's good to be back with ya guys."

"What's your verdict on the situation?" Jade asked.

"They'll be stupid to reject Razor's help," David said. "I may not be too fond of the guy, but I can see what an asset he'll be in taking down the DCs."

"David's right," Keeper interjected. "It'll be a huge win if they have Razor on their side."

"I agree. I'm just not sure how well he plays with others."

"You'll have him under control, Jade," David said as-a-matter-of-factly. "He listens to you."

Jade looked at him in disbelief.

"It's true," Keeper chimed. "He tends to take ya words into consideration." Keeper paused and looked at the door. "Besides, it's not Razor who I'm worried about playing nicely."

"You think Beverly and Jackson are gonna be trouble?" Jade asked.

"More so Beverly than anyone else. Besides, they don't tend to take criticism and orders too easily...and he was involved with killing their father."

"How you know?"

"Come on Jade, Bossman never made a move without Razor. Trust me, he was involved. This is not gonna go well."

Jade nodded. She had to agree with him there. Three alpha dogs were not going to mix well. She was dreading the many arguments that were sure to come. She has never been good at refereeing, but she was going to be a pro when it was all said and done.

Jade got up and gazed at the books on the bookshelf. She was going to miss them. There wasn't going to be any time for reading once they left the safe house. She contemplated on what books she wanted to take with her—just in case. Sherman Alexie. Tim O'Brien. Suzanne Collins. J.K. Rowling. Toni Morrison. Tomi Adeyemi. And the other variety of authors that lived in a collection of short stories anthologies. She wanted to take them all. Sadly, her life was pulling her in another direction. There was no time for lounging around.

It all felt weird to her. A few weeks ago, she was plotting on killing Razor. Now she was planning on taking down the DCs with him. And most importantly, trying to convince Jackson and Beverly to trust him.

It was all just crazy.

A member came to the door, pulling Jade out of her thoughts. "They're ready."

David and Keeper immediately followed him out. Jade waited for a moment. She wasn't ready to leave the room—to leave the books. After she soaked everything in, she sighed and walked out of the library.

Razor and Helena were back in the living room. Jade didn't bother to sit. She leaned against the wall. She read Jackson's and Beverly's faces. They came to their senses.

"We decided to take you up on your offer," Jackson said.

"But you're not allowed on the compound," Beverly interjected.

Razor didn't say anything. He nodded.

"That's good," Keeper was looking a little relieved. "It'll be nice to be at home."

"You're not allowed on the compound either."

Keeper looked at Beverly—shocked.

"What?" Jade couldn't believe that Beverly was going that low.

"He went AWOL."

"To help me!"

"Well, it was a bad call."

Jade walked toward Beverly. "I am so tired of your shit!"

Razor pulled her back before she could get close. "Outside the compound is fine with us."

"Good. You know you're way back. See you then," Jackson walked to the door. "Let's go Beverly."

Jade and Beverly glared at each other for a while before Beverly followed out behind. The other members left out quietly. Jade shook her head as Razor let go of her. She couldn't believe that they would do that to Keeper. Beverly did that just to get to her. If this was how the collaboration was going to start off, Jade wasn't looking forward to going back to HQ with them. She wasn't looking forward to all the attitudes and the arguments. And she definitely wasn't looking forward to Beverly and Jackson throwing their weight around. She was ready for it to be over before it even started.

"What a bitch!" Helena stood up.

Razor turned to Keeper. "It's probably better for you this way. They don't seem to value you."

Keeper looked at Razor shocked. He nodded.

Razor looked at everyone. "Pack what you need. We leave in the morning."

"Not today?" David asked.

"It's a three-day trip to HQ. I'd kill them all if I have to make that trip with them."

David smiled a little. "In the morning it is, then."

~20~

They've scouted four abandon houses that were a mile away from HQ. The houses were all about a half mile away from each other. They picked the house that was closest to the main road that led to HQ. That way should there ever be an attack, they would be the first line of defense. Razor liked to see his enemies coming.

Jade was surprised that all the houses were empty. She thought there would've been a few squatters there. It was the perfect spot. It was a secluded area, and you had the protection of the Black Deficit nearby. Although that really wouldn't have helped.

Sadly, Jade learned the hard truth about the Black Deficit—they were slow to respond. Razor was just now receiving this lesson, and he was beyond annoyed about it. They've been back at HQ for about a week, and they've made no plans on an attack to the DCs.

"What are they waiting for?!" Razor ranted on their second day there.

"Are you kidding me?" Jade said. "I literally had just convinced them to train the prisoners to fight the day you came for me."

By the third day, Razor insisted on all of them staying in the same house instead of being spread apart. Jade didn't understand why.

"We can't fight anyone off if we're separated."

"Yeah, but we can't see if they're coming from another direction either," Jade countered. She really didn't want to stay in the same house as him and Helena. Not that she had a problem with them. It was just weird. Her sister was a woman and married now. They needed their privacy.

"That's why they need more people out here," Razor started pacing. He was doing that a lot lately. "Who doesn't have guards surrounding the perimeter? Fucking amateurs. They're gonna get everybody killed!"

"No offense," Keeper interjected. "But I don't know if anyone wanna volunteer to live near ya."

"Well they're gonna have to get over it. Unless they want to die. Or worse, end up in a DC prison."

"Good point," Keeper admitted. "But try telling them that."

By day five, Razor was ready to march into the compound and give them a piece of his mind. It took all of them, including Helena, to talk him out of it. After that, Razor stopped complaining about Jackson and Beverly, which was scary to Jade. What was he up to? What was running through that terrifying mind of his? Jade couldn't figure it out. David kept telling her not to worry about it—to let the chips fall where they may. But it was like the calm before the storm.

Jade worried how severe the storm would be.

The house they resided in had four bedrooms and a finished basement. Razor and Helena took the master bedroom. Jade, Keeper, and David took the other rooms. They were decent sized bedrooms. Jade made sure she was the furthest from the master bedroom. She wanted to make sure that she couldn't hear anything coming out of that room. She had to get used to living with her sister again.

They all took shifts as a lookout. Jade got the night shift. For some reason, she couldn't sleep at night once they got back to HQ. It was something with being there that made her uneasy. Truthfully, she missed being by herself. She still wasn't used to living with so many people. Jade walked around the perimeter, lost in her thoughts. The two miles seemed to go by fast. She never knew how many times she walked around. By the time she came out of her thoughts, it was time for her to change shifts with David. He hated the fact that Jade was out there alone. He thought they all should be doubled up on turns. But the sad truth was they didn't have enough manpower to pair up.

"I plan on getting more people," Razor said on day seven. It was the first time since his last rant that he talked about the situation.

"How you plan on doing that?" David asked.

"I'll let you know once I come up with it."

After her shift, Jade would wash her face, strip out of her clothes, and go to sleep. She would sleep dreamless dreams. She loved it. Dreams, or nightmares, left her since she was reunited with Helena again. They've been getting along lately. Jade loved that. But she still had an emptiness inside of her. Something was missing. Jade couldn't figure it out.

On the eighth day, Jade was awakened by Razor shouting her name. She jumped up in a panic. This was it. Bossman found them. She threw on her clothes, grabbed her combat mask, and knives. Jade practically jumped down the stairs. She rushed out the front door only to come to an abrupt stop on the porch.

Raina stood about 30 feet away. Jade's heart skipped. She missed her.

She didn't realize how much until now. Raina looked weak. And it looked like she had lost some more weight.

"Raina."

"I heard you were back."

Jade walked off the porch. "Yeah, from who?"

"I was eavesdropping on Jackson and Beverly," she looked up at Razor and Helena. "They mentioned you came back with some DC officers."

Jade slowly walked to her. "My sister."

Raina took Jade by surprise. Before she knew it, Raina jumped in her arms and hugged her tightly. "I was so worried about you."

A few tears escaped Jade's eyes—to her surprise.

"I thought you were dead or something."

"I'm sorry, Raina."

Raina released Jade from her tight grip. She brushed away a few tears herself. "Why you're not on the compound?"

"They've banned me."

Raina nodded. She looked back up at Razor and Helena. Jade followed her gaze.

"They don't bite."

"Oh yeah? From the stories I heard, they do worse."

"They're on our side now."

Raina nodded again. "I'm tired."

"Come sit," Jade picked Raina up and carried her to the porch. She gently sat her on the steps.

"How did you know we were here?" Razor asked.

Raina looked him up and down. She turned her gaze away from him—not wanting to look him in the eye. "I didn't, I just walked until I ran into you."

"And you left without being detected?" there was a little anger behind

Razor's voice.

"...yeah, there was no one keeping watch."

Razor punched the railing on the porch—knocking out one of the posts. Raina jumped. Razor looked at her. "Sorry."

"What's been going on there?" Jade asked.

"Chaos mostly," Raina rested her head on Jade's shoulder. Jade wrapped her arms around her. "The members seem to be a little shaken by something. Now that I'm here, I guess it's because of the two of them."

"Helena and Razor."

"Right."

"Are they at least training the prisoners?"

"Yeah, but it's not that many. Not even half." Raina closed her eyes and took deep breaths. Jade could tell that she was in pain. "I go on some days. When I'm feeling well enough."

"Let me take you inside," Jade picked her up again.

"I'll give ya some medicine for the pain Raina," Keeper said.

Raina gave him a weak smile.

Jade carried Raina to her room. She laid her down in her bed. Keeper came in with some meds. Raina took them and quickly fell asleep. Jade watched her for a while. This whole fight started because of her. Jade felt this overwhelming need to save her. But she feared that she couldn't *really* save Raina. Not from the sickness that was slowly killing her.

Jade's heart sank. She hated feeling useless. Jade and Keeper eventually went back out to join the others.

"She has leukemia," Jade said—answering Razor's questioning look.

"Hard to believe she made it this far," he said.

"Yeah, it is."

"They'll be here looking for her," David said.

"You think so?" Helena asked.

"Yeah, her mother is bound to know that she's missing."

Razor shook his head. "Where was the lookout?"

"Your guess is as good as mine," Jade sat on the steps. She glanced around the wooded area—wondering if Jackson, Beverly, and the members were marching their way there.

Helena sat next to Jade. "Was she the reason you killed that officer?" Jade nodded. "She's cute."

"Yeah she's fucking adorable," Razor said. "She's about to bring a shit load of members to our door."

Jade frowned. "It's not her fault, Razor."

"Didn't say it was," he smiled. "It's exactly what I wanted." He quickly went inside. Confused, David and Keeper followed. Jade rolled her eyes.

Helena looked back and shook her head. "He's crazy."

Jade laughed. Helena laughed too.

"She reminds me of you."

Helena nodded. "I can see that." She ran her fingers through her hair. "Hairdo and all." The two of them burst out laughing.

"I couldn't let them take her."

"I get it," Helena stared off and frowned. "I've seen a lot of people die in DC prisons."

"Hey," Jade put a hand on Helena's shoulder. "That wasn't your fault. You did what you had to do to survive."

"Yeah, at the expense of other peoples' lives."

"There's no point on dwelling on that now. You gotta forgive yourself and move on. Help other people."

A few tears escaped Helena's eyes. She quickly brushed them away. She smiled a little. "You're right."

Jade hugged her and kissed her forehead. She was so happy to have her sister back. The two of them just gazed out in the woods. Both lost in their own thoughts. Someone came outside.

"You should get you some rest, Jade," David said.

Jade turned around to look at him. "I'm ok. I wanna be here when they come."

"Listen to David," Helena said. "Sleep on the couch. I'll wake you when they get here."

Jade looked back at Helena and David. She sighed. "Fine, but be sure to wake me."

"Will do."

Jade went inside and laid on the couch. As soon as her head hit the pillow, she was out.

**

The sun was just beginning to set when someone shook Jade awake. It was from Helena. She looked a little worried for some reason. Jade got up and stretched. She didn't realize she slept that long. The day was almost over. Her shift on guard duty was soon approaching.

"They're here?"

"Keeper spotted them coming on his watch."

"Helena, what's wrong?"

Helena hesitated. "Nothing."

"Now is not the time to be bottled up."

Helena fidgeted with the bottom corner of her shirt. "I don't know what Razor's gonna do," she turned and looked out the window. "And I don't know if they have any prisoners with them."

"Don't worry about it," Jade started walking to the door. "I'll make sure everything is civil."

"How can you be so sure?"

"Cause I'm the only one who sees how vital things are," Jade walked out onto the porch.

Razor, David, and Keeper were already out there. Helena followed shortly after. Jade looked out at the woods. There was no sight of Beverly and Jackson, but she could feel them coming. How was this interaction going to play out? She prepared herself mentally for the shouting match that was likely to occur.

Razor stood leaning on the porch railing. David sat in a porch chair. Keeper was pacing back and forth. Helena joined Razor at his side. Jade took her place on the steps. She noticed that Raina wasn't outside.

"Raina's still sleeping?" she didn't look at anyone in particular.

"She's exhausted," Keeper said. "She traveled on a bad day. There's no way she's going back tonight. She's too weak."

"No one's keeping watch," Jade said to Razor.

"We need all of our manpower here."

"Do we?"

"We don't know how this will go."

"Peacefully."

"I'm willing to be peaceful," Razor gave her a sly smile. "But we don't know how they'll be."

Jade didn't say anything. He was right. She hated when he was right. The sad truth was they didn't know how Beverly and Jackson were going to react. She figured they might use this as an opportunity to show their strength as leaders. They might use this to make an example out of Razor—don't cross them or X, Y, and Z will happen. Not to mention, he was responsible for their father's death. Either way, it wasn't going to be good for them, especially not Jade.

There was a sound of branches snapping. Everyone instantly became on high alert. Jade's heart raced. She hated the unknown. She was just ready to get this thing done and over with. They all heard twigs snapping. They were close. And it sounded like it was a lot of them. It seemed like an army of them. An army? Really? Jade was starting to get pissed. Did it really take all of them to get one person? She didn't even see them, but they were already getting off to a bad start.

Beverly and Jackson broke the tree line first. Followed by Raina's mom, Sarah. A look of worry covered her face. A group of members followed behind. There were about 20 of them. They all were heavily armed and wore the look of combat. Jade was relieved that she still had her knives on her.

"Jackson. Beverly," Razor said nonchalantly. "What brings you and your little army to my doorstep?"

"You know damn why, asshole!"

"Beverly!" Jackson yelled.

Jade and Sarah locked eyes. "She's upstairs sleeping."

"I gave her some medicine for the pain," Keeper added.

Sarah walked over to Jade. Beverly and Jackson tried to stop her, but she shrugged them off.

"First room off the stairs," Jade said as Sarah went inside.

"She had no right being here!" Beverly shouted—trying to gain control.

"You're right," Razor said. "Try telling your team that. She told us there was no one keeping watch when she walked out the front gates."

"That's bullshit!" Jackson said defensively.

"Then how did she get here?" Helena asked.

"That's an excellent question sweetie," Razor walked over and stood behind Jade. "Because we sure as hell didn't just take her from HQ. She came here on her own."

"We're taking her back now."

"She's too weak to make that trip," Jade said.

"Then we'll carry her," Beverly interjected.

"She's not going anywhere," Razor said in a tone that sent chills down Jade's spine. "She's too weak."

Beverly stepped forward. "Then we'll take her."

Razor smiled. "I'll like to see you try."

Beverly began walking toward the porch. Helena quickly hopped off and blocked her path. The two women stood face to face. Jade jumped to her feet.

"Raina's not going anywhere," Sarah shouted from the house.

Beverly looked taken aback. "Sarah!"

"You heard what I said!" Jade could hear Sarah walking back upstairs.

"Run along now," Helena said, smiling.

Beverly looked pissed and embarrassed. She slowly walked back over to Jackson and the members—never taking her eyes off Helena. Once she made it over to them safely, they prepared to leave.

"This all could've been easily avoided," Razor walked off the porch. Jackson and Beverly turned around to face him. "You need people keeping watch out here. In the other houses closer to the compound."

"We're fine with the guards at the gates," Jackson said.

"No, you're not. Bossman and his men can easily walk into your compound and slit everyone's throat."

"I'm not subjecting people to live near you!" Jackson shouted. There was some deep hidden anger behind him.

"Then be ready to die!" Razor shook his head. "Just admit it. You have no fucking clue what you're doing. I've seen the compound, you don't have nearly enough people to take Bossman down."

"We have the prisoners!" Beverly shouted at the top of her lungs. She was really trying to save face in front of the members.

"From one prison," Helena shot back.

"Those prisoners are a raindrop in the ocean compared to the DCs."

"This conversation is over," Jackson spat. "Move out." The group started leaving—Beverly following behind them. Jackson lingered back for a moment.

"What the hell are you waiting for," Razor wasn't done with them. "You need more people."

Jackson didn't say anything. He just glared at Razor.

"I didn't kill your father," Razor admitted. "Bossman did that. And if you want to take him down, you need to play smarter."

Jackson walked away.

Jade sighed with relief. That was way more peaceful than she imagined. She was surprised by Razor's calmness. In their absence he angrily ridiculed them. But to Jade's surprise, he was rather quite pleasant. Jade was thankful for that.

Razor sighed and shook his head once they were out of sight.

"Let's hope that they'll listen," Jade said.

"How quickly do they take advice?" Razor asked Keeper.

"Not really sure," Keeper admitted. "Ya and Jade are the only ones who challenged their leadership."

"That can't be right," Jade said.

"They give people food and a bed. That gets them blind loyalty."

"Yeah," Helena said. "And a death sentence."

~21~

Jade didn't remember falling asleep. In fact, she couldn't recall what happened after Jackson and Beverly left. There was no recollection of her even talking to the others afterward. She must've been exhausted. The sun blinded her as she sat up on the couch and stretched. A small yawn escaped her. She cracked her neck. The sofa wasn't all that comfortable, but her room was occupied. Raina stayed asleep all night. Sarah never left Jade's room—that, she remembered.

Sarah didn't really say anything to Jade. Jade wasn't surprised by it. In all honesty, the only thing the two of them had in common was Raina. They both loved and cared for her. That was as far as their relationship went.

Someone was coming downstairs. Jade turned around to see Razor. He had his trusty machete, and his protective gear on. He was about to take watch.

"You're up."

Jade stood up. "Don't remember falling asleep."

"Yeah, you looked exhausted. Come keep watch with me," Razor walked out the front door. Jade grabbed her knives and her combat mask that was on the living room table. She followed Razor out the house.

It was dawn. It was significantly colder outside. Jade prayed that a snowstorm wasn't on its way. It was toward the end of August, but a blizzard in the summer has happened before. Numerous of times *actually*. Jade dreaded the thought of it. If you thought the strange, hot weather was tough on her asthma; the brief severe cold was a sure death sentence. As if on cue, specs of snow started to fall from the sky.

"How good are you in the cold?" Razor asked, reading her thoughts.

"I almost died during the last blizzard, and that was only a day."

"We'll do a quick lap then."

Jade nodded. She put on her combat mask and pulled out her scarf too. The weather changed fast. You could sometimes experience all four seasons within a matter of seconds.

"I figured out how to get more people," Razor said.

"How?"

"The sweeps."

"The DCs sweeps?"

Razor nodded. "I know the schedules and the locations."

"Do we have enough people for that?"

"We can handle it."

"Ok," Jade was a little leery about the manpower. "When you trying to do this?"

"ASAP. Before Bossman sends out some scouts."

"To where? Here?"

Razor nodded. "We've been inactive for too long now."

"How would he know we're here?"

"Bossman isn't stupid, Jade. He'll know that the Black Deficit is the only place we can go."

"But you said you were the only one who knew about this place."

"It's only a matter of time before they come here. He's probably got some old hunter tracking me now."

"Tracking you? Really?"

"You have no idea, Jade. We've used all kind of resources."

Jade shivered a little. She didn't know if it was from the cold or the images of the things that the DCs did. "You think the debtors are gonna respond well to you?" Jade imagined what she would do if she saw Razor during a sweep.

"You think they're going to try to fight me," it was more of a statement rather than a question.

"I would," Jade could see that encounter. "I sure as hell wouldn't think you were there to save me."

Razor pondered for a moment. "I see your point. But I'm still doing it."

"I'm not saying that you shouldn't. Just don't fight back, ok. Let me or David intervene."

"Fair enough."

The snow was falling heavy now. There had to be at least an inch or two on the ground. Luckily, they were half a mile from the house. Jade couldn't wait to get inside and get as many layers on her as she could. Razor stopped suddenly. He grabbed Jade and pulled her close to him. He held tightly onto her arm.

"Something's wrong," he whispered.

"What?"

Razor gestured toward his ear—indicating that he heard something.

He quickly and quietly lowered himself behind a tree. He never let go of Jade's arm.

They both were very still. Jade tried to focus in on her senses. She didn't hear anything. Razor still looked alarmed—focused.

"Someone's here."

Jade was a little frustrated. Why couldn't she hear anything? How can she keep watch and protect the others if she couldn't hear an intruder approaching? She closed her eyes and took a deep breath. Jade pushed herself to really focus. She was in the middle of counting to 10 when she heard it—the snow crunching under someone's boots. Could it be someone from the house? No. This was someone different. Their walk was very slow—deliberate. The person didn't want to be heard. They sought to catch them off guard.

They were there to do only one thing: attack.

Jade looked over at Razor. She met his eyes and nodded toward the tree. He gave her a signal to go ahead. After slowly peeking behind the tree, Jade saw no one in sight. It was still. It was as if the earth stopped moving, the wind stopped blowing, and the snow stopped falling.

An arrow whizzed pass Jade's face—the tip scratching her cheek. Razor pulled her back just before the next arrow hit its mark. She could really hear the intruder now. They were running toward them. Jade tightly grasped her knives. The intruder was getting closer. About 50 feet. There was another pair of footsteps. And another.

How many were there?

Razor jumped from behind the tree and met the intruder. He swung his machete into the intruder's stomach. The guy looked stunned. Razor ripped the machete out as the guy fell to the ground. Jade could see his guts. She tried hard not to vomit. Another arrow whizzed pass Razor. Jade snapped out of her moment of shock and ran from behind the tree. She ducked just in time for another arrow. Two men were charging at them. One had a sword, the other, a crossbow. Razor went for the guy with the sword. Jade reluctantly went for the guy with the crossbow.

The clanging of metal rung through the air as Razor fought off the intruder. Jade tried to think of how she could get close to her guy without getting hit. She dodged another arrow by hiding behind a tree. Frustration couldn't cloud her judgment. Jade glanced around the tree. The arrows in the attacker's quiver were getting low.

Jade squinted to get a better look. Her eyesight had never been that great, especially from far away. There were about three or maybe four arrows. She just had to wait him out. She checked to make sure that Razor was alright. He was doing fine at backing his man down.

There went another arrow. It landed on the tree behind Jade. She peeked at the guy again. He was turning his attention to Razor now. Jade panicked. He had to keep his focus on her.

Taking advantage of his distraction, Jade launched a knife at the intruder. It landed in his right thigh. The guy buckled under the pain, therefore throwing his arrow way off course. Jade charged at him. He struggled to get another arrow out of his quiver. She threw another knife. This time it hit the guy in the left arm. He screamed out in pain.

Jade grabbed another knife from her thigh strap. A sharp pain went through her arm. The arrow in her left shoulder confused her. Her guy was on the ground, struggling to reload his crossbow. Jade quickly took cover behind another tree. There was another shooter.

Razor and his guy sounded far away now. Jade looked again at the arrow sticking out of her shoulder. Taking a deep breath, Jade looked away, broke the arrow in half, and pulled the tip out from the exit wound. She muffled her scream. She couldn't risk throwing Razor off.

Uneven footsteps were rushing in her direction. Jade crouched down as she waited for her original guy to get closer. Her grip on her knife got tighter and tighter. He rushed from around the tree. Jade plunged the knife into his chest. Then in a swift motion, she pulled it out and slit his throat. She didn't even think about it. The movement just happened so naturally.

There was no time to focus on what she'd done. She had to keep the new shooter fixated on her. Pulling out her knives from the intruder's lifeless body, Jade stepped out from behind the tree.

The new shooter revealed his self. Unlike his deceased comrade, he was all out of arrows. He began running toward Jade. She didn't move. She needed to pace herself. Even though she had her combat mask on, she didn't want to overexert herself. Jade let her attacker come to her.

He threw the first punch. Jade barely got out the way. She stepped back—almost tripping over her victim's leg. The attacker threw another punch. Jade blocked it. They had to keep one of them alive. They needed to know how much Bossman knew and what he was up to.

Jade headbutted him and punched him twice in the face. She needed to knock him out. The guy stumbled back. Jade took that moment to run around him—distancing herself from her lifeless victim. The guy quickly turned around to face her. He charged at her. When he got close, she kicked him in the stomach and punched him in the face again. He remained conscious.

Jade didn't back away fast enough. He managed to grab her by the waist and spun her into him. He wrapped his arm around her neck and started choking her. Jade tried to wiggle herself out of it. When that didn't work, she started elbowing him in the gut. The guy wasn't budging. His grip remained tight. She was getting weak. Desperate, she took one of her knives and stabbed him in his side. He grunted and released her. He stumbled back. She gasped for air. A twig snapped. Jade looked up to see

Razor coming towards her. Her head suddenly flung back. Her attacker was pulling her hair—dragging her closer to him.

"Jade!" Razor yelled.

The guy ripped off her mask. The frigid air hit her face. Cold air went in her nose and into her lungs. Jade lied still—trying to focus on her breathing. The guy took a small pouch off his belt loop. He opened it and dumped dust on her face. Her airway instantly closed. She couldn't gasp for air. Jade frantically tried to find her mask, but she was afraid that that wouldn't even help. The guy stood smug for a second.

Then his head was no longer on his body.

Jade could feel his warm blood shower her as she passed out. Razor was screaming her name.

**

Jade found herself back in her childhood home. She was sitting on the living room couch. Helena sat next to her. They both were bundled up in a cover. They ate popcorn as they watched a movie on TV. The two sisters found themselves laughing hysterically at the comedy that was being performed. Jade heard her mother cooking while her dad kept her company. Occasionally, her mother would laugh at something her dad said. Jade looked around—aware of her situation. This was the happiest her family has been. This was the happiest she has been. She wouldn't feel this way ever again.

"Don't fill up on popcorn girls!" their mother yelled from the kitchen. "Dinner is almost ready."

"We won't!" Helena said between bites.

The girls continued to watch their movie. Jade wrapped her arm around Helena and pulled her close. She kissed her forehead. Helena looked up at her big sister, confused. She was not used to Jade's affection.

"You feeling ok?"

Jade laughed a little. "Yeah. Why you ask?"

"Because you're *super* nice to me."

"I can't show my little sister any love?"

"You usually don't."

"Well, I'm sorry about that."

Helena was completely thrown off by the apology. "That's ok?"

"No. It's not. You deserve better, Helena."

Their father walked into the living room. "I hope you two aren't fighting in here."

"Just the opposite dad," Helena rested her head on Jade's shoulder. "Jade is giving me lots of love."

Their father stood there, watching them. He was glad to see his two daughters enjoying each other's company. "Well isn't that sweet."

"Love you, dad," Jade said. "Love you too, mom!"

Their mother walked out of the kitchen and into the living room. "What's that, Jade?" She took a moment to assess the scene.

"I said, I love you."

Jade's mother smiled. "I love you too, sweetie. I love both of you."

Jade sighed. Soon, all of this was going away. She would no longer see her father's smile. She would yearn to hear her mother's laugh. Her relationship with Helena would never be this carefree.

There was a slight tremble. This was it. Everything was about to change. The slight tremble turned into a violent shake. The girls retreated further on the couch. The TV toppled over. The bookcase came tumbling down. Their parents took cover underneath a doorway.

"It's ok girls!" their dad shouted. "Everything will be alright."

Jade could see a tree falling onto a neighbor's car. A lamp post landed in another neighbor's living room. The ground was cracking. People were running—trying to avoid the gaping hole. Screams were heard everywhere. Everything was not going to be alright. It was far from it.

Nothing was going to be the same.

Nothing.

Helena gripped tightly onto Jade's arm. Jade placed her hand on top of Helena's. It was all she could do to comfort her. A crack began to form in the middle of the living room—separating the girls from their parents. With another violent shake, their house split in half. Their parent's half lowered significantly, which caused them to slide into a hole that was now in their living room. Jade and Helena screamed.

They could hear their parents screams until it slowly faded away. Helena began to weep hysterically. Jade stared at the hole—shocked. The earth still shook. Suddenly Helena went flying in the air. Jade cried after her. And then Jade felt something slam into her chest. Knocking her across the room.

"Come on, Jade!" someone shouted. "Breathe!" Something slammed into her chest again. Her body shook. Air passed through her. "Where's the damn defibrillator?!"

The ground got low. Jade was starting to slide in the hole. The closer she got, the deeper the hole became. Her heart raced. She wasn't ready for this. She wasn't ready to see what was at the bottom. Or worse, she wasn't ready to be stuck falling.

Everything went black.

Jade felt herself falling into nothingness.

It was like an out-of-body experience. It felt like she was floating. Not falling. Not flying. Just floating. It was weird. It felt like she was doing it forever. A bright light slowly started coming into view. The closer she got, the brighter it became. Jade was blinded by it. Suddenly she crashed. It knocked the wind out of her. It took her a while to catch her breath.

Someone wrapped their arms around her and helped her up. Jade was surprised to be looking at her parents.

"Mom? Dad?" her parents stood smiling at her. What did they think of her now? They had to be disappointed in her. She was so selfish and bratty when she left them. She never amounted to anything good.

"I'm so sorry. I've failed you. I was a terrible daughter," Jade cried. Her parents just watched. They never said a word. They let Jade break down privately. Once she finally collected herself, her father walked over to her. He slightly touched her chest, and she went flying across the room.

Jade landed on the floor.

Her mother stood over her. She reached down and touched Jade's chest. A shock went through her body. Her father appeared at her mother's side. He too reached down and touched Jade. They both took turns shocking her.

Jade lied on the floor, withering in pain. She wished it would stop. The shocking kept going through her body. Visions of her parents began to blur. At one point, her father looked like Razor. Jade kept floating in and out of consciousness. Finally, her parents disappeared.

All she could hear was Razor's voice. "Come on, Jade! Breathe!"

There was crying in the background.

~22~

Jade found herself being chased through the forest by headless men.
The chase seemed endless. She tried her hardest to escape them, but
once she thought she was well hidden, another headless man would
come. It was terrifying. It wasn't their lack of heads that scared her, it
was their screams. The screams were agonizing. They were in pain. A
pain that wasn't of this earth. Jade was terrified of that pain. She was
afraid that she would soon be feeling it.

Jade found herself running—running nowhere.

The running never stopped.

Jade woke up under a pile of covers. They laid heavy on her. She was
tightly tucked underneath them. She tried to squirm her way out. Her
chest hurt every time she moved. It was really sore. That attack was the
worst she ever had. Jade thought she experienced all kinds of attacks

before, but that one took the cake. She was surprised that she was alive. After a while, she stopped struggling to get out of the cover entanglement. Jade lied on her back—staring at the ceiling. She let out a sigh of defeat.

"You stopped breathing," Helena sounded terrified and exhausted. Jade could hear the tears falling from her eyes.

Jade squirmed her way up to see Helena. She fought through the pain.

"You stopped breathing for like 10 minutes."

"Sorry," her voice was groggy. "How long was I out?"

"You stopped breathing."

Jade could see how traumatized her sister was. "Come here." Helena snuggled up to Jade. Jade wrapped her arms around her. She kissed her forehead.

"You stopped breathing."

"What happened?"

"We heard Razor screaming. He was screaming your name and asking for help. When I got outside," Helena paused. She was choked up. "He was carrying your lifeless body. You stopped breathing. He did CPR until Keeper came back from the compound with the defibrillator." Helena stopped.

Jade could see tears falling from her eyes.

"He was working on you for so long that people were telling him you were gone, but he wouldn't listen. He couldn't stop. He knew I wouldn't be able to handle it."

Jade nodded. She couldn't believe that Razor was so determined to save her. She was still baffled by him. "Gotta thank him for that."

"I'm just glad you're ok," Helena kissed Jade's cheek. "I don't know what I'll do if I lost you."

"Don't worry," Jade said. "I'm not leaving you again." She meant every word. There was no way she was going to abandon Helena again. She had to survive—for her.

Helena smiled as she laid down. "I'm exhausted."

"Get some rest."

Helena snuggled in the covers. Within minutes she was sound asleep. Jade looked at her for a moment. She couldn't imagine leaving her sister in this hell hole—not again. She was glad that Razor didn't give up on her. There was a light tap on her door. Raina was standing in the doorway. Even in the bed, Jade could see the tears that threaten to leave her eyes. Jade smiled at her.

Jade pulled back the covers and pat the empty space beside her. Raina quickly climbed in. Jade could tell that she still wasn't feeling well. She wrapped Raina in her arms and kissed her forehead. "I'm ok."

"I was worried. I'm glad you're better though," Raina closed her eyes. "I'm really exhausted."

"Get some sleep."

Jade watched the two people she loved the most sleep. But she found herself discontent. She needed to know what was going on. What was their next move? What was Bossman up to? How long has she been out? Did Razor raid one of the sweeps? She sat, hoping that someone would walk past. She wished that she could get up herself. Her body would not allow it. She ached from head to toe. And her chest felt like it was on fire. So, unfortunately, she had to sit there—brooding in her thoughts.

Images of headless men came into mind. Her body count was adding up. Jade never thought of herself as a killer, but she plunged that knife into that guy's chest and slit his throat with no hesitation. Now she was feeling remorseful. Sure, he was trying to kill her, but all she could think about was her parents. What would they think of her?

It was this world.

It was this fucked up environment.

It made her a killer.

Unfortunately, that was the only way you could survive now. It's kill or be killed. And her natural instinct was to not be the latter. Jade could feel herself frowning. She felt useless. She hated feeling useless.

"I see they wormed their way next to you," Razor stood in the doorway.

Jade looked over at Helena and Raina. She smiled a little. "Yeah, they did."

Razor shook his head and walked in. "If they had it their way, they would've been right there when you woke up."

"I'm not surprised."

"How's your condition?"

"My chest is on fire."

"Yeah, sorry. I had to use the defibrillator a few times."

Jade laughed a little—it almost killed her. "I'm not complaining." Razor nodded. "And thank you."

"You don't need to thank me, Jade," he sat on the edge of the bed.

"You saved my life."

"Yeah, that's something you do when you care about people."

"Oh," Jade was shocked to hear him say that. She knew that he cared—his actions told her that. It was just surprising to hear him say it. "You ok?"

"Just restless."

"Yeah, I was trying to keep that guy alive."

"I know. He could've given us some useful information," Razor tensed up a little. "But he did what he did, and I couldn't let him live."

"I get it...how long I been out?"

"It doesn't matter."

"That long, huh?" Jade didn't press the issue. "Have you raided the sweeps yet?"

"Are you crazy? Everyone was too worried about you. Plus, I wasn't sure if Bossman was going to send out more scouts."

"But you plan on doing the raid still?"

"Of course. Your attack hasn't lit a fire under Jackson's and Beverly's ass."

"When you wanna do this?"

"You need to rest, Jade."

"I've rested long enough."

"Take a few days, please."

Jade sighed. "Fine."

"Don't worry, I'll keep you in the loop."

"Thanks. Where's David and Keeper?"

"Keeping watch. We're doing doubles now. No one is allowed out on their own anymore."

"Good call."

"Get some rest," he got up. "We'll be heading out in a few days."

Jade laid down as Razor left out of the room. She tried not to think. Instinctively, Helena and Raina snuggled up closer to her. Jade smiled. She hasn't felt loved in such a long time. She was thankful that she could feel that again. Sleep fell over her. Her body and mind thanked her.

Jade went into a deep sleep. She didn't feel when Helena and Raina left her. And she didn't feel when David laid down next to her. Jade opened her eyes for a moment and saw him lying on his back with his arm covering his face. Naturally, she moved closer to him and laid her head on his chest. He wrapped his arms around her.

"You gotta stop scaring me like that."

"I'm sorry."

He kissed the top of her head. "I'm glad you're ok."

Something seemed to take over her. Something that she had no control over. Before she could think about it, she found herself leaning over to kiss him. At first, he was shocked, but after a few seconds, he kissed her back—passionately. He carefully rolled on top of her—making sure not to hurt her.

It's been a while since a guy's hands caressed her body. Jade enjoyed his hands touching her. Her hands ran down his chest. She pulled him closer to her. He kissed her even harder. This felt so normal to her. It felt like old times. Making out with a guy you liked, and she really liked David. It's been a while since she'd had someone she could depend on. He always had her back, and she found him to be very attractive.

Jade gripped him tighter.

David reluctantly pulled away. "We should stop," he paused. "Until you're feeling better."

"I feel fine."

"Jade, you literally just died. Let's wait until you're back to normal."

She sighed. "Alright."

David laid back beside her. He pulled her close to him. "Trust me, it's hard for me to stop, but I want you to feel better first."

"I get it," she paused—wondering what to say next. "What's been going on?"

"Nothing much. Razor's been on edge...more than usual."

"Why?"

"Well, he thinks that Bossman knows exactly where we're at now."

"Because those scouts haven't reported back."

David nodded.

"He's not wrong."

"Oh, trust me, I know. That's why I wanna raid these sweeps as fast as we can."

"But?"

190

"I'm not sure we have enough manpower."

"No chance of Jackson and Beverly lending us some people?"

"Keeper went through hell just to get that defibrillator. He ended up stealing it."

Jade chuckled. What was it going to take for them to get on board?

"There's no chance of you staying behind, is it?" David asked.

"Not a chance in hell."

David sighed. "I thought so."

Jade knew she was being stubborn, but there was no way she was going to be left behind lying in bed while the others were out there risking their lives. "How long was I out? Razor refused to tell me."

"It really doesn't matter Jade."

"Fine," Jade sat up. She fought through the pain. "Help me out of here." David didn't bother to protest. He got out the bed and gently lifted her up. He carried her out of the room and downstairs.

Helena and Raina were sitting in the living room. Helena was combing Raina's hair. Jade was surprised to see them so close. Raina seemed to take a liking to Helena. Helena turned around when she heard David coming down the stairs.

"What is she doing out of bed?" she scolded. "David?!"

"You try arguing with her."

Helena rolled her eyes. "I swear Jade, you are the most stubborn person I know."

"You shouldn't be surprised then," Jade teased.

"You stay on the couch," she gave Jade a look that scared her. "And that's it!"

David placed Jade on the couch.

"Yes, ma'am." Jade watched as Helena put Raina's hair into finger coils. It was weird seeing Helena nurture someone else. It wasn't because

Jade thought she didn't have it in her, it was because she wasn't used to seeing Helena in such a mature situation.

Jade looked around for Sarah. She figured that she would be close by since she didn't really care for Helena. Jade couldn't imagine Sarah would allow Raina so close to Helena. She didn't see her.

"Hey Raina, where's your mom?"

"At the compound."

"She allowed you to stay?" Jade was a little shocked.

"She said I was safer here with Razor."

"I know. Stunned me too," Helena said, reading Jade's thoughts.

"Well, alright, then."

"She'll be back," Raina winced in pain. Helena was untangling a knot. "She just had to grab something."

The front door opened. Razor and Keeper came walking inside. Razor did a double take. He was surprised to see Jade out of bed. He said nothing to her. He just shook his head. Keeper smiled at Jade. Jade was happy to see him.

"Looks like someone is doing better," he said.

"Or acting like it," Razor retorted.

"Thanks, Keeper, I am," she looked to Razor. "What's the plan on the raid?"

"We can leave out tomorrow if you want."

"Razor!" Helena shot him an evil look.

"You try arguing with her. She's been out of commission for a week. I know she's dying to make a move."

"I knew it!" Jade exclaimed. Helena glared her down. Jade felt like a little kid being scolded. "I knew I was out for a long time," she murmured.

"You wanna kill yourself, Jade, be my guest."

"I'm good as dead if I stay here, Helena."

"Fine!"

"I'll look after her, Helena," David said. Helena rolled her eyes. It was nothing anyone could say to make her ok with Jade going on the raid.

"Alright," Razor said, ignoring all the back and forth. "There's a sweep scheduled for a neighborhood not too far from here. It's going down around noon, so we should set up in the morning."

"Sounds good."

"I hope Sarah is back before we leave. We can't leave Raina here by herself," Helena said.

Razor looked over at Raina and gave her a smile. It was a sweet smile. Jade was taken aback. "She can be our lookout."

Raina giggled.

"Absolutely not!"

"Yeah, I'm with Helena on this one," Jade said.

Razor sat on the floor next to Raina. He pinched her cheeks. "They're no fun."

"Do you know how stressed out I'll be. Sarah would kill us if something happened to her."

"Nothing would happen."

"Plus, she's not well enough to travel."

Razor looked over at Jade and smirked. "Look who's talking."

Jade rolled her eyes and shrugged.

"Razor!" Sarah shouted from outside.

Razor jumped up and ran out the door. Everyone quickly followed. Jade jumped up and instantly regretted it. She shuffled out the door—refusing any help from David. If she was going to be traveling and fighting, she had to get used to her body movement. When she got to the porch, she saw Sarah and about seven other people behind her.

Sarah beamed with pride. "I brought you some people who are willing to fight."

~23~

The people who Sarah brought were considered the troublemakers at the compound—the people who wouldn't fall in line with Jackson's and Beverly's rules. They spent most of their time in the confinement quarters. They went from one prison to another. Sarah broke them free when they were coming back from the showers. She gave them a proposition to help Jade and Razor in exchange for living a little more freely. They quickly agreed.

Their names were Lang, Clay, Rosalind, Danita, Regan, Junior, and Tatianna. Sarah assured them that there was more who were in confinement, but these were the ones she could get to at the moment.

"You did good, Sarah," Razor assured her.

"Just expect a visit from Jackson and Beverly," Helena rolled her eyes at the thought of it.

"Hopefully, we'll be gone by then," Jade shuffled down the porch steps. "Thank you, Sarah. And thank you all for agreeing to help."

"No problem," one of the guys stepped up. "I'm Junior. Saw you fight him that day. You held your own. Impressive techniques."

Jade looked over at Razor. "He was taking it easy on me."

Razor smirked. "She's modest."

"Hey, Jade, I'm Rosalind. I trained with you and David out in the woods."

"Oh yeah," Jade thought back to those days. "You were really good in hand to hand combat."

"And a great shot too," David said. Rosalind smiled.

"Let's get inside, and we'll fill you all in on the plan." Everyone followed Razor inside.

Jade lagged. One of the girls lingered back and watched Jade make her way up the steps. The girl didn't offer any help. She just watched on and smiled a little.

"We heard about the attack," she said. "Sore?"

"Very."

"You going tomorrow?"

"Do bears have claws?"

She smiled. "I can show you some stretches that might help."

"That would be great."

"I'm Tatianna."

"Nice to meet you, Tatianna," they walked inside.

Razor got the newcomers up to speed. He was going to set Rosalind, Lang, and Regan from afar since they were good shots. Tatianna and Junior were to go with the rest of the group while Clay and Danita were to stay behind to protect Sarah and Raina. Sarah suggested that she and Raina go along and wait behind a couple of miles away from the sweep.

Jade agreed with her.

She was worried that Jackson and Beverly would come and take whoever was there away. It was best if no one was there when they arrived. Razor was going to take watch with Clay. He gave everyone shifts and told them to get some rest. Tatianna showed Jade the stretches that would help her with her soreness. Jade tried them all. It was painful, but it helped a lot. She was able to move her body more freely without it hurting too badly.

The thought of tomorrow made Jade anxious. She always felt that way when she was about to encounter the DCs. She prayed that everyone would make it back safely. The thought of facing Bossman again also scared her. It was doubtful that he would actually be at the sweeps, but the possibility of him being there put fear into her heart.

Jade had to shake it off. There was a group of people who were depending on her—some seemed to worship her. It was a little unsettling. She was being praised for killing a guy. Although she'd killed more since then, she didn't want to be admired for that. Junior looked at her in amazement. He called her a grade-A badass. She just thought she was trying to be a decent person.

Razor didn't assign Jade a shift so she could rest. She didn't want to argue with anyone else, especially Helena, so she went to bed. She tried to shut off her brain—she wanted a dreamless sleep. Staring at the ceiling, Jade began to count sheep. The imaginary sheep floated above her. One by one, they jumped over a little wooden fence. Jade was at sheep 47 when she finally drifted off.

**

They huddled in a small garage.

It was about two miles away from the DCs sweep site. They already traveled eight miles on foot. Jade was hurting. She pretended that everything was fine, but she was dying inside. Her body was not prepared for this. But she couldn't just sit behind. She had to be there.

The garage was well hidden by trees. It was the only structure that was still standing in the area. Clay and Danita were going to stay there with Sarah and Raina. Razor thought they all would be fine. The place was well hidden.

Jade sat on a crate while Razor went over the plan again. She focused on her breathing. Jade was glad that her combat mask covered her face. No one could tell how much pain she was really in. Keeper had stocked her mask with medicine, and he improved it after the last attack. Sadly, the improvements weren't helping her at the moment.

Razor and Junior were going to run ahead and scout the area. They were going to find decent spots for Lang, Rosalind, and Reagan to set up and be out of sight. Everyone was to stay put and be on alert. Jade was grateful for the break. She worked on getting her breathing under control. She could feel eyes on her. Helena was watching her. Jade pretended not to notice.

Keeper started passing out some walkie talkies to the group. "Stay on channel 10," he said. "I've been monitoring it for a while, and it seems to have no activity on it."

"Great," Razor took one.

"Sadly, we don't have enough for everyone. So, we'll have to share and stay close to one another."

"Our shooters should get one of their own since they're going to be further away."

"I agree," Keeper gave a walkie to Lang, Rosalind, and Reagan. He also gave one to Clay. "We'll only have one walkie on the ground, so try not to go too far from everyone."

Razor nodded. "We'll be back." He, Junior, Lang, Rosalind, and Reagan all headed out.

Silence fell on the rest of the group that stayed behind. They were all thinking the same thing—please don't get caught. That was a fear whenever you stepped outside. There was a high possibility that you would be imprisoned whenever you went out. They've all experienced and escaped that fate. Now they were under that threat again.

Helena walked over and sat next to Jade. Jade found it calming. Since everything went wrong, she never had her sister by her side. She did now. It brought relief to her. They didn't say anything for a while.

"You ok?" Helena finally asked.

"I feel like shit, but I'm ready to get this done."

"Try to lag behind a bit," Helena suggested. "Let us do most of the work. Only intervene if you have to."

Jade thought about it for a moment. It wasn't a bad idea. She already fought to be here. There was no point of fighting any more than she had to. Her body could definitely use the break.

"Sounds like a plan."

Jade looked over the rest of the group. Fear and concern were in all their faces. Especially Tatianna's. She sat on another crate in the corner— her leg bobbing up and down. Jade didn't mean to stare. She was just wondering what was going on in Tatianna's head. Her fear seemed more significant than the others.

Tatianna looked over at Jade. She gave her a weak smile.

"You ok?" Jade asked.

"I'm scared shitless. You don't know what DC officers do to good-looking women in there." Tatianna was beautiful—she could've been a model if the world wasn't in total shit. Her short haircut brought out the features of her incredible high cheekbones. Her skin was a smooth, mocha color. And her hazel eyes were like staring into stars. Jade could see the water that threatened to escape from those beautiful stars.

"Your sister tried saving me a few times," Tatianna continued. "She threw me in the hole and guarded the door. Sadly, she couldn't be there all the time," she looked at Helena, who was looking down in shame. "Thank you for that."

"Could've done more," Helena mumbled.

"Don't kick yourself. You did what you could," Tatianna said as-of-matter-of-factly. She took out her knife and twirled it around her hand. "Leave the killing to me." Fire blazed behind those beautiful eyes.

"No mercy," Keeper said. "They deserve none."

Tatianna looked over a Keeper for a moment. She watched him for a while—sizing him up. The action made Keeper a little uncomfortable. He looked down at the ground. He tried to divert his look anywhere than in Tatianna's direction.

"I'm gonna make sure they get none."

Silence again fell over the group. It was hard to tell how much time had passed since Razor and the others left. Jade was starting to get a little worried. A part of her wanted to get on the walkie and ask for an update, but instincts told her that that was a bad idea. She wasn't sure what kind of position they were in, and she would've hated to have blown their cover before anything even began. Jade got up and paced a little. She was ready for action.

"They're fine," Helena said, reading Jade's thoughts.

"Seems like we've been waiting forever."

"They'll be here shortly."

Jade felt a little relieved. Razor was Helena's husband. If she wasn't worried, Jade didn't have the right to worry. As if on cue, Razor and Junior came walking into sight. She met them halfway.

"All setup," Razor said once Jade was in earshot. "Let's move out."

Everyone who was going got prepared to leave. Clay, Danita, Sarah, and Raina moved further inside of the garage—making sure they weren't seen by anyone. Before Jade went, Raina made her promise that she would come back safely. Jade made a promise that she would, although she couldn't promise unscathed and unharmed. But she would make it back to Raina either way.

"The two miles go by very quickly," Razor said to the group. "The DCs aren't there yet. Lang will radio us if they get there before we do."

Jade tried not to focus on walking. She decided not to focus on the destination or the events that were about to take place. She tried to clear her mind. This fight seemed never-ending. Her life before this was like a dream. Sometimes she wondered if it ever existed at all. Then Vincent came to mind. She thought back to when they first started dating. She was so in love with him. And he was head over heels for her. They were inseparable. He was clear proof that life before all of this was really there.

It amazed her how two people who were so in love with one another could now hate each other so much. It was this world. It was this environment that drove them there. Unfortunately, there was no turning back from that.

Then there was David, the person she was falling for now.

In this world.

In this environment.

Jade looked over at him. He was walking a few feet ahead—distracted by his own thoughts. How could she be experiencing love now? This was no time for romance. This world no longer allowed it and somehow it managed to creep up on her. She remembered their kiss. His soft lips on hers. She pushed the memories away. This was not the time for sappy

Jade. Warrior Jade needed to get her head in the game. She looked back over at David. He caught her eyes. He smiled at her. She smiled back. David lingered behind, so she could catch up to him. Once she was near, he grabbed Jade's hand and held it in his'.

Jade looked down at their hands, intertwined. A range of different emotions went through her. A part of her was elated for this small piece of affection. It calmed her nerves. The other part was furious and terrified. This was the very thing she was afraid of losing. This could turn out to be a weakness, and she hated herself for it.

David could see the struggle in her face. He slowly let go of her hand.

"Not the right time I suppose," he didn't bother waiting for a response. He walked on ahead of Jade.

"Great," she thought to herself. *"Leave it up to me to screw things up."*

The group had stopped at the edge of a cul-de-sac. Jade walked up to them. It appeared deserted, but Jade knew better. This place was filled with debtors and squatters. All of them hiding. All of them surviving. It reminded her of the house she used to hide out in for months. That seemed so long ago.

"So, what are we gonna do, start knocking on doors?" Jade asked.

"Wait 'til the trucks roll in," Razor said. "Be like smoking out mice from their holes then."

"Nice," Jade said sarcastically.

"Hey, don't get mad at me. It's a technique."

"I wonder who thought of it."

Razor chuckled.

Jade had to remind herself that she couldn't get too mad at him. He *was* playing for the other side now, which was way more beneficial to them since he came up with most of the DCs tricks.

"We'll wait 'til the trucks roll up and for the debtors to start running out. Everyone will try to save as many debtors as they can. Me and Junior will steal the weapons and a couple trucks."

"Both we can really use," Helena said.

"Sounds good."

"Targets are inbound," Lang radioed. It was quickly followed by the sound of roaring trucks in the distant.

Jade's heart was racing. She wasn't sure how this all was going to go down. She just wanted everyone to make it back safe. She also wanted those debtors to be unharmed. Jade took a final look at the group of people she was with.

If she was a scared and confused debtor trying to escape the DC, how would she perceive the group that stood before her?

Razor, Junior, Helena, and Tatianna all looked like threats. They had their war faces on, so she would've avoided them at all cost.

Keeper and David seemed a little more inviting. They had a look of determination on their face, but it didn't seem like they were ready to kill, like the rest of them. Jade didn't know what she looked like, but it seemed like Keeper and David were their best bet.

"I think David and Keeper should stay here and direct the debtors to Clay and Danita," she said quickly. She was trying to make sure this process would go as smoothly as possible.

"Are you insane!" David interjected. "There's no way I'm leaving you."

Razor looked at her. "She's right. Out of all of us, you two seem less threatening."

David shot him a look.

Razor shook his head. "Not like that. You both look like y'all can provide safety. We can't be out here fighting debtors too."

"Just grab their attention and tell them how to get to the garage. Radio Clay, so he knows that they'll be coming," Jade explained.

David was shaking his head. "I'm not leaving you."

"I won't go too far from your sight. Helena already suggested for me to hang back, and I told her I would."

"She's right," the sounds of the trucks were getting closer. Helena turned to David. "Plus, our time is up."

As if on cue, debtors and squatters started fleeing from the houses. Razor excused his self as Jade, and the rest of the group shouted for them to come their way. Keeper got on the radio and told Clay what was going on. Clay said he would be on the lookout for them.

The debtors didn't hesitate for a second. They immediately started running their way. Helena and Tatianna ran off in one direction, while Junior ran after Razor. Jade was getting ready to head in when she was pulled back.

"Stay in sight," David demanded. "And please be safe. I can't take you getting hurt again."

Jade's heart skipped a beat. She could see that he was struggling to fight back the tears. A whole new wave of emotion came over her. Before she knew it, she was kissing him—deeply. The sound of screams and chaos had become their love song.

"I promise I'll be safe," she said once she pulled back. "I love you." Jade took off, running toward one of the houses. She didn't bother waiting for a response. She knew that he loved her too. His actions have told her that. Jade was experiencing a new kind of bravery. She caught a girl rushing out of the house. A DC truck was just pulling up.

"Run toward the woods," Jade directed as she pointed in David and Keeper's direction. David was smiling at her. The girl nodded and ran toward them. Jade moved on to the next house. She kept redirecting people to safety. Helena and Tatianna were just ahead of her doing the same.

The DCs were jumping out of their trucks, confused. One of the officers grabbed a young girl and tried to cuff her. Before Jade could even react, Tatianna was already engaging. There was a lot of pent-up anger there. Tatianna showed no mercy as she slit the officer's throat and was coated in his blood. The young girl looked up at her in terror. Tatianna then quickly directed the girl to Keeper's direction.

Jade kept making her way through the subdivision. She made sure she didn't stray too far from David. She tried her best to avoid the DCs. Every now and then she heard gunshots ring out and DC officers would drop. Lang, Rosalind, and Reagan were doing their jobs. She allowed Tatianna and Helena to engage while she hung back making sure she led the debtors away to safety.

Helena and Tatianna handled themselves very well. Helena was agile and quick. She was able to deliver fatal blows before an officer even had a chance to process it. Tatianna, on the other hand, was more vicious and deliberate. She wanted the DC officers to know exactly what she was doing to them—just like they did to her in prison.

"Jade!" Razor shouted. He was cutting down a sea of officers as he made his way to one of their trucks. Junior, on the other hand, was getting swarmed by another truck, which was why Razor called out for help.

Lang, Rosalind, and Reagan were focusing on the officers who were trying to take away debtors.

Junior and Razor were big guys, but like many, the officers were less inclined to engage with Razor than they were with Junior. Jade was on it. She couldn't stand back and watch Junior get taken down.

"Jade!" Helena shouted. A DC officer got the upper hand on her, and she needed back up. Jade pulled out her bow and arrow.

She aimed.

She fired.

She freaked out for a moment.

Jade was aiming for the officer's back but got his head instead. The officer dropped on Helena—pinning her on the ground. Tatianna rushed over and helped Helena up. The officer's blood covered her neck.

"Thanks," Helena said.

"Sorry," Jade responded as she ran past. She kept her eyes focused on Junior, or what she could see of him. They were all but dogpiling him. Razor was distracted with four officers who decided to gang up on him.

Jade slowed down a little. She took out another arrow. She aimed at the officer that had Junior in a chokehold.

She fired.

She managed to get this arrow through the officer's eye. Vomit threatened to escape her. Her arrows were not at all landing in places she intended—like his arm. Jade wasn't sure if she was getting better or worse with her shot, but they were doing the trick, nonetheless.

The officer's arm slumped off Junior's neck as he fell over. Junior was able to fight off the other officers. A few of the officers turned their attention to Jade. Jade flung her bow across her back as the officers came charging at her. She pulled out her trusty knives.

A slash here.

A slash there.

Jade made contact with every officer that came near her. She was no longer in control of her body. Warrior Jade was now in full control. Jade just sat back and watched as warrior Jade slashed her way to Junior. Regular Jade would worry about her ever-growing body count later. Right now, she had to help Junior. They all needed to make it back.

Junior dropped the last officer once Jade made it to him. He leaned against the truck. He placed his hands on his knees—trying to catch his breath. "Thanks."

Jade put her knives back in her thigh straps. She pulled out her bow and an arrow. She looked around them while Junior was catching his breath. "No problem."

Junior took a deep and final breath before he stood up straight and looked around.

"What's in here?"

"Guns."

"Well, I guess that's why they gave you such a hard time," Jade joked.

"Alright over there?" Razor called out.

"We're good!"

"Good, Junior, take off. Get back to Clay and Danita."

Junior looked at Razor with uncertainty. "Is that a good idea?"

"Yeah, there's a lot of people heading their way. They might need back up."

"He's right," Jade said. "You should go. Tell Keeper to radio Clay before you leave." Junior nodded and got in the truck. He started it up and headed toward the woods. Jade watched him off.

"Jade," Razor climbed into the other truck. "Get back to David."

"Where you going?" she demanded. He was much needed here.

"I'm hiding the truck. I'll be back before you know it," he chuckled a little. "Don't worry. I'm not abandoning you."

She nodded. "Be safe."

Razor took off, and so did Jade. Helena and Tatianna were going into houses together—helping people escape. As she passed people, she continued to direct them to the woods. Jade noticed Keeper on the radio as Junior drove off in the truck. David was giving directions to those who were passing by.

Then she heard a cry.

It stunned her at first. It was a cry she hadn't heard in a long time. Jade looked around frantically, trying to find the source. There he stood. Head full of curls. Cheeks red. Tears streaming down his face as his fingers rested in his mouth. He had to be about three. And he stood in the middle of the street, through the chaos, all alone.

With a baton in hand, a DC officer was making his way toward him.

"Don't you touch him!" Jade sprinted toward him—ignoring her asthma. "Don't you fucking touch HIM!" She brought up her bow and released the arrow.

It hit the officer in the side of his neck. He screamed out in pain. He pulled it out, and blood squirted out profusely. Jade picked up the little boy before the officer fell. Some of the officer's blood hit her face. She continued to make her way to David as the little boy whimpered in her arms.

"It's ok," she said. "It's gonna be ok." Jade finally made it to the edge of the woods. David looked confused as she handed him the little boy.

"Where did yo—"

"Watch him please," she said.

Jade went back looking around. The gunshots were beginning to die out. The screams were starting to go silent. Majority of the DC officers now laid lifelessly scattered on the ground. She was looking for Helena and Tatianna.

"Jade!" Tatianna screamed out. She stood in the front yard four houses down from Jade.

Jade rushed over to her. "What's wrong?" she looked around. "Where's Helena?" Helena came from out of the back yard. Jade sighed with relief.

"We need your help," Tatianna said.

"I hear movement in there," Helena reported. "I'm not sure if it's a debtor or an officer, but everyone else seems afraid to go in."

"I'll check it out," Jade pulled out an arrow.

"We're right behind you," Helena and Tatianna quickly joined Jade as she climbed up the stairs. It all felt eerie. The stair creaked. The doorway was pitch black. Jade's heart raced. She had a bad feeling about this. Someone was waiting for them. She could feel it. She made her steps light and deliberate.

Jade edged her way inside the doorway.

A brick wall hit her.

She went soaring through the air—knocking Helena and Tatianna back along with her. Jade landed on the sidewalk and then rolled into the street.

Everything went black.

~24~

Yelling was heard as Jade slowly came to. Her body ached all over. Blood flowed down the side of her head. She moaned as she tried to get up. What the hell happened? What did she get hit with? Did she really run into a brick wall? That didn't seem likely.

Jade remembered flying through the air—knocking Helena and Tatianna over along the way. Everything around her seemed incoherent. She heard yelling, but she couldn't comprehend it.

"The Queen can't see her reflection!" a guy yelled. "Where's her reflection?!"

"Calm down!" Tatianna said.

"We need help!" Helena screamed at the top of her lungs.

"Where's her reflection?!"

Jade gave up on trying to get up. She slowly rolled onto her back.

"Helena," she croaked.

"Jade," there was severe fear behind her voice. "Stay where you are."

Footsteps came in her direction. Jade froze. Those footsteps sounded huge. It wasn't Helena or Tatianna. Wooziness crept upon her. She wasn't sure if it was from the blood loss or the fear. Jade tried not to move a muscle as the giant towered over her. At that moment, it was best for her to try to play dead. And play dead, she did. Unfortunately, the giant of a man wasn't buying it. She could feel his eyes on her.

He hit his head with his fist. "Where's the Queen's reflection?!" he roared.

Jade couldn't help it. She opened her eyes. Her curiosity got the best of her. She had to see what he was doing. He caught her eye and begin striding toward her.

A gun cocked.

He froze.

"Back...the...fuck...up!" Razor demanded in a tone that terrified Jade. She thought she would never hear it from him—fear.

The giant stood still. He kept glancing at Jade and then at Razor. The giant didn't move away from Jade, however.

Razor stepped forward. "Back the fuck up, or I will drop you!"

"Jade!"

"David and Keeper, stay back!" Helena warned.

Jade could hear the little boy whimpering. David tried his best to console him.

"You got 'til the count of 3!"

The giant didn't budge. He now kept his eyes on Jade, who was just lying not even two feet away from him.

"1...2...!"

"Razor no," Jade managed to get out. The giant was a debtor, that, she knew for sure. He was also mentally disabled. It became more apparent to her. It became more evident to everyone else too. He was a mentally disabled giant who was prone to violence. That was why Razor was so fearful. Jade, on the other hand, was heartbroken. What was this world like for him?

"Stop!" someone yelled. "Please don't hurt him!" A young woman ran up and stood in between the giant and Jade.

"Tell him to back up," Razor was on edge.

The young woman pushed the giant, and he slowly backed up. His eyes never left Jade. Razor walked over to Jade—never lowering his gun. He carefully picked her up off the ground. Jade instantly felt dizzy once she got to her feet. Razor felt her stumble and pulled her close to him so she could stable herself.

"I'm ok."

David rushed over to her—he had given the little boy to Keeper. "Jade," he examined her head. "I'm sorry I couldn't get here sooner."

"He didn't mean it," the young woman said to Jade.

"Sure, he didn't," Razor said sarcastically.

"He just got scared!" she was very defensive. "He would never hurt a woman."

"Tell that to the woman he just tossed across the fucking street!" Helena was livid.

"I'm ok," Jade managed to get out. Her ribs were hurting.

"Where's the Queen's reflection?" the giant cried.

The young woman quickly turned her attention toward him. She rubbed his back as he began to sob. "It's ok, Calvin. It's ok big guy. I know you didn't mean it."

The whole scene broke Jade's heart. What was it like for this young woman? How long has she been looking after Calvin? It seemed like a lot of work. It had to be hard on her—to look after someone who was such a liability. The young woman was a saint. Not everyone would do that.

"I'm ok Calvin," Jade said, trying to help.

Calvin instantly looked at Jade. "Where's the Queen's reflection?"

He kept asking that question. Jade decided to answer. "Right here, big guy."

Calvin nodded and wiped away his tears. "Sorry," he pointed to the blood that was dripping down the side of Jade's head.

"It's ok, Calvin."

"Thank you," Calvin's companion said. "He's on the spectrum." She answered everyone's silent question.

"Autism," Jade confirmed.

"That's my guess. I didn't know him before all of this."

"What's your name?"

"Yoko," irritation quickly came across her face. "And no, I do not have a John Lennon, nor do I know where he is."

"Get that joke a lot?"

Yoko rolled her eyes. "You have no idea."

"Enough chit-chat," Razor was annoyed. "We need to go."

Tatianna looked around. "Yeah, we've been here too long already."

"Jade, can you walk?" Helena asked.

"I think I'll be ok."

"Keeper, go to the truck," Razor said tossing the keys.

"Should Jade ride with me?"

Razor shook his head. "Not enough room. I loaded that thing up with so much equipment." He looked at the child that was in Keeper's arms. It was the first time he registered that a child was there. Disbelief appeared on his face for a moment. "Helena."

Reading his mind, Helena walked over and took the child from Keeper.

"You're ok, cutie."

"You sure you're ok?" David whispered to Jade.

"I can wal—" Jade fell back before she could finish her sentence. She was expecting to hit the ground, but she felt some gigantic arms catch her and scoop her up. Calvin began to quickly walk off with her.

"Put her down," Razor demanded. Calvin ignored him.

"Put her down now!" David shouted.

"He wants to help!" Yoko was losing her patience with them.

"It's useless standing here arguing," Tatianna said. "Let him help. We'll get back quicker if Jade is carried anyway."

"Well tell him to slow down then," Razor said to Yoko.

"Calvin, wait!"

Calvin stopped. Jade was secretly glad to be in his arms. She wasn't so sure that she'd make the journey. Razor and David walked over.

"We're to never leave his side," Razor said to David. David nodded.

"What, you don't trust us?" Yoko was offended.

"Not you," Helena said. "Him."

Yoko rolled her eyes and started to walk behind Calvin. The rest of the group began to make their journey to the garage.

"Where the hell was Lang?" Helena asked.

"It's my fault. I told them to leave," Razor confessed.

"What? Planning to shoot him down?" Yoko retorted. All her patience was gone with them.

"If we need to," Razor said.

"We don't gotta come," she shot back. "Calvin can take Jade to your destination, and we can go our separate ways."

"Sounds good to me."

"No!" Jade croaked. Reading her mind, Calvin turned around so Jade could see the rest of the group. "No one is leaving. Yoko you can't keep doing this on your own. Razor they can be a good asset to us."

"No one's forcing them to leave Jade," he looked at Yoko. "No one's forcing them to stay either."

"That's funny coming from a DC officer," Yoko was determined not to be intimidated by Razor.

Razor chuckled and shook his head. "Yeah, but this DC officer saved your ass."

"NO!" Calvin boomed. Jade jumped. She would've fallen out of his arms, but Calvin tightened his hold on her. The rest of the group stopped dead in their tracks. Tension hung in the air. Jade could see the veins popping out of Razor's arms, neck, and forehead.

"We're upsetting him," Yoko said. "Sorry."

"Yeah, sorry," it killed Razor to say that.

Calvin turned around and stalked off. The rest of the group followed. Silence filled the air for a while. The only thing that occupied the space was Calvin counting his steps.

"51, 52, 53, 54, 55," he murmured.

Jade was beginning to nod off from his counting. It was like counting sheep to her. David would tap her shoulder whenever he saw her nodding off.

"You might have a concussion," he said.

Razor went into his back pocket and pulled out a bandana. "Put this on your head." He handed it to Jade.

Jade held it to the side of her head. She was still bleeding, but it had slowed down a lot.

"79, 80, 81, 82, 83,"

"Does he do this a lot?" Helena was annoyed. She shifted the little boy to her other hip. He was fast asleep. She was annoyed by the weight of the child, more so than Calvin's counting.

"From time to time," Yoko was unbothered by it.

Razor took the child from Helena. The little boy woke up for a moment during the exchange. He rested his head on Razor's shoulder and quickly fell back asleep. "So, we have a child now."

"Jade found him," David said.

Razor looked over at Jade. He raised his eyebrows.

"An officer was coming at him with a baton," Jade explained.

"No worried, screaming, mother around?"

"No. He was all alone."

"Yoko, have you seen him around?" Helena rubbed her arm.

"No, never seen him before," she said. "But then again, I never saw anyone 'round there. We all stay inside for as long as we can."

"So, they're attacking children now?" Tatianna asked.

"They've been doing it. Why you think I killed that first DC officer? He was beating on Raina," Jade quickly thought back to the moment she saved Raina. She remembered how frightened she looked—how ruthless that DC officer was with her. "Are there any children in the prisons?" Jade asked curiously. She couldn't remember if she saw them or not in her brief stay.

Razor shook his head. There was a grim look on his face.

"What happens to them?"

"This world is no longer fit for children Jade," sadness hung in the air as they all took that statement in. This world was no longer fit for anyone.

"15, 20, 21, 22, 23," Calvin had counted to 100 and was now starting over. They all listened to him count as they made their way back to the garage.

**

Most of the debtors cowered in the garage once they saw Razor coming. The sight of a child in his arms didn't make him look less threatening. A few of them took off running in the other direction. Keeper and David scrambled to keep them from fleeing. It took a lot of convincing. Seeing Jade bleeding in a giant's arms didn't help either. Nor did the sight of Tatianna and Helena covered in blood that clearly looked like someone else's. After a while, they finally got everyone to stay and hear them out.

"Look I know you all are scared and confused," Razor said, handing the little boy to Sarah. She gave him a baffled look. Razor ignored her. "All I ask is that you hear me out first before you make a decision."

"He's here to help," Jade awkwardly tried to climb out of Calvin's arms, but he wouldn't let her. "Calvin, I'm ok."

"You should probably sit Jade," Yoko said. She motioned for a guy to get up off a crate he was sitting on. He reluctantly got up. She placed it by Jade. "Put her down here, Calvin."

Calvin gently placed Jade on the crate. "Thanks," she looked at the many eyes that were on her. "As I was saying, Razor is here to help. You all should hear him out."

"Thank you, Jade," he said. "First, does anyone know whose child this is?"

They all were expecting someone to come crying and rushing up to them when they first got to the garage, but no one did. Everyone looked over at him, sleeping in Sarah's arms. Everyone shook their heads. It was no recognition in their eyes.

"Does anyone at least know his name?" Jade asked. Silence. "I found him in the middle of the street."

"Maybe his mother got taken in the sweep?" someone suggested.

"Impossible," Lang interjected. "No trucks left out of there, except for the ones we stole."

"Besides, we didn't leave an officer alive," Helena added. No one said anything. Some just shook their heads and shrugged.

"We'll deal with that later," Razor said. "On to more pressing matters. As you all may see, I am no longer apart of the DC task force. Bossman has made a move against me, and I plan on returning the favor. Now I can't do this alone. If I really want to hurt Bossman, and I mean really hurt him, I'm going to need an army."

"And how you plan on doing that?" one debtor asked.

"By taking him and the DC task force down."

"By shedding our blood," another debtor said.

"No one is going to force you to fight," Razor looked around. "You all can make that decision on your own. I'm just granting you the opportunity to fight back and really do some damage to them."

All the debtors looked at one another with uncertainty. It was looking like none of them were willing to fight. Jade was trying not to panic. It wasn't looking too good for them. They saved a lot of people today. She was hoping that that wouldn't be in vain. Surely there had to be one fighter among them.

"Look at the damage we did to them today," Lang said. "And that was with just a small team."

"And most of us just met yesterday," Tatianna added.

"Just imagine what we can do with an army," Lang's input did nothing to them. Most of them just mumbled some lame excuse under their breath. Some were getting up to go. It was looking like a dead end. It broke Jade's heart. Fear was rooted in them.

"You know there are no children in the DC prisons," Jade said. It was random, but for some reason, she just wanted to share that piece of information with them. "I just learned that today. There are no children in those prisons. What do you think happened to them?"

No one said anything. Jade didn't expect them to. It was a rhetorical question.

"I would think most of them were left abandoned. When their parents were taken away, the officers would just leave them there...all alone...to fend for themselves. That would be the best outcome for them," Jade went silent for a minute—letting her words sink in. It was more to herself than anyone else, but all eyes (and ears for that matter) were on her.

"But you know what I've seen...what I've witnessed? Children being treated as hostile threats. When I saw this little guy here," she looked over at the child who was still sleeping in Sarah's arms. "He was crying and all alone, but an officer came at him with a baton anyway. What threat did he pose? Why was he getting the same treatment as a grown man? Because he *might* be a potential debtor?" Jade's eyes now made her way to Raina, who was sitting next to her mother.

"Do you know the whole reason why I killed that first DC officer? Why they started hunting me down? It was because of her," all eyes diverted to Raina. Tears were escaping Jade. "I was like many of you here today. I kept to myself, and I focused on surviving. That was all you could do in this day and age. But then I saw her. Trying to flee from a DC officer, but she got caught. And she was savagely beaten for it. I couldn't just sit back and survive anymore. I had to fight for life because while we're out here focusing on surviving, we're allowing our children to die."

Most of the debtors looked down with guilt and shame. Jade, sensing that she had them right where she wanted them, slowly began to stand up. Calvin, who never left her side, placed his hand on her back so she could stable herself.

"Razor told me that this world is no longer fit for children. And we are partly to blame. We sat back and allowed ourselves to be oppressed. And our children have paid greatly for that. This world is no longer fit for children? Then I say that we fight and make it so, who's with me?!"

"I will fight Jade!" Yoko said.

"Fight! Fight! Fight!" Calvin boomed behind her.

"I will fight!" someone else said.

"Count me in."

"I will fight for our children!" someone cried out.

More volunteers signed up while others snuck off. They got the people that they needed though. Overall, they got around 50 people who were willing to fight with them. That wasn't a bad way to start their raids.

Calvin carried Jade all the way back to HQ. No one was willing to hear any kind of protest from her. And honestly, Jade wasn't trying to give it. She knew she wasn't going to make it back on foot. Jade barely made it to the raid, and after getting knocked out by Calvin, she knew that the journey back would probably kill her. So, she let Calvin carry her all the way back. She focused on relaxing.

Razor made a little room in one of the trucks so the child could ride back with Keeper. Without the weight of a little kid, the group was able to get back to HQ quickly.

"You showed great leadership back there," Razor said to Jade on their journey back.

"I was just trying to get some volunteers."

"You're too modest. These people look up to you."

Jade snorted. She was no leader. "I dunno what for. I have no clue what I'm doing."

"That may be true, but you're a symbol to them. And that's hell a lot more powerful."

"That can't be true."

"It is," Razor looked around and smirked. "You managed to get two DC officers to fight on your side."

Jade rolled her eyes. "That is not what happened."

"But that's what it looks like," he paused. "And you kind of did manage to get us to fight with you."

"Helena is the reason why we joined forces."

"And that wouldn't have happened if it wasn't for you."

Jade shrugged. She figured that Razor had gone insane for a brief moment.

"Seriously Jade, we can get a lot done if you lead and I come up with the plans."

"As long as we can get this done with less bloodshed on our side, I'm all for it."

"Good, now if you can just stop getting your ass knocked out we'll be good."

"Screw you."

Razor chuckled. "I think David would like to do that," he winked at her and quickly walked off.

Jade was briefly shocked for a moment. She eventually closed her mouth and looked away. Unfortunately, it was in the direction of David. Jade sighed. Razor could be really annoying at times.

~25~

The smile on Beverly's face really annoyed Jade. She wanted to smack it right off. She was sitting on the porch now—along with Razor, Helena, David, and Keeper. Tatianna, Lang, Junior, Yoko, and Calvin stood scattered in the front yard. The debtors from the raid surprisingly were able to fit in the house. Most of them made their way to the basement. Sarah directed them to areas in the home that would hold them comfortably for a brief moment. They were all waiting for Razor to tell them which house they'll be in.

"Thank you for the new recruits," Beverly said smugly. She and a group of members were waiting for them. They were mad about the group that Sarah took, but that quickly went away once they saw the group of people they brought back from the raid.

Razor laughed. "See that's where you're wrong. These are Jade's recruits."

"Yeah, I shed blood for them, so I think they'll be fine here," Jade said.

"You can't possibly hold them all in there."

"That's where those other three houses come in," Razor said. "With people in all four houses, your compound will be well protected...so, you're welcome."

"Fine," Beverly snapped. She looked over at Calvin. "But you'll have to hand over big guy here for me to allow this." She walked over to him, but Yoko blocked her.

"Try to take him, and I'll snap your neck, bitch!"

"Fight!" Calvin boomed.

"Calvin no!" Jade shouted. She feared what he would do to Beverly. Beverly jumped back, afraid.

Razor laughed. "I don't think he'll be going with you."

"You took away some of my people!"

"You had them locked up," Jade shot back. "Clearly they weren't wanted there."

"They couldn't follow the rules."

"Then they're better off here."

"Well, I'm taking someone back!"

"No one is leaving here," Jade got up. "You're gonna have to fight your way through us to get to them."

Beverly knew Jade wasn't bluffing. Everyone went tense—preparing their selves for a fight, should they come to it. Beverly took a good look at the people behind Jade. She knew that the battle with them wasn't going to be easy. Jade was on her last straw with Jackson and Beverly, but mainly Beverly. She hated the way Beverly threw her weight around. She was the boss, and she had to make sure everyone knew it. Beverly's behavior made people feel intimidated. Jade didn't think that was good leadership. She hated bullies, and Beverly behaved like one.

"Well if you *need* to take someone," Razor intervened. "You can take the kid we found."

Jade shot him a look. She wasn't letting the kid go—not a chance in hell. No one was leaving there with Beverly, and Jade meant that. Razor gave Jade a smile and winked.

Beverly looked him up and down in disgust. "I don't want no damn kid."

"Well, I'm afraid there's nothing we can do for you then."

"Let's go!" Beverly and the accompanying members began to stalk off.

"Beverly, wait!" Keeper was in disbelief. "Are ya really gonna deny safety for a child?"

She smirked and looked at Jade. "Yes, the child is your problem. Not mines," she looked at the members. "I said, go!"

They all watched her, and the members march off. Jade's hatred for Beverly grew. She had a strong urge to take her bow and arrow, aim at Beverly, and fire away. It would be so much easier to just get rid of her once and for all. But alas, Beverly wasn't the real enemy in all of this. Despite her "bitchyness," Beverly wanted the same thing—to get rid of Bossman and the DC task force. Their approach to it was just different.

Beverly was a user—it was all about what you could provide.

Jade was a protector—she just wanted to save everyone (whether she knew it or not).

"I hated her in HQ," Tatianna said.

"Damn," Yoko was shocked. She looked over at Razor. "She makes you look like a saint."

"If she keeps this up, she's going to get us all killed."

"Do you really think she'll have an opportunity to do something that extreme?" Jade couldn't picture Beverly ever leaving the compound.

"She's desperate. And as of right now you've been showing her up. She wants to change that."

"What do we do?" Helena asked. "We can't be looking out for Bossman and her too."

"I need to talk to her brother," Razor looked back at the house. "But let's get the debtors settled in first."

Razor was able to divide the debtors evenly between the houses. They ended up with Tatianna, Yoko, Calvin, Sarah, Raina, and the little boy, Levi. They mostly had to share rooms: Razor and Helena; David and Jade; Keeper and Tatianna (it shocked Jade to hear that she wanted to room with Keeper); Sarah, Raina, and Levi; Yoko, and Calvin took the basement. It was crowded, but they all seemed to fit comfortably.

Razor also assigned shifts between all the houses. He mostly gave them all a few days off except for Tatianna and Yoko, who insisted on taking a watch.

They couldn't get any kind of information from Levi. He was only able to tell them his name and that he was four years old. They couldn't even get a birthday out of him, so they weren't exactly sure if that was his real age. Levi seemed to gravitate to Jade. She figured it was because she saved him. He eventually warmed up to everyone else in the house, but he favored Jade a little more. Raina did an excellent job looking after him when Jade was busy. Jade thought she would've made a great big sister. Raina was so used to everyone looking after her, it felt good to look after someone else for a change.

Calvin, on the other hand, seemed a little harder to settle in. He only listened to the women in the house. He completely ignored the men when he didn't perceive them as threats. It took quite some time, and a few scuffles and bruises, for Razor to finally get Calvin to listen to him and the rest of the guys in the house.

It was hard for Yoko and Jade to stand back and not intervene when a scuffling match broke out between Razor and Calvin. Raina and Levi had learned to hide in their room when the chaos broke out. Jade couldn't take it whenever he yelled for her (Queen) during his and Razor's altercations. It was even harder for Yoko, especially when he screamed for his "Koko." During the last dispute, Jade found her crying on the porch.

"You know Razor's not trying to hurt him."

"I know," she said, wiping away a few tears. "He's just trying to help. Trust me, he explains this to me every time."

"I know it's still hard to watch."

"I just feel like I've failed him."

"You did the best you could," Jade said. "That's more than anyone else would do."

"Yeah," Yoko stared off in the distance for a moment. A smile slowly crept up on her face. "You know, he saved me."

"Really?"

Yoko nodded. "I was cornered by two DC officers. The way they looked at me sent chills down my spine. Something just didn't feel right. As they pinned me down, I began to scream at the top of my lungs...to the point that my throat started hurting. Next thing I knew, they went flying across the room."

Jade could imagine it. A flash of her getting tossed across the street came to mind.

"I just saw this giant tossing these guys around like rag dolls. I was scared at first, but then I was just amazed. They couldn't take this guy down, no matter how hard they tried," she looked over at Jade. "I think he broke every bone in their body. Limbs were twisted and angled in ways that didn't seem humanly possible."

Tears began to flow from Yoko's eyes again.

"I broke down crying. Calvin saved me. I knew exactly what they were gonna do to me, and I knew I wouldn't be able to survive it mentally. He spared me from that fate."

The front door opened and closed. The two women turned around and saw Razor standing behind them—breathing heavily.

"You ok?" he asked Yoko.

To Jade's surprise, Yoko started laughing. "Are you?"

Razor laughed breathlessly. There were fresh bruises and cuts on him. He squeezed in between them. "He's actually been taking it easy on me."

"Umm, you sure 'bout that?" Jade couldn't help but laugh a little herself.

"Trust me, I'm sure."

"What does that mean?" Yoko asked.

"I think he's ready to keep watch with me."

"Really?"

"Yeah, this is all about two alpha dogs trying to establish dominance," Razor motioned to his cuts and bruises. "Despite his disability, Calvin is an alpha dog. I'm not trying to take that away from him. I just want him to work with me. I think he's finally accepting that."

"That sounds good," Jade was hopeful.

"Yeah," Razor looked back at the house. "Plus, if we have another altercation, at least we'll be out in the open. I'm tired of scaring the kids."

"Good point."

Jade thought back to how leery Raina and Levi were when interacting with Calvin. He never posed any kind of threat to them. He always referred to them as a prince and princess. Raina loved being called that. But when he had his break down moments, it frightened them.

"I thought you or Yoko should be there during our watch just in case."

"Whatever makes it easier for him," Yoko quickly said. She wanted to help any way she could.

"Now, it's time to go over drills," Razor sighed.

"What drills?"

The drills were in case they were under attack.

It was mainly for Sarah, Raina, Levi, and Calvin. Razor practiced with them for weeks. Sarah, Raina, and Levi were to lock themselves in the basement's pantry. Calvin was to stand guard and protect them at all cost. The key phrase was "defend the castle." Razor figured it would be easy for Calvin to catch on since he had a thing for medieval times.

During random times throughout the day, Razor would scream out the phrase, and they all went into action. Jade wanted to kill him when he did it during the middle of the night—causing them all to run around frantically. The drills brought a new light to Razor though. Helena especially took notice of it.

"He's so fucking sexy," she, Jade, Yoko, and Tatianna were standing on the porch watching Razor and David teach some fighting skills to Raina and Levi. Yoko and Tatianna burst out laughing. Jade did her best not to look disgusted. She still couldn't come around to the thought of Razor and Helena being intimate with one another. Jade was starting to look at Razor more like a brother, which seemed to make it worse for her.

"I gotta admit," Yoko said. "I never really pegged him as being good with children."

Tatianna laughed. "Yeah me either," she looked over at Helena. "No offense."

"None taken. I didn't think he'd be good with kids either."

"I'm not surprised," Jade admitted. Nothing that Razor did seemed to surprise her anymore. Razor was loyal. That's something she quickly picked up on. If you stayed in his good graces, he would stand with you until the end. If you didn't, well, that wasn't good for you.

Junior came into view, and everyone froze. They were expecting to hear some kind of bad news. "Relax," he said, sensing the tension. "I came here to update you on the food ration."

"How's it looking?" Razor asked. One of the trucks that they stole on the raid was halfway filled with food. Razor said that the officers must've loaded up on it at the DC headquarters. He focused on rationing out what they had before asking Jackson for help.

"A little low. We might have three days...four tops."

"I'll go talk to Jackson tomorrow," Razor looked over his shoulder. "Jade, will you join me?"

"Sure," Jade wasn't looking forward to it. It had been a few weeks since she saw Beverly and the members. They thought it best to give them their space. But since they were now the first line of the Black Deficit's defense, the least they could do was provide them food. That's what Jade thought anyway.

**

Jade, Razor, Jackson, and a couple of Black Deficit members stood in the middle of the woods. It was weird, but Jade and Razor weren't allowed near the compound. Jackson, for whatever reason, didn't want to meet them at the house they were staying at. So, they settled with the woods. Razor didn't seem to have an opinion on their meeting spot. Jade was a little offended. Were they that much of a pariah that Jackson didn't even want to be seen with them? But the feeling quickly went away when Jade saw that Jackson didn't bring Beverly with him. She was very grateful for that.

"Make it quick," Jackson said as a greeting. "I need to get back to headquarters."

"We're running low on food," Razor replied.

Jackson gave them a bored look. "And?"

"*And*, it would be nice if you provided us with food," Jade got annoyed.

"Why should we?"

"Because we're providing you with protection."

"We have all the protection we need."

"A little girl was able to walk out of your front gates without being noticed," Razor said.

"You got those people on your own accord. Therefore, you are solely responsible for them."

"When we were out here alone, intruders got less than half a mile from your doorsteps. Jade paid for that by almost dying," Razor was on his last straw.

"I say food is a fair price for that."

Jackson looked at Jade. "I have the prisoners to think about."

There was a long silence between them before Razor spoke. "Forgiveness is a hard thing to do. That's what your father always says."

"Using my father to pivot this negotiation is beneath you," Jackson said. "Like I said, you got those people, so you feed them," Jackson turned to walk away.

"We're not going to get far if we can't work together," Razor said reasonably. His tone kind of scared Jade.

"*You* probably won't, but we'll be just fine," Jackson walked off along with the members.

Jade was stunned.

Jackson was usually the reasonable one. His behavior was so out of character. She expected that from Beverly, but not from Jackson. What changed? What were they going to do now? She didn't expect Jackson to say no. Food for protection seemed like a fair exchange.

"Let's go," Razor started walking back toward the house.

"What are we gonna do now?"

"Leave."

Jade was really stunned by that response. She slowed down a little. "And go where?"

"A few miles east of here."

"You already had this planned?"

"Had to. I'm not about to lose any of my people because of them."

"I don't understand," Jade was baffled. "Why would he say no?"

"I really don't care Jade," there was a little disappointment in his voice. "I thought they were the key to help take down the DC, but I was very wrong. I don't have time to cater to egos. If they're fine like they say they are, then they don't need us as the first line of defense. We can scavenge for food somewhere else."

"Should we run this by everyone?"

"We can mention it, but I'm not voting on it. I'm leaving. The rest can follow if they want."

Everyone was stunned, just like Jade. They couldn't believe that the Black Deficit wouldn't help them. Most of the debtors were naïve, just like everyone else when it came to the Black Deficit. They were a rebel group. Weren't they supposed to help the oppressed?

"Let me get this straight," one debtor said. "They're refusing to help because you didn't get permission to save us."

"And they don't like us," Helena added.

"That's crazy."

"Ya weakened their authority and bruised their ego," Keeper said. "Plus, Jackson feels like ya deeply disrespected his sister." Jade gave him a questioning look. "The members talk."

"Well I suggest we leave," Razor said. "I've scouted an area east of here that's completely abandoned. I say we set up there and scavenge for food in the meantime."

"Some of us can hunt," Lang suggested.

"That sounds like a good start," Razor said. "If you want to stay, you're more than welcome to. But this is my next play. The Black Deficit must learn that we need each other. Personally, I'm not interested in allowing you all to shed blood for that lesson."

Everyone looked at each other and nodded.

"They think they don't need us. So, let them see how far they will get without us." Everyone mumbled their agreement. "We leave out tomorrow morning. Carry only what you need."

Later that day, Jade began packing up all her things. Then she helped Levi and Raina pack their things. She and Yoko explained to Calvin that they would be leaving and going to another place. Jade figured that Razor would be doing drills again once they settled in another house. She was dreading it.

Razor assigned just a couple of shifts to those who volunteered to keep watch. Everyone else was to rest up for the morning. After spending a little time with Raina, Levi, and Calvin, Jade went upstairs to her room to relax. She wondered if they should warn the Black Deficit that they were leaving.

"Screw them," David laid down next to Jade in bed. She scooted over and rested her head on his chest. He wrapped his arms around her.

"What 'bout security? They should double up on it since we're not gonna be here."

"Jackson told Razor that they were fine. He said they had all the protection they needed, so us leaving shouldn't change anything."

"I just can't believe we're calling their bluff like this."

"What do you expect us to do? Sit here and starve."

Jade knew David was right, but it felt wrong leaving and not warning them. Trust, she was beyond pissed with Jackson and Beverly, but she didn't want anything bad to happen to them either. And she was starting to get a bad feeling.

"You're right," she finally said. "I just feel like something bad is gonna happen here."

"They'll be fine if it does Jade."

"That's the problem," Jade thought about the prisoners. She was really hoping that Jackson and Beverly were preparing them to fight. "I don't think they will be."

David sighed. He was thinking the same thing. "Let's hope that they are."

"Have you seen the place Razor's talking 'bout?" Jade saw that David and Razor had been getting closer. She figured it was the threat of Calvin that brought them together.

"Yeah, we took a long walk after one of Calvin's blow-ups and came across it."

Jade giggled a little. She remembered the day he was talking about. David had come up behind Jade and scared the living daylights out of her. Unfortunately, Calvin was there and blew up. He thought David was trying to attack Jade—his Queen. Calvin sent David and Razor flying across the front porch. It was a little joke that went horribly wrong. It was weeks before David could touch Jade in front of Calvin again.

"Yeah," David said flatly. He remembered that day too. It wasn't so funny to him. "I'm so glad he's calmed down since then."

"Me too. I just hope this move doesn't throw him off."

"He'll be fine. As long as you and Yoko are with him."

David took her hand. Jade looked at their hands intertwined. She loved the way his hands felt—they were so soft. It made her feel safe for some reason. She was so grateful to have him in her life. He was so supportive. Living in the world that they were living in now, support was something that you needed.

Jade looked up at David. She leaned over and kissed him. Things had been so chaotic since they got back from the raid, she hasn't really been able to appreciate him.

"What was that for?" he asked once she pulled away.

Jade didn't say anything. Instead, she climbed on top of him and kissed him again. He kissed her back—deeply. His hands caressed her body. Jade's heart raced. Something was taking over her, but she didn't resist it. It's been a while since she's been intimate with anyone.

David's hands found their way up her shirt. He cupped her breast. Finding her shirt being in the way, Jade quickly took it off and unhooked her bra. David tried not to look too shocked when he saw her topless. Jade ran her hands up David's chest and swiftly took off his shirt. She unzipped his pants.

"We gotta be quiet," she whispered.

David smiled at her. "I can do that."

Jade bit the bottom of her lip. She found his smile to be so sexy. She kept going without any regrets.

~26~

Jade woke up before David. A part of her was still in disbelief with what happened the night before. She thought about going further with David for a while, it was just shocking that she had the opportunity to act on it. She looked at him for a moment. He was sound asleep. Jade couldn't stop herself from ogling over David's features. She loved how his brown, scruffy, beard tickled every time he kissed her. The way he looked at her with those beautiful green eyes made Jade feel like he was staring into her soul. She was exposed. David saw every single beauty and flaw within her. Jade loved it.

The sun hadn't risen yet. She thought it would be nice to watch it come up. Jade slipped out of bed and the room unnoticed. She silently made her way to the front porch—carefully not to disturb anyone. Jade sighed with relief once she made it outside, but then she saw Razor.

He smirked. "Morning."

"Hey?"

"So...how did you sleep?" his tone indicated that he knew what she'd done.

"...ok?"

"Really? Just ok?"

"Oh, God."

Razor chuckled. "Yeah, heard that too."

Jade tried her best not to blush. She was so embarrassed. She was sure they were quiet.

"I have excellent hearing," Razor said matter-of-factly.

"Seriously?"

"I swear. I haven't told anyone."

Helena came walking from the side of the house. Once she saw Jade, she beamed. "Someone's glowing today."

Jade looked at Razor.

Razor rolled his eyes. "My wife doesn't count." Helena walked up the steps.

"I'm so embarrassed."

"Don't be. I'm sure David isn't," Helena reassured.

"I bet he's on cloud nine," Razor grabbed Helena's hand and pulled her close to him. He kissed her forehead.

Jade looked at them for a moment. She took them in. She studied the way Razor admired her sister. She noticed the look of love in Helena's eyes. "How do you two do it?"

"That's a weird question to ask your sister, Jade," Razor joked.

Jade rolled her eyes. Sometimes she preferred the mean, scary Razor over the joking one. "I mean being in love."

Helena squealed. "You're in love?"

"Obviously Helena." Helena elbowed Razor in the gut. He hunched over a little. Jade completely ignored them.

"Seems really hard being in love at a time like this."

"Love is never easy, Jade," Razor pointed out. "Not even before."

"But it just seems so effortless for you two. I saw when you first met. It seemed like love at first sight."

"You saw when we first met?"

"Vicky and her crew showed me."

"That bitch is in HQ?!" Helena shouted.

"You were saying Jade," Razor said, bringing Helena back to the main point of their conversation.

"It just seemed like you two didn't fight the feeling. You just went with it. Meanwhile, I'm struggling. It feels nice and so normal, but it's also a weakness. A weakness I can't afford."

"Of course, it's a weakness," Helena said. "You think it's easy being in love with Razor? Everyone wants to kill him. I mean *everyone,* Jade."

Razor laughed.

"I'm terrified that someone will succeed one day, but I don't let that affect the feelings I have for him. If anything, it makes me appreciate him even more."

"It's definitely scary," Razor added. "Especially if you haven't felt that way before. I thought I loved women before, but that was nothing compared to the feelings I have for your sister. And honestly, that makes me more ruthless to my enemies. Because I know that they can use her as a bargaining chip."

Jade nodded—taking all their points in.

"But don't let that stop you," Razor concluded.

"Just enjoy the time that you have with David."

"You're right," the thought of Vincent crept into Jade's mind. "But I have a nasty habit of ruining things."

"David's not Vincent," Helena said.

"Thank God for that," Razor said. "I fucking hate Vincent."

"Who doesn't? Vincent just wanna be on the winning side. It has nothing to do with you, Jade."

"Yeah, he practically sold his parents out once they got to the prison."

"He pretended not to know them."

"Became a bounty hunter and left them there."

"He wasn't even there when they died."

"Trust me," Razor said. "If you were there with him, he would've sold you out too."

"So please don't be afraid to love David because of that asshole Vincent."

"Listen to your sister. She's very wise."

Jade smiled. A part of her was glad that they were there with her. "Thanks."

"We gotcha back, Jade," Helena winked at her.

"We should start getting ready," Razor said. "We'll be leaving out in an hour."

They all walked into the house. Everyone was still sleeping. Razor started waking everyone up while Helena and Jade went upstairs. Helena knocked on Keeper's and Tatianna's door. Jade walked into her room.

David was still sound asleep when she walked in—even with all the commotion. Jade slid into bed and wrapped her arms around him. She rested her head on his back. He stirred a little. Jade didn't move. She wasn't ready for him to wake just yet. She wanted time to just lay there and reflect. Images of last night kept creeping through her mind. She couldn't control it. She didn't want to control it. Everything just seemed so magical. It all felt like a fairytale. It excited and terrified Jade all at the same time. She was in love. And last night made her fall in love even more.

David was so gentle, but still so passionate with her. It had been 10 years since she had sex, and she was only a teenager then. She hasn't been with anyone since. A small part of her was glad that David was the first person she been with since Vincent. He was a fresh palette that helped wipe all traces of Vincent away.

The talk with Razor and Helena was beneficial. Jade had been beating herself up with what happened with Vincent, but now she was ready to forgive herself—even if Vincent wasn't. She still blamed herself for what happened to him and his parents, but she was prepared to move on. And she was moving towards David. Jade wasn't going to let her fears of past love affect the way she felt about David. She was ready to go all in.

David's yawning snapped Jade back to reality. He stretched. She moved back a little to give him room. He eventually turned around to face her.

He smiled. "Good morning."

Jade moved closer to him. "Morning."

"Look like you've been up for a while."

"Yeah, just thinking."

"About?"

"Last night."

"Good thoughts, I hope."

"It was."

David stared at her for a moment. "Is it something you wanna tell me?"

"I'm done holding back with you."

"Were you holding back last night?" he joked.

"I've been scared to really fall for you because of Vincent."

"The shit that happened with Vincent has nothing to do with me. And what happened between y'all wasn't your fault."

"I know," Jade sighed. "I'm just ready to let it all go and focus on being with you."

"I'm glad," he kissed her. "...is there anything else you wanna tell me?"

"Yeah, Razor and Helena know."

"Of course. Him and his scary bat-like hearing."

Jade laughed and then sighed. "Time to make this move."

"Let's do it."

**

The move to the new location went smooth. So smooth that it surprised Jade a little. Nothing was a natural process anymore. But the area was vacant just like Razor said. She wondered why there was no one there. It seemed like a perfect location to be at. Jade could only guess that people usually didn't travel that far out. That was the only explanation she could think of.

The houses turned out to be a little bigger than the homes they were previously in. They all still got the same housemates, but they had a bit more room. It was a lot more houses in the area, but Razor didn't want to spread everyone out. He was still planning on doing more raids so the empty homes would come in handy.

Calvin was able to transition smoothly. He liked his new room in the finished basement. As Jade predicted, Razor went over drills. It was a short process, though. Calvin, Raina, and Levi were able to catch on quickly.

Lang and Junior had set traps around the perimeter to catch squirrels and rabbits. One of the debtors used to be a farmer and was working on trying to grow some fruits and vegetables. They were able to scavenge some canned food and other non-perishable items to hold them over in the meantime. It was looking like the decision to move away from the

Black Deficit had been the right choice, after all.

After a few weeks of getting settled in and managing to stock up on food, Razor began planning for another raid. It was another sweep scheduled in an area 15 miles from their location. Razor was making a list of who was going and who should stay behind. He thought Jade should stay back. She didn't fight him on it, mainly because he wanted Helena to stay behind too. Tatianna made it clear that she wasn't staying behind. Razor didn't disagree with her. Jade wasn't sure if it was because he wanted her to come or if it was because he was afraid to fight her on it. Yoko was going to help with Calvin. Razor definitely wanted Calvin there but knew he wouldn't be able to really look after him. David, Keeper, Lang, and Junior were going as well.

Jade, Helena, Rosalind, Reagan, Danita, and Clay were to stay behind and watch out for everyone back at camp. A part of Jade was glad that she wasn't going. She didn't mind looking after Raina and Levi. Plus, it took a little bit of the pressure off. This had been the longest she had gone without getting hurt. Her asthma had been doing well too. But she was also terrified. She wanted everyone to make it back. She felt like she could make sure of that if she went with them.

Helena was pissed with staying behind, but she didn't say too much. She wanted to be a good role model for Jade. Jade wasn't complaining, so Helena wasn't going to either.

"We can focus on keeping watch," Jade assured her.

"That's a good idea," Razor said. "Rosalind and Reagan can be set up high too."

"Sounds good," Helena tried not to sound too sad. "Just make sure you come back to me."

"Yes, ma'am."

Jade got a sense that this was their first time doing a mission apart. A wave of sadness hit her. She knew it was going to be hard on her sister, but she wasn't worried about Razor. He was going to be ok. Razor would burn down the earth to make it back to Helena.

The night before the raid, Jade sat on the porch. People walked freely around the neighborhood. Jade smiled. It felt like old times. No one was hiding anymore. They all felt safe and confident to roam around. She let the view sink in. This was what she was fighting for. This was what they all were fighting for—normalcy and comfort. She didn't notice Levi until he sat down next to her. He rested his head on her arm.

"I miss mommy," it was the first time he brought up a parent.

"What happened to her?"

"The bad men came and took her away."

"Do you remember how long ago?"

"Long time."

"What about your dad?"

"He was taken before mommy."

"Who were you with before I saved you?"

"No one."

"Really?" it was hard for Jade to believe that he managed to survive on his own.

"I hid in the house when they took mommy away."

"What did you eat?"

"The house had food in it."

"There was enough food in the house after your mommy left?"

"Yes."

Jade figured that his mother hadn't been gone that long then. That was the only explanation. There was no way he managed to live on his own for an extended time.

"You're not leaving me, are you Jade?"

"Course not."

"Will the rest come back?" he was worried about the raid.

"Yes, they will."

"I'm scared."

Jade looked down at him. He was looking out at the street, but he held onto her arm tightly, as if to keep her there. "What are you scared of?"

"Of the bad men finding me."

"Just do what Razor said if that happens."

"But Razor's leaving."

"He'll make it back Levi, trust me."

"Promise?"

"I promise."

Levi didn't say anything else to her. They just looked out at the people in the neighborhood. Eventually, the sun began to set. Levi ended up falling asleep on Jade. She carried him to his room, tucked him in, and kissed him goodnight.

Then Jade made her way up to her room. David was already there in bed. She climbed in with him. She kissed him—waking him up.

"What's wrong?"

"Promise you'll make it back to me."

"I promise."

Jade kissed him one more time and then quickly drifted off to sleep in his arms.

~27~

Jade and Helena walked around the perimeter countless of times. Helena was getting bored. Jade was on the verge of boredom too. The two sisters weren't used to sitting on the sidelines. They both had a thing for the action—whether they wanted to admit it or not.

Despite the butterflies in her stomach, the anxiousness, and her steady body count—Jade felt free when she was out fighting. She had been a sitting duck for far too long. Once she started to take action, there was no turning back. Unfortunately, she had to learn that sometimes you needed a break. It didn't stop her from feeling restless though.

Helena frowned beside her. Jade couldn't help wondering what her sister was thinking. She had to be worried about Razor. Helena did mention how everyone wanted to kill him, maybe she was afraid that today it would finally happen.

"You alright?" Jade asked.

"No."

"Is this the first mission y'all been apart?"

"No," Helena glanced around. "He used to be on missions all of the time before the prison."

"Really?"

"Yeah, it was Bossman's doing."

Jade never really thought about how Helena and Razor's life was before the DC prison. She couldn't imagine it. She always pictured them going straight to the prison once Helena decided to run off with Razor.

"He kept me hidden from Bossman," Helena said. "I think he was afraid."

"Was it because of how innocent you were?"

Helena nodded. "He knew I wouldn't fit in. And he knew Bossman would try his best to tarnish me. To see how committed I was."

"How long did he keep you hidden?"

"Six months."

"Seriously? How he'd manage that?"

"Well, when I was with Vicky and her crew, he was staking us out. He was held up in a house a few blocks away. We stayed there most of the time."

"I'm surprised Bossman didn't grow suspicious."

"Not at first. Razor kept doing his missions like normal. But one of the officers complained about Razor no longer being at headquarters. So, Bossman came looking," Helena rolled her eyes.

"Is that when he said you had to become a DC officer?"

"Pretty much, but Razor said he was planning to marry me...as a last-ditch effort to avoid that."

"I don't understand," Jade was confused.

Helena stopped walking. "Spouses of DC officers can receive the same benefits as the officers."

"And Razor was trying to give you the benefits without you being an officer."

"But Bossman said he would make sure I receive nothing unless I became an officer, so I agreed."

"Why?" Jade asked in disbelief. She couldn't understand why her sister would willingly become a DC officer.

"Razor was killing himself to protect me. He was doing everything in his power to keep his word. I appreciated everything he was doing. I just wanted to make it easier for him. Plus, if I haven't agreed, I'm pretty sure he and Bossman would've been at each other's throats."

"What about the marriage?"

"Well, Bossman called our bluff on that. We couldn't step foot into headquarters without getting married first."

"So y'all got married."

"We didn't have an issue with that. I was head over heels for him. I knew he felt the same way."

"Wow. I didn't know it was so hard for you two."

"You got no idea." Silence lingered between the two sisters for a moment.

"He's alright, Helena."

Helena sighed and smiled weakly. "I know. But I won't ever stop worrying when we're apart."

Jade nodded. She understood—partly. She was worried about David too, but she knew it was nothing compared to Helena.

"Well, at least I'm here now to help you."

Helena walked over and hugged her sister. "I'm grateful for that."

"I'm glad I can help a little."

"Mom and dad would be proud to see us getting along." Jade wasn't as sure as her sister. She didn't say anything. Helena noticed her sister's lack of response. "You don't agree?"

"I think they would be prouder of you than me."

"Nonsense, Jade."

"I've made some poor choices, Helena."

"And I didn't?"

"I'm the oldest."

"So, all of my mistakes are dismissed because I'm younger?" Helena went on when Jade didn't respond. "You really need to learn to forgive yourself, Jade. It's hard for second guessers to survive in this world."

The two sisters continued to walk the perimeter in silence. Jade knew that Helena was right. She had a hard time forgiving herself for her past mistakes. Ever since the world became shit, she became very hard on herself. Jade took what she had before for granted. For some reason, she couldn't forgive herself for that. Everything took one step at a time. Jade was slowly taking them. Maybe one day she'll finally be regret-free, but today wasn't that day.

Jade didn't know how many times they walked around the perimeter. She stopped counting once she got to 20. She wasn't sure she could continue walking much longer. Boredom was taking ahold of her. They had to do something else—soon.

Checking on Raina and Levi seemed like a good idea. Sarah was with them, but popping in on them still appeared inviting. Jade figured the camp would be alright for five minutes. Plus, Rosalind and Reagan were keeping watch on the rooftops. Not to mention, Clay and Danita were making their rounds as well. Everyone would be ok if they took a little break.

"Let's check on Raina and Levi," Jade suggested.

"I can use a break," Helena got on the radio. "Jade and I are taking five."

"Sounds good," Rosalind said.

"Roger-dodger," Clay chimed.

The two sisters began to walk home. Jade couldn't help but think about the people she was keeping watch with. She had gotten to know Tatianna, Junior, and Lang, but the others she didn't know too much about. What was Rosalind, Reagan, Clay, and Danita's situations? Were they debtors or just rebels? How did they get on the DCs radar? These were some of the things Jade wanted to know. They were, after all, risking their lives together.

"Do you know much about them?" Jade asked Helena. "About Rosalind, Reagan, Clay, and Danita?"

Helena frowned. "No, should I?"

"Well, yeah. I mean, we're fighting together."

"Shouldn't that be all we need to know?"

Helena was in a grumpy mood, so Jade ignored her offhand comment. Maybe some food would lift her sister's spirits a little. She hated to see her in a bad mood. If Razor and the rest didn't get back soon, the two sisters would be making a trip to them. Jade pushed the thought of that out of her mind as Raina and Levi came rushing out the door to meet them.

"Is everything ok?" Raina panicked.

"Everything's fine, just hungry."

"And bored," Helena complained as she walked in the house. Jade and the rest followed behind her.

"Can I make you girls a plate?" Sarah asked as they walked in the kitchen. She didn't bother to turn around nor wait for a response, she placed a plate of rice in front of them.

"Thanks," Jade dug in.

Sarah noticed Helena's silence. "Razor isn't back yet?"

"No, it's starting to get late."

"Give them a little more time before you go out there," Sarah suggested. She knew it would be no talking them out of it if they decided to show up to the raid.

"How's it been here?" Jade asked.

"Quiet. I've just been doing a little cleaning to keep myself busy."

Jade nodded. She couldn't think of anything else to say. Sarah and Jade never talked much. Even though they lived in the same house, they never really had a long conversation with each other—especially if it didn't concern the kids.

"Hey," Jade said after a while. "Do you know anything about Rosalind, Reagan, Clay, and Danita?

"Well, Rosalind shared a cell with me at one point."

"Really?" Jade looked over at Helena. Helena shrugged

"But I don't know too much about her. She mostly kept to herself, which is what most of us did in there."

"Oh," Jade was a little disappointed that Sarah didn't know more.

"And I believe Reagan and Clay are brother and sister."

"Wow, they never said anything."

"Well I'm not too sure, but that's what I heard."

"And Danita?"

"No clue, she's timid."

"But not too shy when it comes to fighting," Helena finally joined in on the conversation.

"That's true. Sorry I couldn't be more help, Jade."

"That's ok. You've given me more than I had before."

"Hey Jade, they're back," Clay radioed. "But something's wrong."

Jade and Helena quickly rushed out the door. Sarah could be heard instructing the kids to hide.

It felt like Jade's heart was about to leap out of her chest. *Something's wrong.* That's all she could hear in her head. *Something's wrong.* Were they followed? Was there a group of DC officers knocking at their front door? Was someone hurt? Like really hurt? To the point of death? Or worse, was someone already dead? Did the others just bring back their lifeless body to bury? Who was it?

Please don't let it be Razor. Jade wasn't ready to see her sister hurt like that. It seemed like Jade couldn't get there fast enough. Helena was way ahead of her. Jade never saw her sister run so fast. Not even when Helena chased down the van after she broke out the prisoners. Hate fueled her then. This time Jade saw another emotion—fear.

"God, please don't let it be him," Jade whispered.

Helena had caught up to the group. Jade could see her hugging and kissing Razor. A wave of relief flowed through her, but then Helena gave her a look. Jade's heart stopped. It was a look of sorrow. Only one person came to her mind—David. Jade stopped, and frantically looked around. How could she not pray for him? She was so focused on Razor that for a moment she forgot about David. Where was he? How badly hurt was he? How could she have been so stupid? She still couldn't find him. It felt like her heart was about to jump out of her chest. Her breathing got heavy. Stress was threating to crush her.

"Calvin is carrying him," Razor said.

"Carrying him?"

"I don't know what happened," Razor reluctantly admitted. "Yoko just found him in a house passed out. He must've fallen hard because his head was bleeding."

"His head is bleeding," Jade felt like a mindless zombie. She could only repeat some of the things that Razor was saying. She should've gone with them. Jade should've been by David's side. He was always by hers. Helena came over and wrapped her arms around her sister.

"Keeper patched him up, but we were unable to wake him. We don't know if he was attacked or what. We were just trying to get out of there."

Calvin, Yoko, Tatianna, and Keeper finally caught up.

There was David—unconscious in Calvin's arms. Jade walked over to them. She had to see him. Maybe it wasn't *that* bad. Once she got close, she immediately regretted her decision. David looked so weak and feeble. Something was wrong—it had nothing to do with an attack by an officer.

"I think it's his diabetes," Keeper said, reading Jade's mind.

"His blood sugar must've gotten low."

"Have ya noticed anything strange with him?"

Jade shook her head. "I don't think he would've told me if something was wrong."

"Don't worry Jade," Keeper reassured. "I'll know more once I get back home."

Jade nodded and stepped aside. She watched as they all walked towards home. It felt like she had an out-of-body experience. David was the first person she connected with after spending years alone. He was more than someone she loved—he was her life. She couldn't fathom the thought of living life without him. David provided something that Jade didn't know she needed. Now that she had it, she can no longer live without it. Jade slowly followed the others to the house.

$$**$$

Diabetic coma.

That's what Keeper guessed.

David's blood sugar got really low, which caused him to pass out. Unfortunately, he hit his head pretty bad when he passed out, which probably didn't help. There was no telling when, or if, he would regain consciousness. Keeper hooked David to an IV to help keep his blood sugar at a stable level, but that was all that he could do.

Jade never left his side.

Weeks passed, but Jade remained at David's bedside. She barely left the room unless she needed to go to the bathroom. The others went on two more raids, but Jade stayed put. Helena and Razor tried to convince her to go, but she refused. Jade wanted to be there when David woke up—and she was sure that he would wake.

"Why do I get the feeling you're punishing yourself?" Razor was at his breaking point, Jade could tell. "It's been four weeks Jade. Staying in this room is driving you crazy."

"What would you do if it was Helena?" she asked. "What would you be doing if she was lying in a coma?"

Razor frowned. She had him there. He knew it. It was rare that she stumped him.

"Alright, I won't bother you again about it," he got up to leave. He paused at the doorway. "But Helena is worried about you."

Jade sighed. Another wave of guilt hit her. Pleasing everyone was impossible.

"Alright then," Razor left out without saying another word.

A couple more weeks went by, and David remained unconscious. The others were starting to get a little less hopeful. Jade's hope never wavered. But the others lack of optimism did cause her to stay in her room even more. Sometimes she didn't want to leave to use the bathroom. A part of her was getting annoyed with them. Jade knew that they were trying to prepare her for the worse, but she hated the fact that they were already making plans if he was no longer with them. Jade refused to be ready for that. She couldn't allow them to get in her head, so she kept herself in a little bubble.

One day she woke up to Helena standing over her with oatmeal. It smelled delicious. Jade's stomach growled. Helena laughed. Jade couldn't help but smile a little.

"I guess I brought this right on time."

Jade got up and stretched. Helena handed Jade her bowl once she was done stretching. She sat down in a nearby chair.

"Did Keeper come in yet?"

"Not yet."

The two sisters ate their oatmeal in silence, the sound of the metal spoons clanging against the bowls was the only thing that filled the air. Sarah added some brown sugar and maple syrup to the oatmeal. That was Jade's favorite. She wondered how Sarah knew that. Helena must've told her.

Sarah became the unofficial cook in the house. That title probably came to her because she took care of the kids. When she cooked something for them, she cooked something for everyone. Sometimes the food made Jade feel like a little kid again. The food reminded her of her mother. It's been a while since someone cooked for her.

"We're leaving tomorrow evening," Helena broke the silence. "The officers are switching up the schedule a bit because of the raids."

"And how y'all know this?"

"Razor was able to get his hands on the new schedule."

Jade nodded. She thought about all the people they saved so far. "Do we have any more room for people?"

"It's getting a little crowded, but we can definitely fit some more."

"Ok."

Helena shifted in her seat a little. "You sure you don't wanna come?"

Jade turned her attention to David. She watched him lying in their bed, unconscious.

"I'm just worried."

"I'm ok."

"No, not about that," she paused. "I'm worried about the blowback from all of these raids. I'm worried that they'll eventually come here...when we're gone."

"All the more reason for me to stay."

"Jade..."

"I won't leave him alone and defenseless."

"We can have Clay look after him."

"I'm looking after him, Helena."

Helena sighed. "Alright."

"I'm sorry."

"Don't be. I'd be the same way if I were in your position."

"I know you worry."

"I know you do too."

"I love you."

"I love you too."

The two sisters stared at David for a moment. Jade sat, praying for David to wake up soon. Helena sat thanking God that it wasn't Razor there lying unconscious. Helena shifted uncomfortably in her seat—as if Jade could read her thoughts.

"I think it's getting close for my turn on watch. I'll be back later," Helena said.

"Be safe."

"You too."

Jade continued to mindlessly watch David. She couldn't remember what she thought about, but one thing was for sure—she hated this life. Jade hated the pain and suffering that everyone was going through. She hated the stress and the unknown. At this point, everything was liable to kill you. She wished that the world would just end already.

Darkness was threatening to consume her. Jade was falling into a black hole, she had to get out of it. She got a book and got lost in it. She needed an escape. The room was starting to make her go crazy a little.

Jade reread *The Lone Ranger and Tonto Fistfight in Heaven* by Sherman Alexie. She allowed her mind to be consumed with alcoholism, racism, sex, and drugs. Another kind of pain was better than hers. The pain that Sherman Alexie painted in his stories was a walk in a park compared to what she was feeling at the moment. The world was always filled with pain. There was no such thing as a happy story. Even in fairytales, the main character had to go through some kind of trauma before getting their happily ever after ending. It was all about what kind of level of pain you can take. Jade knew she could take a lot of pain right now.

Jade was almost halfway through the book when she checked on David. He was still lying in the same position. She sighed a little. A part of her was hoping something would happen when she wasn't looking. She watched him for a moment. He looked so peaceful—she never saw him like that. There was no need for him to stress now. There was no need for him to worry. He could relax in his unconscious state. She had to question for a moment if she really wanted him to wake.

Did he really need to suffer like everyone else? Why couldn't he be at peace? If she really loved him, she would want that for him and not wish that he was here with her. Jade sighed again. She always found a way to point out the selfishness in herself.

There was a small knock at the door. Keeper peeked in. "Hey, Jade."

"Hey, come in."

He opened the door wider and walked in. "How's it going?"

"It's going."

"Any changes?"

"None at all."

"Mind if I check?"

Jade put her book down. "Go ahead."

Keeper walked over to David and began to check his vitals. Then he started to stretch David's arms and legs. Jade never knew precisely what he was doing, but she always watched on intently. Keeper wasn't exactly a doctor or nurse, but he had a lot of hands-on experience. Between his sick mother and working closely with Dr. Blackwell, he picked up a lot of things. Still, none of that compared to the 12+ years of training in medical school. Nonetheless, she was grateful that they had someone who had some kind of medical practice, whether it was unorthodox or not.

Keeper sighed. "No change." Jade nodded in disappointment. "I'm sorry, Jade."

"That's ok. It might be better for him this way."

"Don't start getting dark on me, Jade."

"Not dark. Just realistic. There's nothing here for him."

"What about ya?"

"I'm not enough."

"I would have to beg to differ there."

Jade sighed. Keeper sat down next to her. He let out a yawn and stretched.

"Tired?"

"Exhausted."

"Are you going out on the raid?"

"No."

"Why not?"

"Well, we got a lot of people who can go out now. Plus, I want to help ya look after David."

"Thank you."

"Ya welcome."

"What 'bout Tatianna?"

"She's staying behind too."

"Really?"

"Yeah, she wants to help."

"I appreciate that," Jade paused. "What's up with you two anyway?"

Keeper blushed a little. "It's complicated."

Jade laughed. "Then simplify it for me."

"We're not adding a title to it."

"Why not?"

"That's what she wants, and I'm ok with that." Jade looked at him, skeptically. "At this point, Jade, do titles even matter?"

She looked over at David. Did titles really matter? "I see your point."

"He'll wake up Jade. He won't leave you in this hell hole alone."

Jade just nodded.

"I'll come back to check on him later."

"Thanks, Keeper."

"I always gotcha Jade."

Jade climbed into bed as soon as Keeper closed the door. She gave up on getting lost in someone else's pain. She needed the relief of unconsciousness. Sleep was the only thing that was guaranteed to give her some peace.

She was wrong.

**

The forest was burning.

Former prisoners were swarming out of the Black Deficit headquarters. They were all trampling over one another—trying to escape the burning building. They were immediately greeted by gunfire—smoking out mice. They panicked even more.

The Black Deficit members tried to fight back as best as they could, but they weren't prepared for the ambush that the DCs had in stored. Jade stood in the middle of it all—frozen. It all seemed unreal. The DCs was no longer trying to take prisoners. They wanted a massacre. They sought to kill everyone in sight. A small part of her couldn't help but feel that she was somehow responsible.

The screams were agonizing.

It pierced Jade's mind, and she couldn't get it out.

No one seemed to notice her, but she saw them.

The prisoners were terrified. The DC officers were menacing. The Black Deficit members were helpless. The scene was chaotic. The place was hell. Jade shut her eyes and covered her ears with her hands. She tried to block out everything. A terrifying scream of frustration escaped her.

Everything went silent.

Jade slowly opened her eyes. The scene made her sick. She was in the middle of the headquarters. Bodies were lying throughout the hallway. Burned. Bloody. Dead. Women. Men. Old. Young. It all was horrific. Tears streamed down Jade's face. This was all her fault. She knew it.

"Hello, my sweet Jade."

Jade turned to see him standing through an open-door way. His face was covered with blood, but Jade still recognized him. Bossman was smiling at her.

"I was hoping you would come."

Jade started slowly backing away, trying not to trip over a body. She had to get out of there.

"I can't get you out of my mind, Jade. I've been searching for you everywhere!" he walked towards her.

Jade took off running. Her heart was pounding. She couldn't catch her breath.

His hands snatched her back.

~28~

"**A**re you ok?"

Jade shot up out of bed. She looked around delirious. It took a while for her to realize where she was. The memory of her dream quickly faded, but she knew something was wrong.

Razor was in the doorway. "What's wrong?"

Jade looked around for a moment. "Bad dream."

"About?"

"I...can't...remember."

Razor stared at her for a moment—as if her body language would give him a clue. He finally gave up. "Come on down for breakfast. I wanna go over the plan for this evening."

"I slept the whole day?"

"Yeah, we just let you be."

Jade's head was hurting. She slept way too long. "Yeah, sure. Give me a minute."

"Oh," Jade's willingness to leave the room surprised Razor. "Ok, see you down there."

When he closed the door, Jade immediately sighed with relief. She wasn't quite sure why, but she was glad to be awake. Although she couldn't piece together her dream, she knew that was terrifying. Jade felt helpless. She never wanted to feel like that again. Jade did some stretches to try to clear her mind. She focused on her breathing.

Inhale.

Exhale.

Repeat.

After a few minutes, the fear left her. She checked on David. The same. Jade did the stretches that Keeper showed her on David. Then she leaned down and gave him a kiss.

"I love you," she left the door open as she walked out the room.

The sun was blinding. Jade had to squint to see when she walked downstairs. She felt like a vampire. She didn't realize that she kept her room so dark. It felt like forever since she saw the other parts of the house—besides the bathroom. She had closed herself off from everyone. She didn't realize how bad she was doing until now.

Everything felt new to her. She forgot how the house looked. She even wondered if they had new occupants in the house. Her wondering was quickly answered when she walked into the kitchen. The regular occupants were sitting around the kitchen tables. It took three tables to sit everyone. Jade took a seat at the end. Levi quickly sat on her lap. Raina took a spot next to her. She rested her head on Jade's shoulder. Jade gave them both a kiss. Sarah kept them away from her room. She didn't want them to see Jade, sad, and depressed. They both looked at Jade as their hero. Sarah wanted them to keep that image of her.

"Miss you Jade," Levi said.

"Miss you too little munchkin," she tickled him. He laughed. Raina laughed and joined in on tickling Levi.

Sarah sat a few bowls of oatmeal in front of them. "This is the last of it," she announced to everyone.

"We'll pick up some more food on the raid tonight," Razor said.

"Why did the time change again?" Jade asked. Yesterday felt like years ago.

"Because the damage we've been doing with our raids."

"And you just happened to stumble across the new schedules?"

"What are you getting at Jade?" Razor sounded annoyed.

"I dunno if that was by coincidence."

"A trap?" Helena asked.

"Bullshit."

"Why? Because I thought of it?"

"Come on, Jade."

"Razor, how often do DC officers have sweep schedules on them?"

He didn't say anything. Helena glanced over at him. They both were thinking the same thing. "Never," Helena admitted.

"It seems like a trap." For some reason, a flash of her standing in the middle of the forest came to Jade's mind. She shook it off.

"We're still going."

"Razor that's stupid."

"There's a small chance that it's a trap Jade, but we still need supplies and more people."

"But at what cost?"

"We're going!" he growled.

Levi and Raina jumped. They never saw an angry Razor before. Jade quickly gave them a kiss on the forehead—letting them know that everything was alright. The room was silent. There was no point of arguing with him any further. She had checked out. She couldn't come back, undermining his authority in front of everyone. But her gut was telling her that they shouldn't go. It all seemed wrong. Jade knew that wouldn't stop Razor though. His mind was made up—they were going.

Yoko cleared her throat. She quickly gave Jade a sorry look. "What time we leaving out?"

"Around 2. That'll give us enough time to get there, scout the area out, and set up before they arrive."

"Who's all staying behind?" Clay asked.

"We're leaving a few behind this time. I want to have as much manpower as we can."

Every part of her was screaming, that was a bad idea, but Jade was silent.

"Clay, Keeper, Tatianna, Danita, Rosalind, Reagan, and Calvin will stay behind with you, Jade."

Jade nodded and ate her oatmeal. Well, at least Calvin would be there to protect the kids if something went wrong. She tried hard to shake the feeling that something was going to go wrong. She had to trust Razor's judgment on this. Jade blocked out the rest of Razor's plan because it didn't concern her. Her primary focus was on David and the kids. That was all she could worry about at the moment. Helena was safe with Razor by her side. Jade just prayed that everyone else would be safe too.

"You ok?" Helena whispered. Jade didn't realize that she came over and sat next to her.

"Yeah, I'm fine," Jade finished off her oatmeal.

Razor concluded with his plan, and everyone dispersed. Jade lingered behind to play with Levi and Raina a little more. They both filled her in on what they've been up to. They were learning how to fight, and Lang was teaching them how to garden. Yoko had found some art supplies on one of the raids, so they've been painting too. They showed Jade some of their artwork. They made a couple of pictures for David.

"So, he will have something pretty to look at when he wakes up," Raina said.

Jade hugged her. "Thank you," she pulled Levi into their hug. "Thank you both."

"Time to clean your room," Sarah said.

"See you later, Jade."

Jade watched them leave before she got up. Sarah went to clean the dishes. "Thank you for breakfast."

Sarah turned around, a little surprised. "You're welcome."

Jade left out the kitchen and made her way back to her room. She wanted to check on David, and after that, she didn't know. A part of her didn't want to be alone in her room. Between her bad dream and her uneasiness with the raid, Jade was afraid of the dark hole her mind might lead her down.

David was the same when she walked into the room. She really didn't expect him to be awake. She left the bedroom door open. She was done closing herself off to everyone. Jade sat down in her usual spot and watched him sleep. She thought back to when she first met him. It felt like decades ago. He told her to run, and he never left her side since. She missed him. He was right there in front of her, but she was missing him.

It seemed to hit her for the first time, he could actually leave her. Jade never allowed herself to think about that until now. What would she do without him? Jade couldn't imagine it. If she was bad now, how would she be if he actually died? Before she knew it, tears were streaming down her face. He couldn't leave her, not now. It was a selfish thought, but she didn't care. She would be miserable without him.

"I'm sorry."

Jade turned to see Razor standing at the door. He noticed her crying. He paused before he came in. Jade wiped away her tears.

"I'm sorry I blew up at you."

"Don't be."

Razor sat down beside her. He looked over at David.

"I dreamed about Bossman," her dream came back to her.

"I know."

"That's why I'm questioning the raid."

"I know."

"But you're determined to not let that bother you."

"We're not ready for him."

"I dunno if we'll ever be ready for him."

"I hate when you're right."

"I know," Jade smiled a little. She loved that Razor admitted that aloud. Then Razor surprised Jade. He leaned over and kissed her on the forehead—like an older brother would do to a little sister.

"It'll be fine."

Jade looked at him a little shocked and then nodded. He got up and walked out of the room without saying anything else.

**

Jade didn't watch them off. She said her good-byes and wished for their safety before they left the house. She sat in her usual spot and just gazed off. She quickly got bored and started back reading her Sherman Alexie book.

Keeper stopped in as soon as she finished her book. David's condition remained the same. Keeper assured her that everything was fine and then he went to go on his watch. Shortly after, Tatianna stopped in to try to keep her company. Jade could quickly tell that Tatianna wasn't good with comforting people. She kept shifting uncomfortably in her seat. Jade started laughing at her. Tatianna was confused by Jade's reaction.

"Thank you, Tatianna," Jade laughed. "I know you're trying to keep me company, but I'm good, I promise."

"You sure? I don't want you going crazy in this room."

"I'm ok. I really do appreciate you trying."

"You're welcome," she got up. "Just let me know if you get bored."

"Will do."

Tatianna quickly walked out of the room. Jade guessed that she went to go keep watch. Tatianna was one who wanted in on all the action. She was determined not to be left on the sidelines. It seemed like that's what happens to the oppressed when they finally rise. You've spent so long feeling helpless and weak, when you eventually fight back it's exhilarating—freeing. Tatianna wanted all the action she could get. Jade couldn't blame her.

After a while, Jade started to nod off in her chair. She wasn't trying to, but her boredom was making her sleepy. Sleep terrified her. She tried hard to fight it, but there was nothing there to keep her entertained.

Jade found herself back in the woods again.

Alone.

Nothing but screams surrounded her.

It was agonizing. Painful. Terrifying. Jade couldn't take the screams. She had to do something. She ran around, trying to find the source. It was hard to pinpoint where they were coming from. Jade felt helpless. She wanted to help them—save them. She just needed to find them. Her chest was tightening. Her breathing was short.

Jade had to save them.

She needed to.

There was a small knock. "Hey, Jade."

Jade jumped up. Clay was standing at the door. He looked at her, confused. She looked around and saw that she was in her room. She sighed with relief. Her dreams were feeling so real that it was scary.

"Sorry, bad dream," she told him. "What's going on?"

"Nothing, everything's good," he walked in the room. "I'm just taking a break. I thought I would keep you company."

"Oh thanks," she gestured to the chair next to her.

Clay took a seat, and Jade sat down too. "Still no change from him, huh?"

Jade looked at David. "No. Still the same."

"I'm sorry."

"Yeah."

They sat in silence for a moment. Clay fiddled with his hands for a while. He occasionally glanced over at Jade. "We don't really talk much, do we?"

Jade smiled. "No, not really. I honestly don't know too much about you."

"What do you wanna know?"

"Are you a debtor?"

"No."

"But you were in prison."

"Me and my sister were helping debtors."

"Reagan?"

"Yeah, how'd you know?"

"Sarah mentioned it. She didn't know if it was true or not."

Clay nodded. "She's my little sister."

"What about your parents? Are they still alive?"

"Oh yeah. We come from a rich family."

Jade sat up. She never knew someone who came from a wealthy family. Life was very different for the rich. For them, life was normal—like nothing changed. The only thing out of the ordinary was the climate, and they were able to survive that. You could survive anything if you were in the black.

Surviving in the red was almost impossible.

"I bet you're wondering what it's like being rich, huh? Well, it's the same as before. Nice house. Food. A little boring, but stress-free."

"How do your parents feel about everything that's going on?"

"They're all for it."

"Seriously?" Jade shouldn't have been shocked, but she was.

"They believe it's natural selection at work. My dad said it was our way of getting rid of the weak. Only the strong can survive."

Well, that statement was hitting the nail on the head.

"How did you and Reagan get involved with the other side?"

"I never agreed with anything my parents said, especially my dad. As things started getting bad, I began to disagree with them more and more. Then one day I saw this lady," he paused for a moment—reflecting back on that day. "She was a debtor. She was trying to hide out in our neighborhood with her two kids. A few debtors did that. They were less likely to do sweeps in rich neighborhoods. But someone reported her. It was clear that she didn't belong there."

He stopped and stared off. Jade could see that he was fighting back the tears. She didn't say anything. She allowed him to collect his self. It was terrible, she knew it was.

"I remember her screams. It was terrifying. She knew that it was over for her. She knew it was over for her children. She tried fighting them, but it was four officers and one of her. They quickly overpowered her. I couldn't take it. Next thing I knew I was fighting them off, and Reagan was right beside me. Our parents came out to intervene. They convinced the officers not to arrest my sister and me. They did nothing for the woman and her children though, no matter how much we pleaded."

"I'm sorry."

"I later found out that it was my dad who reported the woman."

Jade was a little shocked by that news.

"I was so disgusted with him. I confronted him. It was the worst argument we ever had. After that, I just left. Reagan followed me. Later we got caught up in a sweep. We were trying to save as many debtors as we could, and we were fighting officers. But we got overpowered and taken in."

"What do they do to non-debtors in prison?"

"Offer them to be bounty hunters."

"...and you both declined it."

Clay nodded. "It wasn't bad for us there. Not like the debtors. They kept us in solitary."

"Was Reagan ever alone in there?" Jade knew what happened to pretty girls in prison.

"I made sure they kept us in the same cell. Reagan never left my sight."

Jade nodded. Reagan had the protection of her brother in the DC prison. Other girls weren't so lucky. "I'm so sorry you both had to go through that."

"I'm sorry for what you had to go through."

Jade smiled a little. "I guess we all went through something."

"We're all trying to do what's right. Naturally, we have to go through hell for it."

"That's true," Jade paused for a moment. She thought she heard screams. She listened harder.

There were screams.

Was she going crazy?

She shook her head. Jade could still hear them. She quickly began to hit the side of her head—as if she could beat them out. They were still there.

Clay gave her a confused look. "You ok?"

"I can hear screams in my head."

Clay frowned. "I hear them too."

~29~

The screams got louder.

Jade jumped up and looked out the window. A few people that stayed behind were outside—confusion on their face. They didn't know what was going on, either. Everything looked clear in the camp, so where were the screams coming from?

"Reagan, how's it going out there?" Clay radioed.

"Everything's fine here."

"Rosalind, how's your view?"

"There's no one in sight over here," she paused. "But it looks like there's smoke coming from the Black Deficit's Headquarters."

Jade jumped up. "We gotta go."

Clay nodded. "Reagan and Rosalind stay where you are. Keep a sharp eye out."

Jade grabbed her combat mask, knives, and her bow and arrow. She paused for a moment and looked at David one last time. "Let's go."

Clay followed Jade out of the room. They practically jumped down the stairs. Sarah met them at the bottom. Fear and confusion covered her face.

"What's going on?"

"Not sure," Jade looked around the house. "Clay and I are gonna check it out. Calvin!" Calvin stomped into the living room—Levi and Raina right on his heels. He didn't say anything. He just gave Jade a questioning look. "Protect the castle."

Calvin quickly scooped up Raina and Levi and trudged downstairs to the basement. "Protect the castle! Protect the castle!"

"Sarah, go down with them and don't come out until we say so."

Sarah nodded. "Be careful."

Jade and Clay walked outside. A few people were already at the porch waiting for instructions. They were afraid. It was written all over their faces.

"There's no immediate danger in sight, but I want you all to barricade yourselves indoors until we check it out." Everyone looked at each other. They were anxious. "It's ok," Jade tried to ease them. "Just go indoors for now. And let everyone else know."

"Stay indoors until we say otherwise," Clay said.

The crowd reluctantly dispersed. Keeper, Danita, and Tatianna came up as the group walked away. They were confused like everyone else, but they were ready to fight.

"What's going on?" Danita asked.

"Not sure," Jade briefly acknowledged that this was the first time she talked to Danita. "But Rosalind reported that there's fire coming from the Black Deficit's HQ."

"What?" there was fear and concern in Keeper's voice.

"We're gonna check it out and make sure there's no one heading this way."

"Let's do it," Tatianna said.

"Keeper, I need you to stay here."

"No way!"

"I know you're worried about them, but I need you to look after David."

"Have Sarah look after him," he snapped.

"There's no one here who has medical knowledge like you," Jade paused. She had to be compassionate but stern. "I know despite y'all differences, Jackson and Beverly are kind of like family to you, and I will make sure that they are safe. I swear. But I really need you here with David."

Jade never saw Keeper angry, but that's how he stood in front of her now. He was determined to go with them. The screams got louder and more frequent. Gunshots could be heard in the background. Jade's heart began to race.

"Please, Keeper."

"I still can't see anything," Rosalind reported. "But something is definitely going down at HQ."

"We're running out of time, Keeper."

"Fine!" he snapped. "Just hurry back."

"We will."

Tatianna went over to him and gave him a hug. Then she kissed him passionately. Jade pretended not to see.

"Let's go."

Keeper went into the house as they proceeded to leave the campgrounds. Clay radioed Reagan and Rosalind and told them that they were leaving out. They were to radio Clay if Razor and the rest of the group got back while they were still out. They were also to tell Razor what was going on so they can come as back up.

Jade's nightmare raced through her mind. This was Bossman. Every part of her body was telling her so. She was scared—terrified. All she could think about was the horrible things he was doing to those innocent people. He was looking for her. She knew that. And the people at HQ was paying the price for it.

What was her plan? She knew she couldn't defeat him. Not one on one anyway. She got lucky during their last encounter—very lucky. If it weren't for Razor intervening, she would've never made it out alive. But she had to try to save the people back at HQ. She couldn't just sit back and let them die. Jade would never forgive herself. If she had to sacrifice herself to let them live, then so be it. But sacrificing herself was the *only* thing she was prepared to do.

"What's the plan?" Tatianna asked before they broke through the woods.

"Draw the attack off without leading them here."

"You think it's the DC?" Danita asked.

"Who else can it be?" Tatianna said.

"I think it's the DC *and* Bossman." Everyone stopped in their tracks. "Just a gut feeling."

"What the hell do we do if it's Bossman?" it was the first time Jade saw Tatianna *truly* afraid.

"Nothing, he's looking for me."

"You can't take on Bossman alone," Danita said.

"And we can't lead him here," Jade pointed out. "You all focus on saving the people while I lead the DCs and Bossman away." They looked at one another—unsure. "I'll be ok," Jade reassured. "Besides we don't want someone from HQ accidentally stumbling into our camp with the

DC right on their trail."

"She's right," Clay finally said. "It's the best plan we got right now."

"Alright. Just don't die on us Jade," Tatianna warned. "Helena will kick my ass if I let something happen to you."

Jade smiled. "I'll try my best."

**

They were very quiet and stealth once they entered the woods. They didn't want anyone to know that they were there. They listened intently and followed the screams and the gunshots. Jade thought that the chaos would've died down by now, but it was just as loud and chaotic as when it started. She was not looking forward to facing Bossman. Their encounter was bound to happen again, but she wasn't ready for it. She could never be prepared. It can only be over once one of them died, and Jade wasn't ready to die.

Who is?

But people were dying right now. And it was all because of her. Once again, she found a way for other people to pay for her actions. Jade quickly pushed aside her blame and guilt trip and focused on what needed to be done. Warrior Jade was required. Warrior Jade had been sitting on the sideline's way too long now.

The whole ordeal with David forced her to sit out. She could no longer do that. Jade was preparing to take out as many DC officers as she needed to. That's what life was now. A tit for tat game. You kill my people, and I, in return, kill yours. Jade slid on her mask. Warrior Jade instantly took over. It was irrational thinking that there were two versions of herself, but that's what she felt. It was the best way she could explain it really. Plus, having a different side of her helped to cope with the people she'd killed so far.

The screams were closer now.

To Jade, it sounded like they were about 50 feet away. Jade stopped behind a fallen tree trunk, and she motioned for everyone else to do the same.

"Ok, here's the plan," she whispered. "Once we've killed as many officers as we can, you three lead the survivors back to camp. Take them the long way in case some officers trail you. I'll keep the other officers and Bossman focused on me by heading in the opposite direction."

"What do we do once we get back to camp?" Tatianna asked.

"Hide the prisoners and then come back for me," Jade's voice cracked a little. "Please come back for me."

"Trust me, Jade, we will," Clay said.

"Thank you."

They quickly heard someone running in their direction. They all hid further behind the tree trunk. It sounded like it was a few people. Cries and heavy breathing were heard. Then there was a heavy thud as if someone fell over. Other footsteps kept going.

"Oh, no, no, no! Oh, God, no! Someone, please, help!"

Jade peered over and saw a young man on the ground. A DC officer towered over him with a rifle pointed in his face. Jade threw her knife, and it landed in the officer's neck—right where she intended it to go. A couple more DC officers were further away. Once they saw the officer fall, they began to sprint toward them. Jade and the rest jumped out of their hiding place and greeted them.

They quickly cut through the few DC officers with ease. It appeared that no more officers were close by. Jade helped the young man off the ground once they were clear. It was Paul from Vicky's crew.

"Thank you," he said.

"Paul, what's going on?"

"It's Bossman," he wept. "He's here. They're killing everyone on sight."

"And the fire?" Tatianna asked.

Tears started to fall from his face. "They set HQ on fire. That's how they lured us out of the building."

Jade looked away, ashamed. Her dreams were so vivid that sometimes it felt like they predicted the future. It's absurd, she knew that, but she couldn't help to think that her dream made this into a reality. She looked at Paul. He looked defeated. He's been through hell, that was clear.

"Where's the members and the rest of Vicky's crew?"

"Most of the members are dead," he said. "They weren't prepared at all. It was all an ambush. I got separated from Vicky and the rest of the crew...I hope they're ok."

"And Jackson and Beverly?" Jade had to know. She wanted to keep her promise to Keeper.

"I'm not exactly sure. The last time I saw them, they were chasing after Bossman."

Jade nodded. She needed to find them. "Hide here. Stay hidden until we come back for you."

Paul nodded. Clay helped him find a decent place to hide. Paul was very grateful, and he thanked them one last time before they left.

They continued in the direction of the screams and gunshots. It was starting to die down a little. Fear crept through Jade's body. If the chaos were close to an end, then that meant almost everyone was dead. She couldn't let that happen. She was so tempted to bust out running, but a surprise attack was their best shot of making it out alive. Jade just needed to focus. Focus on her steps. Focus on her breathing. Focus on her movement. Focus on the mission.

They went about a mile before they heard someone else. Again, they hid behind a few trees and waited for them to get closer. It was some DC officers. They were looking for prisoners. They were very stealth—waiting for someone to come out. Jade took out her bow and arrow. It was better to take them out from afar, in case there was another group of officers nearby.

Jade caught Clay's eye and pointed up the tree. He understood what she was about to do and nodded. She climbed up the tree—quietly. It took her no time to get into position. She couldn't be seen. Jade drew back her bow and arrow. She focused in on an officer. Took a deep breath. Released.

The arrow went right into the officer's chest. He quickly dropped to the ground. The other officers began to look around frantically—trying to find the source of the arrow. They couldn't pinpoint it. Jade took advantage of their confusion and drew another arrow back. Deep breath. Released. The second arrow hit another officer—killing him instantly. The officers panicked even more. They immediately dropped to the ground. A few hid behind trees and bushes for cover. Jade managed to take a few more of them out—killing them all instantly.

"Where is it coming from?!" an officer yelled out in frustration. Jade answered the question with an arrow.

The officers were aware that this wasn't a prisoner or a member. They were able to wipe them out with ease. It could only be narrowed down to a few people. Jade was among them. The officers remained still—too afraid to move.

It was time to announce herself. Jade pulled out her knife. She contemplated on who her next victim would be. An officer began slowly crawling. He inched forward and forward. She noticed that he was getting closer to Tatianna's hiding spot. Tatianna couldn't see him so he would take her by surprise. Jade found her next victim.

The officers began to feel at ease due to the abrupt stop of arrows. Some of them slowly got up. Jade couldn't let the one by Tatianna stand up. She focused. She took a deep breath.

Aimed.

Released.

"It's her!" one of the officers yelled once her knife made its mark.

"She's around here somewhere!"

"Alert Bossman!"

Jade's knife quickly struck the officer who tried to run off with the news. Clay and Danita emerged from their hiding spots and began to attack. Tatianna emerged from her place and quickly met the two officers that were nearby. Jade jumped down from the tree. Once they saw her, the DC officers flocked toward her.

She quickly took a lot of them out with her bow and arrow. Some with her remaining knives. When she was down to her last knife, she met the other officers head-on. Jade took a few severe blows to get close to them. Once she was there, she swiftly took them out. Leaving most of them surprised and confused with what just happened.

It seemed like sitting out made her more vicious. It was exciting and liberating. That was a terrible thing to feel, but she felt it. They deserved it. They just killed innocent people. Why shouldn't she take out a few of them for that? The scene they left behind was sure to be horrifying. The officers should pay for that.

Before she knew it, all the officers were lying lifelessly on the ground. She breathed heavily behind her mask. There was blood on her face, she could feel the warmth of it. Jade ignored it and went to collect her arrows and knives. Tatianna, Clay, and Danita picked the dead officers clean of their weapons. Jade took some of their knives.

"We should keep moving," Clay said.

They heard more screams. This time it was really close. They all moved in the direction of the screams. They were getting close. About half a mile.

"Jade and I should go up," Danita suggested once they were close. "Clay and Tatianna should stay on the ground."

"We can pick the officers from afar while you two get the others to safety," Jade agreed.

"Sounds good," Clay and Tatianna hid while Jade and Danita climbed up the trees.

Jade got into position—an arrow on her bow. Danita checked the ammo for the rifle she stolen. She propped the gun on a branch. Tatianna and Clay positioned themselves behind a nearby bush.

The people were close. They were going to run right into them. It sounded like there was a group of them. They were in terror—that much was sure.

Danita looked through the rifle's scope. "There's a huge group of women and men heading this way. Looks like a mixture of prisoners and members," she whispered.

"What about DC officers?" Jade asked.

Danita continued to look for a moment. A few seconds went by before she answered Jade. "They're trailing behind."

A few more seconds went by. The screaming got closer and closer. Jade was getting antsy. Danita had a better view than she did.

"Follow my lead, Jade."

Jade pulled her bow and arrow back. "Just tell me where to aim."

"Give it a few seconds."

Jade couldn't take the screams anymore. It was pure agony to her. Her adrenaline was pumping. She was ready to save them all and get it over with. She slowed her breathing down. There was no reason for her to get all worked up before she faced Bossman. She was just ready to take out as many officers as she could.

Suddenly the group of prisoners, Vicky, her crew, and members came into Jade's view. Following behind was a big group of DC officers. Danita fired off the first shot—hitting an officer dead-center in the head. She continued to fire off more shots, taking out as many officers as she could. Jade didn't start releasing her arrows until they got closer into view. She hit about three officers with her arrows before they all started to take cover. They were struggling to see where the shots were coming from.

As soon as the prisoners and members ran pass the bush, Tatianna and Clay greeted the officers who were chasing right behind them. Once they saw Tatianna and Clay, a few other officers came from out of hiding. Danita and Jade continued their shooting. The prisoners and members stopped running once they saw Tatianna and Clay. A couple of the members and Vicky and her crew attempted to help them.

Jade jumped down from her hiding spot once she shot off her last arrow. There was a moment of confusion. She swore she heard cheers from the prisoners. Her presence made some more of the members willing to fight. Jade didn't have to do too much fighting once she was on the ground. With more people helping, they were able to overpower the DC officers swiftly and with ease.

The officers laid scattered lifelessly on the ground. Danita eventually left from her spot in the tree. They all began picking the officers clean of their weapons. Jade took as many knives as she could carry. Danita loaded up on ammo. Clay and Tatianna divided up the handguns, tasers, batons, and pepper spray among those who were able to fight.

"Glad to see you, Jade," Vicky greeted.

"Where's Beverly and Jackson?"

"They were right behind us."

"I think they got cut off," one of the members said.

"What you mean?"

"I think Bossman and a bounty hunter got to them."

"How far back was that?"

"Maybe half a mile."

"Is there any more back at HQ?"

The member hung his head. "No, this is it."

"Alright," Jade turned her attention to Danita, Tatianna, and Clay. "You three take them back to camp. Make sure to get Paul along the way. I'm gonna try to get Beverly and Jackson."

"Jade," Danita interjected.

"We gotta stick to the plan if we're gonna make it out of this."

"I know," Danita held up a rifle. "I was gonna suggest you take this."

Jade was impressed with Danita's suggestion, but she never really shot a rifle before. She wasn't sure how helpful it would be to her.

"It's kind of similar to shooting your bow and arrow."

"Yeah, but I'm just now getting good with that."

"You'll do fine. Plus, you can spot where they are from afar. It'll keep you from wandering aimlessly around on the ground."

Danita had an excellent point. The rifle would keep her from going in blind—that was something Jade definitely didn't want to do. Danita quickly went over how to properly handle the rifle. She showed Jade some techniques that might help her hit her targets better. Lastly, she gave Jade some ammo for the gun. Jade was well prepared—between her rifle, bow, and arrow, and her many knives, Jade could fight Bossman from afar before getting close to him.

"Good luck," Danita finally said.

"Be safe," Clay followed.

"And don't die!" Tatianna warned.

Jade smiled. "Thanks, I'll make sure not to." Jade glanced around one last time. "You all should get going. Stay alert out there."

"We will."

Jade watched them off. She waited until they were out of her eyesight before she came up with her plan. There was no telling where Beverly and Jackson could be. She wasn't sure what Bossman was doing to them. She just hoped that they weren't dead. The member said they got separated from the group about a half-mile back. That seemed like a good place to start.

It was quiet in the woods. The chaos was over. People were dead. There were only a few survivors. Jade was heartbroken. She couldn't save them all. She wasn't even able to save half of them. She was determined to rescue Jackson and Beverly. They couldn't die—for Keeper's sake.

Jade wondered how she should go about looking for them. A higher view seemed like a good idea. She quickly climbed a tree. It was the tallest one she could find. When she was younger, she was terrible at climbing trees. Once everything went to hell, she got great at climbing them. High ground became a great escape when you were trying to hide from looters.

Jade managed to get to the highest branch. She slowly and carefully positioned the rifle. She mimicked Danita. Jade was glad that she paid close attention to her; otherwise, it would've been hard. She was able to get into a good position, and then she looked into the scope. It was all clear ahead of her. Jade slowly moved to her right. It was all clear there too. She then proceeded to her left. It was clear—at first. She was just about ready to reposition herself to look behind her when she saw Jackson running into her view. Beverly shortly followed.

They were surrounded by DC officers and Vincent. Jade immediately got annoyed. She was hoping that he wouldn't have been there, but that was unlikely. Bossman wasn't there, but Jade knew he was nearby.

Jade gathered all her things and slowly climbed down. She started moving in their direction. She was quiet and stealth. She needed to get closer. There was no way that she could shoot at them from there. Her shooting wasn't that good, and she wasn't going to risk giving her position away too soon. She wanted to get close enough where she could hear them.

It was dead silent for a while—nothing but her heavy breathing. Her asthma wasn't bothering her, she was just afraid. Afraid of how things were going to play out. Afraid of getting caught. Afraid of dying a torturous death.

The silence was starting to alarm her when she heard Beverly scream. She began to move faster but made each step deliberate. She was close enough. Now she needed to find a tree to climb. She found one that was high and had enough coverage. Jade quickly climbed. Her first plan of action was taking out as many officers as she could. That should even out the playing field a bit. Plus, she knew the sudden reign of bullets was sure to draw out Bossman.

Jackson and Beverly could be heard fighting when she positioned herself. Jade made sure that she was secure and well hidden. She looked through the rifle's scope again. Jackson and Beverly were getting overrun. They couldn't fight them off for long. Jade loaded the rifle with ammo and found her target. It was a DC officer who Beverly had difficulty fighting off. Jade took a deep breath. She had to calm her nerves and focus. She locked in on the officer. She held her breath.

Aimed.

Fired.

The bullet made it to the officer's neck—not what she was aiming for, but it did the trick. Blood was squirting out of him. Beverly took advantage of the distraction to finish him off. The other officers paused for a moment. They thought it was a friendly fire.

Jade took advantage of their moment of confusion and took out another officer. This time she got the officer dead center in the head. Jackson and Beverly quickly realized that the shooter was on their side. They began to fight off the officers more confidently. Jade continued to take out more officers—mostly those who were running to join in on the action.

The brother and sister duo were able to fight off the other officers with ease. Jade occasionally took out a few officers that were giving them a hard time. Some of the officers took cover and stayed there—including Vincent. Jade was hoping that he would come out of his hiding spot soon. There was still no sign of Bossman, but Jade had a feeling that he was lingering close by.

She took out a few more officers.

"Find that fucking shooter!" Vincent yelled from behind a tree.

Jade turned her attention to him. His shoulder was in her view. She locked in on it and shot. He screamed out in pain. Jade laughed a little. "Bitch," she mumbled. She stared at him through her scope.

The feeling of hatred ran through her veins. Vincent had to pay for what he did to Helena. He needed to suffer. Jade ignored the other officers. Beverly and Jackson were doing fine on their own. She was getting low on ammo, but there was another bullet with Vincent's name on it.

The guy that she was looking at was no longer the guy she knew. So, she felt no guilt when the thought of killing him entered her brain. Warrior Jade was in full effect. She waited. He had to come out sometime.

Vincent stood there, attending to his wound and shouting obscenities to the officers that were around him. Even from in a tree, Jade could tell that he was annoying them. He ended up arguing with an officer he was sharing a hiding spot with. The officer, now fed up, pushed Vincent out in the open.

Jade had her shot, but another thought entered her mind. Death was too generous for him right now. With what he did to Helena and the people he just helped killed, Jade really wanted him to suffer. She aimed the rifle at his knee—his right one since that was his dominant side. She fired. Vincent dropped to the ground screaming and crying.

Jade continued picking off the remaining officers until she ran out of ammo. After that, she moved on to her arrows. It seemed never-ending. The more they killed. The more officers that came to aid. But they were making a dent in the numbers. Jade could see that. They were slowly, but surely dwindling down.

The officers remained confused. They thought that they had killed just about everybody—Jackson and Beverly being their only exception. Jade's attack was catching them by surprise, which was working in her favor. She was down to her last arrow. The mystery was about to end. Everyone knew that knives were Jade's weapon of choice. It was a sure way to identify her.

Sadly, the only weapon she had left were her knives. Jade now had plenty of them. She could still take out a good amount of them from her position in the tree, but they would be able to zero in on her a little more. She sighed. She released her last arrow. It struck and killed an officer.

Jade then went for her knife.

"It's her!" one of them yelled out once her knife hit an officer. "It's Jade!"

"Alert Bossman!"

"Jade," Beverly whispered. "She came for us."

Jade struck another officer who went running away.

"Find that bitch!" Vincent cried out. "Find her and kill her!"

"She's for Bossman!" another officer spat.

"I don't give a fuck! Kill her!"

Jade responded with a knife going into his left leg. Vincent cried out in pain again. He doubled over on his side. He was breathing heavily—trying to endure the pain. Some of the DC officers started coming out of their hiding spots. They all stepped over him carelessly. They were trying to close in on Jackson and Beverly.

Jade focused her attention on them. She tried to take out as many as she could. Unfortunately, she was only able to injure some of the officers. Jackson and Beverly were able to take them out, but the officers were still able to back them into a corner. The DC officers knew that she was there for them, and they wanted to draw her out.

Jackson and Beverly kept fighting. Jade kept throwing her knives. She was getting low on her spare knives. She had to come down soon. There were two extra knives left. She had to make them count. Jade scanned for her next victim.

Then he spoke.

~30~

"**M**y sweet Jade," the officers stopped moving. Jackson and Beverly did too. "I was waiting for you."

Jade searched around the area. Where was he? Her heart was racing. She knew he was close by, probably watching from afar. He finally decided to step in.

It was silent—only Vincent's groans could be heard.

"Why don't you come out, my love?" Bossman finally stepped into view. There was no telling how long he had been hiding out and watching.

So many emotions ran through Jade. Fear. Anger. Nervousness. Determination. Revenge. She stayed in her position, watching him. Bossman casually walked over to where the other DC officers were. He stepped over Vincent—not acknowledging him. He stood there directly in between Vincent and the DC officers.

"Come on now, Jade!" he was getting irritated. "We don't have all day."

Jade took a chance. She launched a knife his way. He anticipated that. He casually moved out of the way. Unfortunately for Vincent, he caught the knife in his arm. He again wept out in pain. Bossman laughed and shook his head.

"You're getting a little predictable Jade."

Jade needed to come up with an escape plan. She didn't have a chance to make one until now. She picked up the rifle and looked through the scope. She scanned the surrounding area—making sure there wasn't an ambush waiting for them. Everything seemed clear.

The camp was east. She didn't want to lead them there. Her best bet was to go north, back toward HQ. She figured they could lose them that way. There were 15 DC officers left. Plus, Bossman. Vincent was useless at this point. Jade wouldn't be surprised if they left him for dead. If they were able to just take out half of the officers, they would be ok. Jade had her escape plan. Now it was time to execute.

"Jade!" Bossman's patience was now an end. He took out a gun and pointed it toward Jackson and Beverly. "Come out now, or they're dead!"

Jade closed her eyes and said a silent prayer. She prayed that God would be on their side.

"5...4...3..."

"Ok," Jade said. "I'm coming out."

Bossman smiled. "That's my girl."

She gathered up her knives, the rifle, and her bow. Jade climbed down the tree—the backside so she couldn't be seen. She quickly hid the bow and rifle.

Jade stepped out into view with her hands up.

Bossman lowered his gun. He smiled harder. He was genuinely happy to see her. He looked around at the scene. It seemed like the first time he actually took it all in. About 50 dead DC officers were lying about. He laughed and shook his head.

"I must say, Jade, you never cease to amaze me," he looked over at her still smiling. "I mean truly remarkable!"

"Well I try," Jade walked over to Jackson and Beverly. She stood right in between them.

"How does it feel, Jade? Going from one to countless bodies?"

Jade looked at the dead officers lying on the ground. They weren't innocent, but they were human beings, and she took their lives. She quickly reflected on the many innocent lives they took. Anger quickly rose within her.

"Many lives were taken here today, but don't be disappointed," Bossman smiled as he watched Jade conflicted with emotions. "Your so-called righteousness is what's keeping this health industry going."

"...fuck you."

"Jade, don't beat yourself up about it," he laughed. "It's the way of the world. Will it surprise you if I said I couldn't stop thinking about you?"

"Not at all," Jade admitted. "You've been on my mind too."

"Well, that just makes my day. I suppose my friend Razor isn't here."

"No, he's tied up elsewhere."

"I see," he laughed. "Not as smart as he seems. Did you see it, Jade? I was hoping you would see it."

"I did."

"And yet he didn't heed your warning."

"He didn't."

"I wonder who actually made the right call."

"I would say he did. Since I'm here and he isn't."

"Interesting way of looking at it my lovely Jade."

"Kill her already!" Vincent screamed.

Bossman turned toward him. Everyone's attention darted over to Vincent. Jade almost forgot about him. Her focus had mainly been on Bossman since he made his presence known. Bossman walked closer to Vincent. He examined him for a moment. Jade took advantage of the distraction.

"We're heading back toward HQ," Jade whispered. Jackson and Beverly nodded. Jade turned her attention over to Bossman. He was bending down, looking over Vincent's wounds. He stuck his finger into Vincent's shoulder. Vincent let out an agonizing scream.

"Watch for my signal," Jade advised them. She quickly looked around to make sure no one heard her over Vincent's screams.

No one did.

Bossman stood back up. He looked down at Vincent with anger and disgust. He gave him a good kick to the stomach. "Shut it! What good are you?!"

Vincent started coughing for air. Bossman walked away from him without looking back. He turned his attention back to Jade.

"Why not Vincent? What makes him so special?"

Jade looked over at Vincent. "Death is too merciful for him at the moment."

"So vengeful. A lot of people died here today because of you, Jade."

Jade tried not to let her voice crack. "And they will be avenged."

"So will my officers."

Jade nodded. She quickly went for the first officer closest to her. She slashed his throat and went on to the next one. Jackson and Beverly followed suit. They were fighting DC officers left and right. Bossman just stood there—never taking his eyes off Jade.

"Move," Jade shouted.

All three of them began running back in the direction of HQ. The remaining DC officers followed. Bossman lagged. Jade counted about seven DC officers. If they could get rid of them in the woods and lose Bossman through HQ, they would be alright. She had to be realistic with herself, there was no way Bossman was dying today. Even with three against one, he had a better shot of making it out alive than they did. She just needed to escape him again.

Jade looked over and saw Jackson fighting off another DC officer. There were six now. Beverly was trying to outrun an officer that was on her tail. She ended up tripping over a branch. The officer was about to attack her when Jade tackled him.

The officer pinned Jade down quickly. He began choking her. Beverly got up and was making her way over when a gun went off. Everyone paused. Blood started dripping onto Jade's face. It took her a moment to realize it wasn't from her. The officer's grip loosened from her throat. He slowly slumped over. Jade pushed him off her. She and Beverly took cover behind a tree.

"You ok?" Jade asked Beverly.

Beverly frantically looked around. "Yeah, you?"

"I'm good," Jade looked around. No one was in sight. "Jackson?!"

"I'm ok," he said from afar.

"You see what I do for you, Jade," Bossman said.

Jade sighed.

How were they going to get out of this? She was afraid to leave out of their hiding spot. She wasn't sure if Bossman was going to turn his gun on them. Jade closed her eyes and focused on her breathing. She had to stay calm. Stay focused. They needed to take out the rest of the DC officer's and lose Bossman.

Kill officers.

Lose Bossman.

Kill officers.

Lose Bossman.

Jade kept repeating the plan over and over in her head. She was working up the courage to take off running and keep fighting. She had to bring Jackson and Beverly back to Keeper. He had done so much for her. He was always there for her when she needed him. This was the least she could do in return.

"You ok Jade?" Beverly whispered.

"Long day," Jade looked over at Beverly and saw that she was crying. "We're gonna be ok."

"You know the standard protocol is for every corpse to leave out in a body bag," Bossman contradicted her. Could he hear them? "You're not leaving here alive, Jade."

"Just let Jackson and Beverly go."

"Can't do that. They orchestrated the prison break out."

"That was all me."

"A killer and a liar? Where's your virtue, Jade?"

Jade sighed. Beverly wept silently. Jade tried to fight off the feeling of annoyance. It was hard for her to focus and work up the courage to do what needed to be done with Beverly having a break down next to her.

"I still have the scars, Jade," Bossman said. "From our last little encounter. Not a day goes by when I don't look at them. Love scars are what I call them."

There was a whistle.

Jade looked around. She thought she was hallucinating at first, but she heard it again. Bossman appeared not to notice. Jade focused on a bush that was 20 feet ahead of her. Someone waved at her.

It was Razor.

"Now that's just fucking weird," she wanted to keep him distracted while Razor did whatever he had planned.

"You intrigue me, Jade. No one has ever done that before."

"Or maybe they never lived long enough to have the chance to."

Bossman laughed. "Oh Jade, it's gonna hurt me to kill you. Would you believe me if I said I've fallen for you?"

"...well, it has been rumored that you were crazy."

Bossman laughed again. This time a little harder and a little louder. Jade was baffled. He was genuinely laughing at her joke. What was going on? The whole encounter was confusing to her. He liked to chat her up before he tried to kill her. Did he usually do that?

"So, if you were really in love with me," she said. "Why kill me?

"Because you've been made a symbol. A rebel's hero. That's a very treacherous thing during this time."

Jade thought about the number of people who died that day. They all believed in her. She hung her head. "I'm no hero."

"That you are not," Jade could hear Bossman walking. "But you are a killer. A remarkable one at that. I didn't realize it until I sat back and watched you work."

"You've made me that way. You and the stupid government who put this crazy law in place."

"The world is ending Jade. Only the strong can survive."

Jade took a deep breath. Bossman was close. Probably 10 feet away. She pulled out a knife and gripped it tightly. He was more than likely going to shoot. She had to prepare to take a bullet. All she needed to do was lunge the knife in his chest, and Razor could do the rest. Jade crouched down and closed her eyes.

One...

Two...

"You're absolutely right," Jade quickly launched out from the tree.

There was a gunshot. A searing pain ran through Jade's left shoulder. She almost fell back, but she continued to push forward.

Another shot went off.

A bullet whizzed by her head.

Jade plunged the knife into Bossman. Unfortunately, he moved at the last second, so she got just below his collar bone. He let out a groan. They both fell to the ground.

Razor and the others jumped out of their hiding spots. Jade breathed deeply. She was trying to fight off the pain. Fighting ensued around her. Jade continued to lay on the ground. So, did Bossman.

"Jade!" Jackson yelled. He ran over to her. "Are you ok?"

"I got her," Clay came and scooped her up. He pushed Jackson forward. "Move! Move!"

Bossman was still on the ground. He finally moved a little. "Jade?"

Clay and the others ran faster. They were almost out of his eyesight.

"Jade?!" Bossman struggled to get to his feet. She heard him moan out of pain. He locked eyes on her. He came to the realization that she was getting away. "Jade!!!"

There was pure anger in his voice. He yelled and cursed at the few officers that remained. He quickly grabbed his gun and shot them all. He let out an angry scream.

They all kept running. Losing Bossman along the way.

~31~

Helena and Keeper were standing on the porch waiting for their arrival. Jade kept suppressing a scream. Her arm was in excruciating pain. Every little step, or bump, Clay made threatened to make Jade pass out. She didn't even realize that she was also bleeding from her head. The second bullet had grazed her. Being hopped up on adrenaline, she didn't even notice it until they were almost back at camp. She freaked out. Razor had to calm her down and assure her that it wasn't fatal.

Everything was beginning to hit her. The loss of so many innocent lives. The many men she just killed. The encounter with Bossman—again. She managed to escape him—again. The intense feeling of fire flowing through her arm made her focus on all the bad.

"Is everyone ok?!" Helena shouted from the porch. She was holding back tears.

"Jade took a bullet," Razor said.

"Jade!" tears were flowing from Helena now. "Jade!"

"I'm ok, Helena," Jade managed to get out. She was clenching her teeth at that point. Helena ran off the porch, and so did Keeper. They both rushed over to her.

"Be careful touching her," Clay warned. "She's in a lot of pain."

Helena took one look at Jade and began to break down. Razor consoled her and told her that it wasn't as bad as it looks. Helena didn't believe it. Jade didn't want to cause a commotion outside. Everyone was already on edge. They all knew what happened at HQ. She didn't want them to think that it was about to happen there.

"I'm fine, Helena, really." Jade could barely get the words out.

"Let's get her inside," Keeper said.

"The kids," Jade didn't want them to see her like that.

"Yoko and Sarah are keeping them in the basement with Calvin until otherwise."

Clay slowly walked up the steps. The pain wasn't as severe as Jade anticipated, but it was painful, nonetheless. She took deep breaths, trying to focus on something else. Anything else other than the burning pain. Clay sat Jade down on the living room couch. Keeper ran around gathering up things to attend to the wound. Jackson and Beverly slowly walked in—their mind elsewhere. The realization of everything that happened finally hit them too.

"I'm gonna check on Reagan and Rosalind," Clay announced.

"Thanks," Jade managed to say.

Helena sat next to Jade. Razor stood behind her. Jade closed her eyes and leaned back. She just needed to breathe. If she focused on her breathing, the pain would eventually subside.

Inhale.

Exhale.

Inhale.

Exhale.

Repeat.

It was working. The pain wasn't as severe as it was before. Jade wasn't sure if her trick was really working or if it was all psychological. She was leaning more towards the latter, but whatever got her through it, she was all for.

"How you feeling Jade?" Helena worried.

"Been better."

Keeper came rushing back into the room with some tweezers, a needle, thread, a little bottle of vodka, and a bedsheet. He ran over to Jade. She sat up a little. Razor had to help her.

"Don't worry Jade," Keeper smiled a little. "As always, I gotcha."

Jade nodded.

He looked up at her and whispered. "Thanks." Keeper helped Jade take her left arm out of her shirt. He examined her shoulder. "The bullet didn't go all the way through. I'll need to remove it. Luckily, it's not that deep," he reached over and grabbed the tweezers.

"David?"

"The same. Danita's up there keeping an eye on him." Keeper poured a little of the vodka on the tweezers. He shook it dry and looked at Jade. "This is gonna hurt."

Jade took a few deep breaths. She had to prepare herself for the pain. Keeper waited patiently. She counted to 10. "Ok."

It took everything in her not to scream. She didn't want to scare Raina and Levi. Calvin's response concerned her too. Plus, she knew terrified debtors were standing just outside awaiting news. Jade bit down on her lip—so hard that blood was oozing into her mouth.

Razor offered his hand for some form of comfort. She immediately gripped it tightly. Razor tensed a little. Jade tried to think of anything besides the pain. It felt like Keeper was digging around forever. He said it wasn't that deep, but it was deep enough for her.

"Almost got it," he said.

Jade squeezed Razor's hand tighter.

"You're doing good Jade," Razor winced.

She loosened her grip a little. She finally felt it—the tweezer making contact with the bullet. Keeper pulled it out and poured Jade's shoulder with vodka so quickly that it took a moment for Jade to register it. She was so shocked by the sudden pain that a scream escaped her. Helena jumped a little.

"I'm sorry," Keeper said. "It was best not to warn ya." He began to sterilize the needle. "Ya gonna need stitches for ya shoulder and ya head."

Jade nodded. She was preparing herself for a new type of pain. Keeper quickly threaded the needle and began stitching Jade's shoulder. He didn't give Jade any warning, but she was prepared for it. She really needed a distraction.

"I'm sorry," Razor said.

"What for?" she gritted.

"I should've listened to you. You were right. It was all a trap."

"Was there an ambush of DC officers?"

"No. No one. Just a note."

"Saying?" it was hard for Jade to catch her breath. Razor didn't say anything.

Helena finally spoke up. "Gotcha."

Jade managed to look over at Razor. He wore a look of disappointment. She understood how he was feeling. Bossman tricked him. It appeared that Razor didn't know him like he thought he did.

"What made you come back to camp?"

"The note was on a map with the location of HQ circled," Razor paused for a minute. "I realized what it meant, and we came rushing back. Rosalind informed me what happened when we arrived. I was just about to head out to look for you when Clay and the others came back. He told us your plan, so we regrouped and went out looking for you."

"Remind me to thank Clay again," she glanced over at Jackson and Beverly. They were sitting on the small couch across from her—deep in thought. Razor followed her gaze. He immediately knew what she was thinking.

"What happened?"

"We were in the briefing room," Jackson said. "When the smoke alarms started going off."

"I don't know how it happened," Beverly was distraught. "There was so much smoke. People were trampling over one another trying to get out. The screams..." Beverly stared off.

"It was a nightmare," Jackson saw that his sister wasn't going to complete her sentence.

"Where was your lookout?" Helena asked.

"You knew we left, didn't you?" there was a little guilt in Razor's voice.

"We knew you all were gone. Our lookout, which was only a couple of members, were dead before they could even sound the alarm."

Keeper stopped attending to Jade's arm. Those members were his friends—family. They were dead now. Their death was more than likely painful. He felt guilty. So did Jade.

Razor shook his head and sighed. "Why didn't you have more lookouts?"

"We thought we were safe. No one knew the location of our

headquarters beside you."

"If I could figure it out then so could Bossman. It was only a matter of time."

"They locked us in," Beverly rejoined the conversation. She was completely out of it—broken. "The place was on fire, and we couldn't get out. We managed to break out a window, but everyone couldn't get out in time...the screams...." She broke out crying hysterically. Jackson comforted his sister.

Keeper quickly snapped the thread and tied the end of it. Jade winced a little. He went to sterilize the needle again. He threaded it and cleaned the gash on the side of Jade's head with the vodka. Jade barely flinched. She didn't say anything—to any of them. They were all thinking about the horrible deaths of all those people.

Jackson, Beverly, and Keeper were a lot closer to them than she was, but Jade felt their pain. Despite her differences with the leaders, everyone was kind and caring to her. They didn't deserve to die the way they did.

"As soon as we stepped outside there were gunshots," Jackson resumed. "We barely had any weapons, so we ran. People were getting shot left and right. We didn't have any kind of evacuation plan."

Beverly wiped away her tears and cleared her throat. "We fought off a few officers and were able to take their weapons."

"We were finally able to fight back, but we lost a significant amount of people."

"It was all hopeless at that point. The gunshots. The screams. The terror. We were just running, trying to survive."

Jade glanced over at Razor. "I think this all might've been our fault."

"How so?"

"The raids," Jade couldn't believe it wasn't apparent to him. Or maybe Razor just didn't want to admit it. "Bossman was gonna respond to them at some point. We should've had a plan for it. Or at least alerted them on what we were doing."

"It's our fault," Beverly admitted. "We were just so stubborn. We didn't want to take any advice from anyone. Let alone you and Razor."

"She's right," Jackson chimed in. "It was our arrogance that got everyone killed."

"Let's just agree that we're all to blame here," Razor admitted. No one disagreed with him. The room was filled with guilt.

Keeper was done stitching up Jade. He fashioned the bedsheet into a sling and put Jade's arm in it. Jade sighed and leaned back. She was finally able to relax a little.

"Thank you, Keeper."

He didn't say anything. He cleaned up the area and wiped everything down.

Helena got up to alert Yoko and Sarah that everything was ok. Tatianna went over to comfort Keeper. The day was filled with anguish and loss.

"Jade, you got hurt again," Raina said once she came up from the basement.

"I'm ok little munchkin."

Raina walked over to her. "No, you're not. You're covered with scars."

Jade sighed. "That I am."

"Come on, Raina. You and Levi can help me with dinner," Sarah intervened. Raina gave Jade a kiss and followed her mother into the kitchen.

"What do you think Bossman's next move is?" Jade asked Razor. Razor gave her a weird look. She couldn't tell what he was thinking. He stared at her for a while—to the point that it was making her uncomfortable.

"Why you looking at her like that?" Helena asked.

"Just thinking about their conversation in the woods."

"You heard that?"

"All of it."

"What he say?" Helena was annoyed with being out of the loop.

"He confessed his love for your sister."

"What?!"

"You don't think he actually meant any of that, do you?" Jade just thought they were doing a bit—kind of a back and forth thing. She never once took him seriously.

"It would explain a lot."

"Bullshit!" There was no way Razor could be serious. Jade was sure that he was messing with her.

"He had countless opportunities to kill you, Jade, but he didn't."

"He shot me Razor."

"A non-fatal wound."

"That's because I came at him low!"

"Something he could easily predict."

"Are you fucking serious right now?!" Jade couldn't believe what he was saying. She looked around the room. Everyone was looking at her weird.

"That would explain why he shot that officer who was choking you," Beverly added.

"And why he shot his remaining men instead of us," Jackson chimed in.

Jade shook her head. This was ridiculous. It was all just utterly ridiculous. There was absolutely no way Bossman could have feelings for her. The feeling of hatred, maybe. Surely not anything romantic like love.

"I'm just saying, when it comes to dealing with you, he's been acting way out of character," Razor explained. "Having feelings for you would explain why he's been so unpredictable."

"I can't believe you right now," for some reason Jade felt exposed.

"Sorry, but that's just how I see it."

"What do we do now?" Tatianna chimed in. "If Bossman is unpredictable?"

"Well not totally unpredictable," Keeper pointed out. Everyone looked at him with a questioning look. "We know he'll be looking for Jade. I don't think he will stop."

"That's true," Razor stood up. "We're tripling up on security."

"Jade!" Danita came rushing downstairs. Everybody jumped up— preparing for a fight. Danita ignored them all. She looked right at Jade.

"He's up."

~32~

It was all overwhelming. Especially since everyone in the house was cramped inside of Jade's room. She never considered herself to be claustrophobic, but she was feeling like it at the moment. She sat right next to David on the bed. He was curious about her arm and the long scar she had on the side of her head. They convinced him to tell them what happened the day he fainted.

"It's not really all that interesting," he admitted. "I just haven't been keeping up with my blood sugar levels."

"Why not?" Jade asked.

"Honestly, there's been so much going on. Between the raids and the constant patrolling, I sometimes forgot to check. I did that day."

"Do you remember what happened?" Razor asked. "What you were doing? Was there anyone in the house with you?"

"No. No one was there," David paused. He was thinking back to that day. "I was scavenging for supplies. I was feeling weak that whole day, but I chalked it up to being tired. I was heading upstairs to look through the medicine cabinet when I just blacked out."

Everyone looked at each other. There were a few skeptical looks. David noticed them.

"What?"

"We just wanna be sure that you weren't attacked or anything," Razor said.

"I'm telling you I wasn't. If I was, why would they leave me alive?"

"That's a good point," Tatianna said. "Why would a DC officer leave him alive? We sure as hell wasn't leaving any of them alive."

Razor contemplated on Tatianna's statement and agreed. "We just needed to be sure."

David nodded. "So how many days was I out?"

They all exchanged uncomfortable looks. Jade wasn't sure who was going to tell him. Most of them threw glances her way. She sighed and cleared her throat.

"Umm, it's been close to two months, David."

He wore a look of disbelief. "That can't be right."

"Well, when you fainted, you hit your head pretty badly. We think the combination of your low blood sugar, and how you fell, contributed to how long you've been out."

David remained stunned.

"But I'm glad that you're finally up and with us now," Jade assured. "I was worried."

"So, what's happened?" he noticed Jackson and Beverly in the doorway. "Why are they here?"

They filled David in on what happened that day. He went from shocked, to sad, to angry. It was all overwhelming to him. Jade knew how he felt. It was all overwhelming for her, too, and she was there to experience it. Everything seemed to get worse. When it looked like they were finally winning, they were finally able to fight back, the DC came along and knocked away all hope again. It was useless and a never-ending cycle.

Silence fell on the room once they were done.

"Surely you're joking," David finally said. "Bossman can't really be in love with Jade. That's impossible."

"It would explain a lot," Razor said.

"No, you're wrong."

"That's what I said," Jade agreed.

"Look," Razor was over the whole back and forth. "Our main concern right now is figuring out what to do next."

"Well, we know what's next for us," Jackson finally said. "Canada."

"You can't be serious," Jade said. "You wanna flee? Now?"

"This is a losing fight," Beverly defended her brother.

"How can you say that?!" Jade was stunned at how low the siblings could go.

"Look at all the people we just lost!" Beverly cried. "We're way over our heads here! We can never be *that* vicious."

"This was never really our fight," Jackson admitted. "This was our dad's fight. We just tried to carry it on when he died. We never knew what we were really doing. And because of that many people lost their lives. At this point, I just need to look out for my sister. Canada is the place where I can do that."

Jade sat there with her mouth open. She couldn't believe what she was hearing. The idea of the Black Deficit was always a beacon of hope for debtors. They were the rebel group—something that could fight back. If they leave, all hope would be lost. It would be devasting. Debtors would start laying down and accepting their horrible fate.

"I can't believe you two," Keeper said. "You sold everyone a dream that you never believed in."

"We did what we had to do to survive," Jackson said coldly. Their revelation left everyone stunned—except for Razor, who seemed to know the truth all along.

"I wouldn't recommend you leaving just yet," Razor said. "Let it die down first." Jackson and Beverly agreed.

Jade looked at them with disgust. She just couldn't believe that they were going to leave everyone behind. A part of her was regretting the decision to save them. They should've died right along with the people they got killed. Jade instantly felt sorry for thinking that. She didn't want anyone to die, but she didn't want anyone running away like cowards either. At least when you died, you died a hero. That was way more noble than fleeing.

"I'll show you both where you can stay," Razor said. "And we should let Jade and David rest."

Everyone slowly walked out of the room. Jade was glad when everyone was gone, mainly Jackson and Beverly. She didn't want to look at them anymore. A small part of her was hard on them, but she didn't care. They said that they didn't ask for this. No one did.

No one wanted to be hunted down like animals. No one wanted to be treated inhumanly. No one wanted to fear for their life. This was the world they were living in now. And you had to deal with it. You had to adapt to survive. That was life. No one could just run from it. There was no escaping it *unless* you fought back.

"Apparently Bossman is in love with you," David said once everyone was gone.

"Yeah, I don't really believe that."

"But what if he is?"

"He shot me."

"That doesn't mean anything."

"Oh, because that's a sure-fire way of showing someone you love them?"

"He's a psycho Jade. Who knows how he shows his love?"

"He doesn't love me, David, and I'm tired of talking about it."

"Sorry."

Silence fell between them.

"You scared me," Jade admitted.

David smiled a little. "Now you know how I feel."

"You just had to show me, didn't you?"

"I felt like it was my turn for once."

"I never left your side."

"I know."

"Do you?"

"I felt your presence."

Jade rolled her eyes. "Bullshit."

David laughed. "I always feel your presence." He leaned in and kissed her. It was gentle at first, and then it turned passionate. A wave of fear hit Jade so hard that tears escaped her. David pulled away, confused.

"What's wrong?"

"What if it's true?" Jade was starting to panic. "What if he actually thinks that? He'll try to kill you."

"Wouldn't he try to kill me anyway?"

Jade shook her head. "It'll be worse."

"It won't happen Jade."

"You don't know that."

"I'm not letting that affect how I feel about you. I love you. And I would die feeling that."

Jade couldn't help herself. She began crying. It was a little dramatic, she knew that, but the whole day was just overwhelming. Shit hit the fan—fast. This was the first time that day that she could catch her breath. And sadly, she could only think about David dying.

David chuckled and kissed her again. "Stop being silly."

Jade wiped away her tears. "I love you."

"I love you too."

~33~

The next few weeks were tensed. Everyone was on edge. Razor tripled up on security. Lang, Reagan, and Rosalind held shooting seminars. Clay and Danita taught combat fighting to anyone interested—everyone was interested. Razor ran drills non-stop. He ran drills for different kind of scenarios. If Bossman tried to burn down the camp. If the lookouts were taken out. If they were attacked in the daytime. If they were attacked at night. If they came from the east, west, north, or south. If they came when it was raining, snowing, or sunny. He ran so many drills that everyone was exhausted—and paranoid.

Although Jade was finding it annoying, she appreciated it, nonetheless. It was better for them to be over-prepared than not prepared at all. She didn't want the people at camp to experience the same fate as those at HQ.

Jade and David took the time to get some rest. They needed to be 100 percent if Bossman was to come again—and he was going to come. It was just a matter of time before he figured out where they were hiding. He had time and manpower to do so.

Jackson and Beverly stuck around, to Jade's surprise. She thought that they would've fled once a week went by, but they stayed. She wasn't sure why. In her opinion, it was risky for them to stick around. Bossman wanted them just as much as he wanted Jade.

After a week, Jade was able to bear the pain in her shoulder. She stretched it and made sure she worked her left arm. She was afraid of it locking up on her at the wrong time—like in a life or death moment. Tatianna helped her with stretching her arm. There were times where Jade was ready to kill Tatianna. She pushed Jade hard—extending her arm further than Jade expected. In the end, it worked. Jade's arm was back to normal in no time.

After being out for two months, it took David some time to get back into the groove of things. His main battle was the overwhelming feeling of exhaustion. Exhaustion and getting his body back to functioning correctly. It all started off slowly, but as the days went by, he slowly began to become more his self.

Keeper came to work with him. The key goal was managing David's blood sugar level properly. Keeper gave him an ear full about neglecting to maintain it appropriately, especially with the unique gadgets that he made for David to dispense insulin more conveniently. What was he making them for if David wasn't going to use them? Jade completely agreed with Keeper. She needed him to be on top of that. She couldn't take one more thing to worry about.

Jade was back keeping watch two weeks after the attack at HQ. She couldn't sit out anymore. She spent her first day back on patrol with

Razor. They haven't really spoken to each other since he made the claim that Bossman was in love with her in front of everyone. Jade hasn't been necessarily avoiding him, but she hasn't gone out of her way to speak to him either. People began looking at her funny after he made that accusation. She felt completely exposed. A small part of her blamed him for that.

"Mad at me?" he asked after they walked around the perimeter a few times in silence.

She hated the way he could read her mind. "A little."

"I was just telling the truth."

"Did you have to do it in front of everyone? Now everybody is giving me funny looks."

"Fuck'em."

Jade sighed and rolled her eyes. He didn't get it. It was already hard enough to accept that Bossman may have some weird romantic feelings for her. It was even harder to accept it when everyone looked at her funny because of it. They already believed it to be true. Therefore, they perceived Jade to be a threat.

"I'm sorry," he said. "You're right. That's something I should've told you in private. I was just shocked by it all. That's something that I never expected from him."

"Come on, he had to be with women before."

"Well yeah, he had sex with his share of women. But he was just as ruthless to them as he was to debtors."

"So, you're saying, out of the whole time you've known him, you've never seen him in love?"

Razor shook his head. "Some people aren't capable of love Jade."

"Exactly, and I don't think he is now."

Razor laughed. "Whatever helps you sleep better at night."

Jade rolled her eyes. Razor really annoyed her sometimes, but she was very grateful for him. "Helena told me what it was like for y'all before the prison."

"Did she?"

"Don't know if I said it before, but thank you for taking care of my sister."

"Don't get mushy on me now."

"I'm serious. It seemed like Bossman put you through a lot over Helena."

Razor tensed a little. It looked like he remembered what he went through. "Bossman put everyone through a lot."

"Well, I know it wasn't easy," Jade looked over at him. "Y'all were really close, right?"

"Thick as thieves."

Jade knew it was a touchy subject, but curiosity got the best of her.

"After falling in love with your sister, I saw things differently. I saw how vicious he really was. I wanted to shield Helena from that."

"And how did he feel about that?"

"Betrayed."

"How so?"

Razor sighed. He hated that they were talking about this, but he entertained Jade. "Before Helena, my purpose...my mission was the DC task force. I was very appreciative and loyal to it. After having her in my life that changed. Bossman saw that. He felt like I could change her. Make her one of us if I was so keen on having her in my life. But I loved her because she was so different. I wasn't willing to do that. I guess he felt betrayed by that."

"Is that why he sent you out on missions?"

"Yeah, but he was starting to finally trust and accept her until he got word that she was helping women prisoners who were being sexually abused."

"What you do then?"

"Took a lot of finessing on my part, but he ignored it, until…"

"Until what?" Jade knew that he was holding back something.

"Nothing. Just forget it."

"No, tell me."

He sighed. "Until you killed that DC officer."

Jade stopped walking. She never really thought about how much that affected them.

"There are a lot of DC officers who have debtors as family members. And there are quite a few officers whose family members injured or killed one of them."

"What happened to them?"

"Well, the officers had to accept the fact that their family member was gonna be killed," he paused. "It was hard for Helena to understand that and that's what made Bossman keep a tighter watch on us."

Jade didn't say anything for a while. She regretted opening this dialogue. She finally worked up the courage to speak. "I'm sorry."

"My relationship with Bossman was destined to come to an end. You were just the vessel for that to happen."

Jade appreciated Razor downplaying her actions. "I don't get it."

"I was working on an escape plan, for all three of us," he looked over at her. "I couldn't let you die. Helena would've never forgiven me. But then…"

"I broke out the prisoners," she really did make things harder for him.

He chuckled. "Yeah, I was pissed and a little amazed at you for that one."

"So, the torture room?"

"That was all show for Vincent," he admitted. "Although Helena's part was a little more real."

Jade already knew that. "Those punches felt pretty real to me."

"Well, I couldn't pull them too much, Vincent would've noticed."

"Why would you care about that?"

"Because he was reporting everything back to Bossman. He wasn't one of us, but he wanted to be very bad. He thought spying on me would help him with that."

"And after the whole prison break?"

"Bossman took Helena and demanded that I bring you to him. He knew that if pushed, I would get you. He knew that I would do anything for Helena." Razor looked sad and defeated when he said that. Helena. That was his only weakness. He quickly shook off the feeling. "There. Is your curiosity satisfied now?"

Jade smiled a little. She was hitting him with a whole lot of questions. "Yeah. Thanks. And, umm, sorry."

Razor laughed and shook his head. "You should probably go check on Loverboy."

"My shift isn't up already, is it?"

"Time flies when you're interrogating someone."

Jade smiled at him and walked off.

~34~

The passing of time did not make things calmer at the camp.

With each passing day, people got more and more paranoid. Everyone was just counting down the days to the next attack. The few survivors from HQ made everyone at camp even more paranoid. Every loud noise made them jump. They had nightmares. Sometimes everyone would go into a panic when a few survivors screamed in their sleep at night. It was driving Jade crazy.

It was suggested that Beverly and Jackson should talk with them, but they were too ashamed to. Jade and Razor tried talking with them, along with Vicky and her crew, but that still didn't seem to help any. Jade couldn't really blame them for how they felt. What they experienced was unimaginable. Most of them saw their family and friends get burned alive or shot to death.

Who wouldn't have nightmares about that?

Jade began pushing herself. She exercised. She practiced her shooting—both with her bow and arrows, and her rifle. Razor and Clay went back to get her bow. Razor insisted that it would be riskier to go without it.

Jade practiced her combat fighting—mostly with Razor. He was the only one who was as threatening as Bossman. She insisted that he didn't take it easy on her—Bossman wouldn't. She had to prepare herself properly. She and Razor argued a lot about that.

"You're gonna be useless if you're all bruised up and sore Jade."

"I need this, Razor. How else am I gonna be able to fight him?"

"Just let me handle him."

"You seriously think I can avoid brushing elbows with him?"

He sighed.

"If you won't do it, Clay agreed that he will."

"Really?" Razor's tone suggested that he would change Clay's mind.

"Reluctantly, but he knows how important it is to me."

"Fine," he snapped. He knew that it was a losing battle. Plus, he knew that Jade was right, and he hated when she was right. "Don't say I didn't warn you."

It didn't take long for Jade to start regretting her decision. There was a vast difference between Razor holding back and the *real* Razor. The first few sessions didn't last five minutes—because of Jade getting knocked out instantly.

Helena and David were furious. They weren't too thrilled about the sessions. It took a lot of persuading on Jade's part. They eventually accepted it, although they weren't too happy about it. They knew it was no talking Jade out of it.

The next few sessions Jade hung in there a little longer, but she still got knocked out. She would come to with Razor kneeling next to her. He looked sad every time. Razor was hating every moment of it.

"You can't take me out head-on," he said in their last session. "Or Bossman for that matter."

"I gotta," Jade groaned. She tried to stand up. It almost killed her to do so.

"Stay down, Jade."

Jade slowly got to her feet. She needed to catch her breath once she was up.

"Damnnit Jade! Can you stop making me do this?!"

"Razor, please."

"That's enough for today."

"No, I can keep going."

"We will start again tomorrow."

"No Razor!" He turned to walk away. Jade glared at him. She couldn't give up now. She refused to. She knew he hated this, but he agreed to it. He couldn't walk away. Jade grew furious. The next thing she knew, she was charging at him.

Everything went black.

Jade woke up in her bed. David was sitting on the edge. There were ice packs on her chest and stomach. She didn't need a mirror to show her that she was black and blue. David struggled to look at her. It was hard for him to see her like that. The feeling of guilt rushed through her. She just had to make things hard on everybody.

"I'm sorry," she croaked.

David looked over at her. He smiled weakly. "Don't be. I should've expected it."

"How so?"

"You did the exact same thing when you thought Razor was coming after you."

"That feel like ages ago."

"It does, doesn't it?" he looked out the window. "I think it's a coping mechanism for you."

"Really?"

He nodded. "To prepare yourself for what's to come."

Jade never thought of it that way, but it made sense. She felt safe when she was prepared. And in this chaotic world, you need to be ready.

"It just upsets your sister and me to see you hurting yourself like this. It's not easy on Razor either."

"I know," she admitted. "But it'll hurt more if I'm killed by Bossman."

David sighed. "Point taken."

Jade's eyes got heavy. Keeper must have come and given her some pain medication when she was knocked out. Sleep overcame her. She dreamt about ways to take out Razor.

**

Jade woke up early the next morning to exercise. She wanted to clear her head and get an early start on her day. Her nerves were getting worse as each day pass.

Was this the day Bossman would come?

Jade slowly got out of bed, trying not to disturb David. She went into the bathroom and washed her face. After stretching, she headed out to run laps around the perimeter. She had been slacking on pushing her lungs. Jade grabbed her inhaler instead of her combat mask. With her sessions with Razor, she had been pushing her mask to the limit. She needed to save that for when she really fought Bossman.

No one was up when she left out of the house. It was still dark. It was quiet out. There was no one outside—just the people who were scheduled to keep watch. Jade said hello to them as she ran her laps. No one bothered to ask what she was up to. They all thought she was weird. Here she was, black and blue, and running laps around the camp.

Her sessions with Razor confused them the most. Who would volunteer to take a beating from Razor? They didn't understand. Jade wasn't bothered with getting them to understand either. What she was doing was necessary. If she wanted her and her loved ones to survive, she had to do some irrational things. Bossman was crazy. She had to match him.

Jade was able to run around the perimeter twice before she needed to use her inhaler. The next lap around was tough, but she pushed through. She used her inhaler again after the third lap. Then again in the middle of the fourth lap. She told herself to keep going. Her chest was killing her. After her fifth lap, she stopped. That was enough for her today. She would be useless if she had an asthma attack. She took a couple puffs of her inhaler and headed back toward the house.

Clay was just about to start his round as lookout when Jade came walking up to the house. He looked at her and smiled.

"I see you're getting ahead start," he shook his head once her bruises came into full view. "You're really pushing yourself."

"I gotta."

"...you know people are starting to look at you crazy."

"Trust me, I know."

"I understand why you're doing it though."

"Well, you seem to be the only one that does."

"No, Reagan does too."

"I'm surprised she even talks."

Clay laughed. "Only to me."

"I see. Well, I'm glad she understands too."

"Are you taking a shift today?"

"I think I will. Give Razor a day off. I'm sure he'll like that."

"I'm sure the others will too."

"How so?"

"It's scary for them," he said. "To see him in action like that. It brings back bad memories for them. He may be on our side now, but he wasn't always. They remember that."

Jade never took that into consideration. There were people there who had run-ins with Razor before. She never considered how scary that must've been for them. To see him in that cruel matter with someone at camp had to be tough for them. Jade felt bad. How could she be so inconsiderate? She had to end it soon, but not before she could figure out a way to beat him head-on.

"I never thought about that," she admitted.

"I know. Don't beat yourself up about it. We've got bigger things to worry about."

"Thanks."

"See you around, Jade."

Jade continued to make her way home. Razor was standing on the porch when she got there. He was leaning against the railing, deep in thought. He gave her a puzzling look when she walked up the steps.

"Ran some laps," she said. "I'll take a shift today. Give you a break."

He nodded.

"Let me know when it's my turn." She went upstairs to lay down. Jade quickly fell asleep as soon as her head hit the pillow. Dreams about defeating Razor consumed her.

**

Jade found herself annoyed.

She wasn't sure if Razor did it to punish her, but she found herself keeping watch with Beverly and Jackson. Jackson was paired up with someone else from camp, which left her with Beverly. Jade has never been a fan of Beverly. She wasn't fond of the cocky, arrogant version and she couldn't take the weak, cowardly version of Beverly now.

Beverly lost all hope of potentially earning Jade's respect the moment she and her brother decided to leave everyone behind. But they couldn't go just yet. They were trying to give it time to die down a little. So, while they stayed, Razor made sure they earned their keep by taking shifts as lookouts.

They didn't talk much.

Jade mostly thought about fighting combos that could possibly knock Razor out. She also was secretly praying that nothing happened while she was on watch with Beverly. Unfortunately, she viewed Beverly more as a liability than an asset. If they were attacked now, Jade would have to worry about saving herself *and* Beverly. She didn't want to take on that pressure again. Jade couldn't shake the memory of Beverly sobbing next to her while she was struggling to figure out how to get away from Bossman. She didn't want to go through that again.

"You're awfully quiet," Beverly said.

"Thinking about ways to take out Razor." Beverly didn't say anything. "Think I'm crazy?"

"I always thought that," Beverly paused. "I've seen your sessions."

Jade didn't like Beverly's tone when she said that. She knew Beverly was about to accuse her of doing something wrong. Jade rolled her eyes.

"You know, you're scaring everyone here."

"I've been told."

"Maybe you should have those sessions off-campus. You know, if you're so keen on doing them."

"In case you didn't notice Beverly, you're no longer in charge. You've gladly neglected that duty," Jade instantly regretted saying that. She didn't like Beverly, but she never really wanted to hurt her. The look that Beverly made told Jade that she did that. Jade sighed. "I'm sorry. You didn't deserve that."

"But your right," Beverly sighed. "Look, all I'm saying is that the people are rattled enough. They don't need to see Razor in action like that."

"They're gonna see a lot worse when Bossman comes."

"How do you know if he's even gonna come?"

Jade stopped in her tracks. "Are you kidding me?" Beverly didn't say anything. "Trust me he's coming."

"You know what this reminds me of? That time you warned us that Razor was coming for you. You did the exact same thing. You were practicing your knife throwing, your shooting, and you were fighting with the members. You were also terrifying the prisoners. And here we are now, full circle."

Jade didn't say anything. Beverly was right. She did the exact same thing before. Maybe that was a coping mechanism for her. At least she was prepared when her crazy ravings became true.

Beverly sighed. "You know what? Forget what I said. You seem to have a better handle on things than I do."

Jade was a little shocked by Beverly's comment. It completely caught her off guard. "Trust me, all of this is way over my head."

That seemed to cheer Beverly up a little. "To be honest, I'm surprised you're getting knocked out so much. You've been able to take down Razor with ease before."

"That's because he was going easy on me."

Beverly shook her head. "But you're quicker."

Jade looked at her, confused. Did she seriously not hear when Jade said Razor was taking it easy on her?

"Trust me, he wasn't prepared for your speed that day. He may have been holding his punches, but he wasn't holding back the speed of his movements."

Jade reflected on her words. Beverly had a point. Razor had been holding back that day, but Jade's swiftness did catch him off guard. He couldn't hold back his reflex. She had been so focused on matching his strength, which she could never match, that she never thought about anything else. Her only advantage was his slow reflex. Jade just had to be quicker—catch him completely off guard. Strike before he can even register what happened.

"Thank you, Beverly."

"You're welcome."

They finished up their shift with no issues.

Jade came up with combat combos that focused more on her speed. She needed to try out her theory—quickly. It never surprised Razor to see Jade coming out of nowhere to attack him. He was always prepared for it. And it always ended with Jade laid out on the ground unconscious. Jade wanted to change that today.

Jade, Beverly, and Jackson were walking back to the house at the end of their shift. Razor came walking out. They both locked eyes. They both read each other's mind. Razor and Jade charged at one another at the same time.

This time, however, Jade picked up speed. She pushed herself to the limit. Before Razor could register anything, Jade was on his back. She had her legs wrapped around his waist, and her forearm locked on his throat. He thrashed around for a moment—trying to fling her off. Jade applied more pressure on his throat. She unwrapped one her legs, and with all her strength, stamped on his knee. Razor quickly fell on his side. Jade ignored the pain of hitting the ground. People came rushing outside to see what all the commotion was about.

"Jade!" Helena yelled from the porch.

Razor was getting weak—she applied more pressure. Jade could feel him slipping into unconsciousness. He suddenly stopped struggling. Jade could hear him snoring. She stayed in her position for a few minutes. Was Razor faking? A few more minutes passed. Jade couldn't believe that she really did it. Did she really take out Razor head-on? It seemed too good to be true.

"Jade, what did you do?!" Helena screamed. The terror in Helena's voice told Jade that she really did it.

Jade slid out from under Razor. She rolled him on his back. Although she heard him snoring, Jade checked his pulse. The terror in Helena's voice made Jade a little scared. She was just trying to knock him out. She wanted to be sure she didn't go overboard.

Jade kneeled beside him. Helena came rushing over. "Relax Helena, I just knocked him out."

Helena punched Jade in the arm. "Don't tell me to relax!"

Jade rubbed her arm. She looked up and saw Beverly smiling at her. Jade smiled back. A couple more minutes passed, and then they heard Razor cough.

"Razor!" Helena was relieved. "Baby, you ok?"

Razor chuckled. He looked over at Jade. "Well, I'll be damned. You did it."

Jade smiled.

Razor slowly sat up.

Helena smacked him. She punched Jade in the arm again. "You two are done with this shit!" she got up and stormed off. The rest of the crowd dispersed.

Razor sat rubbing the side of his face while Jade rubbed her arm. They both looked at each other and burst out laughing.

~35~

The next couple of weeks was nerve-wracking for Helena. Jade and Razor were constantly sparring with each other all the time, no matter how much Helena and David protested. Now that Jade knew her advantage, she wanted to brush up on it so she would be flawless at it by the time she encountered Bossman. Now aware of his weakness, Razor wanted to strengthen that so he would know how to beat someone who had speed over him.

Eventually, Tatianna got in on the action. She wanted to sharpen her fighting skills as well. Yoko, Clay, and Lang joined in. After a while, the whole camp was sparring with one another. It was a skill that they all needed to brush up on. It was common to be on patrol and see a sparring match break out between a couple of campers.

For the first time, in what seemed like the only time, Jade felt prepared.

She has never been with a group who was fully equipped, but that's how it felt at camp. Could they actually have a chance against Bossman and the DC? It was beginning to look like they did. Jade was able to breathe a little. Now all they had to do was sit back and wait for Bossman to make the first move.

One night, after a long day of sparring with a few people, Jade sat on the porch. She was waiting for David's shift to end before she went to bed. As of lately, she was having a hard time falling asleep without him. It was something about the way she felt in his arms that made it easy for her to fall asleep. His arms felt secure. Like nothing in the world could touch her when she was in them.

As soon as Jade sat down, Levi came rushing out of the house and into her arms. He quickly fell asleep. She didn't bother to take him inside. He was okay in her arms. Levi was very clingy to her lately. Jade wasn't sure what was causing it, but she allowed him to be clingy. With all the fighting that's been going on lately, she felt like she owed him that. It was probably scary for him—seeing all of that.

After a while, Sarah came out and took Levi, so she could put him in bed. Raina came out to take his place. She sat right in between Jade's legs. Jade played in her hair and aimlessly looked around.

"Sometimes I feel like all of this is my fault," Raina said.

Jade frowned and looked down at her. "How so?"

"This all started because of me."

"Raina, this world was fucked up before you were born."

"If you weren't wanted, those people at HQ wouldn't have died. And you were wanted because you killed that DC officer to save me."

"I'm not sure if you noticed Raina, but I'm a debtor, I was wanted long before I met you."

"I just feel guilty."

Jade kissed the top of her head. "Stop being silly, my little munchkin."

Raina smiled a little. "Do you ever regret it? Saving me? I mean Bossman wouldn't care who you were if you hadn't killed that officer."

That was true, if it weren't for Raina, Jade would've never been on Bossman's radar. She would've continued hiding out and avoiding sweeps. She would've been scavenging and all alone. Jade would've only had to worry about herself and not a camp full of people.

But she also would've never found love. She wouldn't have seen her sister. Jade wouldn't have known Razor—who was turning out to be an excellent brother-in-law. She wouldn't have met Keeper. In the past, the one thing that Jade was terrible at was relationships. Since her encounter with Raina, she became better at that.

She owed that all to Raina.

Jade stood Raina up and turned her around. Raina's eyes were glossy. She was on the verge of crying. Jade stared right into those brown eyes. She took them in. Her heart began to race. Apart from her sister, Raina was the first person that Jade truly loved through all the chaos.

Jade was on the verge of crying herself. She cleared her throat. "Never," she said sternly. "In fact, if I had to do it all over again, I would. No hesitation. You're worth it, munchkin."

Raina blushed as she wiped away her tears.

Jade kissed her cheek. "I love you with all my heart and soul."

"I love you too, Jade."

"What's with the waterworks?" David asked.

Jade didn't see him walk up. She was preoccupied with easing whatever guilt Raina was feeling away. None of what was happening was her fault, Jade wanted to make sure that she knew that. Raina had enough burdens to deal with in her young life. Guilt shouldn't be one of them.

"Just declaring our love for each other," Jade wiped away the few tears that escaped her.

David came and scooped Raina up. "Oh yeah?" he kissed her cheek. "Did I tell you how much I love you?"

Raina laughed and nodded.

"Well, I think I'll tell you again," he started tickling her. Raina doubled over laughing.

Jade smiled at the view. She stood up. "We should head inside." David followed her inside with Raina in his arms. They tucked Raina in her bed and kissed her goodnight.

They then went to their room. Jade stripped out of her clothes and got into bed. Her body thanked her for the rest. She didn't realize how sore she was until she laid down. David got into bed with her. Jade quickly wormed her way into his arms. She laid her head on his chest.

"She was just feeling a little guilty earlier."

"About what?"

"She feels like all of this is her fault."

"Nonsense."

"That's what I told her."

"How you feeling?

"I'm good."

"Really?"

"Really. I've never felt so prepared."

David smiled. "That's good. It's always good to be prepared." He leaned down and kissed her. Their kissing turned passionate. David quickly rolled on top of Jade and allowed his hands to explore her body. Jade lost herself in their lovemaking. All her stress and worries swiftly melted away.

Jade swiftly fell asleep shortly after that.

**

The next day Jade found herself a little discontent. She wasn't sure why. She figured she woke up on the wrong side of the bed. She didn't sleep great. It wasn't a nightmare or anything like that. The night just consisted of a lot of tossing and turning. When she woke up, she found herself in a bad mood—even after some good lovemaking. Jade was over the day before it even started. Her body felt utterly drained. Her spirit felt the same.

Jade shook off the feeling. She got up and began her day like usual— went running, sparred with a few people, went home to change out of her sweaty clothes, ate breakfast, started her shift as a lookout.

"Someone's in a bad mood," Razor said when Jade snapped at him about something.

"I'm sorry," she said. "I dunno what's wrong with me."

"Don't worry about it."

"Have you ever had a moment when you thought life was going just way too good?" Jade wasn't sure where that question came from.

"Like the way it's supposed to be?"

"You know what I'm talking about. Right?"

"Of course, I do."

"I think that's how I'm feeling right now."

"You think?"

"That's the only way I can explain it."

Razor looked at her and sighed. "Maybe you should just stick around at the house today. Spend some time with Raina and Levi. That always seems to cheer you up."

Jade nodded. Looking after Raina and Levi would help improve her mood. It was something about their innocence that made her forget momentarily what type of world they were living in. It was like old times with them. She could use that. Jade left Razor and went back to the house. She passed a lot of people on her way back, but she ignored them all. She was afraid of snapping at them like she did with Razor. No one else deserved to be subjected to her bad mood.

Sarah looked confused when Jade walked into the house. Usually Jade didn't come in until dinner time, with the occasional snacks and bathroom breaks here and there. This time Jade came in and sat down on the couch. Only Sarah, Raina, Levi, and Calvin were usually at the house all day.

"Everything ok?" Sarah asked.

"Yeah. Just not in the mood today. I was thinking about keeping an eye on Raina and Levi. Give you a break."

"Really?" Sarah seemed shocked.

"Yeah, go relax."

"Thanks," Sarah called for Raina and Levi. They came rushing out of their room. Once they saw Jade, they both raced to sit on her lap. "Jade's gonna be watching you today." They both screamed with excitement.

"Enjoy yourself, Sarah," Jade said as Sarah was rushing out of the front door.

"There's food in the pantry in case they get hungry," she called out as a form of goodbye.

"So, what are we gonna do today, Jade?" Raina asked.

"What you wanna do?"

"Draw!" Levi shouted.

"Draw?" Jade asked Raina.

"Ok, and then I get to pick."

"Sounds fair to me."

Raina and Levi ran into their room to get their drawing supplies. All three of them spent a few hours drawing things. Jade was no artist, but she found coloring to be therapeutic. It felt freeing. She was instantly feeling better as she colored across the paper. It all was just a random blend of different colors, but it looked so beautiful and serene. It gave Jade a sense of peace.

Levi called it scribble. Raina disagreed. She thought it was magical. They both bickered back and forth about it. Jade sat back, laughing a little. Their bickering put her in the mind frame of siblings. She thought about all of her and Helena's bickering sessions when they were little. The arguing ended up getting a little intense, and Jade eventually had to break them up. Calvin finally made his way up from his room in the basement when Jade calmed the two down.

"The Queen is in her castle!" Calvin boomed once he saw Jade. "The Queen is in her castle and is here to stay!"

"That's right Calvin," Jade got up from the couch. "Now, come eat lunch with the Queen." Jade hated referring to herself as the Queen, but Calvin wouldn't listen to her if she didn't. She felt so narcissistic every time she said it.

Calvin followed behind her right along with Raina and Levi. They all sat at the kitchen table and ate stale peanut butter cracker sandwiches. They were dangerously low on food. Everyone was too afraid to go out scavenging. There was a great fear that Bossman was lurking behind every corner. Jade made a mental note to bring up the issue soon. They all couldn't just sit around and starve to death.

"What's next?" Jade asked once they were done eating.

"Don't know," Raina admitted. It was her turn to pick an activity, but she couldn't think of anything.

"How 'bout hide-and-seek?" to Jade's surprise, Raina and Levi never heard of it. Jade was a little stunned. Hide-and-seek was so basic, she thought every kid knew how to play it. She was wrong. They were quickly able to catch on once she explained it to them.

"Oh, so basically what we do when the DC officers do a sweep," Raina said.

"...yeah," Jade said uneasily. "But for fun."

"Ok, let's play!"

"Yeah, play!" Levi chimed.

"Ok, I'll count while you three go hide somewhere in the house." Jade didn't want to even think about them playing outside. She could feel the imaginary heart attack just thinking about one of them being lost. "I'll start looking once I count to 20."

Jade closed her eyes and began counting. Levi and Raina ran away giggling. Calvin's big footsteps quickly walked away too. She got to 20 and started looking. They were all pretty easy to find. They went straight to their rooms and hid in there. Jade explained to them that all the rooms were available for them to hide in. After that, the game started to get more competitive—except for Calvin of course.

They played the game for a couple of hours. Jade found it to be amusing. She hasn't played a game in ages. A small part of her felt like a kid again. The game brought out a different side of them, especially Raina. Raina had a little conniving side to her.

When it was Raina's turn, she would always try to find Calvin first (because he was the easiest to find). She quickly learned that if you called out his name, he would answer back—giving away his position. After a while, Levi called out the unfairness of it, and Jade had to agree. Finding Calvin no longer counted.

The new ruling brought on another bickering session between Raina and Levi. Jade just shook her head, smiling. She realized Sarah needed a break from them a lot sooner. Sarah definitely had her hands full looking after them.

Jade eventually moved them outside. She sat on the porch while Raina and Levi played in the front yard. They took their bickering sessions up a notch—in the form of stick fighting. They each grabbed a small branch and began swatting it at each other. Jade thought it best for them to fight it out. It looked like they were having fun and wasn't hurting each other. They seemed to be letting out some frustration as well. Jade gave them pointers as they continued to fight. Eventually, their petty name-calling turned into laughs and giggles.

Calvin joined in on the fun. He scooped them both up with great ease and began spinning them around. They laughed with delight.

"Faster! Faster!" they both screamed.

Calvin spun them around faster until he lost his balance. He put them down, and they all slowly laid down on their back. They laid there on the ground. In the front yard. Staring up into the sky.

Jade laughed. She was enjoying her time with them. "Tired?"

"Very," Raina said breathlessly.

"The ground won't stop moving," Levi groaned.

"Round and Round," Calvin confirmed.

Jade chuckled again. The delights of being a kid. And then Jade frowned. She tilted her head a little.

What was that noise?

It was strange.

It was the sound of small wheels—a lot of them. It was heard throughout the camp. Jade quickly stood up. The noise was vaguely familiar to her. She had definitely heard it before—a long time ago. She rushed off the porch and over to Raina and Levi.

They quickly got up and ran to her side—fighting through their dizziness. Other people around the camp began looking around curiously.

Then Jade finally saw them—remote control cars. The last time she saw one of those she was a preadolescent. They had something shiny on top of them. Some of the people began walking up to it to see what it was carrying.

Levi was so amazed by the foreignness of it that he wanted to examine it closer. Raina remained at Jade's side—afraid. Calvin quickly got to his feet.

Something was wrong. Who was controlling these cars? Jade quickly pulled Levi back—just in time.

She saw orange.

She felt heat.

They all flew back and hit the ground.

Screams resonated throughout the camp.

~36~

Jade groaned as she struggled to get up. The wind got knocked out of her. She had to get to her combat mask—fast. Agonizing screams were raining throughout the camp. Various explosions kept going off. Levi and Raina were crying. Jade quickly got to her feet. She tried hard not to focus on the pain.

"Talk to me! Y'all ok?" Jade rushed over to the children. She looked them over. They only had a few scrapes and bruises. She got them to their feet. Jade looked around for Calvin. He was closer to the house. "Calvin?!"

He slowly got to his feet. "The knight is ok my Queen."

Jade had to get to her weapons and her mask. They were in the house sitting on the living room table. The windows were blown out. There was some smoke coming from upstairs. She looked over at Raina and Levi and then back at Calvin. They had to go with her. They never prepared for a scenario where the house caught on fire. Every scenario involved Calvin protecting the children and Sarah in the basement. Jade grabbed Raina's hand, who in turn grabbed Levi's hand. Jade led them into the house.

"Come on, Calvin," she called over her shoulder. Calvin quickly followed. Once inside, Jade gathered up all her things. Raina and Levi looked around terrified. The screams and the chaos outside were scaring them.

"Jade, what are we gonna do?" Raina asked.

"Go grab your weapons. Quickly," Jade demanded. She looked over at Calvin. "Gather up your weaponry, my brave knight. Hurry!" Calvin rushed downstairs.

Raina and Levi came out with their batons. Razor had taken a few of them from a raid and taught Raina and Levi how to fight with them. In case they ever encountered an officer, they would be able to incapacitate them and run and hide. Calvin came upstairs with his weapons. One of them was a sword that Yoko found scavenging one day. Jade had never seen Calvin so happy. He felt like a real knight with a sword.

"Orders my Queen."

Jade planned to get Levi and Raina far away from camp as she could. "The town is being attacked. We must protect it."

"Protect the castle!" Calvin boomed.

"No, Calvin," Jade pointed to the smoke that was slowly descending downstairs. Something was definitely on fire now. She could smell it. "The castle is burning. You must leave and follow your Queen."

"Follow the Queen!"

"Protect the prince and princess at all cost."

Calvin quickly scooped up Levi and Raina and nodded. "Protect the prince and princess."

Gunshots began to ring out. Levi and Raina jumped a little.

"Hey, you two," Jade said. "Everything's gonna be ok. I won't let anything happen to you. You understand?"

They both nodded.

Jade looked at Calvin. "Let's go."

They rushed out of the house. The scene reminded Jade of a war zone. There were people strewn about with a part of their body missing. There was a lot of random limbs in odd places. Legs hanging off a branch. Arms in a bush. A foot was on a porch. While someone's decapitated head was on a roof. People were running and trampling over each other. People were trying to help the injured. And people were bleeding to death. The scene was sure to haunt Jade's dreams if she made it out.

"Close your eyes my little munchkins," she advised. They quickly obeyed.

Jade's first objective was to find Sarah. Once she saw her, she was going to send them all off with Calvin. Their best play was to hide out at HQ. Jade was sure that Bossman and the DC officers wouldn't bother to go back there. If she makes it out of this, she will come back for them.

Once she sent off Sarah and the children, she was going to find Helena, Razor, David, and Keeper. She was going to lead Bossman away while the others had a chance to escape. That was as much of the plan she could come up with. But she had a strategy. She tended to deal with things better when she had a strategy—no matter how loose and vague it was.

Jade began to make her way through the camp. Calvin was right on her heels. Unfortunately, she couldn't stop to help anyone—not with Raina and Levi with her. They were her number one priority.

More gunshots began to ring out. This time much closer. Calvin and Jade hid behind a tree for cover. The people that ran by them weren't so lucky. Most of them were shot to death. Jade took the rifle off her back. She wanted to save her ammo, but she couldn't let everyone die. She waited until the officers reloaded before she started firing back.

Luckily, there were only a few of them, so Jade had no trouble taking them out. She and Calvin still hid behind the tree for a moment before moving. She wanted to make sure there were no other officers nearby. Once she was convinced that the coast was clear, they continued to make their way across the camp.

Jade had one guess as to where Sarah could be, and that's near the lookout area. Sarah only felt safe near Jade, Razor, Helena, and David. Razor was out patrolling. Sarah had to be with him. Now all Jade needed to do was get to them. They came upon a group of DC officers savagely beating on a group of debtors. They were so preoccupied with their beating that they didn't hear them approaching. Jade pulled out her knives. She didn't want to use her ammo or arrows if she didn't have to.

Calvin stayed behind—protecting Raina and Levi. Jade took a deep breath and took off running. She slid in between the officers and debtors. She quickly slashed all the officer's ankles and then their throats once they were at her level. Jade was coated in their blood.

"Are those eyes still closed, my little munchkins?" Jade asked breathlessly. She couldn't imagine if they saw her like this. She tried to wipe away some of the blood. It was useless.

"Yes," they said in unison.

"More invaders my Queen!"

Jade looked and saw a few officers were heading their way. The debtors quickly got up and began to run off. Jade gripped her knives. She waited until they got closer. Once they were close enough, she threw one of her knives, and it landed in an officer's neck. The other two officers got attacked by Yoko and Tatianna—who had been lying in wait.

The remaining officer came charging at Jade. He was a big guy, so Jade used her fighting tactic that she'd been using on Razor over the last several weeks. She sped up and quickly jumped on his back. She stabbed him repeatedly in the chest. He fell to the ground, landing right on top of Jade. Yoko and Tatianna quickly got the officer's dead body off her. Tatianna helped her up.

"Well done my Queen."

"What are they doing here?" Tatianna asked, shocked.

"The house was on fire."

Tatianna shook her head. "We didn't prepare for this."

"Who knew they'd have explosives?" Yoko stated.

"What's your plan, Jade?"

"Right now, to find Sarah and get the kids out of here," Jade retrieved her knives.

"And go where?" Tatianna pressured.

"Hideout at HQ."

Tatianna shook her head. "Rosalind said that they got us surrounded in a semi-circle. Starting back west by the house, and then north and south."

"They're pressuring us to go further east."

"There's a trap there then," Jade stated. "We need to be going in another direction."

"Razor said our best hope is to go further east," Tatianna said.

"Is Sarah with him?"

"Yeah, everyone's there at the border of the camp. We were sent to look for you."

"Ok, let's go."

They all kept running east. They encountered a few DC officers along the way, but they were able to quickly take them out. They managed to save a few more debtors too. It was much easier to do now that Jade had Yoko and Tatianna there for back up. They were getting close to the camp's border when they ran into Rosalind and Reagan.

"What are you two doing out of your nest?" Tatianna asked.

"Razor told us it's time to evacuate," Reagan said.

Tatianna looked at Jade and Yoko, surprised. "She speaks."

"Duck," Reagan ordered. They all took cover. Reagan quickly shot and killed a group of DC officers that were heading their way. She looked at them. "Enough chit-chat. Let's move out."

"You heard her ladies," Jade said.

They all followed behind Reagan. It wasn't too long before Jade could see Razor, Helena, David, Keeper, Clay, Lang, Sarah, Danita, Junior, Beverly, and Jackson at the border. Sarah and Beverly were directing debtors out while the others were fighting off DC officers. The few debtors that Jade and the others managed to save quickly followed Sarah and Beverly's instructions and headed out. Jade and the others joined in on the fight.

"Good, y'all made it out!" Razor said in between fighting.

Calvin took his place by Sarah, but Jade could tell that he was itching to join in on the fight. She knew that he was getting antsy watching her. He viewed her as his Queen—he wanted to protect his Queen.

"Beverly, help look after the kids!" Jade ordered as she fought off an officer.

Calvin didn't need any more orders after that. He quickly put Raina and Levi down and drew his sword. He charged and began slashing every officer he saw. The scene was a little horrifying. Calvin decapitated a few officers. A few more lost their arms. Blood was spurting about everywhere. They quickly finished off the DC officers once Calvin joined in on the fight.

"Thank you, Calvin," Jade said in between breaths. She was tired. She did a lot of fighting and running for today. Sadly, they weren't close to being out of danger yet.

"We gotta keep moving," Razor instructed.

They all started heading out. Jade quickly hugged Helena. She was glad to see that she was ok. David rushed over to kiss Jade. He then tried to clean some of the blood off her face.

"Are you ok?" he asked.

"I'm fine. Just a little exhausted."

They all crossed the border of the camp. They ran for about a mile. The surviving debtors were in their line of view, but they were a mile or so ahead of them all. Jade wasn't sure where they were going, but it seemed like the debtors had a good idea.

Jade was a ball of nerves running through the forest. Bossman was drawing them out east for a reason. That reason couldn't be good. She had to trust Razor, though. If there were anyone who knew how Bossman thinks it would be Razor. Razor matched his crazy. They needed that.

Jade and the rest of the group were slowly catching up to the group of surviving debtors. They were scared. They weren't prepared. They knew that death was coming. Jade could see all of this just by the way they were running. They needed to be brave. They needed to be strong. There was no way they all were going to survive if they didn't stick together.

Then one of the debtors tripped on something.

There was a loud bang.

Jade and the others stopped dead in their tracks. A cascade of blood and guts rain through the air.

Jade screamed.

~37~

Everything seemed to be going in slow motion. A debtor tripped. A fiery cloud shot up and engulfed the group of debtors—including Vicky and her crew. The fiery cloud quickly turned red and pink. A shower of blood, guts, and limbs cascaded through the air. It flew back toward Jade and the rest of the group.

Screams.

Gunshots.

More screams.

That's all Jade could register as she took cover behind a tree. At first, she couldn't tell where the screams were coming from. The debtors? No, they all died instantly. There was no way anyone survived that explosion. The screams were coming from Jade. And Helena. And Beverly. And

Sarah. And Raina. And Levi. It was the screams of shock and total fear.

David held onto Jade tightly as they took cover. As bullets whizzed past them, he reassured her that everything was going to be ok. They were going to get out of this just fine. Jade froze. Everyone did. They were shocked by the sudden death of the debtors. It was just them now. 19 of them against Bossman and the DC officers.

They were no match.

"Stop!" Bossman screamed. "If one of you bastards killed her, I'm gonna split you open right here!"

The gunfire quickly ceased. Jade caught her breath. She didn't realize that she was holding it all that time. This is what he wanted. He wanted her to run right to him. Jade took her bow off her back and loaded it with an arrow. She closed her eyes and focused on her breathing.

"My sweet Jade, are you there?"

Jade didn't answer. She continued to focus on her breathing. She had to mentally prepare to encounter Bossman. This time David was by her side. She wanted to get rid of him. Jade was worried about his safety.

"Jade, please answer me."

Jade looked over at David, who was looking back at her. There was fear in his eyes. He didn't want her to respond. He didn't want her to face him. She could see that he was about to do something stupid—like run out and try to attack Bossman. He couldn't do that.

"I love you," she whispered to him.

David frantically shook his head as she stepped out from behind the tree. Bossman was standing just a few feet away from the tripwire that killed the debtors. He smiled once he saw her.

"Here I am."

"And unharmed. Looks like I won't have to kill any of my officers."

"Not yet, anyway."

Bossman laughed. "My officers weren't so lucky during our last encounter."

"Because you shot them all."

"They were proven to be useless. I don't like working with useless people."

"Apparently."

"Well," Bossman sighed. "I must give you some unfortunate news. I killed Vincent."

Jade didn't blink. "Good ridden is what I say. He was becoming a little bit of a nuisance to me anyway."

Bossman boomed with laughter. Jade recognized the irony of her statement, which was why she said it. For whatever reason he found her humorous, she wanted to keep that going.

"Oh, Jade!" he shook his head. "You are funny."

"Thanks, I'm here all night."

Silence fell between them. Jade didn't know what to do. She was trying to give the others time to escape. But she couldn't figure out if she should begin attacking Bossman or not. Again, she was trying to see what he was playing at. Her interactions with him were always curious.

"Sadly, good help is hard to find," Bossman admitted. "The only person who was more than useful to me is now on your team."

Jade didn't say anything.

"Are you there, my wonderful friend?!"

"I'm here, Nick," Razor stepped out of his hiding spot. Jade quickly looked back at him. Their eyes met. Jade had so many questions.

Bossman laughed. "Christ, I haven't heard that name in such a long time. I didn't realize we were on formal terms, Ryan." Razor grimaced when Bossman said his legal name. "He was so loyal and passionate to my program, Jade. Until he met that fucking sister of yours. He went from being my apprentice to my ace in the hole."

"Well, she has a way of changing people."

"That she does. Turned my best man into a lovey-dovey sap."

"I wouldn't call him a lovey-dovey sap per se."

"You don't know him like I do Jade," he began to pace a little. "He was vicious. Cruel! One of the cruelest I've ever seen."

"What's your point?" Razor was getting impatient. He was ready for Bossman to make his move.

"My point is that I trusted you! And you betrayed me!"

"Happens all the time," Razor said nonchalantly. "Move on."

This seemed to really piss off Bossman. Jade looked back at Razor. She wondered what he was doing. Why piss off Bossman? They needed to get out of this alive. That would less likely happen with a raging, mad, psychopath after them. Again, she had to trust Razor. He's had way more experience dealing with Bossman than she did. She just had to look out for a signal from Razor.

"Then you should be prepared to accept the consequences!"

It appeared that the DC officers were waiting for their cue too. They quickly began to shoot at Jade and Razor. Razor swiftly took cover. Jade rolled to the ground and hid behind a fallen tree trunk. She managed to shoot and kill an officer with her arrow as she took cover. Bossman yelled at his men to cease fire again.

"Jade," he sighed. "I'm sorry. I lost my temper there. Are you hurt?"

Jade didn't say anything. She focused on her breathing. Her mask was delivering a breathing treatment. She deeply inhaled the medication.

"Answer me, Jade!"

Raina and Levi rushed into her mind. She needed to get them out of there. They had to be afraid, listening to all of this. Bossman couldn't know that they were there. If he doesn't know, then they were safe. She just needed to give a message to Sarah and Yoko. Once the coast was clear, they needed to get Calvin and the children out of there. She tried to think of ways to deliver the message to them.

"Jade answer me, or I'll kill that boyfriend of yours!"

The mention of David quickly made Jade refocus. How did he know about David? Had spies been watching them? She glanced over herself. There was blood trickling down from her right upper arm. It looked like a bullet grazed her.

"Just a little graze from a bullet," she replied. A gunshot went off. Jade jumped a little. He just killed an officer. She cursed under her breath. What was wrong with this man? She couldn't understand his weird fascination with her.

"Not sure if he was the one who shot you," he said. "But you get the gist."

"Shit," Jade mumbled. Bossman was becoming too unpredictable for her.

"What about you, Ryan? Alive and kicking over there?"

Razor didn't respond. But Jade could see him moving a few trees away.

"That's great," Bossman continued on. He knew that Razor was just fine. "I want to be the one to kill you. I want to be the one to kill you both."

Jade sighed. She really needed to come up with a plan. She had to get Raina and Levi out of there before Bossman noticed them.

"I spend time admiring my new scar. You seem to really favor the collar bone area," Bossman paused. He noticed that Jade was ignoring him. He got a little choked up. "Jade?"

"Well to be fair," she said. "I was aiming for your heart. But you keep moving."

He chuckled a little. "That seems fitting."

"Sorry."

"Don't be, my lovely Jade."

Jade sighed. She realized that there was only one more move left. "I dunno about you, but I don't got all day. Should we just get on with it?"

Bossman sighed also. He too came to the same realization. "It appears that we should," he paused. "Ready?"

"I was born ready."

Bossman chuckled.

Gunshots rained.

Tatianna was the first to move. She took advantage of the distraction of Jade's and Bossman's conversation and caught a few officers by surprise. She stole their guns from their lifeless bodies and retook cover. Tatianna returned fire from behind a tree. This was really personal for her. A couple of the officers there were the same ones that abused her.

The others took Tatianna's lead and began to fight back. Sarah stayed hidden with Calvin and the children.

Jade decided to wait it out. She figured that the officers had to run out of ammo at some point. She just needed to keep her ears open in case they decided to walk around the tree trunk. Gunshots began to rain out from above. Lang, Rosalind, and Reagan were high in the trees. They were picking off the DC officers quickly. There might be some hope for them, after all.

Now she just needed to figure out how to escape Bossman. She was sure that Razor was coming up with a plan on how to kill him, but she had to admit that that option was seeming improbable. The best and the most likely option was to incapacitate him and live to see another day.

Then Jade heard something that terrified her. It was Raina. She let out a piercing scream. It was a scream of fear—and possibly pain. Jade just reacted instinctively. She jumped out from behind the tree trunk and began running towards Raina's screams.

"Raina!" Jade was beginning to panic. Raina let out another scream, this time it was joined by Levi's screams. "RAINA!!"

Why were they screaming? Were they hurt? Where were Sarah and Calvin?

"Jade!" Raina called out.

Jade rushed to the scene to see Calvin trying to fight off three officers. It appeared that Sarah, Raina, and Levi had tried to help him. Sarah had a black eye, and Raina and Levi both had busted lips. Seeing that they couldn't help, Raina began to scream to draw out assistance. Calvin was having trouble, so Jade prepared her bow. Then something hard knocked her to the ground.

Raina screamed out in fear again. "Jade!"

Bossman was on top of her. He had been waiting for Jade to come out. Jade quickly registered what was going on. She grabbed her knife before he had a chance to pin her arm down. She swiftly shoved the knife in his upper thigh. He screamed out in pain and punched her hard in the face. He toppled over. It took everything in Jade not to pass out. She slid away from Bossman's grasp. Blood was oozing out of his leg. He focused his attention on that. Jade noticed that he cracked her combat mask. She could feel her medicine escaping out.

"Shit," she mumbled.

The three officers now had the upper hand on Calvin. Jade quickly grabbed her bow and took one of them out. Shots from above took out the other two.

"Jade!" Raina screamed again.

Unfortunately, Jade couldn't move in time. Bossman had her by her hair and was dragging her away from the group. Bullets whizzed past her as Lang, Rosalind, and Reagan tried to take him out. Jade struggled to get her hands on one of her weapons. They were moving fast. Surprisingly fast, considering that Bossman had a knife sticking out of his leg.

Catching a glimpse of the knife, Jade saw her opportunity, she quickly began to punch the knife's handle—driving the blade further into his leg. He screamed and immediately let her go. He fell to the ground. Seeing another chance to get the upper hand, Jade took her bow and slid behind him. She pressed the handle against his neck and began choking him with it.

Bossman was stunned for a moment. He then began to elbow her—with extraordinary force. Jade focused on remaining strong, but each blow was agonizing. She had to stay strong. She was very optimistic, but it could all end for them right here and now. If she just remained strong, she could kill him, and all their fears and worries would vanish. They could finally breathe. They could finally live.

She just needed to wait him out.

Bossman was starting to get weak. The blows were getting light. Then he suddenly stopped. Jade didn't move. She kept holding the bow with the same force. He was still breathing. She could feel it. She wasn't moving until she felt him draw his last breath.

Sadly, that wasn't happening anytime soon. Bossman used all his force to headbutt her twice. It felt like Jade was hit with a brick—twice. It left her briefly stunned. That was all Bossman needed. He quickly had his hand wrapped around Jade's throat. Jade's eyes got big by the sudden turn of events and the sudden lack of air.

"Fight all you want, Jade, but healthcare will be aggressive!"

Jade struggled for air. She was beginning to make a strange gurgling sound. Her chest was tight. The veins in her face were protruding. She was in severe distress. She had to think—quickly. Jade couldn't leave Raina and Levi. She couldn't leave Helena. Not like this. Not until they were safe.

"See what you make me do?" there was water behind his eyes as if this was something hard for him to do.

He was pinned to her closely. So close that there was no space in between them. Jade just needed him to back away a little, and she could strike. She could move her feet. The knife that was in his leg was resting against her knee. Jade jerked her leg as hard as she could multiple times. Her knee was able to hit the knife. Bossman didn't loosen his grip, but he did move back from her, giving her enough space.

"This is the best deat—"

Jade had her legs around his neck before he could finish his sentence. She locked on to his neck tightly. She tightened her grip like a python.

Luckily for Jade, Bossman loosened his grip. She was able to breathe just a little. Jade's sudden leg chokehold totally caught him by surprise, but not for long. He quickly had her in the air and slamming her repeatedly. Unfortunately for him, Jade's grip never loosened— determination was flowing through her veins. If she was to die here today, she was making sure that Bossman was going with her.

Jade was in the air, in what seemed like the 100th time, when someone came tackling Bossman. This knocked Jade off him, and she went flying in the air. She hit the ground hard and rolled a little. Jade began coughing for air. Her body instantly felt relief.

"Jade!" Helena was quickly at her sister's side.

Jade looked over and saw Razor fighting with Bossman. Bossman was weak, so Razor had no trouble getting the upper hand. Blood was trickling down Jade's face. A few branches cut her when she went flying in the air.

"Are you ok?"

Jade nodded. "Raina?" she rasped.

"They're ok."

Jade began coughing again. It hurt for her to talk. She didn't realize how tight of a grip Bossman had on her throat until she was free. Jade took off what was left of her combat mask. It was all but in shambles and useless at this point. She went into her pocket and took out her inhaler and her old red scarf. She always carried her scarf—like a backup and a form of security. After taking a couple of puffs of her inhaler, Jade wrapped her scarf around her nose and mouth. She felt like her old self.

Once her breathing got back to normal Jade got to her feet. Bossman and Razor were still fighting. Bossman had managed to knock Razor to the ground. He was kneeling, catching his breath and preparing to get up. Jade couldn't allow him to get to his feet. She ran and kneed him in the face with all her might. Bossman flew back. He laid stretched out on his back. Blood oozing from his nose.

He chuckled. "Cheap shot Jade."

Jade caught her breath. "Like hair pulling?"

"Touché."

Jade looked over at Razor, who was getting back to his feet. He nodded at Jade, indicating that he was ok. Jade nodded back. She felt weird without her combat mask.

"How's your breathing my sweet Jade?" there was concern in Bossman's voice. "I don't want you dying on me from an asthma attack."

"Fine, no thanks to you."

He chuckled again. "Sorry about that."

Jade looked at the knife that was now barely visible in his leg. "Yeah me too."

"I deserved it."

"Along with many other things," Tatianna said, walking up. The others followed behind her, including Lang, Rosalind, and Reagan. Jade was relieved to see that David was ok.

Bossman looked at her carelessly. "I assume my officers are dead."

"They are," Jackson said with satisfaction.

Bossman shrugged. "I have more on the way."

Jade knew he was telling the truth. They all needed to leave before his backup came. There was no telling how many more of them there would be. They barely made it out of this attack alive. She wasn't confident that they could make it out of another.

"We gotta move," Jade said.

"Not until he's dead," Jackson charged at Bossman. Bossman quickly got to his feet. He tossed Jackson around with ease.

Everyone wanted their shot at Bossman. He was the primary source of their problem. He was the reason why they lived in such fear and stress. This was their shot to end all of that. They all got their licks in when they could. But even by his self, Bossman was proving to be tough to take down.

No one could match him. The only two people that gave him a little trouble was Razor and Clay. Noticing that, Razor and Clay began to double team him while the others got in cheap shots that could help them finally kill Bossman.

Jade lingered back—along with Helena, David, and Keeper. Keeper attended to fixing Jade's mask, while Jade, Helena, and David looked out for Bossman's backup. She was a nervous wreck. She had enough of Bossman for one day. She wanted to leave and regroup. There was a bad feeling about staying. She understood why everyone was focused on having an opportunity to kill Bossman. He made this world unbearable to live in. She'd experienced the same fear that everyone else experienced.

The countless amounts of torture, abuse, and deaths. They were all on his hands. But for whatever reason, at this moment, Jade couldn't kill him. It was the thought of Raina and Levi that held her back. Their safety was her number one priority. They needed to get out of there—fast.

Bossman noticed Jade's hesitation. He never took his eyes off her as he fought. It was something about the way he looked at Jade that terrified her. This seemed to be what he wanted. They were playing right into his hand, and all of this was a trap. Jade panicked a little when the thought crossed her mind. The children were with Sarah, Yoko, and Calvin. That wasn't enough to fight off a DC army. She had to end this—quickly. Something was telling her that the backup was nearby. She looked around and noticed Calvin watching them. She had an idea.

Jade pulled out her inhaler and took a couple of puffs. She rewrapped her scarf. Then she charged at Bossman. She ran as fast as she could. It was easy to run pass Bossman—he was preoccupied with Razor and Clay. She executed the exact move she did on Razor. Jade jumped on his back, wrapped her legs around his waist, and her arm around his throat. She took her leg and stomped on his injured leg.

Bossman fell to the ground.

"I see you keep finding ways to get me in between your legs," he joked as he struggled to breathe. Jade wrapped her forearm around him tighter. "They're here, Jade," he croaked.

"We won't be," she said confidently. She looked up and saw Calvin pacing back and forth. He was antsy. All he saw was Bossman on top of Jade. "Calvin! Protect your Queen!"

Jade never saw Calvin run so fast. Before she knew it, she was up in the air right along with Bossman. She quickly untangled herself from him and dropped to the ground. She landed on her back—hard. The pain caused her to cough a little. Razor swiftly helped her up.

Bossman didn't stand a chance against Calvin. Calvin tossed him around like a rag doll. Jade never saw somebody get viciously tossed around so much. The sight of Calvin in action scared her a little. Bossman lost consciousness once Calvin threw him sideways against a tree.

"Well done my brave knight," Jade said. "Now come, let's go."

Tatianna pulled out a knife. "Time to slit his throat."

"We gotta go," Jade said.

"Not until he's dead," Jackson demanded.

"There's an army of DC officers coming."

"Jade's right," Razor said. "We need to leave."

"Not until he's dead!" Jackson and the rest of the group began walking towards an unconscious Bossman.

Bullets whizzed past them.

"Shit!" Tatianna yelled out of frustration.

They all took off running. They ran into Yoko, Sarah, and the children along the way. Jade was happy to see that they were alright. She was ready to get them out of there. The day consisted of nothing but fear and death. It was way too much for the children to experience. She wanted to provide them safety. That seemed impossible.

All she was able to provide was the real-life version of hide-and-seek—along with fleeing for your life. And that's what they did.

They ran.

They ran until they were out of breath.

They ran until the bullets stopped flying.

~38~

They found refuge in a run-down factory. Jade wasn't sure how far out they were from the old campgrounds. It had to be far, though. They were well into the night before they found the place. Her whole sense of direction was off. Most of the day consisted of running, hiding, and fighting that she felt all turned around. Her body ached as soon as she was able to sit and rest. She was sore. Her sides, her head, her legs, her arms—every inch of her was in pain.

No one said anything. They all reflected on the events of the day. The many lives lost. They had built themselves a small army, and now that was all gone. They thought that they had prepared themselves for any kind of attack. They were very wrong. No one can prepare themselves for the craziness and viciousness of Bossman.

David and Jade didn't speak. He seemed a little distant to her. She didn't understand what that was about. She wondered what he was thinking. What was he planning? After the events of today, Jade was sure that he had to be planning something. After a while, he finally turned his attention to her.

"You ok?" he looked her over.

"Yeah. You?"

"I'm alright," he suddenly got up. "I need to talk to Razor."

Jade was a little surprised by his sudden need to consult with Razor. "Ok."

David quickly walked off. Jade watched after him. Once he was out of sight, she closed her eyes and sighed. It was a long day. She didn't have the energy to worry about what he was up to. She took deep breaths.

Inhale.

Exhale.

Repeat.

Jade then noticed that someone was crying. At first, it was quiet and very subtle, but over time, it began to get louder and out of control. Someone was breaking down from the events of today. She got up and began searching for the source. She was stealth. She didn't want to alarm anyone. After everything that happened today, Jade wanted to break down and cry herself. For some reason, she couldn't. The tears just wouldn't come.

Jade was surprised when she stumbled across Tatianna. She had her knees up to her chest, and her head rested on her arms. Tatianna was sobbing uncontrollably. She didn't see Jade walk up.

"Tatianna?" Jade said with caution. "You ok?"

Tatianna jumped up, surprised. She quickly wiped away her tears. "I'm fine."

"I'm sorry I stopped you from killing him."

Tatianna shook her head. "It's not that."

"Then what?"

"All this shit seems so pointless. We spent time preparing, building. And then he comes and wipes it all away." Jade didn't say anything. Tatianna had a good point. "I mean, is it even worth it anymore? Should we keep fighting? Look at all the people that died today. We were no better than the Black Deficit at HQ."

"You're absolutely right," Jade admitted. "I've been wondering the same thing."

"I don't know what to do anymore, Jade."

"You're preaching to the choir. But I'm not ready to give up just yet."

Tatianna shook her head and laughed. She was amazed by Jade's persistence.

"Not until he's dead."

"I don't think that's even possible."

"Trust me," Jade said confidently. "He bleeds, just like the rest of us."

"Well, this won't end until one of you are dead."

Jade nodded. She definitely agreed with that statement. It was hard for her to live with Bossman alive. She couldn't live in peace with him roaming around. And it appeared that he felt the same way. It might be better for everyone if they both died. As long as he was gone, she was okay with dying too. She wanted peace for everyone.

"Or maybe if we're both dead."

Tatianna looked at her, confused.

"I'm prepared for that.

"Yeah, but I don't think everyone else is."

"Well, they should."

"Jade?"

Jade was surprised to see Raina and Levi walking up to them. She hoped that they hadn't been there long. She didn't want them to know that she was preparing to die.

"Damn everyone is sneaking up on me tonight," Tatianna admitted.

"What's wrong, my little munchkins?"

"We just wanna be with you," Raina said.

Jade motioned for them to sit, and they both sat on her lap. She cringed when they did. Her body was in a lot of pain, and the weight of them didn't help much. Tatianna just laughed at her. She knew Jade wasn't going to tell them to get up. Not after the day they had. Tatianna felt like Jade spoiled them too much, but after today, she understood why.

They all sat there silently for a while. Raina and Levi held on to Jade tightly. They were beyond afraid, and Jade had become their security blanket.

"Jade," Raina finally spoke again.

"Yeah."

"Thank you for protecting us."

"Yeah, from the big bad man," Levi said.

"Hey!" Tatianna was a little offended. "I helped too!"

Raina and Levi giggled. Tatianna pretended to be mad even more and began tickling them. Jade thought she was going to pass out with the two of them squirming around in her lap. Tatianna eventually noticed the look of pain on Jade's face and stopped.

"Sorry."

"It's fine," Jade gritted.

Tatianna couldn't help herself. She began to laugh a little.

"Screw you," Jade couldn't help but laugh a little too. Raina and Levi joined in on the laughter also—although they didn't understand why they were laughing.

"There you two are," Sarah said, walking up. "Come on. It's time for bed."

"Can we stay with Jade please?" Raina begged.

"They're ok with me."

"Actually, I'll rather they go with Sarah," Razor interjected.

"Damn is everyone convening at my hiding spot!"

"We need to talk."

Jade dreaded those words, especially when they came from Razor. *We need to talk.* No good news ever came after that. She sighed. She was ready for the day to be over. She was ready for her life to be over. Jade gave Raina and Levi a kiss goodnight. They reluctantly went with Sarah. Tatianna stood up and helped Jade off the floor. They both walked off with Razor.

They found the rest of the group, besides Sarah, Calvin, and the children, in what used to be the employees' breakroom. They all sat around with the look of sadness and defeat. There was no more hope left in them. Jade and Tatianna hung out by the doorway while Razor went to the center of the room.

"So, what's the next big plan?" Tatianna asked.

"Honestly," Razor admitted. "There isn't one."

"What?" Jade couldn't believe it. They had to think of something. They couldn't just hide out there and wait to be found.

"The only other thing I can think of is getting them to the border," Razor said gesturing to Beverly and Jackson.

"Fleeing then?" Tatianna said. "That's our next move?"

"Helping those who want to flee, yeah that's our next move."

"Who's all fleeing?" Tatianna demanded. A part of her was annoyed.

Rosalind raised her hand. "I'm tired of fighting."

"Sarah and the children need to go too," Jade said suddenly. That was how she could keep them safe. Once they were across the border, they would be out of Bossman's reach. They would be safe. They could live in peace. She can then focus on taking him down.

"What?" Helena was surprised and a little hesitant. She didn't want to be away from the children.

"Will you take them with you?" Jade asked Jackson.

He nodded. "We'll look after them."

"Jade, you sure this is a good idea?" Helena persisted.

"I can't focus when they're here, Helena. I held back way too much because I was thinking of them."

"That you did," David mumbled.

Jade looked over at him. She was a little shocked. "What's that supposed to mean?"

"We had our chance to kill him, and you stopped us."

"There was an army coming."

"We could've taken them."

"Don't be stupid, David. We barely made it out of there alive."

"It seemed like you were looking for a reason not to kill him."

Jade stood stunned and speechless.

"Enough Loverboy," Razor interjected. "Jade made the smart play. And she only did it because she was thinking of Raina and Levi. I agree, they go across the border."

Jade was fuming. She couldn't believe David. How could he accuse her of such a thing? Why on earth would she want to keep Bossman alive? That was insane. She wanted him dead just like everyone else. It upset her when they couldn't kill him when they had a chance. But she thought about Raina and Levi. She thought about the many DC officers that were armed and ready to kill. A different decision had to be made. She wasn't proud of it, but she would make it again if it meant that it would keep the children alive.

"What about those who are staying behind?" Clay asked. "What's the plan for us?"

"Right now, we just focus on getting the others across the border safely."

"Which way is the best to go?" Lang asked.

"Straight across the river. Everybody knows how to swim?"

"The Detroit River?"

"Is there another river between Detroit and Canada?"

"Detroit is heavily guarded with officers," Jade couldn't see how they could get around that.

"I know a way," Razor said confidently.

"And does Bossman?" Jade couldn't help but ask. Bossman had been in Razor's head a lot lately. She noticed that David rolled his eyes at the mention of Bossman.

"I know what you're getting at and trust me he doesn't."

Jade didn't say anything.

"Now, does everyone know how to swim?" Everyone said they did. Razor continued, "We'll rest here for a couple of days and then make our way to the border."

"Is that it for tonight, Ryan?" Tatianna joked. Razor gave her a deadly stare. She quickly retracted. "Sorry."

"That's it."

David was the first to leave out. He brushed pass Jade without looking at her. She watched him as he stormed off. His behavior toward her left Jade baffled. She didn't ask for any of this. This was just her life. She thought he understood that. Apparently, she was wrong. Everyone else filed out beside Razor, who was lingering behind to talk to Jade.

"Don't worry about him," he said.

"He's starting to hate me."

Razor laughed. "God Jade not this again."

"What did you two talk about?"

"What?"

"He told me he was gonna talk to you. What did you talk about?"

"I never talked to him."

"Stop lying Razor."

"I never talked to him."

Jade sighed and rolled her eyes. "Fine. Be that way."

"He's just probably upset at the way Bossman was flirting with you."

"Oh, so attempting to strangle me to death is his way of flirting?"

"This is Bossman we're talking about."

"Honestly Razor, I dunno much about him. I dunno what he's capable of. All I know are the rumors."

"And I'm telling you the rumors are true."

"He's not gonna stop looking for me, is he?"

Razor shook his head. "He's obsessed with you."

Jade figured that out already, but she still sighed out of frustration. She sat on the counter in the breakroom. Razor sat next to her.

"How did you get your nickname anyway?"

It was Razor's turn to sigh. He knew people were going to be curious about his name once Bossman used it. "I'm amazed at your curiosity."

"Oh, come on! You had to know I was gonna ask. I feel stupid thinking that your name was really Razor this whole time."

"It is," he shot back. "My dad always called me that."

"Your dad?" Jade perked up a little. She was always fascinated with Razor's past.

"Yeah, my parents were pretty old when they had me. And I was a very wild child. I was always in some kind of trouble. I got into a lot of fights and had some serious anger issues. My dad called me Razor because I was sharp and always on edge. I think he was just trying to make light of the situation. My mom and I didn't get along too well."

Jade knew the answer before she asked, but she couldn't help herself. "Are they still alive?"

"Of course not. My dad died in one of the natural disasters, and then my mom shortly after."

"Sorry."

"It was a long time ago, Jade."

Jade sighed out of frustration. "What are we gonna do?"

"I'm honestly, not sure. I never saw him obsessed with someone like this."

"I feel like we're all out of options."

"Well, there's one option."

"What's that?"

"Canada."

"Seriously? You wanna flee while others are here suffering?"

"I said it's an option."

Jade didn't say anything for a while. She felt completely lost. She didn't know what to do anymore. She couldn't go back to just surviving but trying to fight back was proving to be just as useless—and helpless. There was just this urge to try to save everyone. It seemed like the more she tried, the more people that died. That burden was starting to take its toll on her.

Razor stared at her for a while. "To be completely honest with you, Jade, my only main concern is protecting Helena and you. No one else matters."

"I know."

"So, how about you focus on that, instead of trying to save the world," he paused. "Because I don't know if you noticed, but the world has ended. There's not that much to save anymore."

"I know."

Razor got up. "Get some rest."

"I'm gonna hang back for a little while."

Razor nodded. "Don't be too long."

**

They only found themselves at the factory for a few days. They didn't want to wait around too long before they fled. Jade was glad to be starting the journey. She had spent the past few days with people who were angry at her. David was still mad at her about the whole Bossman thing. And now Raina was upset with her. She didn't like the idea of being separated from Jade. Sarah did her best trying to convince Raina that Jade was only looking out for her safety, but Raina didn't believe it. She didn't understand why Jade would choose to stay behind.

"You won't be worried about me, but I'll be worried sick about you," Raina said. "Why would you want that for me?"

"I don't want that for you," Jade explained. "I want you to be safe."

"I want that for you too!"

Jade understood what Raina was saying, but fleeing was not an option for her. She had unfinished business to attend to. Raina felt like Jade was being selfish. Those words hit Jade hard. She hasn't been called selfish in a while. The words brought Jade back to the last conversation she had with her mother—or argument rather. It brought tears to Jade's eyes.

"She's a child," Razor said once he saw Jade crying in the break room. "She'll get over it eventually. Besides, you don't need to explain yourself to a child."

Jade didn't say anything. There was nothing that she could say. Raina might've been right. Jade was selfish and a little stubborn by staying behind. It just felt like something that she needed to do. Levi, on the other hand, was sad but understood. He didn't want to leave Jade behind, but he also wanted to get away from the big, bad man. Jade explained to him that Bossman couldn't get to him once they were across the river. Levi was excited about that. He was also excited about getting a chance to be in the water. He never experienced it before and was looking forward to it.

"Sometimes you gotta be prepared to make decisions for those you care about without their permission," Razor continued. "They won't always understand what you're doing. You gotta accept that they might end up hating you."

Jade listened and nodded. Out of everything that's happened, she was comforted by the fact that Razor was always on her side. She never realized that until now—even from their rocky start. He always stood behind her decisions. Although there were times when he challenged some of them, he had her back, nonetheless. Jade was grateful for that. She was thankful for him and Helena. If she had them, then she would be alright.

The journey to the Detroit River was going to take about three days. It mainly would take that long because they would be making multiple stops for the children and Jade. Keeper was still working on her mask, and she was trying to ration out the few inhalers she had. They all found it unfortunate that all the trucks they stolen from the raids were now destroyed. It would've made the trip much more comfortable and less awkward for Jade. She tried to strike up a few conversations with David along the way, but she was met with stone-cold silence.

"What am I guilty of?" she was frustrated. "Can you at least tell me that?"

"It seemed like you enjoyed it," David finally said. "The way you interacted with him...I can see why he's obsessed with you."

Jade stopped walking. She stood there for a moment in disbelief. "Are you serious?"

"You asked."

"You're punishing me for something I didn't do!"

"You didn't see what I saw."

"And you didn't feel what I felt!"

David didn't say anything. He continued to walk on.

"You never even gave me a chance to explain myself!" Jade stood there, fuming. Tears began to form. She was feeling a strong urge to just leave. Maybe things would be a little easier if she was just alone. Relationships were complicated, and life seemed a lot simpler when she didn't have them. She quickly regretted having that thought. There was no way she was going to leave her sister again. But maybe that was the way—just her, Helena, and Razor. That would be just as easy.

Again, Jade regretted that thought. She couldn't leave Keeper behind, and she was growing closer to Tatianna. Jade sighed.

Relationships.

The group was well ahead of her and didn't appear to hear her and David's conversation. She wiped away a few tears that escaped her and moved on.

Jade was afraid of going into Detroit again. She hadn't been there since the DC officers set up there—that was about eight years ago. People began fleeing across the border as debtors were getting mass incarcerated. A good number of debtors had fled before Bossman set up patrols at the borders of every state that was across from another country. He didn't want anyone to escape.

During Jade's last trip to Detroit, she almost got caught. She was looking for Helena when she had a bad asthma attack. She took a trip to the hospital and was hunted down for days when she tried to escape. Eventually, she lost the officers through a group of protestors who were trying to repeal the new medical law. People were still brave during that time. Bossman hadn't snuffed out all the hope from them yet.

On the first night of their journey, they all cramped inside this small rambler-style house. They all took turns keeping watch. It was very deserted in the area, but they wanted to be safe. The patrol was limited to the porch because they were few in numbers. Jade couldn't sleep so she agreed to keep first watch. Jackson volunteered to keep watch with her. They both sat on the porch in silence for a while.

Jade wasn't in much of a mood for conversation. She was feeling depressed and wanted to be left alone. Jackson, on the other hand, was a little uncomfortable in the silence. It seemed like he wasn't used to it. This was their first time alone. It never occurred to them before, but they never had a one on one conversation with each other. In fact, Jade couldn't say that they were even friends.

"How's your asthma?" Jackson asked, trying to make conversation.

"It's ok right now." Jade readjusted her scarf. She did it out of habit whenever she thought about her asthma.

"Sorry about your mask."

"Yeah me too. I hope Keeper can fix it."

"He will. Trust me. He's good with that kind of stuff."

"Why did you and your sister mistreat him?"

Jackson got uncomfortable.

"Sorry, I was always just curious about that," Jade explained. "He's so loyal. I don't think y'all appreciated that."

"We didn't," Jackson admitted. "He was close with our father. Our father always appreciated his inventions. We only saw Keeper for that after he died."

"Well, he's much more than that."

"I know. I realize that now."

Jade nodded. "I'm sorry. I'm not trying to be judgmental or anything."

"I know he's your friend. You're just sticking up for him."

They fell back into silence for a moment. Jackson was figuring out what else to say while Jade was thinking about relationships. It was ironic how she was criticizing Jackson for his friendship with Keeper when she was having issues herself. She decided to shift the conversation a bit.

"Do you miss your father?"

"Everyday. Although as of lately, I've been finding myself angry with him."

"Why?"

Jackson looked uncomfortable again. "Because me and my sister didn't want any of this. We didn't want to be in a war. We just wanted to live our lives in peace. We were in good health. We weren't on the DCs radar."

Jade didn't say anything for a moment. She was a little surprised. She wasn't expecting him to admit any of that, but she understood where he was coming from. And she couldn't blame him either. It was interesting, though. Clay and Reagan were in the exact same position as Jackson and Beverly, but Clay and Reagan chose to help and fight and didn't seem to regret it any. Jackson and Beverly didn't seem to have a choice.

"I get it," she finally said.

"Really?"

"Not saying I agree with it, but I understand."

"It's just, by the time our father died, he had so many people following him. Once he was gone, all those people naturally looked to us. We didn't want to disappoint them or our father's memory, so we took over and pretended that this was something that we wanted."

"Now I know why y'all didn't do a lot of rescue missions."

"I'm sorry."

Jade sighed. "Don't be. Just promise that you'll actually look after Raina and Levi."

"I will. That's the least we can do for you, Jade."

"Thank you."

"And don't worry about Raina being mad at you. She'll come around."

"Thanks."

"And so will David."

"Does everyone know about that?"

"He's been giving you the cold shoulder. Of course, we've noticed."

Jade was a little relieved. She felt the need to pick Jackson's brain a bit. "He says it seemed like I enjoyed my interaction with Bossman. Did you notice that?"

Jackson was silent for a moment—as if he was thinking back to that day. "You two did seem to feed off each other. I wouldn't say that you enjoyed it, though."

"What you mean feeding off each other?"

"Your energies seemed to match. It was definitely clear why he's fascinated with you."

"It is?" Jade just wasn't getting it. What did they see?

"He brings out a different side of you, Jade. And to be completely honest, I don't think Razor matches his crazy. I think you do."

Jade was a little stunned by that. "What?"

"Well, let me take that back a little, I think you have the potential to match his crazy."

"I still don't follow."

"You never saw yourself in action. That day when HQ was burned down. You were terrifying in those woods. I was just glad that you were on our side. You were showered with DC officers' blood."

Jade didn't say anything.

"And you were covered in more blood a few days ago."

"I was just trying to save everyone."

"We get that, but you look vicious all the same."

"But you all killed people too. Everyone was ready to slit Bossman's throat," Jade was getting a little offended. Why was everyone starting to look at her as a monster?

"By all means, I'm not saying that we're innocent. But seeing how you and Bossman look. And seeing how you both interact with each other. It just put somethings into perspective," he paused. He looked over at Jade's disappointed face. "Just give him time. He'll come around."

Jade sighed. "I'm afraid there won't be any."

Jackson didn't say anything.

Jade had a point. The only thing that none of them had enough of was time. She didn't want to end things with David on a bad note. She loved him. It would break her heart if something happened to one of them, and they didn't have the chance to make up. But she couldn't keep going on with him giving her the cold shoulder either. She was stuck between a rock and a hard place. It was very frustrating.

"Are you still mad that Beverly and I want to flee?" Jackson eventually asked.

The odd question pulled Jade away from her thoughts. She looked over at Jackson, who was looking back at her. He wore a look of curiosity. He seemed to really care about what she thought. That baffled and intrigued her.

"No, why do you ask?"

"Was just wondering. You were really pissed when we first announced that we were."

"It felt like all those people died in vain by you both giving up," Jade explained. "But now, with everything that's happened, I get it. Everything feels so hopeless."

"But you're not giving up."

"Trust me, I wanna, but I just can't for some reason."

"Is it pride?"

"Seems more like stubbornness," Jade had been analyzing her reasoning over the past few days. That was the only conclusion that made sense to her.

Jackson laughed a little. "I'm surprised you admitted that."

"Just being honest."

"I can appreciate that."

"I don't think any less of you and Beverly for wanting to leave," Jade looked over at him. "I just want you to know that."

Jackson nodded. "Thanks, Jade."

The rest of their shift went by fast and uneventful. Jackson started to doze off. Jade let him sleep. She stared into the pitch darkness of night. A part of her wondered if some of Bossman's spies were watching her right now. She knew that she sounded paranoid, but she had a weird feeling.

"You alright?"

Jade jumped. She quickly turned around and saw Razor standing at the door. She sighed. "Yeah, I'm good."

Razor walked out on the porch and raised his eyebrows. "You sure? Your frown says otherwise."

"Just a stupid thought. I'm fine, and I don't wanna talk about it."

"Fair enough," he kicked Jackson. "What a wonderful way to keep watch."

Jackson looked around, embarrassed. "Sorry. Didn't know I dozed off."

"I was fine," Jade said.

"Ok, well, your time is up. Go inside and get some rest," Razor demanded. "Clay and Reagan are up next."

Jade followed Jackson inside. He took a spot by his sister while Jade headed toward the back of the house. She found a place closest to the back door. She tried to make the hardwood floor as comfortable as possible. Once she found a comfortable position, she began to drift off to sleep. Then someone snuggled up against her. They were small.

"I'm sorry," Raina whispered. "I love you, Jade."

Jade couldn't help herself. Tears escaped her eyes. "I love you too munchkin," she was happy that someone eventually came around.

~39~

The next couple of days on the road went by smoothly. They hid out in an abandoned store once they got to the border of Detroit. They needed to scout the area out and the path to the Detroit River. Jade was antsy. She didn't know how this was going to go. They were overwhelmingly outnumbered. They all might not make it out of this alive. Or worse, they would get caught and get imprisoned. Jade dreaded that thought. Razor reassured her that everything would be fine. She tried to find comfort in that, but she couldn't.

"We'll get through it," he said again.

"I hope so."

"Jade, it isn't good for morale to be doubting everything."

"Sorry," she looked across the room and saw David talking to Keeper.

Things had not gotten any better between them over the past couple of days. "Do you think I'm like Bossman?"

Razor sighed. "Jade."

"Jackson mentioned that he thinks I have the potential to be just like him."

"I really need you to focus," Razor had a lot on his mind about their current mission.

"Sorry, you're right." Razor was always there for her. She could at least do the same for him. "What's the plan?"

"Me, Clay, Junior, and Lang are gonna scout out the area. At least five miles up and see how the patrol is."

"Ok. What should we do here?"

"Nothing. Just keep watch until we get back."

"Sounds good."

Razor looked at Jade for a moment. He sighed again. "Everything will be ok, I promise."

Jade just smiled at him and nodded. Razor went off to get ready. Jade tried to refocus herself. She had to get Raina and Levi across the border safely. That was her main mission, and that was what she had to focus on at the moment. Everything else had to be put on the back burner. What they were about to do was incredibly dangerous and scary—especially for the children. She wasn't sure how she felt about the whole thing. Jade was relieved that they were going to be safe, but she was going to miss them terribly.

They all divided up a time to keep watch between them. Jade agreed to keep watch by herself because they were a person short. Of course, everyone disagreed with that notion, but she ignored them. She wanted to be left alone. She was tired. Tired of plans and missions. Tired of being on patrol and keeping watch—just tired of it all.

Honestly, she had a strong urge to get Raina and Levi to safety and then turn herself in. She needed to be realistic, she couldn't spend her whole life being on the run.

Who can live like that?

The answer was everyone.

Everyone who was a debtor and everyone who decided to help them. It was no kind of life to live, but sadly, it was a life that everyone was living in.

Jade took her bow and arrow, wrapped her scarf around her nose and mouth, and armed herself with her knives. Then she took her shift on patrol once Razor, Lang, Junior, and Clay left. They were to keep watch only up to a half a mile from the store, but Jade went a little further. She really wanted to get away from everyone.

It felt like she was slowly falling into a depression, which was very bad—especially at this time. She knew what the cause of it was. David. He told her that he wouldn't let Bossman alter his feelings toward Jade. He lied. He saw one interaction with them, and everything changed. It broke Jade's heart.

Was she that unlovable?

It seemed like she had a knack for turning lovers against her. Maybe she was a monster, after all.

Jade walked around aimlessly for a while. It was eerily silent. No one ever wondered in major cities anymore. Even the few rich people stayed clear—in fear that they would mistakenly get identified as debtors. The silence was oddly peaceful to her. So much had been going on recently that she could use a little quiet. Most of the recent noises have been screams and gunshots, which all indicated terror. The silence meant peace, Jade appreciated that. She was desperately in need of a few quiet moments.

After some much-needed time passed, Jade made her way back to their hideout. Reagan and Yoko were standing out front when she got back. It was no telling how long they had been out there waiting. Jade didn't care at that point.

"Everything good?" Yoko asked.

"All clear."

"Don't really think we'll come into much contact with people out here," Reagan said. "I'm betting all of the action will be closer to the river."

"I think you're right," Jade admitted.

"Well get you some rest, Jade," Yoko said. "It's our turn for watch."

"Alright, be safe ladies."

"We will."

Jade walked inside the store once Yoko and Reagan walked out of her sight. Although it was daytime, the store was very dark inside—and dusty. Jade tighten her scarf. She had to make sure she couldn't breathe in any specks of dust. They couldn't afford her having an asthma attack now. Her mask wasn't close to being fixed, and she just lost the ample supply of inhalers at the camp. It was hard for her to get used to her scarf again. She was so accustomed to having her combat mask that she found the air from her scarf to be quite stuffy.

Just about everyone was sleeping in the store. No one stirred when she walked in. Jade found herself a spot in the back of the store and sat down. She watched as everyone slept. She wished that she could sleep, but she was way too antsy to rest. All she could think about is if Bossman would be there.

Did he know their next move?

Did he know that this was the only move they had left?

Flee.

Jade was a ball of nerves. She really could use a drink. Ironically enough, they were currently hiding out in a liquor store. The liquor, however, was long gone. Along with anything else useful that once occupied the store.

Eventually, someone began to stir. Jade looked over and noticed that it was David. He stretched and slowly got up. He let out a silent yawn and paused once he saw Jade. She quickly diverted her eyes. She was embarrassed. She didn't realize that she had been staring. To her surprise, he got up and walked over to her. He took a seat beside her.

"Hey."

"Hey," she hated to admit it, but she felt giddy. This was the first time in a few days that he actually talked to her. And he was the one to initiate it.

"How was it out there?"

"Quiet."

"Not surprised. No one in their right mind will come this far."

"Yeah, it's a little peaceful though...to me anyway."

"Compared to the last few days, I can see why you'd say that."

Jade nodded. She didn't know what else to say. She had so many questions for him. Was this it? Did he want nothing else to do with her? Once Raina and Levi were gone, would he leave too? Was he fleeing to Canada?

To home?

Jade never once thought about that. How could she be so stupid? For the first time, in a long time, David would actually be close to home. He had spent so long trying to get back once everything happened. This would be the first time he could finally go back. A wave of emotions hit her. She no longer had to ask. He was leaving her.

An awkward silence hung in the air.

"I'm sorry I turned out to be a monster," Jade didn't want him to leave thinking of her that way.

He frowned. "I never said you were a monster."

"I know, but you think differently of me."

"We all have issues, Jade."

"But mines isn't something that you can look over, is it?"

David sighed. "I admit it. I do see you in a different light."

"It's not something you can love?"

"I never said I stopped loving you."

"You definitely haven't been treating me the same."

"I know."

"You're leaving, aren't you?"

David was silent.

"Is that why you've been acting so distant toward me?"

"Partly."

"...Bossman has to die David."

"And we had that opportunity, but you didn't take it."

"I was thinking of Raina and Levi."

"And I think you were using them as an excuse."

Jade looked at him in disbelief.

"You keep saying that we all would've died that day if we killed him," David said. "But I know you, Jade. I know that you would be willing to die if it meant that you could kill him in the process. We all were willing to do that. Once he was dead, Sarah and the children would've been safe. You stopped us for another reason. Maybe one day you'll figure out why, but I already know," he stopped and paused. It looked like he realized the reason all over again. "So, I think it's best for me to finally go home and try to live in peace."

A few tears fell from Jade's eyes. "I understand," she knew there was no way to talk him out of it.

His mind was made up. Who would be willing to turn down an opportunity to live in peace? He definitely deserved it. Asking him to stay behind would've been selfish.

David was right, though. She was not willing to flee and leave Bossman alive to terrorize everyone else. It wasn't right. It wasn't fair. Jade was tired of living in a world of unfairness. At least now, Raina and Levi would have David to look after them. It would also make the transition for Raina a lot easier too. She knew David just as long as she knew Jade. Raina would find some comfort in that.

"I'm gonna miss you," Jade wiped away her tears.

"Me too."

Keeper sat up. Helena did too. Jade and David no longer said anything to each other. They started to look aimlessly around the store. Jade did her best to try to look normal, but she was hurting inside. She really was heartbroken. She had a feeling that things were coming to an end with her and David, but it hadn't been confirmed yet. Jade was able to live in the bliss of ignorance for a little while.

Sadly, all of that was shattered now, and she was left with nothing but pain. Keeper got up and stretched. Helena quickly followed. They both noticed David and Jade sitting in the back of the store. They took in the scene.

"Ready to go?" Keeper finally asked David.

"Yeah," David got up. "Let's see if they're back yet."

David and Keeper walked out of the store. Helena headed back toward her sister. She didn't acknowledge David or Keeper when she passed them. She quickly took David's spot next to Jade.

"I'm sorry Jade," Helena said once David was out of the store.

"Don't be."

Helena paused. She was going back and forth on whether she should ask her next question. She decided that she should. "Thinking about giving up?"

"Turning myself in."

"Don't."

"I won't," Jade meant it. "There's no way I'm leaving you again."

Helena stared at Jade. She searched her eyes. She finally nodded—accepting that her sister was telling the truth. "Thank you."

"No point of thanking me. You're my world, Helena."

Helena smiled. "I love you too, Jade.

**

They all waited for the dead of night to make their way across the border. It was the best chance they had. The blanket of darkness could conceal them from the DCs eyes. They needed all the concealment they could get. Hopefully, it would make the trip a whole lot easier.

Razor came back and reported that the next five miles up were clear. There was no kind of patrol going on there. Lang took his rifle and was able to scout out the area a little further. Again, it appeared that there was no patrol going on.

"You think it's a trap?" Jade asked Razor. She was really concerned with the lack of security. This area should've been crawling with it.

Razor shook his head. "They're focusing on catching people by the border."

"Are you sure? It would seem easier to catch them before they got to the river."

"They can't charge them with illegally fleeing if they never get close."

Jade sighed. That seemed like a good point. You can't really prove that someone was trying to flee if they're still miles away from the border. She just had to be sure.

"Ok."

"Try to rest up as much as you can," Razor suggested. "It's gonna be a long night."

Jade went back to her spot in the back of the store. She tried lying down. Getting comfortable was hard. She was quickly tired of sleeping on hardwood floors. She missed her bed back at camp. It didn't hit her how cozy her camp life had been. She really didn't appreciate it until it was gone.

There was no telling if they could get back to that kind of lifestyle again. None of them realized what they built until now. They had a community—something that has never been done in a while. Now all of that was gone. It didn't look like it was coming back either.

Jade tossed and turned while trying to count sheep. She was exhausted and could really use some energy. She just needed to focus on calming her nerves and clearing her mind. The imaginary sheep kept running through her mind. The sheep usually helped her fall asleep, but it was taking its time that day. Jade was up to 200 when she eventually started drifting off.

Sadly, she couldn't fall into a deep sleep. She was sleeping, but still aware of her surroundings. She heard everyone's conversations. People snoring. People exchanging shifts, and more. By the time it was ready to get going, Jade had found herself even more exhausted than before. It was annoying.

The river was roughly 10 miles from their current location. The plan was to split up. Those who were staying behind were going to draw off the guards while the others tried to cross the border unnoticed. Razor was confident that the distraction of the guards would be easy once they saw Jade. The officers would be so focused on her that the others should slip by undetected. Easy peasy—at least for those who were crossing the border.

The plan was still unclear on how the others would get out of there. They just planned on winging their escape. Jade wasn't too worried. As long as Raina and Levi were alright, nothing else really mattered to her.

Surprisingly, the trip to the border went by fast. Everyone was silent along the way. Even Calvin, who usually counted his steps, was quiet along the journey. He carried Raina and Levi with ease. Jade tended to stick by him during the most part of the trip. Raina and Levi were asleep, but Jade felt the need to be by them. This was the last time she was going to be with them.

The realization hit her hard. She was more than likely, never going to see them again. She fought back the tears. It surprised her when she heard someone sniffling beside her. Jade looked over and saw Helena crying. Her sister was thinking about the same thing. Helena was going to miss them just as much as she was. Jade wrapped her arm around her sister to comfort her—and herself.

The second half of the trip Jade found herself near David. They didn't say too much to each other, but he did reach out and took her hand. The simple act of them hand-holding made Jade's heart race. She was grateful for any kind of affection. She looked up at him. He was looking at her.

"I love you," he whispered.

"I love you too," Jade felt closure. She was happy that this would be the last words they'll say to each other.

They got to the area where they were to split up quickly after that. Jade and David hugged and kissed for the last time. Jade took in how soft his lips were; how firm his hands were pressed against her lower back.

Calvin slowly handed off Raina and Levi to Jackson and David. The children woke up during the exchange. Jade hugged and kissed on them as much as she could.

"I love you my little munchkins," she managed to say. "Be safe."

Raina started crying. "I love you too, Jade. Please make it back to me."

"I will."

"Love you too, Jade," Levi mumbled in sadness. "Miss you."

"I'll miss you too little man."

"Alright. Time to move," Razor said. Everyone else quickly said their goodbyes, and they started going their separate ways. "Watch out for our signal," Razor said to Jackson.

"We will. Be safe."

"You too."

They all walked off.

Jade took a deep breath. She prepared herself for the final battle.

~40~

The smell of a storm was coming—Jade could feel it. They've experienced so many crazy storms over the past 10 years that you can sense when another one was approaching. Jade found herself to be afraid. She hated experiencing a storm during the night. It was something about the darkness that made it seem a hundred times worse. She just prayed that it would hold off until the others made it safely. It could be helpful for their escape, though.

Razor, Helena, Jade, Keeper, Tatianna, Yoko, Calvin, Clay, Reagan, Danita, Junior, and Lang all hid behind trees and bushes as DC officers passed on patrol. Jade had never seen so many officers before. There was no way they were going to get out of this alive. There was only 12 of them. It had to be over 100 officers there.

"Don't worry," Razor whispered. "I know a way around them. We just have to take a few of them out first."

"And then what?" Jade whispered back.

"We head for the tunnels."

Jade had no clue what tunnels Razor was talking about, but she nodded. A few of them were going to sneak up on some officers and kill them. They needed their badges to get into the tunnels. Taking their weapons would also come in handy too. Razor encouraged Jade to stay hidden. He didn't want her presence to sound off the alarm too early. He also worried about what his presence would do.

Reagan came up with a suggestion. Razor, Clay, and Lang got in position. She borrowed Jade's bow and arrows. A group of officers came walking by. Reagan took each of them out before they had time to sound off any alarm. She was so swift and smooth that it kind of scared Jade. The guys quickly retrieved the bodies before anyone saw. They relieved the officers of their badges and weapons. It all went smoothly, which made Jade a little antsier.

Razor led them toward the tunnels. The tunnels led you right to the river walk. The river walk led you to a pier right on the river. No one knew about the tunnels beside the officers. They were built when an overwhelming number of debtors began escaping across the border. Bossman had them made so officers could get to the debtors before they could cross the river. The tunnels worked. No debtors ever escaped once they were built.

Jade wasn't sure what the penalty of illegal fleeing was. She figured it would be death. Death seemed to be the penalty for most things. Death was already after her. This current criminal act wasn't going to change any of that.

"Razor," Jade whispered. "Won't the tunnels be filled with DC officers?"

"Yeah, we'll just have to wait it out some."

It wasn't a great plan, but the point of it all was for them *to* get caught. They needed all eyes on them so the others could escape. Jade was just trying to hold off on an altercation as long as she could. They continued to hide behind trees and bushes once they were in sight of the tunnel's entryway. They paid close attention to how often officers went in and out of the tunnels and how regularly the surrounding area was patrolled.

It had been a while since Jade was close to a large body of water. The smell of the river brought back so many memories for her. Mostly of her parents, and the family vacations they used to take. They had a summer rental house right off Crooked Lake. Jade and Helena would spend hours in the water. Sometimes their dad had to drag them out. The two sisters would be all prune-like by the time they came out, but they loved it. It all felt like another lifetime. It didn't feel like a life that Jade once lived.

The waves were crashing violently. Jade was sure that a storm was coming. She just wasn't sure what kind or how bad it would be. You never knew how bad a storm could be anymore. She was ready to get it over with. Jade watched, along with the rest, as the officers walked in, out, and around the entrance to the tunnels. It was a highly active area. There was no way they could go undetected.

Jade weighed the pros and cons. Would it be better if they got caught outside the tunnels or in? She favored the latter. If they got trapped outside, they had to deal with the outside guards along with the guards inside the tunnels, steadily streaming out as back up. If they got caught inside, however, they could disable the doors, which could hinder any more guards from getting inside. Now the question was, how do they get inside unnoticed?

Jade was too far away to get Razor's attention. She was wondering if he had a plan. She was currently sharing her hiding place with Reagan. Jade looked over at her to see if she had any thoughts. Reagan was taking the scene in with a frown on her face. Jade wasn't sure if she was angry or just focused.

"I think it might be best if we got inside undetected," Jade whispered.

"But how?"

"I'm not sure."

Reagan stared on again and then suddenly, there was a small expression of excitement on her face. "Ask Keeper if he still has some vodka and matches. I have an idea."

Jade whispered to Lang, who whispered to Tatianna, who whispered to Keeper Reagan's question. Razor looked over at Jade in confusion. Jade mouthed the words "she has a plan." Razor nodded his head in understanding.

The items got passed along, and Jade handed them over to Reagan. Jade didn't say anything. She watched as Reagan worked. Reagan borrowed Jade's bow and arrows again. She took two arrows and dowsed the tips with alcohol. Reagan struck a match and lit one arrow. She aimed in a direction that was far away from them. She released it, and it landed on a pallet that had some items tied down with a rope. The ropes quickly caught on fire. Some officers rushed to the scene.

Reagan took the next arrow and paused before she lit it. She was searching for her next target, but it appeared that she was having trouble. Jade quickly scanned the area. She spotted a DC truck. Maybe they could get that to explode. Jade announced her suggestion.

Reagan lit the arrow on fire. "The chances of it actually exploding are slim," she explained to Jade. She released the arrow. "But it'll cause the same reaction all the same."

The arrow landed, and it was followed by an explosion, which in turn caused another explosion. Reagan looked over at Jade in awe. "So yeah, that was some movie shit."

Jade smiled in return.

The explosions caused the DC officers to swarm to the three different spots. A swarm of DC officers began rushing out the tunnels as well. They all waited for the last officer to run out before they rushed inside undetected.

"That plan turned out better than I thought," Reagan admitted once the tunnel doors closed.

"Great job, Reagan," Razor said.

"Now, where do we go?" Jade asked.

"Out to the Riverwalk."

"Do you think the others took advantage of Reagan's distraction to head for the border?" Clay asked.

Razor quickly looked around them. The others followed suit—they were in the clear. "Let's hope so."

Jade's heart was racing. She was trying to keep herself calm. She didn't want to cause an asthma attack. It was the smoothness of the mission that was concerning her. The security seemed to be a little lax here. Were her and the others that good? Or was someone making it easier for them? Jade tried to refocus. She was paranoid.

How could he know they were coming there?

The better option for them was to go further into hiding. Not take on the DC task force more. But Jade couldn't shake the feeling that something was very odd about this situation.

There was a slow rumble beneath them. They all stopped and looked around. Was there something headed toward them? The shake kind of reminded Jade of a big truck or tank passing by. However, there was no way that a truck or tank could fit in the tunnels. Jade wondered if it was coming from outside, but they all could feel it under their feet.

They all resumed walking again—this time at a much faster pace. The rumble happened again. It was more violent this time. It almost knocked Jade over. Tatianna and Yoko did fall. Keeper and Lang quickly helped them up.

"Shit," Jade mumbled.

"Earthquake!" Razor announced. They all took off running with Razor leading the way. They had to get from the underground. That was the worst place to be during an earthquake—especially an unnatural one.

They quickly approached the doors that led them to the Riverwalk. Razor swiped the stolen badge, and the doors opened. They ran out of the doors and was met by a group of DC officers. It all seemed so chaotic. It took a moment for Jade to take everything in. They were dodging cracks, large debris, and bullets. This seemed more like it—shit hitting the fan.

This was what she was used to. Chaos and unplanned interactions. They all began fighting—trying to survive. Jade couldn't remember her interactions with the officers, but she was, once again covered in blood with her knives clutched in her hands. Warrior Jade made yet another appearance.

It didn't take that much to overpower the group of officers. The earthquake took the ones they were unable to kill. They just needed to be quicker than them. It worked to their advantage. Razor led them to the pier. The alarms started to go off once they made it on there. Jade could hear a swarm of officers running in their direction.

Unfortunately, for the officers, and them on the pier, the earthquake hadn't let up just yet. In fact, it got a little more intense. The dock shook violently. Jade was wondering if it was a good idea for them to run on it while the ground was still shaking.

They all couldn't keep their balance for long on the shaky pier. They found themselves gripping on the wooden railings for dear life. Jade prayed that the earthquake would end soon. She could feel her hands bleeding because she was holding on so tightly. She couldn't hold on much longer. Her next trip would be in the water, and she was sure that she wouldn't do well there.

The ground shook for another minute before it stopped. It took another few minutes for everyone to recollect themselves. Then another minute passed before they all came back to their interrupted situation.

The officers who survived the earthquake came rushing toward Jade and the rest of the group. More fighting quickly ensued. Jade had to promptly toss her bow aside because she used up all her arrows. The others immediately ran out of ammo from the stolen rifles, and they hadn't taken out a tenth of the DC officers that were there. They were slashing their way through officers, but they still found themselves backed onto the edge of the pier.

Jade hadn't noticed that they'd gotten so close until Danita almost fell in. Jade quickly caught her. An officer took advantage of the distraction and cut the side of Jade's abdomen. Jade screamed and dropped to her knees. She still managed to keep a firm grip on Danita. Seeing Jade get hurt, Danita quickly pulled herself back onto the pier.

Jade quickly put her hands on the cut to try to stop the bleeding. The officer attempted to go in for the kill when he suddenly dropped. A bullet went through his head. Jade quickly looked around. The shot didn't come from any of them. They were all entangled up in their own battles that no one noticed that she was hurt.

Danita tore off the dead DC officer's shirt and wrapped it around Jade's stomach.

"Shit," Jade panicked. "He's here."

Danita tied a knot on the make-shift tourniquet. "That should hold you."

"Danita he's here."

"Don't worry about that right now, Jade." Danita quickly went to fight off an officer that was heading their way when he suddenly dropped. She and Jade looked around frantically. She swiftly helped Jade to her feet. Jade let out a groan. Danita looked at Jade's side. "You ok?"

"I'll live," Jade gritted. She scanned the area for Bossman. He was there, Jade knew it. Who else would start shooting their own men? Especially when she got hurt.

Bossman had to be looking on from afar. Jade tried her best to fight off more of the DC officers, but she had a hard time fighting through the pain. The more she moved, the more blood flowed out of her. If it weren't for Danita and the mystery shooter (who was sure to be Bossman), she more than likely would've been dead.

After a while, Jade dropped back to her knees. She was feeling weak and dizzy. Danita's tourniquet was soaked in blood. Jade could feel it dripping down her side. It took everything in her power not to pass out. She focused on her breathing.

Danita quickly rushed to Jade's side. She assessed Jade's wound and then quickly looked around. She wanted to try to get Keeper's attention, but he was preoccupied with fighting off the swarm of DC officers. It was looking hopeless, and then another alarm went off. The sound of a PA system came on.

"Enough!" Bossman's voice rang out. All the officers quickly obliged.

Razor and the others looked around trying to see if they could find Bossman. Jade let out another groan. Helena looked over at her and saw that she was hurt.

"Jade!"

"Here Jade lay down," Danita suggested. She helped ease Jade down on her back.

Helena rushed over to Jade's side. She assessed the situation. "Oh God Jade."

"I'm ok," Jade managed to say.

Danita went over and ripped off a few more shirts from a few more dead officers. She rushed back over to Jade and pressed the shirts against Jade's cut. "I think it might be deeper than I thought. It's hard for me to tell."

"Drop your weapons, and I will send over aide," Bossman demanded.

Razor and the others circled around Jade as protection. "Don't do it!" Jade called out. She was sure it was a trap.

"Don't be silly, my lovely Jade. I don't want you dead just yet."

"We're not releasing our weapons," Razor shouted.

"I can just as easily kill all of you and get to her myself," Bossman said casually. "I've had you all in my scope for a while now."

They all turned around frantically—still searching for him. Bossman laughed. It made it even eerier. Jade closed her eyes. She couldn't decide what to do. There was no way she could go on with the cut bleeding the way it was. But what would happen when the aide was done attending to her? Would they kill her right then? That didn't make sense. Why patch her up if they were just going to kill her? Will they kill the others then?

Jade didn't want to risk the lives of the others. There were just too many unknown variables. They had unfortunately reached the flawed part of their plan—time. How much time would have to pass for the others to cross the border? And the bigger question was: how would Jade and the rest of the group know if the others made it across?

"Tick-tock Jade," Bossman said. "Or I'll start shooting."

"We can't drop our weapons," Razor whispered.

"Razor," Helena said. "She's hurt pretty bad."

"We're all gonna get hurt, Helena."

"Razor!" she snapped.

A gunshot went off.

Everything seemed to happen so slowly. Jade saw the bullet whizzed through the air. She watched as it slowly entered in the center of Lang's head. The back of his head exploded as the bullet exited out—along with blood and a little brain matter. There was a brief moment of shock before life went out of his eyes. Lang's lifeless body dropped into the river.

Jade let out a terrifying scream.

"Fuck," Razor said in frustration. "Drop your weapons." A few of the others could be heard weeping as they all dropped their weapons.

Jade couldn't stop crying. She wasn't sure why. It was something about Lang's final look that resonated with her. Was that the look that she would wear when the time came? Will Helena? Will Razor? There was a sudden moment when she envisioned their death. This upset her even more.

"Patch her up," Bossman ordered. "Quickly!" An officer began walking over toward them. "Let's make it interesting and fair. Drop all of your weapons."

The officer paused, then reluctantly complied. He resumed his journey over toward them. Once he was close, he pulled out a surgical staple gun and loaded it up with staples. Helena held onto her sister's hand for comfort. The officer kneeled beside Jade, and Razor towered behind him— watching him closely.

The officer removed the layer of shirts that Danita had made. He dowsed Jade's wound with alcohol aggressively. Jade screamed and cried even more. He then started to staple the wound without any hesitation or warning. Jade tried to focus her mind on anything else besides the pain. Sadly, that wasn't working. The officer made his last staple, and then he covered the cut with bandages and wrapped it with gauze.

The officer quickly stood up. "Done."

"Good," Bossman let off another shot. Like Lang, the officer was stunned. He too fell into the river.

"Shit!" Helena shouted.

"He could've been gentler with you Jade," he said.

Jade sighed. She was wracking her brain, trying to figure out how they were going to get out of this one. She looked up at Razor. He appeared to be thinking the same thing.

"Jade and Razor are not to be harmed," Bossman ordered. "Everyone else is fair game."

The wave of guns cocking was overwhelming. If anyone went for their weapon now, they were sure to get shot. Even if Jade and Razor were to reach, the others would probably be dead before their weapon got to them.

What were they to do now?

Mother nature decided to intervene once again. An aftershock hit and caused Jade and the others to fall into the water. A few officers fired off some shots as they too fell in. The aftershock caused the pier to break off. Jade dodged the debris that fell into the river. Madness quickly ensued.

Jade struggled to see where everyone landed. She tried not to panic. She managed to spot Razor not too far from her. He was snapping a few DC officers' necks and taking their weapons. Jade managed to spot Helena after a while and saw her trying to fight off an officer. Jade quickly swam toward her.

The officer was trying to hold Helena underneath the water. She was fighting with him, but she was also trying to avoid the falling debris from the pier. It was hard for her to focus on both. Jade swam faster. As Jade got closer, the officer was finally able to pin Helena under the water. Jade dived deeper into the water.

The officer didn't notice her, so she was able to get close and stab him in his arm. He still didn't loosen his grip on Helena. Jade tried to physically loosen his grasp, but it was hard. She quickly went back up and locked herself on his back. She started choking him with her arm, but the officer still wasn't budging. Worry consumed her. Helena couldn't hold her breath underwater much longer. Jade managed to pull the officer under with her, and she swiftly slit his throat. He finally released his grip from Helena.

The two sisters came up for air.

"You ok?" Jade asked.

Helena nodded while coughing for air

Bullets spewed across the river. Jade and Helena went back underwater for cover. They swam further and deeper all while trying to avoid the bullets. Jade was able to use a dead officer's body as a shield for the shots they couldn't outswim. Then the river shook.

Jade had no clue what was going on, but being underwater didn't seem like a good idea anymore. Jade took Helena's hand, and they popped back up to the surface. She looked around, trying to find out what caused the river to shake. Jade didn't see anything out of the ordinary.

She looked over at Helena again. "Good?"

"I'm fine Jade," Helena looked around frantically. "Where's Razor?"

"Duck," Razor said behind them. The two sisters took cover back underwater. They waited until Razor signaled them that it was ok to come back up. Once they reached the surface, Razor looked over Helena. He made sure that she was ok. Once he was satisfied, he turned his attention to Jade. "You alright?"

"I'm good, you?"

"Peachy," he fired off some more shots.

Jade could spot the remaining surviving group: Yoko, Tatianna,

Keeper, Calvin, Reagan, Clay, Junior, and Danita. They all began making their way to Jade, Razor, and Helena. Once everyone was close, they all huddled around each other in a circle. Yoko and Tatianna gave Jade and Helena a couple of rifles they taken from some officers.

"What's the plan?" Tatianna demanded. "Do we all die here in the river?"

"I'm working on it," Razor growled.

"Well work harder," Tatianna shot an approaching officer.

A few patrol boats sped toward them. They were coming from three different directions. They were going to have them surrounded.

"Shit!" Tatianna screamed out in frustration. "It just keeps getting better and better."

"Did you expect a walk in the park?" Reagan came to Razor's defense.

"I'm not going back to no fucking prison!" Tatianna cried.

"I don't think prison is in store for us," Junior pointed out.

"Focus!" Razor was getting annoyed with the chitter-chatter. They didn't have an escape plan, and that frustrated him.

It frustrated Jade too. She took in the scene. An army of DC officers was standing on the shore. A good number of them were in the river. And it was hard to tell how many of them were on the three patrol boats, but she was sure they would still be outnumbered.

Jade quickly wrecked her brain for options. Sadly, she could only come up with one, and that meant she would have to break her promise to Helena. That wasn't an option. Jade was not leaving her sister again. She would die first. Unfortunately, that scenario was probably going to come true soon.

The patrol boat that was in front shined a floodlight on them. Jade was blinded by it. It made it harder for her to see anything.

"Jade, my love," Bossman called out from the boat. "I know what you're up to."

"Oh yeah, what's that?" the best plan was for her to keep him talking. Their conversations usually kept him distracted. At least, that's what she guessed. "Just a dip in the river?"

He chuckled. "Oh, Jade. You know, you really hurt me during our last encounter. I mean, unleashing that big guy on me," Bossman shook his head. He was reflecting on his last encounter with Calvin. "That was just petty."

"Well, you were trying to fucking kill me."

He sighed. "That I was. Seems like that's all our relationship consist of. But you see Jade, you were holding back on me."

"Was I?" Of course, she was. Jade just didn't think that Bossman noticed.

"You know you were. I found myself...after I regained consciousness, of course, thinking about why you were holding back. It seemed like something was keeping you tied down. Something was keeping you from being free."

"Besides you?"

Bossman ignored her last comment. "So, I found myself doing some research—a comprehensive research on you. Of course, I knew about your asthma, and I knew about your debt. Vincent told me all about that years ago. No, I was curious about the reason you killed that DC officer in the first place. What drove you to start fighting?"

Jade froze in the water.

Her heart was pounding out of her chest.

She tried to focus.

Jade tried to calm herself down, but her body just reacted. Her asthma was starting to flare up—her chest began to tighten. Jade knew the reason why she started fighting. She knew who inspired her to fight back. Jade wanted to save her. And if Bossman figured out who that reason was, then she was no longer safe. Jade prayed they made it across the border.

Another light flickered on the boat.

There she sat...

...Raina.

She was tied to a chair with tears streaming down her face. Raina was shaking with fear. Levi sat next to her. He was bound to his chair as well, and they both had tape over their mouths.

Jade launched forward, but Razor quickly pulled her back. He locked her in his arms. Jade struggled to get out of his grasp.

"I found your reason, Jade," Bossman said casually. "I found what's been tying you down."

Helena and everyone else froze with fear and shock. What were they going to do now? Where were the others? What was Bossman about to do?

"As I said before, Jade, I know what you're up to." The floodlights on the other two boats came on. To their left Jackson and Sarah were held at gunpoint. To their right Rosalind and Beverly. They all were bound and gagged. "I found someone else too," Bossman pulled David into view.

Jade struggled harder against Razor to no avail. Bossman pulled out a gun and pointed it to David's head. Tears blinded Jade's vision.

"Do you know what the penalty for illegally crossing the border is?"

David found Jade's eyes. She never realized just how green his eyes were. It was like she was seeing them for the first time. They shined bright—even in the dark of night, they stood out. Water was on the verge of spilling out from those gorgeous eyes, but they remained teetering on edge. David looked at Jade bravely and mouthed the words "I love you." The next moment felt surreal. Jade didn't feel like herself. Blood, bone, and brain matter spewed out of David's head. The brightness of his eyes slowly faded out. It felt like Jade's eyes were deceiving her. She screamed out in anguish.

The scream seemed never-ending.

David's body slumped over the side of the boat and made a splash in the water. His lifeless body sunk for a moment and then floated back up.

Jade felt weak. She felt herself slipping. If it wasn't for Razor holding her up, she was sure she would've sunk to the bottom without the desire to come back up. Jade couldn't stop herself from crying.

"It's ok, Jade," Helena whispered, crying. She held onto her sister. "It's gonna be ok."

"Death," Bossman said, answering his own question. That was the officer's cue to penalize the others. Gunshots rang out, and one by one, the others' bodies made a splash in the water. Jade cried even more— along with some of the remaining survivors.

Razor held on tighter to Jade. "Focus, Jade. I need you to focus," the water in the river was receding back.

Jade nodded as she tried to pull herself together. She had to think. She had to figure out a way to save Raina and Levi. Then she saw Bossman pull out two machetes and walked over to the children. Jade panicked. Before she knew it, the words were coming out of her mouth.

"Just take me. Please, just take me instead. I surrender," Jade broke her promise to Helena, but it was the last play she had left. Helena didn't bother to protest.

Bossman stopped and looked at Jade. "I don't want you to surrender my love. You don't understand. I'm not doing this to hurt you. I'm doing this to free you...to heal you...to be the woman you were born to be," he walked behind Raina and Levi. "You're tied to them, and that's hindering you. Because of their innocence, you hold back on who you truly are. You consider them with every action you make. You don't see the amazing woman you can become, but I do."

The blade from the machetes stuck out of Raina's and Levi's chest. They both had a look of awe, confusion, and pain. Raina's eyes bulged as blood slowly poured down the tape that covered her mouth. She never took her eyes off Jade.

The look haunted her.

Levi's body twitched from the pain. It all was unbearable to watch. Jade stopped breathing. There was a brief moment when she passed out altogether. When she came to again, they were still in the same position. Levi's body slumped over, and Raina's head tilted back.

"No, no, no, NO!" Jade wasn't ready to accept the fact that they were gone. "No, God, please, NO!" It couldn't be real. This was all just a vivid nightmare. Jade would wake up and find them sleeping soundlessly in their beds. She would hug them, kiss them, and hold onto them tightly. She would never let them out of her sight. And Jade would never entrust someone else to protect them. All she had to do was wake up. But no matter how hard she pinched herself and no matter how many times she opened and closed her eyes, she found Raina and Levi in the same position with machetes sticking out of their chest.

Bossman pulled out the blades and nonchalantly tossed their bodies in the water.

The careless act enraged Jade. This was no nightmare. This was reality. "You fucking BASTARD!" she screamed at the top of her lungs. "I'm gonna kill you! I'm gonna watch you die slow!"

"Yes, Jade, yes!" he was elated. "You see, it's working already."

"I'm gonna fucking kill you! You coward! You child killer!" Jade didn't notice that Razor was slowly pulling her back—toward Canada. She also didn't see that the water in the river was becoming shallow.

Jade was blinded with rage and tears. Raina's last words kept ringing in her ears.

Please make it back to me.

Jade had to make it back to her. And Levi. And David. Jade promised. She needed them back. She had to get them back. The thought was ridiculous, but maybe, just maybe, she could get them back when she killed Bossman. All she had to do was get to him. Jade kept trying her hardest to get out of Razor's hold. She needed to kill Bossman. She needed to make him suffer.

"Razor, please let me go!" she finally noticed where he was headed. "No! Razor I have to kill him! Please, Razor, let me kill him!"

Razor ignored her. In fact, he tightened his grip on Jade and took Helena into his other arm. He had a plan, and he knew Jade wasn't going to like it. But his main focus was getting them out of the situation safely. The others began to follow his lead. Bossman was so tied up in Jade's anger that he didn't notice what the others were doing.

"Stop! Razor please!"

She realized she would never hear Levi's laugh again.

Jade fought harder.

She realized that Raina would never cuddle up to her again.

Jade fought harder.

She realized that she could never kiss David again.

Jade fought harder.

"Stop! Please! Please!" Jade was defeated. She knew it. She let out another scream of anguish and heartache.

"Kill the others," Bossman ordered.

There was the sound of rushing waves. Jade looked over to see a wall of water cascading toward them. She prayed that it would just take her. They all were quickly engulfed in them. The waves hit Jade hard. It knocked her out of Razor's grasp. Jade allowed herself to float toward the bottom. She was ready to give it all up. She was ready for it to end, but it wouldn't. Razor quickly grabbed her again and started swimming toward Canada. The others were right on his tail.

Another rush of waves hit. The boats were knocked over along with everyone on them. The wave launched Jade and the others closer to the shores of Canada.

"Jade! Jade!" Bossman yelled out in anger once he saw how far they've gotten. He started swimming after them—even though they were far ahead.

Another wave launched them even further. Jade choked on the water. Suddenly she felt the bottom of the river on her feet. Razor quickly carried her and Helena up on the shore.

"Jade!" Bossman kept swimming. Another wave engulfed him. Jade didn't see him come back up.

Razor continued to carry Jade and Helena away from the shore. He was determined to put as much distance between them and Bossman. Jade laid in his arm, defeated. Weak. Every ounce of fight in her fleeted.

They all were about a mile away from the shore before Razor stopped to rest. They all sat against some tree logs. Everyone tried to catch their breath. It seemed impossible. Most of them couldn't stop crying.

The skyline of Detroit stared back at Jade. Tears ran down her face. She thought about the people she loved who was now dead in that river.

Raina's smile.

Levi's rosy cheeks and head full of curls.

David's soul-searching eyes.

Every ounce in Jade's body wanted to give up, but she couldn't—she wouldn't. Raina and Levi didn't deserve to die the way that they did. They were true innocence. She had made it her mission to protect the innocent—to protect the children. She failed, but she would correct it. Jade would avenge them. And she would make this a world worth living in. She would make it safe.

No one would no longer live to just survive.

"Goodbye, my little munchkins," sorrow, despair, anger, and determination flowed through Jade's veins. "I love you."

The End

ACKNOWLEDGMENTS

This journey has been five years in the making. What started as a short story series has blossomed into a dystopian novel series. Although this world is riddled with hopelessness and pain, I find it so intriguing. It makes one ask: what are we willing to do to be a decent human being? Are we willing to fight for the weak and the oppressed? To even kill for them? This world explores the thin line of becoming the very thing that we hate. It explores the many flaws of human beings, but also shed light on our courage and bravery. When it's all said and done, I believe that we will choose to help one another in the end.

So, I would like to thank you the reader for taking time out to explore this world that I have created. I hope that you will continue this journey as more books are released in this series.

I like to thank everyone who helped me put this book together, to the cover artist, beta readers, proofreaders, editors, my husband Fred, family, friends, and more. Your support has meant so much to me.

Lastly, but *never* the least, I like to thank God for guiding me on this writing journey. I thank you for pushing me whenever I began to get complacent.

Until the next time,

Jana' Chantel

ABOUT THE AUTHOR

 Jana` Chantel is a full-time writer from Detroit, MI. After graduating from Grand Valley State University with a BA in Creative Writing, she went to work for an indie publishing company as a publishing assistant. From there, Jana` wrote and published her first book entitled *Into My Mind*, which was a collection of personal essays. Most recently she has written and filmed a sci-fi TV pilot with her husband entitled *Fault: Gamma*, which won the 2017 New York Film and TV Festival for Best TV Series Concept for a TV pilot. When she isn't writing, you can find Jana` on a film set with her company Thirty Four 26 Studios. *Surviving Red* is her first debut novel.

www.janachantel.com

Facebook.com/SurvivingRed

Instagram & Twitter: @survivingred

www.ingramcontent.com/pod-product-compliance
Lightning Source LLC
Chambersburg PA
CBHW020241110726
47898CB00004B/1344